THE STRINGS OF FATE

Book Two of the Freedom for Rhethos Series

HANNAH R. LYON

THE STRINGS OF FATE
Book Two of the Freedom for Rhethos Series

Copyright © 2024 by Hannah R. Lyon

Inspired Legacy Publishing is a division of (DBA) Inspired Legacy, LLC
PO Box 900816
Sandy UT 84090-0816.

All rights reserved. No part of this publication may be reproduced distributed or transmitted in any form or by any means including photocopying recording or other electronic or mechanical means without proper written permission of author or publisher, except in the case of brief quotations embodied in critical reviews and certain other noncommercial uses permitted by copyright law.

ISBN 979-8-9877883-2-5 (paperback)
ISBN 979-8-9877883-3-2 (hardcover)

Printed in the United States of America.

WHAT PEOPLE ARE SAYING

"Lyon's characters inspire me to keep going in my own life and bring magic into each day."

—Janet Cheney, MA English Literature, bestselling author

"Hannah Lyon is a top-notch writer. I couldn't put this book down. It's easily my favorite new fantasy novel I've read all year."

—Jared Godfrey

"Lyon's masterful story-building takes you on a journey to unveil the dark secrets of Rhethos."

—Finn O'Malley, bestselling author of the *Keeper of Elements* series and GLOWup series

"Hannah is a magnificent storyteller who builds an incredibly realistic world and a deep web of intricacies."

—Jerel McLain, author of *Mixed Tape: The Soundtrack of a Life*

"This book brought me into an amazing space of intriguing fantasy!"

—Deborah Wiener, feng shui consultant, international award-winning speaker

"There is always a cost to gain freedom and equality, even if you wear rebel violet. In Rhethos, that price is often paid in blood, but even a Goddess might go too far."

—David Walker

"Prepare to be hooked—again! *The Strings of Fate* is a high fantasy adventure with teeth, engaging character development, and plot twists that will make you ponder your own destiny and choices."

—Bridget Cook-Burch, *New York Times* bestselling author, founder of Your Inspired Story

"Here is a captivating fantasy novel offering a vivid, thrilling, immersive story."

—Maureen Ryan Blake, TV host, international bestselling author

DEDICATION

To all of my fellow conspirators who've ever been
silenced, undervalued, or broken.
Each of you has the ability within yourself to speak freely,
shine brightly, and encompass your full potential.
This part of the journey is for you.

CONTENTS

CHAPTER ONE

HOODS UP AND HEADS DOWN

Angelyn McKinlee had never been colder in her entire life. The freezing Rhethosian countryside ate into her bones while a chill unrelated to the weather sent uneasy waves of ill omens straight to her heart.

"Keep it moving, McKinlee."

Marselle's feminine voice commanded her from their supply wagon's driver seat. Despite being several hours into the return journey to the rebel camp and being soaked with rain, when Angelyn glanced up at the southern Rhethosian lady turned rebel spy, she still had flattering curls in her red hair and determination in her eyes.

Angelyn quickened her pace as she walked beside the supply wagon, her hand pressed lightly against its worn edge. With the weight of the barrels she'd salvaged from the cove, their going was extremely slow, and she knew Marselle was eager to get off the road.

She squinted down the empty gray land, south to where Will and the rebel army were laying siege to Lorington. Part of her wanted to know so badly about how the battle was going that her feet slowed once more.

West is where the people are who need these supplies most, she reminded herself. *Josh is back West, though he probably hasn't thought of me once. All he cares about is being free and experimenting with those Goddess Touched runes that Will gave him.*

She hoisted herself unceremoniously into the wagon's bed and sidled past the six barrels that sat as high as her chin so she could stand next to Belka.

The poor girl, a young, inexperienced rebel who was trying to prove her worth, was shivering uncontrollably in the tiny space between the back of the driver seat and the last of the massive barrels. Despite being new to the cause herself, Angelyn could tell Belka was completely out of her element.

Belka stood with her arms wrapped around herself. "Is that smoke?" she asked suddenly. She pointed over the driver's seat toward the southern horizon. Her breath formed in anxious clouds that puffed out across the dismal, wet landscape.

"No, it's mist," Marselle dismissed. "The same dismal fog that covers fifty miles in every direction."

Angelyn, however, had that chill rise in her chest again, one that could be ignored just as much as the freezing weather. Shivering, she strained her eyes. Her new, black dress had never really dried since Marselle pulled her out of the waves, and when she glanced at her fingertips, Angelyn found they were tinged blue. *Not good.*

She climbed over the wagon's edge and into the driver's seat next to Marselle on the freezing planks. "I see something."

"Not you too, McKinlee," Marselle grumbled and halted their progress. The worn wheels of the wagon sank into the muddied earth. "Just because your men are risking their lives down there . . ."

"Look again," Angelyn insisted, ignoring that last comment. She didn't have a "man," not since her husband had abandoned her almost two decades ago, and though the rebel leader had had the gall to kiss her once in her old home . . .

Deliberately, Angelyn cleared her throat and pressed an insistent hand onto Marselle's shoulder. At the peak of one of the distant hills, she saw plumes of black. Not white but an ominous, destructive shade of darkness.

"Oh no," Marselle whispered.

"Something's wrong," Belka said. "We should ride south and help!"

"What are we going to do, girl?" Marselle said, cold realism in her emerald eyes. "There are bloodthirsty armies that way, and a towne with granite walls the heights of which you've never seen. Three women and a month's supply of food and salt should ride up to all of that?"

"But if the men are in trouble, then—"

"Then there's nothing we can do!" Marselle snapped. "McKinlee's the only reason you're here, so I suggest you sit down and keep quiet."

Angelyn couldn't help but silently agree. If they changed their course and rode toward Lorington, a full day away, they'd have to find shelter to avoid freezing to death in the fog. If they rode on, back "home," they would be warm, safe, and would feed many hungry people before nightfall. *And I could see my boy.*

Her heart began to warm at the idea of seeing her sandy-haired teenager when she spotted movement on the horizon. It was closer than the cloud of smoke and lower to the ground. The dots of movement shifted toward them, solidifying into the forms of men and horses as they broke through the fog.

"Marselle . . ." Angelyn began. "Men. On the horizon."

Marselle snapped her attention south. Her gloved hands tightened on the reins. "There shouldn't be any patrols this way right now. I can't tell what colors they're wearing, can you?"

"No," Angelyn said. *And there's nowhere to hide in this bleak countryside if they aren't wearing rebel violet and instead bear Rhethosian Blue, men serving our enemy, the Lord Bradford.* When she looked at Marselle, she knew the woman was thinking the same thing. They were on the edge of rebel territory, and there was no telling who they could meet.

The group of riders stopped where the country roads diverged and looked around. Angelyn's heart sank into a waiting pit of fear when she saw them point toward their wagon.

"Looks like we've got their attention," Marselle sighed, and she renegotiated the wagon so it faced the southern road. "Hoods up and heads down, girls. I'll speak to these bastards."

Angelyn held her sodden hood against the sides of her face, pressing back the damp braid of her dirty blonde hair. Two situations warred in her mind, one where she sighed with relief at the rebels who had news about the siege, and one where she crawled back into her old Rhethosian shell to survive against military guardsmen.

She was confused when she saw that the approaching horses had violet leather wrapped around their tack, but the men riding them wore Rhethosian Blue tunics under their armor. The rider in the lead slouched against the neck of his beast. Angelyn thought she saw blood on the man's gloves.

"Where are you boys heading in such a hurry?" Marselle asked. She pressed her forearm in front of Angelyn, shouldering forward in the wagon's driver seat to keep the riders' attention solely on her.

The man in the lead clenched at his horse's mane, as if his grip was the only thing keeping him in the saddle. His black hair was plastered against his head, and Angelyn thought she saw a reddish tint to the wetness along his hairline. Her eyes darted down to his mount's legs, which were slick with sweat, as if the rider had forced the horse nearly to a breaking point.

"What's in the wagon?" the man demanded. His voice was deep and harsh for one so young, and Angelyn knew where that kind of tone came from: a boy turned into a brutal man by the Rhethosian army.

"Nothing but salt, dried fish, and a few barrels of wheat, Master," Angelyn said before Marselle could stop her. She kept her eyes down, looking at the man's collar as rainwater dripped onto her face from the hem of her hood. "We're on our way to Lorington for our monthly trade."

The man craned his neck to see in the bed of the wagon where Belka sat. Angelyn watched calmly as the dampness of his tunic stained a darker shade than rainwater. He motioned, and all three of his companions shifted their horses forward to make an arc around the wagon.

"You'd best take the lids off those barrels," ordered the man in the lead.

"Really, Master—" began Marselle.

"You can't go on to Lorington," started one of the others. "We'll escort you to Kaylyn instead, where it's safe."

Marselle gave the riders an appreciative smile. "Our business is south, not west. Why wouldn't one of our Lord's greatest cities be safe?"

Angelyn wondered why these men were bothering. Wasn't the blood on their leader's uniform cause enough to move along quickly to shelter and a healer? Now that she was outside of her loyal Rhethosian cage, she saw the absurdity of the guardsmen's power-hungry attitudes.

"My lady," spoke the man leaning on his horse's neck. "You're dangerously close to rebel territory, and trust runs thin up here."

"Why shouldn't we go south?" Belka demanded suddenly. Angelyn felt her heart skip a beat as Marselle glanced back at the girl incredulously.

"The rebels tried to camp outside the great city, but we marched from Kaylyn with the lieutenant to clear them out with a bit of fire," the guardsman explained shortly.

"Fire?" Belka repeated, and Angelyn saw terror in the girl's bright blue eyes. "What about our men?"

"'Our' men? *Lorington's* men are still safe behind their walls," snapped the man in the lead. "Where did you say you're from, girl?"

Belka's jaw fell slack. She stuttered a bit, then Marselle reached back and slapped her with the back of her hand. Belka cried out and the men's horses shied back several steps.

"You'll have to forgive the child," Marselle said smoothly. "She is quite simple, and never learned to keep her Lord's silence."

"It seems so," replied the leader. The bite in his voice told Angelyn he was nearly out of patience, but what the guardsman said wasn't adding up. *If they set a fire to harm Will's men, why are they retreating? And where is Sarrett? What went wrong for which side?* Her heart twinged painfully when she thought of the rebel leader, and she resisted the urge to put a hand up to the amethyst pendant at her throat.

Belka whimpered, gingerly pressing her fingers to her reddening cheek. Angelyn saw anger bubbling in the girl's eyes, and a recklessness that she knew would break their situation into pieces. She felt a slight movement against her leg and saw Marselle quickly raising the hem of her gown to reveal the hilt of a knife strapped to her calf.

The leader of the guardsmen motioned to the others with a grunt, and two of them drew swords from their hips. The man closest to the wagon pointed the tip of his blade at Belka, whose eyes went wide. Angelyn saw the girl running her hands along the floor of the wagon, gathering remnants of wet sand into a hard ball.

"Belka, don't—" was all Angelyn had time to say before the girl threw her makeshift weapon at the guardsman's face. He swore, and at the same moment, Marselle unsheathed her blade.

Angelyn instinctively ducked when Marselle flicked her wrist and sent her knife flying into the lead guardsman's neck. The armed man to Marselle's left swung at her head, forcing her to dive to the wagon bed's floor.

"Tell me you have another knife!" Angelyn cried as the unarmed guardsman on the right side of the wagon dismounted and limped toward them. She could now see that his left thigh was burned badly.

"Actually . . ." Marselle began and swept up the silk of her gown to unsheathe a second blade. She met the next swipe of the guardsman's blade to her left.

Angelyn didn't have time to see Marselle's next move because the man to her right grabbed hold of her ankle and yanked hard. She kicked back, slamming the heel of her boot against his chest. His fingers grasped and twisted the thin fabric of her soaked dress and the seams began to split.

"Get away from me!" Belka screamed. Sounds of a struggle pounded against the wagon's wall, but Angelyn couldn't see the girl or her assailant.

Angelyn twisted sideways and aimed her next kick low. She connected with the burned leg of her attacker, who howled and let her go. When she glanced at her boot, the sole was covered in melted chunks of red and black flesh.

She snapped her attention to Marselle, who still held off her opponent before returning her gaze to her own. The man curled on the ground by Angelyn's side of the wagon was screaming, clutching at his exposed bone. She heard Belka shriek again and jumped down so she could sprint to the wagon's rear.

Belka knelt in the middle of the wagon bed, her arms spread to bar the guardsman's access to their barrels. The guardsman stood above her with his back to Angelyn. He swung his sword in wild arcs, laughing each time he made contact with Belka's arms. Splashes of the girl's blood stained the worn planks.

Angelyn sprung onto the wagon's bed, hot anger coursing through her freezing muscles. She threw her arms around the guardsman's neck from behind. He staggered as Belka pressed her back against the barrels, clutching her injured arms.

"Bitch!" snapped the guardsman, flailing wildly to try and reach Angelyn. The man tottered for a moment, then pitched forward toward the barrels and Belka.

Angelyn slammed into the wagon bed, then felt her heart freeze as Belka let out a piercing scream from somewhere beneath her. With a desperate burst of strength, Angelyn grabbed the back of the guardsman's jacket and forced him off of Belka. Jutting out of Belka's gut was the length of the man's sword.

The guardsman laughed hoarsely, clutching at his sore throat. Angelyn was paralyzed with horror as Marselle jumped into the space next to her, and with one swift motion, she knelt and cut the laughing guardsman's throat.

"Belka," Marselle began, wiping her knife on the dying man's sleeve. "Damn it . . ." She barely touched the hilt of the blade held firmly in Belka's stomach, and the girl cried out in further pain.

Angelyn looked away as blood quickly seeped into the wagon's bed. Outside, beyond the back of the driver's seat, she could see the leader of the group slumped lifelessly on his horse, Marselle's first knife in his neck. When she craned her neck, she saw the other two men were dead on either side of the wagon.

Seeing those corpses oddly didn't give her any satisfaction, but when she glanced at the body in the wagon bed, a wave of gratification flowed through her that terrified her more than anything else.

"I'm sorry," Belka was saying, looking up at Marselle who knelt next to her. "I was thinking of Darren . . ."

Marselle shook her head and placed a hand on Belka's stomach, applying pressure around the sword. "I know," she replied, an unusual softness in her voice. "I'm the one who taught you to speak up."

"Go south," Belka begged, her voice dangerously weak. "Find out . . . what happened."

Angelyn pushed herself forward and grabbed Belka's hand. The slashes all over her arms had almost stopped bleeding. "We will," she assured her, ignoring the look Marselle was giving her. "We'll find the rebels, flying violet banners."

Belka nodded, her face deathly pale. Angelyn wasn't sure if she heard her, but the girl's eyes closed and her lips fell slack. Marselle swore under her breath, and Angelyn felt her throat clog with bitter tears.

A new sound met Angelyn's ears, and she gripped the wagon's edge with trembling fingers. On the horizon, beyond the reach of the mist, she saw a new group of riders headed toward them.

CHAPTER TWO

STANDING AGAINST THE TIDE

The mechanism of Lorington's massive city gates shattered under the incredible force of Devaki's Blessing Runes, and the siege that Will expected to take months ended in one night. It should have been a moment of victory for him, as much as his men who cried out triumphantly around him, but Will kept his guard up.

Nothing was going according to the rebel leader's plan, and the sudden appearance of his Goddess Touched daughter was only the beginning of the chaos that threatened to ensue next.

A groundswell of cheers erupted from hundreds of men as they flew past Will, heedless of the commands of their rebel Masters, pouring into Lorington's streets and wreaking havoc. Fires had already started to blossom in the west district, and instead of the organized welcome Will wanted, he heard screams of distress and curses shouted against his army.

After making his way through the army to the gates, Will found Rowlann, the leader of his elite forces and one of his most trusted men. Holding onto the arm of Will's coat amongst the chaos was Devaki Tarran, the Armellan daughter he'd never met.

Will had to keep glancing down at her to truly comprehend her abrupt existence, her dark skin spattered with blood in the moonlight. Protectively, he pressed her against the edge of the inner courtyard, beyond which Will could see the clay roofs of thousands of buildings.

"Will!"

Over the roar of the rebels and the Rhethosian guardsmen clashing with them on all sides, Will heard his name. Irvin rode toward them, working his way past the centerpiece of the gray courtyard: a towering statue of the First

Bradford, whose face was cemented in Rhethosian history as the man who saved the kingdom from Cybarys' chains.

Will thought he saw Irvin spit at the statue as he went by, showing his current distaste for the entire regime. Irvin sidestepped his mount around the soldiers in rebel violet and viciously swept his blade down on all others, leaving death in his wake. The former Towne Master, one of Will's first supporters, killed with ease.

Devaki flinched next to Will, and when he glanced down at the girl, he saw a film of shock over her deep brown eyes. Her traditional golden Armellan silks and studded leathers were torn, and dried blood caked her arms up to her elbows. Along with the wave of pity that hit him, Will felt sickening nostalgia grip his heart. *Her eyes are the same shape and color as her mother's.*

"We need to get you a horse!" Irvin shouted when he reached him. His high cheekbones and sharp jaw were accented by the torchlight spanning the courtyard. "There's a lot of initial push back from Moore's guardsmen here, but I don't know what it'll look like farther into the city. Let's keep this as short-lived as possible, shall we?"

Will agreed grimly. The smells of fire and blood were too strong here. He knew he needed to let his men into Lorington so they could earn their victory after years of waiting for battle, but he also needed to show the Rhethosian citizens that the rebel cause was different from the violent military leaders of The Bradford's long-held regime.

A group of rebel fighters formed around Irvin's horse, protecting its flanks from the rush of Rhethosian guardsmen who continued to try and push the invaders from their city. Will put a hand on the bridle of Irvin's mount, holding it steady amongst the waves of motion and torrential sound.

A flash of red light exploded in front of them, and the thousands of men pressed together in the courtyard scrambled back in terror. Rowlann and several of his company appeared amongst the spatters of magic remnants that flew through the air like dying embers. He raised one arm above his head, wrapped in violet cloth, showing a path for the rebels to charge deeper into the city.

She cut Protection Runes into the armor of his company, Will thought, perplexed. *I've never seen the passive magic used in such a way.*

"There's as good a chance as any!" Irvin declared, and Will barely heard him over the renewed shouts of the rebel fighters as they moved forward. Irvin whistled shrilly, catching the attention of several rebels on horseback, and beckoned until one made his way over to the courtyard's outer wall.

The men formed a circle around Will and Irvin, blocking any enemy attacks and allowing them a moment to speak. They certainly didn't expect to be in an enemy city so quickly, but gaining peace between its people and his was paramount.

"Do you remember the city's layout?" Will asked Irvin, thanking the man who handed over his horse. It was a sacrifice in the waging battle, and Will appreciated it. He needed a mount to get where he was going.

"How hard is it to remember a square block of granite?" Irvin laughed. He swept an arm up, clad in his typical show of rebel violet, pointing away from them. "Southern corners are barracks and businesses, west district is high-population slums, and the lovely eastern and northern ends of the city are my kind of people."

Will nodded, sheathed his sword, and climbed into the saddle. A wave of dizziness almost overtook him when the wound that ranged along the left side of his ribcage leaked under his tattered shirt. The burn he'd acquired while failing to save the supply wagons from the lieutenant's sabotage would not flex, and he ignored the sticky, seeping wetness.

"Tell Rowlann to head straight for Towne Centre in the northern district," Will commanded, brushing off the concerned look in Irvin's eye. "Half his men should stay with the troops as they station themselves around the city to keep the peace. The rest go with him to take Moore and his family alive. We will secure our victory within the hour."

"I'll head east?" Irvin proposed.

"I thought you'd prefer that neighborhood," Will agreed, then ducked instinctively when a loud crash filled the air and high-pitched screams echoed toward them from further in the city.

He turned his attention to Devaki, who stood with her back still pressed against the courtyard wall, her eyes following the thousands of movements all around them with shocked precision. He watched as she twisted her brass prayer bracelets around her wrists, her slim, blood-soaked hands shaking.

"Devaki," Will began. "Don't be frightened–"

"Uh, you need to leave her with someone, out of sight," Irvin began, urging his horse closer to Will's as Will offered Devaki his hand. "You know how these people will react if they see her with you."

"She stays with me," Will stated, and he helped Devaki into the saddle behind him.

"That's not the first impression we want to make here," Irvin insisted strongly. Armelle's people, their faith, and their Goddess' magic had been outlawed in Rhethos for centuries, so everything his daughter stood for made her a target amongst all Rhethosians.

"Neither is letting the men get out of hand," Will retorted, and he yanked the reins of his horse away from Irvin. "Once we've secured the streets, return to the courtyard. Tell Rowlann I want Moore and his family at that statue."

"Right. Best of luck, brother!" Irvin said as he rode off, scattering rebels and Rhethosian soldiers alike. After passing on Will's instructions to Rowlann, Irvin headed toward one of the side streets on the east end of the courtyard, and many rebel fighters followed after him.

Will twisted as far as his wounds would allow him to glance back at Devaki. "This is almost over," he said. "I promise."

Devaki nodded, though Will noticed her eyes drifted to Rowlann's men and the jewel-like remnants of magic that sparkled on the stones around them. *I never thought I'd see Blessing Runes cut into rebel armor,* Will thought as he turned their horse to face west. *That must be considered blasphemous amongst Armellan Goddess Touched.*

Will spurred their horse forward, clearing his head and shouting for his men to follow him. The courtyard's stone wall split in a delicate iron archway ahead of them, well-lit in the moon's brilliant glow. They rode under it at a pace that the fighters on foot could follow, and Will tried to memorize all of the details of the city as they flew past them.

Of the many northern Rhethosian townes that he had studied, Lorington was the largest and most prosperous. It reminded Will of the southern townes of his early childhood; he saw their architectural ingenuity and modern details in Lorington's curbed streets and structured tenements.

The market district, he thought as he steered his horse through many narrow blocks of individual business and rows of shops with homes stacked on top. Even though the cacophony of the courtyard faded behind them, there were still a few shouts from the streets around them and up ahead.

Will slowed when he saw a dozen of his men on the upcoming corner, beating down the doors of several businesses. Despite the pristine condition of the white-washed stone and Rhethosian Blue awnings that shaded each storefront, the walkways were covered with shattered glass that sparkled in the moonlight.

"What do you think you're doing?" Will shouted, and he felt Devaki jump behind him. Each man turned to glare at Will, then recognition dawned on their faces when they spotted his dark hair, broad shoulders, and unmistakable green eyes. They scrambled for words as the hundreds of rebels following Will through the market surged past them, though many stopped to watch their leader's reaction.

"We are here to share our *cause*, not loot these people's homes and businesses!" Will continued, raising his voice so it carried around the market and into the side streets. "We are here to create change, not burn their homes like the Rhethosian military!"

The man nearest Will glowered, keeping his sword raised. "We didn't think anyone would—"

"You didn't think I'd be right beside you?" Will cut in, bemused. "Just like I have been from the beginning? Put your blade down; everyone here bears rebel violet."

"You heard him," spoke up another of the rebels on the marketplace corner. He flipped his sword around so the hilt faced downward. Will had no doubt he'd been using the butt of his weapon like the others to break locks.

Will's right arm reached back without him thinking and acted as a shield for Devaki. The rebel wasn't holding his sword in an offensive stance, but some latent instinct in him woke and told his body to protect his child. He'd always felt the need to help others, but this natural inclination was completely different.

"Look up," Devaki said quietly, and he glanced at the tenements on the second levels just in time to see drawn back curtains fall into place. Will let a smile touch his lips for a moment. His daughter had sharp eyes, and Lorington's people were watching.

"What were your orders?" Will demanded as he moved his horse closer to the dozen men on the corner.

"Station ourselves in twos at every corner till the city is taken," replied the same rebel who had spoken before. He looked uninjured and his blade was clean. "Run down any guardsmen in our way and await instructions after the Towne Masters are captured."

Will nodded. "Then you should get moving," he said. "And I have a special task for the twelve of you: repeat those orders to every rebel you see and make it clear that no other actions will be tolerated."

"Yes, Master Will!" The response echoed amongst the men on the corner, and many others who were making their way into the western district.

The man in front of Will's horse craned his neck to see around the rebel leader. "So, is she our secret weapon or something?" he asked, jerking his head at Devaki. "Did she make the pagan magic that broke the gates down?"

"I said move," Will growled, and he spurred their horse directly at the man, forcing him to dance backward several steps. He turned his attention back to the roads that led deeper into the city, where the market district turned into the poorer sections of Lorington.

Through the remaining hours of the night, Will made sure fires were quenched, riots were diffused, and now he could barely keep himself in the saddle. He looked over his shoulder, back toward Lorington's central courtyard in the distance. The dead of night was finally over, and Lorington's battlements were stained with the pale pink of the coming morning. It was time to regroup with Irvin and Rowlann.

Behind him, Devaki, who had thus far held her own, eventually rested her head against his back, between his shoulder blades. It was an odd feeling to be close to her, and a bit of discomfort rose around his heart.

Will yanked his equally weary horse into the gutter so the last rows of rebels could continue. They were in the heart of the poorer area of the city now, and here the ramshackle housing rose precariously.

He craned his neck to look back at Devaki, who was shaking a haze of exhaustion from her eyes, sending tufts of her curling brown hair bouncing off her cheeks. "It's dawn," she said, glancing at the barely visible orange light that attempted to vault the city walls. "I need a minute to pray."

Will grimaced; it had been decades since anyone had spoken to Cybarys around him. Even though he felt an immediate connection with this girl, Will was bluntly reminded how different Devaki's world was from his. He shifted the reins to his left hand and wrapped his right arm around to place pressure on his aching ribcage as he gulped back his distaste. "Go ahead."

Devaki gave him a smile and slid out of the saddle. Battle shock and brutal trauma had sat upon the Armellan girl's shoulders like suffocating weights, but when he watched her twist her traditional ring off the fourth finger of her right hand, it was as if it all dissipated and revealed the smart, vibrant teenager he knew well from their letters over the years.

Devaki turned the sharp edge of her ring toward a Guidance Rune on her forearm, its scar tissue just visible through the dried blood on her skin. She traced the symbol without drawing blood.

"Dear Mother," she murmured, "show us in the light of a new day how to be closer to your loving arms." A warm touch of desert heat emanated through the air, and a soft red glow issued from the rune on Devaki's arm.

Will raised his eyebrows, not sure what to think. He was impressed at the immediate strength of his daughter's magic. "You called forth that energy from Cybarys without offering blood?"

Devaki nodded, giving him a plain expression, as if wondering why this was an odd thing for him to point out.

"I have never seen a Goddess Touched pull on a magic source without cutting open their skin," Will pointed out. "Have you?"

"I suppose not," Devaki said. It didn't seem to bother her. She pressed the rune ring a bit harder into the Guidance Rune shape till blood did leak down her arm. The maroon glow and heat amplified instantly.

Usually, it takes either a lot of faith or a lot of blood to use that much power so easily, and she's barely bleeding, Will thought. *Whatever she did to Rowlann's armor was just as powerful. Blasphemous, and traumatizing for her, especially because she had to bleed to keep the spell active. Why would—?*

"Dear Goddess!" Devaki exclaimed suddenly. Before Will could ask, she stepped further into the slums.

"Where are you going?" Will demanded.

"We *have* to go this way," Devaki replied, renewed vigor sparkling in her eyes.

"Why?" Will asked cautiously.

"I felt an enormous pull in this direction," she explained. Her silk shoes kicked up clouds of filth from the pathway's edge where she walked to avoid the flow of men and horses on the road.

"Devaki—" Will began.

"Usually, I get only small hints from her that I need to decipher," she continued, and Will could barely hear her as she rushed forward, now dozens of paces in front of him. "But now I feel her hands literally on my shoulders telling me to go this way!"

Devaki halted and gestured wildly down the street. Bits of magic remnants leaked from the cut on her arm, sprinkling to the packed dirt.

"You're not in Valsara anymore," Will started angrily, staring down at the girl. "You cannot cut runes and run wherever you please."

"You *know* I didn't run anywhere across the sea," Devaki replied. "I think there's something down here we need to see. And," she added, lifting her chin a bit higher, "I don't care what your men think."

"During a battle you never rush forward without knowing what you're heading into," Will reasoned.

Devaki crossed her arms over her chest and gave him a challenging look. "Are you going to come with me, or stop me?" Her bloodied fingers drifted over a Strength Rune on the inside of her wrist, poised with expert ease.

Remembering how she had effortlessly summoned so much magic moments ago, Will swiftly caught her meaning. He shook his head and offered her a hand up. "At least ride in front of me and tell me where we're headed. And try not to spray those Bloodgems all over the city; you're attracting too much attention."

As Devaki climbed into the saddle in front of him, he thought he heard her giggle. "'Bloodgems'? That's a pretty old-fashioned term," Devaki said. "I can't remember the last time I heard that."

"I can't remember the last time I said it," Will confessed. Everyday terms of magic and Armellan phrases were long in his past, pieces of himself he had chosen to forget in order to scorn the place and its deity who'd scarred him deeply. Now, the words tasted like molded bread on his tongue.

As they cantered further into the heart of the western district, Will kept the horse at a steady walk as the streets were clearer and easier to navigate. He noticed that Devaki kept the Guidance Rune on her arm open, drops of blood staining her filthy pants. She leaned forward in the saddle, practically over the horse's neck, all shock and weariness forgotten.

"Master Will!"

Will pulled up on the next corner, in front of one of the rebels stationed there who was waving his arms frantically. He had streaks of silver in his short, black hair and lines of strain on his tanned neck. "You should stay back," the rebel cautioned.

"The locals down here are cursed!" added the man next to him, and Will saw this rebel couldn't stop glaring at Devaki. "There's contagious Armellan Blood Magic in the earth here."

"What is that supposed to mean?" Devaki snapped. Will put an arm around her.

The rebels stared hard at the exotic teenager, looking her up and down for a moment before spitting in her direction.

"Pagan filth!" one of them yelled.

"We should cut down the Blood Goddess bitch!" suggested the other, and with alarm, Will recognized hatred and fear in the eyes of his men. In a city now full of rebels, having brown skin was as dangerous as wearing Rhethosian Blue.

"Leave her be," Will commanded. "Explain yourselves to me." There were no connections between Armelle and Rhethosian townes, only rumors of ancient magic or "curses" that Northerners perpetuated like bedtime tales.

"The folk we've seen are heavy with fever," explained the older rebel. "They barely noticed us as we set up patrols. I don't think they even saw our rebel violet."

"They keep saying one thing before stumbling into their homes," the second man contributed. "'Stop digging.'"

Will felt unease creep through his weary body. "Curse" might be a word Armellans didn't associate with their magic, and he knew no Goddess Touched dwelled in Rhethos, but. . . all rumors came from *some* fact.

Those without Cybarys' magic or without faith couldn't travel through the Goddess' Woods. People in the brother townes of Patten and Morely, so close to the ancient trees, had been stricken with fever in the past and then executed by The Bradford to keep the disease contained.

What will Irvin think when he hears about a sickness here in Lorington so similar to what took his family in Patten years ago?

"Let's go," Devaki insisted, breaking Will out of his worrisome thoughts. She tugged on his hands wrapped in the horse's reins.

"Stay at your posts until you hear from myself or Master Irvin," Will said to his men. "Escort any other locals to their homes with caution, but do not harm them."

"Understood, Master Will," replied the older rebel. "Though we wish you wouldn't head down there. It doesn't look safe."

Will said nothing, squeezing his boot heels against his horse's side to move them forward. *What is happening here?* he thought. *And why does the Goddess want Devaki here?*

Several blocks later, Will realized that the homes on either side of them, and the dozen levels of residences above them, were abandoned. Doors hung open, windows looked in on dark, empty rooms, and belongings lay scattered in the dusty streets.

"What happened here?" Devaki murmured.

Will was about to tell her he had no idea when they rounded the next corner, and he had to yank them to a sudden halt. He put a hand on Devaki's shoulder to steady her as their horse shook its head violently.

"Dear Goddess!" Devaki whispered, and Will choked back several less-than-savory exclamations of his own.

Before them, the edge of the western district broke off like the edge of a cliff. The street was cut in a precise line that extended to either side for dozens of blocks, forming a large rectangle of expertly dug-out space. Homes along the sides of the excavated area looked as if they'd been demolished hastily and without much care, with exposed pieces of framework and roofing hanging like permanently suspended afterthoughts.

"Can you see the bottom?" Devaki asked, her voice weak with wonder.

Will craned his neck, cautiously looking over the horse's head and into the sunken digsite before them. Walkways had been cut into the dark soil, trodden to solid ramps of earth that rimmed the area's edges. The scent of sandy earth was starkly out of place within the granite walls. Debris from scrapped homes littered the descending paths, and many digging tools had been left abandoned.

"No," he responded wonderingly. "But I do see. . . sandstone."

"Really?" Devaki questioned and tried to get down from their horse. Will caught her arm, keeping her firmly in the saddle.

"Lower than the initial walkways," he explained, pointing over her shoulder, "there are buildings. Or at least they used to be whole buildings. And they must be Armellan sandstone bricks."

"Let me go," Devaki insisted, pulling at his grip. "Can't you feel that?"

"Yes," Will agreed. "And I don't like it."

It had been a long while since he'd felt the Goddess' presence, but Will felt the unmistakable pull of Cybarys when he looked into the digsite, especially when he squinted hard enough to see the remains of sandy bricks toward the bottom. He shivered and renewed his hold on Devaki's upper arm. *Something about this isn't right.*

"We have to go down there!" she insisted, twisting to look up at him. There was excitement in her dark brown eyes, and a little desperation as well. "There's something here She wants us to see."

Will was about to object, but he could tell from her face that this was an argument he could not win. Devaki loved her Goddess, and because of her faith, she could wield her Touch with more power than Will had ever seen. That magical pull was a beautiful sign to Devaki, but it set a heavy weight of distrust in the pit of Will's stomach.

As if to make her point even more clear, Devaki broke open the bit of blood that had dried over her recently cut Guidance Rune. A sudden desert breeze touched Will's skin, and the glow around the symbol on his daughter's arm was stoked back to life like a dying ember.

Then agony split through the middle of his skull.

Will cried out and hunched forward in the saddle. He dropped the reins and gripped the edges of his head, reeling with sudden, overwhelming pain. He felt Devaki crumple forward against the horse's neck, an anguished scream erupting from her mouth.

The pain blinded Will, reducing the world to a shattered haze of red and white. He was aware of wrapping an arm around Devaki's shoulders to keep her in the saddle. It felt like a lance was driving its way through the center of his head, then expanding with what felt like enough brutal force to split him in two.

Keep your young magic away from here.

Several voices spoke in Will's mind, echoing the command simultaneously. He trembled, ready to collapse. Their horse stepped dangerously close to the cliff's edge.

We protect Cybarys' ancient secrets. You are not welcome here.

Devaki whimpered, and Will felt her start to slip from the saddle. Gritting his teeth, he grabbed blindly forward till he brushed the leather of the bridle. He yanked hard to the left, forcing the beast to turn away from the giant, rectangular hole in the ground. Mercilessly, he kicked the horse's sides, sending them in a gallop back where they'd come from.

The searing pain in his head subsided, and he was able to see again. Every part of him ached like he'd been beaten by a dozen guardsmen. Will urged their horse onward, hoping the farther they retreated, the less effect that place would have on them.

I have never felt magic like that before, Will thought when he could stand to collect his thoughts. *Whatever they are digging for down there, the Goddess doesn't want people near it. So. . . why would the Goddess bring Devaki to that pit's edge?*

Will swore under his breath. This was an unforeseen conflict he couldn't address right now; his focus was the people of Lorington and their Masters. His army now covered the city, and Moore would be forced to speak with him about the future. That was what mattered.

Devaki sat up slowly in front of him, steadying herself with the saddle horn. Will watched her shoulders rise and fall with deep, slow breaths. "Did you hear them?" she asked.

"Yes," Will admitted. "And we should probably heed their words."

"But she led me—"

"Listen to me," Will cut in.

"No!" Devaki insisted. "Why are you so afraid of her?"

Will pulled up tight on the reins, bringing them to a halt. With care, he dismounted and looked up at her. They were at the edge of the western district, back into the wider, cleaner streets of the marketplace.

"Do you honestly feel like that horrible pain came from your loving Mother?" Will demanded. He was aware how crass his words were, but he continued anyway. "You must understand that things in Rhethos are harsher than your home. If you can't tell, the people here fear you and hate your magic, and who knows what waits in that hole?"

"You don't know anything about my 'home,'" Devaki began, her eyes watering. "And I came here for you."

Will grimaced, holding back many remarks that he knew would break his daughter's heart further. He'd written to her for so many years about how he felt, and she had never responded with scorn or disapproving judgment. But now, with her sitting atop his horse, staring down at him with fresh tears in her gaze, he couldn't help but question the core reason behind why he fought in the first place. It was for her.

"Look who's being a lazy son of a bitch!" declared a familiar voice, and Will rotated in the street to see Irvin riding toward them. "Why are you standing around?"

Will cleared his throat, not intending to answer. "How does the east side look?" he asked instead.

"I've finished taming that mess of rich ingrates," Irvin declared proudly. Will glanced at his friend's right hand, which held a freshly bloodied sword. He noticed several small slashes on Irvin's legs, though none of them were bleeding anymore. "And our rebel masters have reported that they've imprisoned some guardsmen in the southern barracks while the rest are being hauled away in corpse wagons."

Will nodded. "The western district is managed as well. Let's head back to the courtyard and meet with Rowlann."

"Oh, I've already done that," Irvin said with a smile. "You've been out here for quite a while, so I came to find you. Rowlann's got Moore, his family, and a few others at The Bradford's statue waiting for you."

"None of them were harmed?" Will asked.

"They all look much better than Sarrett does at this point," Irvin replied smoothly.

Will eyed his friend. "What did you do?"

"First of all, Will, find a place to stash that girl," Irvin said, jerking his head toward Devaki, "and let's go finish taking control of this Rhethosian shithole."

With more effort than it should have taken, Will pulled himself back up into his saddle. When they reached the edge of the marketplace, he stopped beside several of Rowlann's men stationed along the courtyard's outer wall.

"You two," Will began. "Keep an eye on her."

"Really?" Devaki insisted, but she didn't protest further when Will helped her down from their horse next to two large men with bloody Blessing Runes on their armor. He knew they were the only ones he could trust with the girl's life.

"Stay out of sight, and I will find you later," Will assured her. "I promise."

Without giving her a chance to reply, Will turned away in relief from Devaki and took a deep breath to clear his mind. The coming moment was one that he wanted spoken about throughout Rhethos, about how a single man with a force he had mustered in the name of freedom peacefully convinced northern Rhethos' largest towne to fly rebel violet banners . . . at least, that was the story he'd make sure was told.

This is a dawn of a new beginning, Will thought, dismissing any attention he'd been placing on the odd existence of violent Armellan magic in this towne, and how it was calling to his only child. He squared his shoulders as he made his way through the rows of cheering rebels, under the iron archway, and back into Lorington's courtyard.

CHAPTER THREE

SECRETS OF SAHMA

Joshua McKinlee launched himself off the nearest ledge without looking down. His boots hit the platform beneath him, spraying frost into the dawn's icy light. After spending two weeks free of the confines of his mother in the rebel's hidden camp, he knew The Fort's raised walkways and pulley systems by heart. Each creak of water-worn wood was a greeting under his boots, and every rough piece of rope, spattered with melting ice, was a welcome familiarity in his grip.

Joshua slowed his progress at the nearest net of knotted rope when he heard an approaching group of footsteps, shattering the early morning's silence. Peering east, he shielded his deep brown eyes from the dusted beams of sunlight as a group of the camp's children barreled toward him. Joshua had to stop himself from waving when he saw a few familiar faces. Only a week ago, they would have asked him to race with them.

Now, the eight boys breezed past Josh, who had to press his tall, thin frame against the makeshift railing of the platform to avoid being knocked off. They glared distrustfully at the leather gloves he now wore. Ada, one of his mother's former barmaids and also one of his few remaining friends, had suggested donning these a little too late.

"Joshua," she had said worriedly, standing with her hands on her slim hips in the makeshift common hall, "Everyone can see those pagan marks on your hands, and I know what you're up to in those trees every morning. You should spend less time out there before your head softens."

He tugged the gloves Ada had given him up further on his wrists, though not to avoid the pre-winter cold. Normally, Ada would have flashed him her prettiest smile and playfully teased him about how things had changed so much since his recent sixteenth birthday. Yet when Will had left him with a list of the Blessing Runes that would create his newly discovered magic, Joshua had felt no reason to be ashamed, even though Ada seemed to think he should be.

The only other person who could potentially understand and help him was a stranger. Mistress Merheene rarely left her small living space at the very back of The Forts. Joshua had only met her briefly on the first morning of his "free life," astounded to see an old Armellan woman in Rhethos. No one knew why she was there, save for the whispers around camp that she was a passionate supporter of Will, a woman who tried to take on the exclusively male role of monk across the sea and who had found a safe place to worship her Mother far from her home in peace.

These are rebels fighting for Rhethos' freedom, he reminded himself, waiting and watching a few more puffs of hot breath issue from his mouth to give the group of boys plenty of time to get further ahead of him. *They don't follow the Armellan Goddess; in fact, they hate her and want this war to have nothing to do with her magic. Pretty outdated beliefs for people trying to move the world forward.*

Joshua shook his head, throwing back the dirty blond waves of hair that kept falling in his eyes. His mother used to cut his hair regularly, but now she was gone, and Joshua was glad for the distance from the woman who had lied about his Goddess' Touch his entire life.

Joshua's hand darted to his pocket, where his gloved fingers fished past the compass he always carried with him to the list of runes Will gave him before leaving. His favorite so far was a series of loops that came together in a long knot, one that Will notated as meaning "Protection."

"Cut the rune," he had instructed in a whisper, *"say a prayer related to its meaning, and feel a connection to the Goddess. As long as your blood flows, so will Her gift of magic to you."*

A few days ago, Joshua had gathered enough courage to trace the shape of it into the skin of his upper arm. It had seemed gruesome at first. The pain of it didn't bother him much, but the feeling that it sent coursing through his body was disconcerting. It reminded him of his mother and the guardsmen from Kaylyn at the same time; overbearing, yet comforting in a sour sort of way.

But the heat pressed in when Joshua squeezed the cut like Will had taught him, and blood pulsed down his pale skin in thin lines. That made the odd, negative feelings attached to the Blessing Rune fade, and, if he concentrated on what he wanted, he could do things he had never had the power to do before.

Now, in the quiet of the northern Rhethosian morning where he found the most peace and courage, Joshua unsheathed the dagger Will had given him the night his home burned to the ground. He glanced around and, relieved, found the walkways empty of any women, children, or elderly rebels, then rolled up his tunic's thick sleeve to reveal the freshly scabbed Strength Rune.

"Please don't let me break any bones this morning, Goddess," Joshua muttered as a "prayer," and used the dagger's tip to break open his skin again. After quickly sliding the weapon back into its home, he took a deep breath and continued his exciting yet solitary run through the ramps and ropes. When he'd run with the other boys not long ago, he'd learned which pieces of the walkways were most stable, and which to avoid until someone was ordered to repair them. He recalled the fall he'd had on his first day in the camp, and he tightened his grip on the nearest line of rope on his left.

The system had been built high above The Forts for speed of travel and better use of the limited space in the camp's elongated niche of previously deserted land. This run was the fastest way to the Goddess' Woods that others avoided, the place where he spent most of his time when not in training with the rebel Master Orton, who had stayed behind with a small number of men after the army left to protect the remaining families.

Joshua gained speed as he went, leaping after he counted the memorized number of steps between each section of platforms so he wouldn't have to glance down. The fresh blood on his arm started to dry on his goose-bumped skin, and suddenly Orton's gruff bark echoed in Josh's head: *You are an idiot if you think you can balance both sides. I can't teach you to fight, to kill, while you're wasting your time with pacifist magic. One cut throat, and you'll be just like Will with your pagan Touch gone. . . and good riddance.*

Swearing under his breath, Joshua dismissed the logic of Orton's words. He soared across a gap between two long, thin planks and grabbed onto a knotted rope that hung from the edge. Instead of working his way slowly down to the ground twenty feet below, he swung for a moment, twisted the Protection Rune on his upper arm enough to feel fresh blood, and let go.

In the midst of his freefall, two combatting temperatures raged across Joshua's body: the freezing breeze of the morning air and the bright heat of the Goddess' magic that glowed off his skin. Less than a breath later, his feet slammed into the ground. Soft dirt, soaked with last night's rain, melted into mud beneath him. A spray of gem-like magic remnants burst out in a wave. He cringed at the jolt to his entire body, even cried out, but there was no pain, and definitely no broken bones.

"No way," Joshua muttered and laughed shakily to himself. When he stood up straight, however, his body started to vibrate with an uncontrollable rush of delayed adrenaline. He had to crouch back down to the mud, not realizing how fast his heart was racing. *I had no idea if that would work,* he thought shakily.

But there was no one to tell him to be more careful. For the first time in his life, Joshua could go where he wanted and do whatever he pleased. *At least within the boundaries of the rebel camp.* He kept every appointment to spar with Orton, and he helped Ada each night clean the camp's common hall so he'd have someone to talk to. These tasks were enough to satisfy Orton and the other few men in charge.

Yet he was losing connections to the humans around him the more he explored his new gift. He felt this incredible bond with Cybarys since learning about his Touch, something that both excited and scared him. Who could he share that feeling with? Only a small part of Josh wished he could confide in his mother like he used to. She had to be back soon, though; the food that the rebel camp had wouldn't last forever, and Joshua knew all too well how unhappy people could become when they were hungry.

Joshua stood up when the backflow of adrenaline stopped shivering through his limbs. He strode toward a place beyond the edge of the camp, along the border of the Goddess' Woods. This early, he knew Orton was up in the watchtower, and Joshua waved one cautionary hand above his head as he passed under it, walking across the bit of solid ground that the tower's legs stood on, surrounded by an open trench. He was sure that the rebel Master had seen the shower of magic remnants Joshua had created, but at that moment, he didn't care about the consequences.

When he walked under the cover of the trees, everything seemed to dissolve into a peaceful haze of cool green and gray. His favorite spot was not far into the woods, far enough for him to still see the camp's border torches but in a tall enough section of crisp underbrush to hide him from anyone's view. Joshua sat and concentrated, eyes scrunched shut. He focused on the breeze to begin clearing his mind. Each wave of air came forward, tickling the leaves, caressing the bark. . . then it all stopped with a gradual smoothness.

He found that the experiments he'd been trying with the cuts on his knuckles worked best when his mind was clear. Joshua let out a slow exhale, then took off his gloves. *Balance,* he thought. *I can find the balance.* Glancing down, he examined the eight Protection Runes he'd sliced into his skin in the smallest patterns possible.

Help me figure this out, Cybarys. I need you to tell me what to do with this gift.

Joshua stood, brushed wet leaves from his pants. He glanced worriedly at his hands, anticipating the damage he might do today, then murmured, "Orton is going to kill me." He shook himself to relieve the tension in his muscles and faced the closest tree. Forming tight fists, he forced the Strength Runes on his knuckles to break open. Without thinking further, he punched the oak tree in the center of its trunk.

Red light sparked briefly when he made contact, and, when his knuckles didn't crack beneath his skin, Joshua swung at the tree with his left fist. Bits of bark chipped off the tree and cascaded to the forest floor. This was only the third time he'd tried this after getting the crazy idea the night after his mother left: if killing another person made him lose his gifts, what would happen if he learned how to fight only to defend himself? How far could he push the rules?

Every time his fist connected with the trunk, a fresh thought went through his head, and the impact embraced it for one moment, made it real, then shattered it, and let it fall to the ground with the splintered pieces of wood, no longer a burden on him.

Crack.

This is why Mum kept the Goddess' Touch from me; because she's scared of what she can't control or understand.

Crack.

This is why Will can't use his Touch anymore; one blow like this to the wrong part of a person and they would die.

Crack.

This is why Ada doesn't like me anymore; I'm not like anyone else in Rhethos, and that's not what she wants. She wants someone like Will--older and braver and stronger. But Mum is the one who likes Will. I saw it so clearly in her eyes before he left.

Joshua let out a cry, spun, and crashed all his momentum into the tree.

A fissure split up the length of the bark, launching up into the branches above. Joshua stepped back, pulses of residual pain echoing up his arm. Blood leaked from the Strength Runes, yet there was not even a scrape on his knuckles. His fingers, however, were starting to swell.

That's never happened before, he thought, and in wonder and confusion, he took a step closer to examine the damage. *If I use both Strength and Protection Runes together, would I be able to throw more punches? Or does it matter more what I "pray" before I cut the runes? I wish Will was here. Or, better yet, if only I could find him and help him wherever he is right now.*

"The magic will not heal your bones, little Rhethosian."

Joshua whirled, sweat and bright red magic remnants flying from his face and arms. He couldn't stop the look of shock that spread across his face when he saw Mistress Merheene standing alone at the forest's edge. It looked as if it had taken a lot of effort for her to make her way to where she stood, leaning heavily on one of the ancient oaks. Though her clouded eyes seemed to focus on his feet, the old Armellan woman's lips split into an uneven grin as if she could see the surprise on Joshua's face.

"I only mean, use caution," she clarified, her words slightly weighted with an accent that hung heavily on her *o*s. "Our Mother wouldn't want you breaking yourself to pieces, especially at the expense of one of Her beautiful trees."

Joshua lowered his fists, wiping blood on the nearest wet bunch of leaves. He almost reached for his gloves to cover his hands out of habit, but then he remembered that this woman couldn't see him or wouldn't judge him like the rest of the camp was beginning to. There were so many things he wanted to ask her. Jumbled in his head was each bit of knowledge he yearned for to help make a difference in this war.

"I didn't mean to . . ." he began, then frowned and tried again, "I actually don't know what I meant. I'm just trying to . . ."

"Find balance?" Mistress Merheene finished as she adjusted her thick, blood-red robes against the cold. "It's difficult to choose a side, isn't it?" She nodded as if she were aware of the battle between Joshua's ears.

"I . . ." Joshua said, then cleared his throat. He wasn't used to talking about his feelings, especially his inner conflicts as of late, and yet here was the woman who could at least answer some of his questions. Why, out of all the mornings he came out here alone, did she join him now? He thought back to the prayer he'd said to Cybarys, in this place of power. *I asked for help. Did the Goddess tell her to come find me?*

"How did you know to find me here?" Joshua questioned aloud. "What do you know about the Goddess' Touch? And who *are* you?" Everything started spouting from his lips, and he quickly clapped a hand over his mouth, embarrassed.

The Armellan woman laughed, a light, pleasant sound that was jarring coming from a wrinkled old mouth. "Sit with me, little Rhethosian. Our Mother weaves our Fate's Strings in an ever-moving pattern, and right now She has chosen to connect ours."

Though her words only confused Joshua more, he stepped over to help her sit in the chilled underbrush till her back rested gently on the oak beside her. He noticed how, when he helped her, the edges of her robes were painted in a series of runes that shimmered in the morning sun. They scrawled in geometric lines around her wrists, collar, and the hem at her feet.

"Now," Mistress Merheene began, and when she turned her head toward Joshua, he had to swallow unevenly when he focused on her milky eyes. "Across the sea in Valsara, Cybarys' servants are called monks. These important members of society are all male, and when a woman chooses to try and fulfill this role, well, she is frowned upon, to put it kindly. Master Will, however, has no qualms with female monks, thus you find me here, where I can serve and worship my Mother in peace."

Joshua raised his eyebrows, surprised to hear that someone from what was supposed to be a peaceful kingdom could be driven away to a place like Rhethos where her race and her religion were outlawed.

"But don't let me bore you with my history," Mistress Merheene smiled, and she reached out to pat Joshua's leg where he sat next to her. "*You* are the one chosen and blessed by Our Mother."

He stared at the Armellan woman, finding his gaze focused on the wrinkles around her mouth. Was she referring to his Goddess' Touch? Was it really that special, after he had been told his entire life that those with this "curse" were supposed to be killed at birth? Somehow, Mistress Merheene's voice was both sweet and foreboding, and Joshua hung on every word with frightened precision.

"You want to fight for your family and for your kingdom, but you also want to keep your Touch," the old woman continued. "You want to be independent from your mother for the first time, but you miss having her close by. You want to understand and balance all of these things, but there is always a price, little Rhethosian. What is your price for true freedom?"

Joshua froze, then felt his mouth fall open. "How do you know the things you know?" he stuttered. This was the first question that surfaced amongst the tempest of demands and confusion in his head.

"Cybarys connects all of us, as a loving mother to her children," Mistress Merheene replied. She gestured around her at the forest's edge, and several of her long, white braids slid down her robed arms. "In places like this, where Her power is strongest, we feel those connections more powerfully. . . *if* we are open to them. They only frighten and sicken most. But if you open your mind, our Mother will answer you and guide you toward whatever you want to know."

"How?" Joshua demanded. Everything he'd run from since the night his home was engulfed in flames was a tangle of elated confusion. He hated his mother for hiding his magic from him and smothering him with her fear for sixteen years, but now she was away. He loved Will for setting him free and giving him something to fight for, but now he was gone, too. All that was left was this tool, this connection to a higher power that he had been taught to despise his entire life.

"That's why Cybarys told me to come see you this morning," Mistress Merheene said. "To show you the 'how.'" She reached into one of her sleeves and pulled out a dried bundle of leaves. The dark yellow plant was bound in an artful spiral that was already burned on one end. "This is Sahma," she explained. "Monks across the sea, as well as Goddess Touched, use it to speak directly with Cybarys. I do not have much of it, for it only grows well in dry heat, and northern Rhethos is always cold and wet. Therefore, use it sparingly."

Joshua reached out hesitantly. He knew, in Kaylyn, that his mother's main competition sold a wine that was infused with the oil of the Sahma plant, making it a highly addictive, hallucinogenic drink. Flashes of angry, babbling drunks and stupidly grinning addicts who tried to disrupt his mother's common hall came to mind, and his fingers shied away from the bundle of leaves.

"Its smoke will not harm you, little Rhethosian," Mistress Merheene said, and she let the bundle fall into Joshua's lap, untouched.

"Why do I need this?" he asked unsurely. "Can't I just. . . pray here?"

Mistress Merheene shook her head. "There are rules, and spaces of energy that separate this realm from the Goddess'. I know Sahma has been misused in this kingdom, so know this a tool that you can use whenever you are ready. Your Mother is always waiting for you."

Joshua held back, unsure. Then he carefully grasped the bundle of leaves in his right hand, admiring the way they were layered together with the winged tip of each piece of the plant facing outward. He held it up to his nose, inhaling the sharp smells of blackened plant life and earthy musk. Despite his trepidation, it was hard for him to resist walking over to the dying torches along the borders of The Forts not far away, impatient to try.

After all, he'd wanted help, and the Goddess had brought him someone who would not judge him. He'd wanted answers, and the Goddess had brought him a tool to reach out to her. Surely this was right.

Joshua found his gaze kept settling on the freshly clotted cuts on his knuckles. The sore spot on his arm reminded him of what he'd tried with the Protection Rune this morning on his run. He could be capable of so much more, maybe even find a balance between fighting for his kingdom and connecting with the powerful Armellan Goddess.

Mum would tell me not to do this, he thought angrily, remembering how she had told him to keep his head down, keep his mouth shut, and let others make his life's decisions for him for sixteen years. With that thought clear in his head, Joshua found his feet and made his way over to the torches.

Only a brief kiss of flame set the bundle to light, and Joshua held it under his nose for a few seconds before shaking out the slow-burning leaves. Smoke enveloped his face, permeating his mouth, nostrils, and eyes. The world became a warm haze of brilliant colors that flexed and bent with each breath he took.

Joshua tried to speak, but found that his lips were heavy. A bit of panic touched his chest, like the cold embrace of a wave when the tide rolled in. That wave could engulf him if he wasn't careful. He wavered a bit, then took a deep breath, and thought of all the answers he felt he had the right to. *Cybarys,* he began in his mind. *Why do I have this magic? What am I supposed to do with it?*

Everything hung still, his heartbeat echoing like a slow, steady drum in the length of each of his bones. He felt the thrum of the world around him, and it was both comforting and massive, an empty vat of silence that was quickly filled with his disappointment. No one was going to answer him . . . and besides, how could he tell, in this state of mind, what was real or not anyway?

Then, a voice echoed back in his head, first in a warbled wave that he had to strain his senses to hear. *"Fate's Strings, little one, are woven throughout all of my children."* The feminine sound grew in strength, filling the confines between his ears. It was warm and strong, like a hug from his own mother, layered with a power that he knew was fully capable of crushing him. *"Some strands mingle briefly, others are intertwined until they end, and many knot as they struggle against their destinies. Yours shines brighter than others."*

Joshua's mouth and throat were suddenly very dry. *What am I supposed to do with this magic?* he thought once more. *I want to fight, like Will, but I don't think I want to kill anyone.* His head spun and he reached out to grab the stake holding up the torch next to him. He could feel Mistress Merheene's stare from where she stood not far away, observing him.

His eyes widened when he noticed that his fingers shimmered with coral red and deep blue streaks of light, and the runes on his skin ached like hot bruises. Then he admitted something he wasn't aware of until the words echoed in his head: *I don't know what to do.*

"Blood cannot be shed unless it is in service, little McKinlee. You are not meant to take lives, only protect them, and bring them to a free world."

Joshua reeled, overcome by the warm light of the world in the Sahma glow, along with the strength of the Goddess' voice in his head. *He* was supposed to protect and lead people? Wasn't that Will's job?

"There is much more underneath the surface of Rhethos' current conflict. Walk with me, little McKinlee, and we will truly set this kingdom free."

CHAPTER FOUR

FACING THE BRADFORD'S SERVANT

L orington's courtyard was much more subdued now. Its torchlight blended with the arriving dawn that revealed congealing pools of blood and surrendered weapons along the white cobblestones. Though the circular space was filled with thousands of Will's men, there were subdued groups of Rhethosian citizens also present.

Will was sure Irvin kept some of the locals here so there would be witnesses to the way their Lord's lieutenant and Towne Masters would be treated. *Master Irvin Colwell, always putting on a show where he can shine.*

The locals stared up at Will as he rode by, fear filling their eyes as they whispered to one another. A low murmur of resentment bubbled through the crowd, and Will felt it hit him like a tide. That wave would be up to his neck before he knew it, and then he'd be sputtering for air unless he could persuade Moore to see reason, under much more stressful terms that he had hoped.

Irvin rode up next to him and pointed to the group of men at the very center of the courtyard, standing near the base of The Bradford's statue. "We have the three most important ones on display," he whispered. "The Trade Master is the one in furs on the right, Master Torald. To the left is Moore's older son, Adlar, the Gold Master. And, of course, we have Master Jeras Moore himself, The Bradford's servant, front and center. Tough bastard, despite how feeble he looks."

Will took in each man's appearance quickly, creating mental notes on top of the bits of information Marselle's spies had told him in the previous weeks. "Put your weapons down," Will said to his men, who were holding their blades against their prisoners' throats.

They obeyed as Will dismounted, still doing his best to ignore the burn that ran along his left arm and ribcage. He needed everyone to see a strong image of him and flinching at the pain that lanced across his body every time he tried to turn too far wasn't an option.

Adlar Moore may hold the more lucrative title, but Torald is the real power here, Will thought as he observed the men. *Lorington's trade is its lifeblood, and with the northern rebel townes not supporting them and the southern Lord cutting off all trade routes, Torald and his tradesmen have been suffering in the middle.* Still, he withheld any compassion from his face for the moment.

Master Moore took a small step forward, restrained by Rowlann himself. His frame was quite thin, but Irvin was right; he held his head high and his rich fabrics of Rhethosian Blue and deep orange were disheveled as if he'd fought his captors significantly despite his age.

"Master Moore," Will said, giving the man a smile. He raised his voice so everyone present could hear him, and whispers of the impending exchange rolled back among the thousands, beyond what Will could see. "My name is Will Tarran. I'd like to speak with you privately about how my men and I can help solve many of your problems."

"I denied your treaty missives for a reason," Moore began, his voice low and controlled. "Your lies of a peaceful alliance don't mean anything to me; I know I'll end up like Sarrett over there soon enough."

Will glanced at Irvin, who now stood behind him several paces. Irvin jerked his head behind Moore and the other Towne Masters, toward the granite statue of The First Bradford. When Will stepped sideways to see the Rhethosian lieutenant, his throat constricted.

Jonathan Sarrett was strung up by his wrists, several lengths of rope running up the legs of the statue to keep him barely suspended above the ground. The rebels had removed his military uniform, leaving him in his underclothes with his bare feet brushing the stones beneath him. Dried gore plastered his arms and his curled brown hair. Will was unaware if Sarrett hung his head in shame or was merely unconscious.

"We thought it was fitting to display him beneath The Bradford's backside," Irvin spoke up proudly. "Right where that ass of a man belongs."

Will stared at Irvin, trying his best to keep his face neutral. Brutality was a tactic of the old regime he did not want to repeat, but his burns reminded him that it was because of the cowardly lieutenant that almost all of his supplies were gone and many of his men lay dead.

"Sarrett is paying for his crimes," Will began, turning his attention back to Moore. "His disgraceful tactics forced us to use violence against your towne. But you have done nothing wrong, save for letting men like Sarrett and his masters rule you. We've kept the peace with your people and accepted your men's surrender. You owe me at least one civil conversation before we resort to stringing you and your family up with the lieutenant."

Moore's gray eyes darted momentarily to an elderly woman and one young man standing by her side on the opposite end of the courtyard. It was a mere instance, but Will caught the glance.

Unexpectedly, Will found himself wanting to look toward his own child. Even though he wanted her as far away from this mess as possible, there was an inherent need to protect her. He also thought of Angelyn McKinlee, briefly recalling how she always stood with her son proudly at her side no matter the danger.

"I've brought you here to show your people they don't need to be afraid for you or for their towne," Will said, turning in place as he spoke so all could hear him. "We're here to bring peace, and changes that will benefit everyone in Rhethos."

"Murdering rebels!" spat Master Torald from his spot next to Moore, and when Will looked his way, he saw pure abhorrence in the middle-aged man's dark eyes. The rebel holding him pressed the tip of his dagger back against the Trade Master's throat.

"We will wait for our Lord's Captain to come save us," Master Moore began, and Will felt his heart sink. "I do not have any desire to speak with you."

"I assure you—"

"No matter what you threaten, The Bradford will honor our loyalty, especially with the pagan Blood Goddess on your side," Moore snapped. "I have nothing more to say."

Irvin cleared his throat loudly. Though he still wore his boiled leather armor, stained with sweat and blood, he flourished an imaginary cloak with his wrist and bowed before Moore. Will opened his mouth to intervene, but Irvin stepped in front of him.

"I don't believe the Colwell family of Patten ever had the chance to work with you," Irvin said, raising his fake politeness to a volume that was meant for a long speech. "But your honorable reputation reached us in the northern mountain townes nonetheless. If you won't reason with Will, I have a feeling you and I can come to an understanding."

Whispers rose in the gathered crowd, bleeding from the edges of the courtyard back into the streets. People down alleyways stood on their tiptoes or climbed along the edges of carts to get a good look at the former Rhethosian Towne Master now addressing their leader.

"Colwell," Moore mused, chewing over the old family name. He shrugged carelessly. "That means nothing to me."

Irvin slapped Moore across the face. The blow was hard enough to make the Towne Master's head snap back, blood issuing from his lips. Rowlann jerked Moore's arm to keep him standing. Out of the corner of his eye, Will saw Moore's wife start forward, although one of the boys next to her held her still. A wave of sound rippled through the locals and the rebels alike.

"Your time is through here, you old son of a bitch," Irvin snarled, and when Will clamped a hand on his shoulder, he felt Irvin seething. "Give the official surrender of the towne to us, or we will cut your youngest son's throat first."

Will placed himself between his friend and Lorington's leader. "This last night has been long for all of us. We will allow you to discuss what you think is best with your fellow Masters and your family. By sunset tomorrow, we will meet."

For a moment, Will thought Moore was going to spit in his face. Instead, the man turned his head to the right, away from Rowlann, and let a mouthful of blood fall to the stones at his feet. It was as close to acquiescence as Will thought he'd get.

"Rowlann," Will continued, "take Moore, his sons, and Torald to the central barracks."

The crowds began to disperse, and the rebel soldiers were peacefully emptying the courtyard. Several men from Rowlann's company approached him, and Will immediately noticed Devaki walking between them. He swore under his breath.

They did their best to keep her hidden, but she stood out so clearly with her dark, rune-scarred skin. The rebels in the courtyard who noticed her glared in her direction, though they kept their hands from their weapons when they saw Devaki headed toward their leader.

Now that the chaos of the battle had faded, Will knew he needed to find out how to explain her to his rebel Masters who previously had no indication of any Armellan Goddess Touched involved in his cause. Rumors were already spreading.

"Master Will," spoke one of Rowlann's men. "We have a casualty count, an assessment of what's left of the supplies, and reports from scouts that were sent south of the city to share with you and Master Irvin."

"Good," Will replied, then cleared his throat, glancing down at his daughter. He somehow knew that, given the chance, she would slip away from Rowlann's men and try to head straight back to the western district. "I need you to take her to Master Rowlann personally. Tell him to find her suitable accommodations within the barracks, away from entrances into the city."

Devaki stared up at him. The exhaustion and shock he'd first seen on her face was setting back in, now that her magic and the drive of seeing the mysterious digsite had worn off. "I want to stay with you," Devaki began.

"That's not possible right now," he cut in. He couldn't, amongst all else that needed to be handled, conquer the idea of speaking to the girl he'd had to abandon the night she was born. "I'm sorry, but I need—"

"To hide me away?" Devaki cut in. Her body trembled as she spoke, but she stubbornly held her ground. "So I won't see you string up Moore and his family like that lieutenant? Rowlann said you were *different* from the rest of Rhethos."

Will gave her a cold stare, not ready to take her pacifistic judgment. "Sarrett will be taken down and put in a cell where he belongs soon enough," Will replied.

"And you want to put me away, too!" Devaki snapped. "Because you don't want to see me? Because you want to ignore Cybarys' presence here?" She took a step forward, then stumbled as her legs collapsed wearily beneath her.

Will lunged forward and grabbed one of her arms. Red sparks flew between their Goddess Touched skin, attracting stares from the rebels still clearing the courtyard. "You need to rest," Will said firmly. While she found her balance, Will quickly pulled the Rune Ring from his daughter's hand. He passed it to one of Rowlann's men. "For now, do not give this back to her. And keep anything sharp out of her room."

Rowlann's man glanced at Devaki, as if he was afraid of what she was suddenly capable of. Devaki, however, merely let her arms fall to her sides and turned away from Will.

The remaining two of Rowlann's men led him to where Irvin was no doubt waiting in the barracks, a short walk away from the main courtyard. The buildings where Rhethosian guardsmen were usually housed were stout, organized blocks of stone that ranged around the southern curve of Lorington's walls.

Will touched a hand to the side of one of the barracks as they passed, trying to remember the last time he felt the rough cut of granite like this. To him, it was a sign of truly moving south, where the material was plentiful and adorned every street and castle in Clancy by the sea.

"Where would you like us stationed, Master Will?" one of Rowlann's men asked as they cleared a path through the rebel fighters further into the heart of the barracks.

Will shook his head, bringing himself back to the present and taking his fingertips off the stone. Instead of the salty breeze and the whip of fresh canvas sails that were echoing in his mind from his past, he focused on the marching of feet, the organization of weapons, and the shouts of his commanders that filled the space around him.

"Guard the Towne Masters," Will replied. "I want two of your company always with Moore and the others."

The men nodded, and they stopped in front of the nearest stone-clad structure. It was slightly larger than the rest, and the Rhethosian Blue banners that whipped above its corners caught his eye. The Bradford's sigil was something he hadn't seen in a while, but he could make out the blazing sun and dark raven in the dull light.

"Take those down and burn them," Will commanded, then stepped inside.

The square space before him was already well-lit with many candles, its plain walls lined with shelves full of military correspondence. The stone's cool surfaces had absorbed countless hours of pipe smoke, judging by the stale, earthy aroma of the room. At its center was a worn desk where Irvin sat, rubbing his hands tiredly through his thin blonde hair.

"I've been told Lorington's commanding officer did not survive," Will said, shutting the door behind him.

Irvin sighed. "Pity," he replied shortly. "We could have questioned him about this mess."

Even though Will wanted nothing more than to collapse and sleep for days, the information contained in this room's walls brought fresh motivation into his blood. *This* was what he could base changes on, between the haughty rulers of this city and the working class beneath them, just as he'd done in townes like Irvin's twelve years ago.

"Oh, don't delve into that yet!" Irvin protested when Will stepped over to the desk and began examining the nearest stack of letters. "Now that we have a moment, I want to celebrate."

Will noticed a bottle of whiskey and several cups on the windowsill behind Irvin. When Irvin poured him a glass and handed it over, Will took it but did not drink. It was tempting to dull the pain in his side, but he wanted a clear head above all.

"I didn't expect to be inside these walls for nearly another month! That is an accomplishment, brother. Though. . .I do have a confession to make," Irvin began in the stiff silence. "I suppose I didn't have to slap him."

Will gave Irvin a hard look.

"It was a clear insult, though," Irvin insisted. "As if he doesn't know my family name. . . Are you going to drink that or should I help you out?"

Will shrugged. "Take it," he said, and he offered the whiskey back to his friend.

Irvin began to pace. "Just say what you're thinking already, please," Irvin mumbled after draining his cup.

"All right," Will said and met Irvin's eyes soberly. "You might have ruined our chances of peacefully taking control. What were you thinking?"

Irvin shook his head. "How do *you* think you can make this entire towne fall for you without shedding any blood? Behead Moore and the rest instead of wasting time getting him to trust us. There are bound to be others who hate him, too. They probably loved seeing their rich figurehead take a hit."

"Regardless," Will insisted, "I want to gather all the correct information to bring this city together under rebel violet. Now, Rowlann's man mentioned updates, so I'd like to hear what you've been told and see written reports."

Irvin set his drink down on the desk's corner. "Well, we lost five hundred men at the supply line fire," he grumbled. "Another eight at the gates. That's a sharp cut, in my opinion, off our ten thousand soldiers. Almost all of the Rhethosian officers stationed in this district were killed.

"These barracks and several more guardsmen's stations up north hold all of the troops that we want Moore to give over to our command. We could add twenty-five thousand more to our ranks. It would be quite time-consuming to have to kill them all instead."

Will nodded slowly, sorting through what he could do with this information.

"Are you ready for the rest?" Irvin asked. He held up two sealed reports and handed them to Will.

Breaking them open, Will read the latest information with a knot in his throat. "So," he began, "here are the worst parts. Thanks to Sarrett, we barely have enough supplies to feed the army for three days."

Irvin grimaced as his pale blue eyes scanned the papers. "We need to take what we want from this city before we have rebels and locals starving."

Will felt a chill run through his body, and he took a seat behind the desk. "And, according to that second report, the Rhethosian Captain and his army are three weeks away, a month if we're lucky."

"Lovely," Irvin spat, as if the word were a curse. "That's all we have before Caldrell and fifty thousand men arrive in Kaylyn, less than a day from here, and turn that little seaside shithole into our worst nightmare."

Will exhaled. "Right. First, send word to Marselle," he began. "I want an update about the latest supply runs and what she can filter to us; that should be our priority before worrying about Kaylyn and the Captain."

Irvin nodded, though the corners of his mouth twitched. "Do you really want to chat with our lovely smuggling queen Marselle, or her current co-conspirator, Miss Angelyn McKinlee?"

Will smiled wanly. "I won't lie to you," he said. "I do want her here."

"Dare I ask why, Will?"

With a straight face, Will replied, "She has a unique perspective."

"The only perspective you're really interested in is under her skirt."

Will frowned. "I have always been focused on the cause," he began calmly. "I've never been distracted. Why are you so concerned now?"

"You've changed," Irvin said, and Will noticed sparks of jealousy leave Irvin's eyes. All that was left was the reasoning of a good friend, one that Will knew he couldn't discount. "Everyone has seen a difference in you since you went to Kaylyn."

"The rebellion has evolved since I left Kaylyn," Will countered. He held up his hands to either side, as if this were something he shouldn't have to explain aloud. "We're moving forward. Having Angelyn beside me is a change that will benefit our people, I promise you that."

Irvin grimaced, and Will saw many retorts flicker across the man's thin face, passing by like bits of torchlight in the night. He formed counterattacks in his own head, poising them against the backs of his teeth.

But the response Irvin chose was one Will didn't have a weapon to block with:

"Then forget Angelyn. The real problem here is your daughter."

Will took the blow, trying not to show any pain on his face. He stood slowly from his seat, walked toward Irvin, and stopped directly in front of him. "I did not tell her to come here." He didn't really hear himself; a noise was rising in his head, a tinny murmur in his subconscious that was telling him to either punch Irvin across the jaw or wrap his fingers around the man's long neck.

"I know, brother," Irvin said. "She's brought a factor into this fight that almost everyone in Rhethos hates: magic. A distrust of the Blood Goddess runs deep in our bones."

Will knew it was true. Over the last ten years, he had formed alliances with many, and he'd always been open about his past. Yes, he grew up in an Armellan temple, and yes, he had the Goddess' Touch. No, he did not worship the ancient Mother, and no, he did not use her magic because he constantly abused the rules of its creation and hated the idea of using it even if he could.

"Devaki came here because she believes it's her destiny to help free Rhethos' people," Will began. "But I've spent a decade telling everyone that we could do this on our own, without the outlawed faith and its deity."

Irvin let out a breath, apparently letting go of a lot of tension judging by the way his shoulders slumped forward. "We took the towne because of her runes, and I can't deny I'm grateful for that," he said plainly. "But word of an Armellan child using Blessing Runes is already spreading through the ranks, and pretty soon, on top of winning Lorington's people, we'll have to reassure the loyalty of our men."

"We won't earn Lorington's trust by murdering their Towne Masters." Will said this more strongly than he intended, and it lit fresh opposition in Irvin's eyes.

"You see, *that's* McKinlee talking!" Irvin responded, rolling his eyes. "The people are defiant, and we don't have time to woo them over till they parade around in rebel violet. The only way to move forward is by showing them we are in charge. Removing the Towne Master's head is the only solution. I will do the dirty work for you, Will. I always have, and you know it."

Will grimaced, not wanting to acknowledge some of the things Irvin did "behind his back" that he was aware of and chose not to concern himself with. "It's not happening."

"What will you do instead, then?" Irvin demanded, exasperated.

"I will reason with Moore in a day's time. You'll help me, just like the old days with the northern townes."

Irvin grimaced, crossing his arms as if unconvinced.

"We'll point out all that we can provide that The Bradford never could," Will continued. "We'll make fair deals with Torald and his tradesmen, and the Loyals as rich as Moore will have no choice but to follow suit. Angelyn can help me with that, all the way down to the farming families outside the walls."

"All right. I'll do my best to back you up, brother. Let's *not* mention to Moore how close the Insane Captain is."

"Or the giant pit in the western district," Will added, running a nervous hand through his hair.

"The *what*?" Irvin snapped, eyes wide.

"It's not important," Will replied, though he knew that was a lie no one would believe, especially himself.

"Will, you *know* this is weak," Irvin reiterated. "Unless we secure this towne and press on now, Caldrell will shore up Kaylyn like a garrison and stop us from moving any further down the coast!"

"You keep saying words like 'weak,'" Will began, "as if behaving in any way other than what The Bradford would do is doomed to fail. Mercy is not weakness. Empathy is not a form of surrender. I've come this far by listening to the people and helping them with my two hands. That won't change now."

"You've been listening to *me*, too, Will," Irvin insisted. "That's why you've been able to—"

"I think I'm done doing that for now," Will cut in firmly. "Regardless of Angelyn or Devaki or the Goddess herself, this is *my* fight. And I will swing the sword when I choose."

CHAPTER FIVE

BEYOND FREEDOM'S GATES

Shock pinned Angelyn down in the bloody wagon bed. She couldn't move, and she couldn't let go of Belka's stiff, blue fingers. The new set of riders was getting closer, and with Marselle's weapons discarded and nowhere to hide the bodies of Sarrett's men, Angelyn's glance at her friend was bleak.

"I . . ." Angelyn began weakly. "I don't know what to do."

She watched Marselle, noticing her eyes were hard green flints in the flat countryside's pale fog. Her gaze was on the half-dozen men approaching them on the deserted road. She saw no compassion in Marselle's countenance, only quick calculation of what to do next.

This is it, then, Angelyn thought, and it took all of her resolve to wrench her fingers from Belka's and stand next to Marselle in the wagon bed with her shoulders back. If these were more of Sarrett's men, she only wanted her last thoughts to be devoid of the fear that had ruled her whole life like a sweet poison she had willingly consumed.

I wish I could have seen my son one more time, but I know he'll be fine without me, she thought with conviction. *He's finally free of me, like he wanted. And Will . . .*

Angelyn's chest constricted with a warm tightness. Never before had someone both infuriated her and inspired her beyond what she assumed were the confines of her heart. Now, when truly faced with the idea of never seeing the rebel leader again, she found herself feeling something entirely unexpected.

"Son of a bitch!" Marselle swore suddenly, and Angelyn stared at her. Rarely had she heard the Rhethosian lady curse, and those certainly weren't the last words she'd thought she'd hear Marselle utter in her eloquent vocabulary.

"What?" Angelyn demanded.

"That's Master Novak!" Marselle exclaimed and waved an arm above her head.

"*Who?*"

Marselle leaned heavily on the nearest supply barrel, some of the tension leaving her body. She nodded forward with a small lift of her chin. "See the man on the left, with the auburn beard? He's one of the oldest rebels I know." She let out a sigh and put a hand on Angelyn's shoulder. "Relax, McKinlee. We aren't dying tonight."

Angelyn reluctantly loosened her fists; the men who pulled their horses up in front of the wagon looked as menacing as Sarrett's guardsmen, and none of them bore a color except black. She waited as they scrutinized the bodies, noticing herself that she and Marselle had blood drying on their arms and dresses. The man Marselle had waved to dismounted, a smirk rising on his lips under the tangle of his long beard.

"My lady," he began, his thick eyebrows raised knowingly. "This is an excellent reminder as to why I'm glad you're on our side."

Marselle flashed a grin, full of charm. "Master Novak. Your observation skills are impressive."

"They've kept me alive so far," Novak replied with a humorless bark of laughter. He glanced briefly at Angelyn, and for a moment the familiarity in his chestnut gaze went cold. "You usually don't run this far south on the roads. What are you ladies doing out here in this weather? You could lose some fingers and toes if you're not careful."

"Unexpected storm flooded my supply drop," Marselle explained. "And tore up our usual roads. I must say we are glad to see you, as opposed to more of these."

She kicked at the body of the guardsman in the wagon bed at her feet and Angelyn grimaced. Belka's lifeless form was just as close, though the riders couldn't see due to the high wagon walls.

"Looks like you ran into Sarrett's stragglers," one of the rebels with Novak commented. He dismounted and made his way around to the back of the wagon, his nose wrinkled. He glanced up at Marselle and Angelyn, as if trying to process how women had killed four Rhethosian guardsmen.

"If we're sharing, I'd love to hear *your* story, my friend," Marselle prompted Novak.

Novak jerked his head at the other rebels as he talked, and they gathered the weapons and boots of Sarrett's men. Angelyn felt her jaw drop as she listened to all that had transpired outside and inside Lorington's gates.

"Wait," she interrupted suddenly. "You said someone broke into the city with *magic?* Someone used Blessing Runes?"

Novak nodded. "It's a disgrace, if you ask me," he grumbled and spat to the side of his horse's neck. "We don't want that evil Blood Goddess anywhere near our cause."

Angelyn gripped the wagon's edge with her numb fingers. "Marselle!" she blurted. "Josh must have—"

"There's no way your boy could have made it down there," Marselle cut in, her voice almost a whisper.

"But who else could it be?" Angelyn replied.

"Did you just say your son is Goddess Touched?" Novak snapped, and the other five riders raised their eyebrows, looking carefully at Angelyn.

Angelyn swallowed, mentally chastising herself for recklessly speaking about something she knew needed to be hidden, even amongst Will's rebels. The idea that her son, who refused supervision of any kind, had ridden south with Will to be used as a tool for the rebel cause was now all she could think of.

"That doesn't matter if you have a starving army to deal with, it seems," Marselle pointed out, shifting the rebel's attention.

Novak let out an impatient sigh and urged his horse forward. He held out a gloved hand, indicating that Marselle needed help getting back into the driver's seat. "Correct. Master Will now needs your supplies and your assistance, my lady," he said shortly. "You can send word to some of your other girls to route supplies to The Forts; we need this wagon in the city by sundown tomorrow."

"Seems like we don't have much of a choice, do we?" Marselle agreed and climbed over the partition into the front seat, without Novak's assistance. "McKinlee, get up here. You don't need to torture yourself anymore back there. I still need you."

Angelyn stumbled on her freezing feet, her mind too busy whirling with freshly imagined horrors to object. Belka had wanted to ride toward Lorington, toward the smoke on the horizon, and she was getting her wish in the worst way possible. Trembling, Angelyn placed an old blanket over the girl's body.

There's no way Will would have let Josh go to war with them, she told herself as one of the rebels took off his heavy riding cloak and offered it to her to stay warm. *He can't be there, where there are fires and soldiers and chaos and death. He's just a boy!*

Their going was as slow as before when the wagon jerked forward, but Angelyn felt none of the comfort that she should have with a rebel escort now at their side. She hardly heard Marselle chatting quietly with Novak as the wagon bumped along the rough road for hours. She hazily heard Marselle mention loyal family names down in her home towne of Clancy, what several of her spies were up to when Novak inquired, and what the situation was regarding their tactics in Lorington with the unexpected taking of the city.

All she knew was that Belka was dead, Joshua could be in danger, and when she thought she was ready to make a last stand, she was now riding toward a towne full of her new enemies.

"It'll be best if we ride up slowly."

Novak said these words an unknown amount of time later, and Angelyn blinked rapidly as Marselle shook her shoulder. She didn't remember drifting off, but under the warmth of the cloak given to her, she rubbed her hands together and focused her disoriented mind. She glanced up at the gray sky and noticed that the sun was now beginning to set.

They had spent almost the entire day riding to the crest of the hill where the wagon and the half-dozen rebel scouts now rested. Ranged below them, haphazardly coated in waves of twilit fog, was an expansive field. At its center was the beginnings of a fortress the likes of which Angelyn had never imagined.

"Master Will is speaking with the Towne Master this evening," Novak was explaining to Marselle. "Before we rode out last night to secure the borders and find you, rations were already dwindling amongst the army."

"And they'll have to take food from the people before long," Marselle sighed, rolling her neck and displacing a few of her curls. Angelyn noticed Novak's gray cloak draped over Marselle's black gown. "Let's keep this wagon, now worth its weight in gold, up here with your men while we sort out how to handle this mess you've all made."

"I'll take you both down," Novak agreed, and he motioned for one of his men to dismount and hand his horse over to Marselle and Angelyn. "Though,

I have to warn you it won't be pretty; there hasn't been much time to clean anything up."

Marselle nodded and mounted the horse in one swift movement from the driver's seat into the beast's saddle, a feat in itself in her newly acquired cloak and heavy skirts. She held a hand out to Angelyn, a grim expression on her thin lips.

"Belka . . ." Angelyn began, hesitating.

"She'll be taken care of, and her lover will be told where to find her," Marselle replied. "We have the living to worry about now. Let's sort out how to help these men because they certainly can't do it themselves."

Novak grunted at that, but he said nothing as Angelyn took one last glance at the wagon's bed before climbing into the saddle behind Marselle. She knew that Marselle wanted her help because she, of all people, knew not only how to sort and store supplies as she did in The Forts but also how to manage hungry, angry people.

As Marselle kicked her heels and followed Novak down the hill, Angelyn struggled to get a handle on her thoughts: she wanted to face this new challenge of the rebel cause she'd embraced, especially because it was one she felt she could excel at. That spark of importance, of having a purpose, began to flicker back to life in her chest. *But I also need to know Josh is all right.*

Her worries about her son's whereabouts were temporarily eclipsed by the sights of the area surrounding Lorington. The only comparison of this scale of violence she had was the skirmish with Sarrett's men on Kaylyn Field the night her home burned, and that was a blur in her mind. She couldn't recall if there were any similarities between the two stretches of countryside.

This place, however, was much larger than the spot outside her old home. The destruction wreaked upon it assaulted her eyes and nose. Streaks of charred land cut across the back of the field where the rebels' wagon line had sat, dark blooms of soot and debris being all that remained of their vital supplies. Their horse shied away from the area, avoiding the burnt land that smelled of musty, blackened wood. The closer they got to Lorington, the more the ache in her stomach grew.

She shrugged her borrowed cloak closer to her body and forced herself to look up at the walls of the city. The sheer scale of the carved stone was daunting. Instead of the feelings of safety and power she was sure the walls were meant to project, Angelyn felt a nasty wave of imprisonment wash toward her.

This place is enormous. She watched as Novak shouted up to the tiny shadows of men atop the battlements. *We have to make this work for the rebellion to survive.*

"We'll wait here for a moment," Novak said, and his strong voice was instantly absorbed by the massive walls before them. "They've got to manually open the gates for us."

"Why's that?" Marselle asked.

"Not quite sure how because there were tens of thousands of men out here in the chaos. But word is Master Rowlann broke the mechanism. Some say he has pagan runes cut on his armor," Novak grumbled, and Angelyn glanced at him when she heard a bit of fright in his voice.

She watched as the massive gates were jerked backward in uneven motions till enough space was cleared for their horses to pass through. Novak rode in first, but Angelyn put a hand on Marselle's shoulder so they stopped halfway. Something on the ground caught her eye.

Gathered in bunches around their horse's hooves were sparks of deep red light. Some were buried beneath the surface of the mud, but many of the gem-like orbs lay like streaks of unmined ore at Lorington's feet. She blinked several times, wishing the unnatural glowing specks would disappear.

It didn't make sense. She thought of the pacifistic rules of the Armellan kingdom that her friend and mentor Gabriel Chapman had shared in whispers back in Kaylyn. Seeing the Goddess' Touch used for destruction like this was confusing.

Josh? she thought, panicking. *Did Josh do this?*

An unexpected memory pressed itself to the forefront of her mind, of the last time she had seen magic remnants.

At The Hamond, sixteen years ago, she lay covered in sweat and blood. Every muscle in her body quivered, ready to give up and never move again. But the baby in her arms kept her breathing, even after what Gabriel had just done to the fragile little boy. "The Blood Moon" was an occurrence that only cursed Rhethos every twenty-five years, and it shone in the sky the night Joshua chose to join the world.

Her fingers brushed over the rune Gabriel cut in the smallest shape possible at the base of Joshua's skull. "Protection," he whispered reverently as the crying baby's blood began to clot. "It will keep him safe from the guardsmen who take every child for fear of them being Goddess Touched, as long as I bleed for Cybarys while they are examining him." Angelyn couldn't take her eyes off the bits of red light that were scattered across the bloodied bedspread. Deep maroon specks that pulsed with unnatural light had appeared after Gabriel cut the rune.

No matter how skeptical she was of magic, those specks were real.

The remnants of magic at the feet of their horse were also real, and for a moment both instances blended together in Angelyn's mind, forcing her to accept the Armellan Goddess as another powerful variable in this fight for Rhethos she had joined.

"McKinlee," Marselle began, her voice unusually subdued. "It can't be your boy. He's safe, far away from here." With that, Marselle led their mount forward into Lorington's courtyard.

When the gates slammed definitively shut, Angelyn couldn't help but marvel at the sheer size of everything around her. Two weeks ago, her life had consisted of the small, declining towne of Kaylyn, and places like Lorington, despite their relative proximity, were distant dreams. Everything from The First Bradford's statue to the thousands of buildings that barreled beyond the courtyard's walls was overwhelming. The granite expanse was unsettlingly silent and void of people, save for the occasional rebel soldiers on patrol.

"Master Will would like to see you this way, in the barracks," Novak instructed.

"Not so fast," Marselle said, and she glanced sideways at the bearded rebel. "I have old friends inside these walls who I haven't connected with in a long time. McKinlee would do fine speaking with Will in my stead."

"Going out there wouldn't be the best idea, my lady," Novak cautioned. "The streets are secured, but the locals are still loyal to Moore and The Bradford. It's not safe."

Marselle gave Novak a shallow smile, one that Angelyn had quickly learned meant the woman was nearly out of patience. One kick of her heel and a flick of her wrist made their horse sidestep up against Novak's mount, pressing Angelyn's leg against the rebel's saddle. Marselle leaned over and gently placed her hand on top of Novak's thigh.

"You know," she whispered, "I am rather bored with men telling me when I'm safe or not. I've found that . . ." Angelyn barely saw Marselle's grip dart down the rebel's leg to the sheath strapped to his outer calf. ". . .I have myself well taken care of." She pulled his knife free and tucked it against the horse's saddle. "Off you go, McKinlee. Say hello to that handsome rebel leader for me."

Angelyn slid off the back of the horse while Novak grunted several curses under his breath. She'd never seen Marselle interact so brazenly with Will's men; to behave freely around her girls in the rebel camp was one thing, but these were rebel soldiers, and, more importantly, former Rhethosian men.

Now they're Will's men, Angelyn reminded herself as Marselle rode off, leaving her alone with Novak in Lorington's courtyard. *Will, who these men obey, and who listens to each of them and treats them as equals, not monsters or minions.*

"That woman astounds me," Novak grumbled, tugging at his beard as he shook his head. "It's Miss McKinlee, yes?"

Angelyn nodded, then jumped as the rebel pulled a folded piece of violet cloth out from under his cloak. He tossed it at her.

"You should at least get the blood off of your face," he muttered. "Would you rather walk or ride there?"

Angelyn ran the cloth along her cheeks and forehead, trying not to think about what she must look like. She steadied herself, taking a deep breath that was filled with ash and the coppery aroma of blood. "I better keep moving on foot. Why is Master Will in the barracks? If he's captured Lorington's leaders, why not use the Towne Master's suites?"

Novak gave her an exasperated look, one that twisted his mouth in an ugly grimace. "You don't know our rebel master very well at all, do you?" he chuckled darkly. "Follow me."

Well enough, she thought, grumbling to herself.

After dismounting, Novak led his horse through the iron archway of the courtyard into the organized blocks of barracks that ran along Lorington's southern wall. Here, the eerie quiet swelled to a bustling of sound as they approached where the rebel army had spent the last night and entire day taking control of the city.

Novak handed the reins of his horse to a nearby stable hand as they walked. In between the rows of stout, stone buildings were smaller courtyards where fires burned, weapons were cleaned, and echoes of many different victorious songs met Angelyn's ears.

Just as the first time she'd entered the northern rebel camp beyond the Goddess' Woods, she expected riotous monsters of men abusing their new-found power, yet all she saw was subdued, respectful pride in the men around her. Once again, these people surprised her, as their leader had.

"Watch your head," Novak barked, and Angelyn focused on the path in front of them. The rebel had led her into a large, square building in the center of the barracks, lined with detailed white stone. The slanted awning in Rhethosian Blue at its entrance was low to the ground, forcing Angelyn to duck as they approached what must have been the former Rhethosian commanding officer's home. Angelyn had to stop and press herself against the wall to her right to avoid a group of men marching by.

Novak put his ear against the double doors before them, listening. "Well, this is it, Miss McKinlee," he began, glancing back at Angelyn. "Best go give that report."

Angelyn felt her throat go dry. Who was she, really? She thought of hesitating until Marselle came back but dismissed all of her unsure thoughts. Will himself told her to make her own choices and determine her own future. So instead of obeying her fears, Angelyn grabbed the door handle and showed herself inside.

"Sarrett's in a cell now, as you wanted," Irvin was insisting, his back to the door. "Though the men all agree only one day of public humiliation isn't a fair punishment for his crimes."

The small, square room was packed with shelves lining the walls and a short desk set centrally on the stone floor. Will stood behind the desk, one hand set against its surface, the other pressing over his eyes, no doubt in reaction to Irvin's displeased tone. When he pushed his fingers back through his hair, that nervous habit of his that Angelyn recognized, he spotted her and froze.

That moment hung for longer than it should have, suspended for several heartbeats. Angelyn held Will's gaze, observing all the emotions that flew over his features: shock at her sudden appearance, relief, then the overwhelming pressure of his current predicament.

Despite this wave that swelled from his spot in the room to hers, Will's lips ended up curving into a smile. Angelyn smiled back, though the expression faded immediately when Irvin spun, blinked away his surprise, and glared at her.

"Oh, you've got to be joking!" he sighed. "Dare I ask why you're here instead of our dear Marselle? And whose *blood* is that?" He wrinkled his nose, frowning at her stained dress and cloak.

Angelyn broke eye contact with Will, something that was harder than she thought it would be, and gave Irvin her attention. "I'm here on Marselle's behalf," she explained. "And. . . you know what?" she added angrily, "I bet it was *you* who brought him down here. Where's Joshua?"

Irvin stared blankly at her. "Your boy? Will insisted he stay behind. But you're right; if I had a choice, he'd be here proving his worth."

Angelyn caught Will's gaze again, silently begging him to tell her the truth. He nodded, and Angelyn felt her shoulders relax. It still didn't make sense; two people in Rhethos had the Goddess' Touch, and only one of them could use it. If Joshua wasn't here, who broke the gate mechanism?

"Look, love," Irvin began with a condescending smile before Angelyn had a chance to ask. "While you and your new sisters-in-arms have been traipsing around the countryside, we've been managing the siege and submission of this towne. It would be best if you'd just—"

"A girl died at my feet for the cause," Angelyn cut in, and she took an aggressive step toward Irvin. He had no idea what had happened on the road. Belka's face flashed across her mind, and Angelyn's temper flared even higher. "This is her blood, not mine."

"Irvin," Will intervened. "Leave her be. We'll meet with Moore and the rest soon, but in the meantime, I'll speak with Miss McKinlee."

Irvin grimaced. "Right. I'll see what Novak has to report." Irvin marched past Angelyn, though he stopped a step behind her and lowered his voice. "You know," he sneered, "I bet he'd take out Sarrett's guts string by string if *you* asked him to do it."

Angelyn stared, speechless, as Irvin left. She understood, from what Novak summarized, that the lieutenant had hurt the rebellion badly. When she looked back at Will, she realized something: he had spared Sarrett's life, and that was something he never would have done before meeting her.

She did understand Irvin's side, however; a dark piece of her heart wanted to abandon Marselle's task and find where they were keeping the man who had killed her best friend and burned down her home. Rhethosian Justice, in all its cold "one cut throat for another" barbarism, sounded appealing.

She shook her head, clearing her thoughts. "Irvin is as pleasant as ever," she observed once the door had shut.

Will grimaced. "I'm sorry." He cleared his throat and shifted his weight from his spot behind the desk. "Would you tell me where Marselle is? Who did you lose?"

Angelyn watched Will shift a hand to rub against the length of his rib cage on his right side. Through his dark tunic, Angelyn could make out the extra bulk of layered bandages: a new wound, evidence of him placing himself in harm's way side by side with his men.

"Who did *you* lose?" she questioned back.

It didn't take long for both of them to speak their tales of what had transpired since they'd last seen each other. When silence fell, Angelyn stepped forward, aware of the space closing between them. Her feet stopped at the foot of the desk, its span the only thing keeping them apart.

Glancing down, she saw piles of parchment detailing supply counts, innumerable lists of local family names, and many maps of Lorington's four districts. It seemed overwhelming. When she looked back at Will, Angelyn saw his gaze flick to the amethyst on her neck that had belonged to his mother.

"Will. . .?" Angelyn asked after a moment. "What's *really* wrong?" She thought she saw something else troubling him, beyond the worries of the city, some deeper secrets that she was barely able to notice but wanted to learn more about.

Suddenly, as if triggered by a physical blow, Will put a hand over his mouth, gripping the edges of his jaw and the rough shadow of his beard. He clenched his eyes shut, and when he looked at her again, Angelyn almost thought she saw a haze of tears. Her hand strayed across the desk, brushing against layers of thick paper. When she gripped the tips of his fingers, he grasped back tightly.

"It's Devaki," he said softly, the words muffled by his hand. "She's here, and I have no idea what to do."

"Who?" Angelyn asked.

A harsh knock came at the door, and two rebels stepped into the office without any further warning. Angelyn pulled her hand back, though she noticed Will almost made it impossible to do so.

"Master Will," spoke one of the men. "There are reports of fighting up in the northern district. People have died on both sides."

Angelyn looked quickly to Will, who had straightened his shoulders and hidden all sense of fear or frustration from his face. "How many?" he asked sharply, stepping out from behind the desk. When he stood next to Angelyn, she noticed how he favored his right side, leaning ever so slightly into his hip with his elbow pressed toward his ribs.

"Six," the rebel responded. "We know you said not to harm citizens, but they killed two of ours first. Some accusations were made of stealing food."

"Find Master Korgan, or Creel. One of them and their men will go up with you to keep the peace," Will said, and both the rebels relaxed noticeably. "Take army rations with you to replace anything that was taken."

"There's not much left," the man spoke anxiously, his tone becoming a bit defensive.

Will glanced at Angelyn and briefly put a hand on her shoulder. "Thanks to her, that's about to change."

CHAPTER SIX

BEING KEPT IN THE DARK

Sarrett felt the withdrawal setting into his bones but refused to give up hope. Even though he'd lost his senses on the battlefield, willingly losing his high ground and shouting at a hallucination of his dead sister in front of his men, they would save him. Even though he'd been shamed like a disobedient animal in front of northern Rhethos' largest towne, his Captain would come for him. Even though he now shook uncontrollably, discarded like spoiled meat in the back corner of a cell, *someone* was on their way.

He was a Rhethosian lieutenant, after all. He knew things. He had value. He demanded fear and respect and prestige in his life!

Sarrett knew in his current state there was no way he could escape on his own. His body shook and shook and shook. Every part of him vibrated with fury and the all-consuming need for Sahma wine. Since his discovery of the drink in Harling's cellar in Kaylyn not six months ago, he hadn't gone eight hours without a small glass.

He hated that it had escalated, giving him both brilliant ideas and haunting nightmares, always calling him back for more. A man with his talent and family name didn't belong here, within stone walls with narrow bars and hardly a torch for light or warmth.

Sarrett's bloodied hands moved thoughtlessly across the dirt floor as if in search of something he knew wasn't there. *How long have these rebel bastards had me down here? A night? A week?* His trembling fingers examined the bruises on his arms, the scrapes on his knuckles, and the large bump on his head where the rebel leader had knocked him unconscious. His body jittered with a nauseating range of emotions, returning to one fact: *someone will save me.*

"No one's going to save you!" scoffed a harsh voice, full of merciless laughter. The rebel who left him dried meat and lukewarm water continued to guffaw, and Sarrett realized that he had, at some point, spoken his thoughts aloud. He hadn't heard himself over the chattering of his own teeth and the quivering of his eyes in their sockets. One glance at the tin cup made him ache for what his heart truly desired.

"Then why keep me alive?" he roared as the man retreated.

Caldrell will be arriving up here soon, Sarrett reassured himself, but each time he thought on it, the more his addled mind had trouble making sense of it all. *But. . . why is he coming? Because I failed to capture Will? He did threaten Mayra and my children, didn't he? I swear to The Lord I put them somewhere safe. Or is there something else that the Captain wants for his master in northern Rhethos? Something more that I can't remember?*

His brain pulsed in demanding knocks against his skull. Surely Harling's wine had made it to Lorington; it was *too* good to be confined to a shithole like Kaylyn. All he needed was a sip and the pain would cease. The comforting, brilliant haze would take over. Without the wine, all the memories were coming back of times he wanted to drown, just like Lily had. The Sahma oil turned his concerns into passable pleasantries, and his deepest fears into conquerable whims.

He groaned and turned toward the wall.

"Pride, brother, is forever your ugliest quality."

Lily's sweet, young voice tickled at his mind. Sarrett shut his eyes, refusing to look toward the other end of his cell where he knew she was waiting. After seeing her blue-skinned expression of shame on the battlefield, he could hardly stand looking at her in a place like this.

"If you could only let it go, Jon, you would see the clarity that comes with sobriety and repentance."

Sarrett couldn't help glancing, briefly, in the direction of the cell that was suddenly filled with a dull, blue-gray light. The shimmer of a girl barely in her teens stood pressed against the wall in a sodden, dusty blue dress. Long, lank dark hair hung in front of her saddened eyes, river water leaking from her swollen lips.

"The only thing in your way is your delusional pride."

Sarrett let out a whimper and snapped his attention to his bare, soiled feet. "You don't understand, Lily," he murmured. "You were too young. This is all I have. I cannot let go."

"What did they do to you?" Lily asked, her watery voice warbled with pain. *"You deserve to go back to how you were when I knew you. Was it your Captain? Or was it this drug that scarred you beyond recognition?"*

Sarrett refused to look back at his saddest mistake. Everything after Lily didn't matter; every bit of his soul that he soiled, every bit of his dignity that he destroyed, was worth it.

So he would not give in to his captors. His pride for the military that gave his family name purpose was too strong to betray to the likes of Will Tarran. In his heart, however, he knew that if that damned man walked in wearing his black and rebel violet, holding a bottle of Harling's wine, Sarrett wasn't sure what he'd do.

It wasn't just Lily. He needed it to press back the memories of years before he came to Kaylyn and what happened in his training in the south. In the darkness of his cell, Sarrett futilely fought a torrent of images that the Sahma wine had kept buried.

Heartbreak in his mother's eyes when he brought Lily home . . .

Vomit bursting through the fingers clamped to his mouth . . .

Reports of men being forced to dig, far north . . .

Pride on his captain's face, his teeth stained with wine . . .

None of it made sense, and Sarrett ignored the flashes that kept appearing in his head. He clasped his arms about himself, cradling his head and his chest, including the remains of his lieutenant's jacket.

Over and over, he reminded himself that someone would save him, wouldn't they?

CHAPTER SEVEN

POWER IN CONSISTENCY

Will stopped gathering evidence when he lost the daylight. From his seat in the former Rhethosian officer's building, it took tremendous effort to look away from the stacks of public dispute records and military reports to summon a messenger.

When a member of Rowlann's company arrived, Will told him to take Moore, the Trade Master Torald, and Moore's sons up to Towne Centre, the massive castle centered in the northern district.

"Escort them with dignity," Will clarified. "I've seen the looks around the barracks the last day from our men and Moore's, and you can tell them why these leaders get such good treatment."

"Why is that, Master Will?" the man questioned.

"Respect," Will answered, "is vital to our success. Let Moore know that he's welcome to choose whatever chamber he sees fit for our meeting."

Rowlann's man nodded, taking several others with him for the transportation of their most important prisoners. No doubt many of the rebels assumed he and Irvin would make good on their threat to hang Moore and his followers soon enough.

Will faced the faded glass of the former commander's quarters. One month. Those two words rang against the inside of his head like an incessant death toll. If he was lucky, that was all the time he had before Caldrell could fortify Kaylyn and have fifty thousand Rhethosian soldiers less than a day's ride from Lorington. What could Will achieve in such a short time that would ensure the crucial foothold of his cause?

He sighed, pulled the strip of leather out of his hair, and ran his fingers through it one more time. His torn jerkin, burned vest, and bloodied trousers had been replaced with a clean set of black garments salvaged from the supply crates.

There was a fresh wrap of violet cloth on his upper left arm, and seeing it reminded him of the night he'd arrived in Kaylyn a mere month ago. It was odd, observing his reflection the same on the outside, yet the inside of him felt so different. He knew, in his heart, it was because of the woman he'd met there.

"Ready to chop off some heads, brother?"

Will gave Irvin an exasperated look, taking his friend's dry sense of humor with a grain of salt. Irvin stood in the doorway, and Will noticed, despite how much they'd handled in the course of their first night and the entire last day, Irvin had found the time to completely redress himself in as much finery as possible. He swallowed a question as to where Irvin may have acquired such clothing.

The splendor of his intricately patterned doublet, laced cuffs, and pressed trousers echoed the prestige of when Will had first met him in Patten, a lazy, egotistical Towne Master. Irvin tapped the toe of a neatly polished boot impatiently.

"I've sent them ahead, as planned," Will began. They had discussed their strategy for the night less than an hour ago, but he still felt the need to reiterate its beginning stage.

Irvin nodded, adjusting the hem of his spotless, silver-gray sleeve. "Moore's eldest is here to join us on our walk, as you requested." He jerked his head to his left, and Will stepped away from the mirror to get a clearer view of the exit where he spotted Adlar Moore, and four of Rowlann's men behind him.

"My father has chosen the west hall," Adlar Moore said, his thin lips barely moving, as if speaking to them was painful. "Though I have to say we didn't expect to see our castle again."

"Things are changing, my friend," Will replied. "You should learn to embrace the unexpected."

Adlar stared blankly at him, blinking with a furrowed brow. A day's worth of research about the Moore family confirmed that the oldest son was arrogant and a bit dim-witted, and Will intended to use both these character flaws to his advantage.

Will motioned for Rowlann's men to lead Adlar alongside him as he made his way out of the barracks. The gaze of every rebel soldier was drawn to them, and Will couldn't tell if he saw more distrustful eyes or hopeful ones.

They're torn, too, between Irvin's bloodier, easier path and the more peaceful yet difficult one I constantly preach.

He glanced briefly at the section of barracks where his man had retained the majority of Moore's guardsmen. There were so many soldiers in this place, now imprisoned in the buildings where they were stationed because they remained loyal to their Towne Master.

"I've never walked along this street," Adlar commented as they made their way along the main thoroughfare that ran north through the city. The polished white stones of the street were still deserted, barely touched by the day's last light.

Will glanced sideways at Adlar, pretending not to have noticed what he'd said. A younger version of his father, Adlar's thin frame and sharp facial features were visibly strained. He clearly wasn't used to people not hanging respectfully on his every word.

"It's not as if we have time to ride, let alone stroll through every district of the city," Adlar added, more strongly than Will expected. He stared pointedly at Will, eyes demanding a respectful response, but neither Will nor Irvin did much but shrug. Heat rose on the young man's cheeks.

The two rebels stationed on every corner nodded as they passed. Each direct route that appeared, Will made sure to lead them down a side street instead, much to Adlar's annoyance. When Will glanced up at the residences, he saw faces staring down from between Rhethosian Blue drapes. Word would no doubt spread fast of his "amicable stroll" with Jeras Moore's heir, like he wanted.

Will caught Irvin's eye. Over the years, they'd grown accustomed to persuading people to their cause as a team, and it was an easy pattern to fall back into even under new circumstances.

"It must be nice," Irvin began in the silence, "to walk these streets so safely."

"Meaning. . .?" Adlar said slowly.

"Meaning it must be hard to keep the peace, as of late," Will clarified, "with how your great city has been caught in between the boycotts of the south and the rebellion to the north. People have surely been suffering within your walls."

"Not the people who matter," Adlar smiled. "Lorington can hold its own. . .always has."

Irvin gave Will a pointed stare, eyebrows raised. If the formality of persuading the Towne Master and his people to their cause did not work, they could potentially work with those in the city walls who were considered less (and populated more).

"I've no doubt of the strength of your home," Will said, not bothering to look at Adlar as he spoke, "though there has been trouble in your western district."

"Not trouble, just sickness," Adlar replied. "The poor are always sick and always expect their betters to save them."

Will's mouth tightened into a thin line as he nodded subtly to Irvin: having a man who used to rank higher in Loyal status than Adlar himself respond to that comment would be best.

"Such an entitled bunch, aren't they?" Irvin sighed, getting an enthusiastic nod from Adlar. "I had a similar situation in my old home. The Rhethosian Captain and his men didn't arrive to help until the illness had spread through most of towne."

Adlar rolled his eyes, then muttered, "Well, it's hard for our Lord to protect us from such things when he's busy dealing with rebels like you."

Irvin grunted, and Will barely heard him say, "There's always an excuse not to help."

Will slowed his step to focus on the form of Towne Centre that loomed larger before them. Letting Moore and his family decide where to hold the evening's meeting in this historic location was a courtesy he hoped would earn him some sense of diplomatic cohesion. This could be such a turning point in his cause that Will had to take a moment to breathe in.

"The castle was commissioned by the First Bradford himself," Adlar said, his chin raised with pride. Now that Will and Irvin had given him the attention and responses he wanted, Adlar didn't seem to want to stop talking.

Moore's eldest son's gaze was also on the stacks of mighty square turrets that rose higher than Lorington's walls. Their decorated granite forms layered inward, each massive structure skirting the main building like a stone collar. "It is the largest and oldest Towne Centre in this central part of Rhethos."

Will nodded, knowing the history well. Seeing the castle and the clear superiority on Adlar's face told him he was used to jaw-dropping admiration around himself and his family. *That makes him blind to more important things.*

"It was all about size with those bastards, wasn't it?" Irvin commented. He sounded unimpressed, but Will knew better. On the inside, Irvin was itching to explore the impressive structure and make its gilded halls and extravagant rooms his own. When Will saw Irvin's step quicken, then relax into a confident saunter, he knew the man's tell: this was his element, and he was happy to be back in it.

Despite his clear animosity for them, Adlar took Irvin's comment as a compliment, one somehow directed at him and his family. "These walls have housed my family for hundreds of years," he said pointedly.

Will couldn't help but marvel at the size of the enormous stone steps that led to the Towne Centre's towering doors, and the west-facing windows that slowly received the setting sun's rays. One could never tell that any battle had taken place outside Lorington's walls the night before. From a place like this, the ideas of bloodshed and Blessing Runes seemed impossible.

Moore's son was still rambling, mentioning how there used to be more guards, more servants, and more welcome decor until recent times. "And there's practically no food left," Adlar added.

That comment made Will halt. "According to your ration reports in the army barracks, the food stores up here should be plentiful."

Adlar scoffed, then licked his lips. "Lies," he said, as if it was something to be proud of. "Your comment, Master Colwell, about suffering reaching the entire city is true. With our Lord so far and you rebels so near, trade is nearly at a standstill. Whatever your lot brought into these walls is probably more than what you'll find in winter storage centers throughout Lorington."

Will and Irvin gave each other concerned looks. *I knew food was an issue,* Will thought as they continued walking, *but this is an actual crisis.* He added it to his list of items to address in their meeting with Moore.

While listening to Adlar's further comments, Will scrutinized their surroundings for more details of the towne's recent history. His attention was on every inch of this place as he appreciated the fact that, in this powerful, loyal towne, his violet-bearing men guarded its doors and now led him inside. The receiving hall boasted a high ceiling with stone-patterned staircases encircling the surrounding walls. The bones of the castle spoke as strong of a statement as the outside.

"The castle is impressive," Will added after one of Adlar's rambling sentences about his grandfather's additions in the east towers.

At first glance, everything in the receiving hall, along its walls, and by the staircase they now climbed was magnificent. Encased in aged yet plain gray-speckled stone on the outside, the shock of the grandeur indoors was easily overwhelming. Shortly, however, Will noticed that Lorington's Towne Centre had evidence of neglect that no one had had a chance to hide.

The rugs are nearly threadbare, he thought, noticing their thin feeling under his boots. *Every tapestry and painting is dusty. The furniture on display is stained and does not match. Where are those who usually would upkeep such things?*

Will was wondering if Irvin was also seeing these signs of neglect, but instead an old memory came up, causing Will's steps to slow; eight years ago, when he went to Patten Towne to persuade its Master, Irvin Colwell, to his cause, Will had seen similar issues.

Patten was a prime towne to turn its colors because The Bradford neglected its needs. Being so close to the Goddess' Woods, winter illnesses were blamed on curses from Cybarys. When Irvin called for food, healers, and other supplies, he was ignored. Is something similar to Patten happening here?

Will had to clear his head as he, Irvin, Adlar, and Rowlann's men reached the end of the hall. They stood before an ornate door that opened on a long, rectangular room. The majority of space was taken by a slim table, bathed in the sunset that streamed through a wall of windows behind it. It had been many years since he'd been in a place as fine as this, fresh clothes included. Will squared his shoulders to meet the challenge he knew he'd be facing in the room.

Jeras Moore sat in the center of the table, opposite the entrance so the sun shone in over his shoulders. Will acknowledged this position of power and let Moore have it. Despite the glare off the polished wood, Will took a seat across from Moore, nodding at the old man, who stared stonily at him as Adlar sat on his right.

Torald, the middle-aged Trade Master, sat on Moore's left. Once Rowlann's men filtered into the room and shut the door, Will noticed Rowlann himself standing in the corner, his hand on his weapon. Next to him was Moore's younger son, who showed no inclination of sitting. In fact, he looked quite distracted, as if he couldn't care less what was about to happen here.

Finding it odd that he was still standing, Will motioned to a chair on Moore's side of the table, but the young man shook his head dismissively after flicking his eyes to his father. *His name is . . . Gardain,* Will recalled. *The one who stopped his mother from running into the courtyard the night Irvin struck his father. Why won't he sit? Or. . . will Moore not let him?*

"It was a waste to bring that one up here," Moore began when he noticed where Will's attention was. "Gardain's better suited for. . . other tasks. Now, can we get through this? Your gesture to meet with us up here, where my family has worked so hard, one last time is not lost on me."

"Well, you're welcome, then," Irvin sighed. He swiftly kicked two chairs out from under the table next to Will, one to sit in and one to prop up his new boots on. "This really is a lovely place. And this doesn't have to be the last time you see it."

Moore placed his hands on the dark wood of the tabletop, knitting his long, wrinkled fingers together. His frail shoulders straightened against the back of his chair, as if his opposition didn't need to be vocalized yet again.

Will glanced at Adlar, who, despite his constant bragging on the way here, was now completely silent in the presence of his father. Torald, for all his defiance in the courtyard the previous evening, also followed the Towne Master's lead.

This is a different dynamic than the northern townes, Will thought, *where all the towne's Masters share power and respect. Here, the Moore family is either completely loved and obeyed, or more likely, Jeras has something over them to command such loyalty.*

"Your family has done a lot to care for this towne," Will began, keeping his attention on Moore. "And because you seem to value as few words as possible, I'll be brief: it's clear to me that your towne hasn't been thriving as much as you'd like to imply. Your son actually shared many details with us and showed us the recent disrepair of this castle on our way here. Thank you for that candor, Adlar."

Moore glared at his eldest son, clearly embarrassed by this error. Out of the corner of his eye, Will noticed a small smile touch Gardain's lips. *He won't sit with his family, and he's aware of his brother's blind arrogance. Interesting . . .*

"You are right that a place like this is hard to upkeep," Moore admitted smoothly.

"I can relate to that," Irvin spoke up. "But these are things we can easily fix if we work together. There's merely the formality of you announcing an official surrender to Master Will and his cause and placing violet banners on your beautiful castle turrets." He looked to Will, who gestured for him to continue. "Oh, and the use of your army against The Bradford and his captain, of course."

"If you and your people agree to our terms, there will be no more bloodshed between us," Will began. "This comes with more freedom and prosperity than you could ever imagine having under your Lord and his military monsters. You'll open trade with the whole north of Rhethos, which will easily bring a small towne like Kaylyn and all its sea traders into our cause, too. You'll become the booming central commerce of Rhethos once more. Everyone within these walls wins."

Torald glanced at Moore, then fidgeted in his seat. "The lack of supplies from the north *has* been devastating," he admitted. His voice was high-pitched and nasally as he further confirmed what Will knew. "And not six months ago The Bradford cut off all trade from the south as well, as if punishing us for merely being near your rebels—"

"Master Will," Moore cut in, stemming Torald's all-too-honest words. Despite the slight tremble in his hands, his deep voice held its normal baritone strength. "I'm afraid you overestimate how dire our situation is."

"I don't think so," Irvin countered. He tapped his heels on the chair next to him for emphasis. "We don't need to knock on every door to see that some districts are suffering immensely, while you and your Loyals are doing just fine, albeit the wear is starting to show on you as well."

Will looked sideways at Irvin. "We have your commanding officer's reports from the barracks," he added in support of his friend's bold assertion. "And we think it's best if you see my cause as a solution to your troubles. The hammer of the Rhethosian military cannot cripple anyone else if we stand against it together."

Moore's expression hardened, and Will felt the tension in the room rise palpably. Rowlann only had to glance at his men for each of them to put hands on their weapons. Will noticed Gardain Moore lower his head to stare intently at his feet, fresh sweat on his brow. *He doesn't like conflict,* Will noted, adding this observation to what he'd already learned about the silent, second Moore son.

"Whatever you may have glanced at on your way here doesn't form some bond of comradery in hard times, Master Colwell," Moore began, his tone tight as he looked at Irvin. He stood from his seat, slowly but deliberately. The fur-lined sleeves of his robes rested on the edge of the table as he gripped its carved lip. "We do know your family's name, and we are well aware of what happened in Patten before you turned against our Lord."

Will winced, knowing this wouldn't end well. Moore was obviously turning the discussion away from the persuasion of his towne to the rebel cause by picking on Irvin's past. Even Torald, who seemed open to negotiation when trade benefits were mentioned, had his attention on Moore's antagonizing of Irvin.

"Brother," Will started and put a hand on Irvin's arm. He noticed how stiff the former Towne Master's muscles were, though Irvin shook off Will's grip with one sharp movement.

"My situation is an example of how The Bradford does nothing in anyone's interests but his own," Irvin said in a calm voice. "Many died in my towne, and—"

"And you took what little was left for yourself," Moore interrupted. Adlar sneered next to him, dutifully matching his father's expression. "You hoarded your meager winter supplies and let your people starve out of spite to your neglectful ruler. But who could blame you, after the Blood Goddess' illness took your own wife and daughter?"

Irvin rose swiftly, his jaw tight as the color drained from his face. Against the orange glare of the setting sun, he looked like a flaming torch ready to consume the room with his anger.

Will had to hold back an urge from times past to reach for his nearest weapon; he knew what his friend had suffered, and what he now fought for in the name of his lost family. Silencing Moore's ignorant tongue by cutting it out would be an easy solution, but he would no longer stoop to such a level. When he renewed his restraining grip on Irvin's arm, Will felt him try to pull back, his hand in a readied fist.

"No need to strike me, Master Colwell," Moore added quietly. "You don't have much of an audience this time."

Will stood, clamped his other hand on Irvin's shoulder, and forced him back into his chair. "We are not here to insult one another," he said, raising his voice to an authoritative tone that echoed off the intricately wood-paneled walls. He looked at everyone in turn, willing his firm yet peaceful attitude into the eyes of those assembled on each side of the table.

"Master Moore, let me be clear," he continued, his voice clipped. "This is a formality to give you the chance to stay alive and keep ruling this towne under rebel banners with my men. A decent man would welcome the opportunity to unite his people and keep his title in this kingdom's rebirth."

Torald raised his eyebrows, wrinkling the graying patches of hair at his temples and along his forehead. He seemed to want to speak in favor of a compromise. Even Adlar Moore, despite his thickness, opened his mouth for a moment. Will noticed Gardain shift, almost taking a step forward, but with the current tension in the room, Rowlann put out an arm, barring any further movement.

"I'm sorry to have wasted your time this evening," Jeras Moore rebutted coldly. "A forgotten traitor with no heir does not frighten me. Neither do you, Will 'Tarran,' falsely carrying around the Armellan family name. I will tell you the truth even though you've chosen to avoid the subject: you may have 'solutions' to our problems, but we know you are really pagans of the Blood Goddess. My people saw the outlawed magic sparks outside the gates. You are only here to lie and bring us back into Cybarys' chains."

There were too many red flags in that small speech to address, so Will let them pass over him, choosing to prioritize and address them later. He refused to let the Goddess into his fight, or anywhere near his current set of challenges. Why, though, was a northern Rhethosian Towne Master so afraid of a deity only found and worshiped across the sea?

"You know our goal is to keep you alive, don't you?" Will found that he voiced the question through gritted teeth.

Moore did not seem disturbed in the slightest. "Master Will, none of this matters," he stated, crossing his arms over his sunken chest. "You've slowly persuaded northern townes to embrace your color over years. But you're out of time in this respect; The Bradford is sick of your annoyance and is sending his Captain to destroy you. You're desperate to—"

"There is no desperation on our end," Irvin cut in. His temper had cooled now, and he crossed his legs casually on the empty chair next to him once more. "Caldrell is not an issue; your city walls are now keeping us and our men safe. It's merely a matter of whether you and your family would like to enjoy Lorington's defenses or swing from its battlements on the end of a rope."

Will bit his tongue, letting Irvin's threat sit for a moment. "You are right, Master Moore," Will said. "We don't have time. And that's why we're moving forward."

Moore glanced at Torald, who had almost managed to speak up again, a hopeful expression on his face. Instead, the Trade Master ground his teeth silently as Moore stared him down. Moore straightened the outer layer of his robes, his chin held high. "Your 'cause' is a path straight back into Cybarys' slavery. I'll stay under The Bradford's protection until I die as my family has always done."

Will stopped himself from wincing at another mention of the Goddess, and he heard Irvin sigh, shaking his head and muttering something under his breath. "And I don't suppose you're going to share with me how the Goddess' energy is connected to the digsite in the middle of your western district?"

Moore sneered at Will. "I have no idea what you're talking about."

Rowlann cleared his throat to show he was ready to remove the prisoners whenever Will was done with them.

Moore is still holding back on why he thinks Cybarys is involved in this situation, Will thought. *He's biding his time, waiting to see me fail.*

"Master Rowlann, that's enough for now," Will said. "Take Jeras and his sons back where you found them." He stood, inadvertently pressing his arm to his aching side. He had done his best to ignore the healing burns, but the movement brought their pain back to the forefront of his mind.

"Master Irvin," Will added, "Speak privately with Master Torald in the meantime. Give him an opportunity to enlighten you on the condition of the current tradesmen in the city. Ration distribution between our people and Lorington's needs to begin soon. Food is something I've found is always a good way to make peace. See if you can come to an understanding."

Rowlann nodded as his men gathered the Towne Master and his sons. Moore stared at Torald, wrinkles sharpening his gray eyes to vicious points. "Don't you dare speak a word in that traitor's favor," he snapped. "You know what will happen if you do."

Torald grimaced. Irvin rose, giving Will a pointed look. Irvin gave Torald a small bow, a bright grin now plastered on his face. "Looks like we need to find somewhere to talk," he said with his usual charm. "Preferably somewhere with wine; you know this castle well enough, don't you?"

Torald reluctantly nodded and left the room with Irvin, their voices echoing back toward the meeting hall. Rowlann's group was almost out the door when Will spoke up. "Gardain Moore. Stay with me for a moment."

The youngest Moore blinked curiously when he looked up from the floor in Will's direction. Jeras shot a glance over his shoulder as one of Rowlann's men pushed him through the doorway. He caught his younger son's eye for a moment, and Will saw distaste and distrust in the old man's gaze.

We're unraveling the truths of this towne, Will thought, *and I know I'll have better success speaking to this young man, one second son to another.*

CHAPTER EIGHT

TWO SECOND SONS

Will tried to catch Gardain Moore's eye as he took a seat in his father's recently unoccupied chair, but the young man kept his gaze locked to the tabletop. Despite Jeras leaving the room, Gardain still seemed unable to speak.

A memory from his childhood shone across his mind, as glaring as the blood-orange tint of the setting sun that ranged across the hall. It had been more than ten years since he'd thought of his older brother, Mic, and how, when he was six and his brother was ten, they had sat on the deck of their family's trading galley in the deepening light.

Mic thrived under their father's tutelage, learning how to navigate the ship, command the men, and keep the company records, while Will was expected to listen but stay silent. It took only a question or a wrong recitation to earn him a harsh rap on the side of his head or worse.

Will stood and rolled his shoulders to fend off the unexpected emotions that had arisen since he noticed the same behavior between Jeras and Gardain Moore. He walked behind his chair to look out the row of windows, considering how to address the young man. As the sun continued to melt below the city walls, the last of its color graced the gardens along the west side of the castle. Not far beyond were beautiful manors, each a miniature castle of its own.

"Your city's Loyals live out here, yes?" Will began. He turned from the opulent view to see Gardain merely nod. "They are important folk, to live so well despite what I saw in your western district." He paused for effect. "You and your family don't spend much time out there, do you?"

Gardain's back straightened in indignation, as Will expected. "As I'm sure you can tell," Gardain spoke rigidly, "the family and I are rather separate entities."

Will nodded. "I have a feeling there's always been something more important than you in your father's life."

Gardain shrugged one shoulder, trying and failing to be flippant. Even though he was twice the young man's age, Will remembered himself making that same gesture as if it were yesterday. "Second sons are an ignorable necessity," Gardain replied. "The lack of pressure is actually quite nice."

Will watched Gardain keep his gaze down on the gilded edge of the table. "Perhaps," Will agreed, "but the lack of a voice really isn't."

"A voice?" Gardain repeated. He pushed his hands up either side of his head, messing his light curls out of his face. "I'm not sure that really matters, if you are hanging the family soon enough for not supporting you."

"The" family, Will confirmed mentally. *Not "my" family.*

"Regardless," Will said, "it looked like you had something to say several times this last hour, but you stayed silent. I want to give you the opportunity to speak now, free of the judgment of your father and brother. Amongst the men who follow me, no voice is left unheard."

Will waited, but when Gardain only clenched his jaw and lowered his fists into his lap, he realized that his words weren't really reaching this young man. Gardain's body language belied a person not used to being spoken to directly, let alone being allowed to contribute to the outcome of an important conversation. Will singling him out was a bit too much, it seemed.

Will couldn't help but compare the way his father always spoke *with* his elder brother Mic, and always spoke *down* to him. His way of physically and verbally dismissing his second son was deliberately cruel.

"Sorry to disappoint, Master Will," Gardain mumbled. "But your 'opportunity' is really lost on someone like me. I don't think anything I could say would help you."

Will frowned, rethinking his initial strategy. *I need to speak to him about what intrigues him, personally, since no one has ever done that before. Then I can get this one to trust me.*

Gardain shifted against the back of his chair, as if Will's lack of an immediate response was making him uncomfortable. Will noticed that every time he moved his arms or repositioned his hands, Gardain's eyes followed them, focusing on Will's leather gloves. When he glanced at Will's arm resting on the chair's back, the sleeve of his new, black jerkin was pulled back enough to show part of his wrist and forearm. *My rune scars,* he thought, and smiled. *That's what interests him?*

"They're pretty to look at, but these markings don't mean anything, you know," Will said. He took his seat once more and removed his gloves to fully expose the rest of the Blessing Runes. "I can't use them anymore."

Gardain's gray eyes widened, and he sat up straighter. Part of Will thought that the young man might grab his hands to examine them more closely. In fact, Gardain's fingers twitched forward, then he seemed to restrain himself.

"That's such a waste of a gift!" Gardain suddenly exclaimed, startling Will. There was much more emotion in his voice than any utterance so far. "'Strength,'" he continued, gesturing to the shape along one of Will's wrists. "And *that* one, on top of your right hand is unmistakable: 'Blood.' You must have had your Blood Fortune read when you were a boy, yes? In Valsara? That's such a special spell that you can only use once per person's lifetime."

Will's grin softened, thinking briefly of the day that magic was cast, the girl who was there in the temple beside him, and the deadly consequences that followed. "You're well-read in modern Armellan culture for the son of a Rhethosian Towne Master," he observed.

Gardain blushed, bright pink touching his high cheekbones as he nervously touched his ashy-blond hair once more. "I . . . find it interesting, I suppose," he murmured, burying his passion behind what sounded like well-practiced shame. "It's just that someone like you, despite your faults, is fascinating to me."

Will wasn't sure if Gardain meant his loss of Blessing Runes as a "fault," or the fact that Rhethosians took every precaution to not have children when Goddess Touched blood could appear in them. And yet, here he was, someone who shouldn't exist in this kingdom. "Something tells me educating yourself on the rules of outlawed magic and the culture associated with it isn't a pastime you're praised for," Will pressed on casually, pulling his hands back toward his side of the table.

"Correct," Gardain said with a nod. Now that Will had gotten him to talk, he found that Gardain was extremely blunt as if social subtleties were lost on him. Gardain's gaze stayed on Will's rune scars as he continued, "but you'd be surprised at the resources sitting in this old towne that no one cares about.

And with no attention from my brother, and no love from my father, it gives me a lot of time to absorb those resources."

Will raised his eyebrows, wondering if Gardain was being purposefully vague. *What "resources" on Armellan magic can Lorington possibly have?* Gardain was shy, but he certainly wasn't stupid.

"Gardain," Will began, and he crossed his arms over his chest as he leaned back. With the Blessing Runes hidden once more, the young man finally made eye contact. "I have a feeling we can help each other. That's why I wanted to speak with you alone."

Gardain tilted his head from side to side, as if weighing options. "I know," he began, his tone very practical. "I must look rather easy to manipulate from where you're sitting. Ignored, pitiful, desperate for attention, even from a rebel?"

"I didn't say that," Will replied calmly. "I'm not like your father; I'm not here to play games."

"This whole life is a game, Master Will," Gardain said, and a humorless smile touched his lips. "You're playing whether you want to or not. What do they call it across the sea? Destiny? 'Cybarys weaves our Fate's Strings, and we just dance'?"

Will nodded, not trying to hide how impressed he was; this young man really did know more Armellan phrases than he expected. He leaned forward again, making sure Gardain could see that he meant to emphasize his next words. "There is a reason I lost my Touch, Gardain; I do not follow the Goddess, nor do I respect her teachings. I'm here to break the twisted Rhethosian ways of lying, manipulating, and betraying each other that The Bradford promotes. If you'd let my people show you, we are honest fighters working to make peace and real freedom possible."

"Forgive me if that seems childishly naive," Gardain replied. Will had had others spit that response in his face for over a decade with anger and fear, but Gardain's tone was one of casual practicality; he didn't mean to offend Will in the slightest. The young man did, however, snap his gaze back to his lap, as if he'd shocked himself with his own brazen response.

"How can I show you my honest motivations, Gardain?" Will asked. "What can I say or do that will help convince you of the value of my cause?"

Gardain's eyebrows shot up into his curled bangs, clearly not expecting to be given this option. "I suppose . . ." he started slowly, then sat up straight as his thoughts came together. "Yes, there is something. Master Will, I want you to tell me where these came from."

He reached below the table, fumbling with one of the pouches tied at his belt. Cold instinct took over Will's senses, and he touched the hilt of a knife on the inside of his arm, ready to draw and throw it if necessary.

Gardain, however, didn't seem to notice; he was slipping on a thick glove, and when he placed his hand back on the table, it was held in a loose fist. Instantly, Will felt the warmth of the Goddess' magic fill the room, hotter and more encompassing than the retreating light of the sunset.

"I can't touch these or they'll fade away to dust," Gardain began, "but from what you've said about your relationship with Cybarys, you couldn't have made them." He opened his gloved hand, and dozens of magic remnants sprinkled across the tabletop. Their gem-like forms glowed with a blood-red light. "These were collected outside the towne's broken front gates."

Will felt his throat go dry, cursing himself for not ordering someone to destroy those. He wanted no trace of what Devaki had created to be found, and yet, amidst the chaos of taking control of the city, that detail had been forgotten.

He reached across the table, grabbed a couple of the magic remnants, and rolled them between his bare fingers. Apparently, even though he didn't possess the Goddess' Touch anymore, her magic was still in his blood and allowed him to hold the magic remnants. He glanced back at Gardain, patiently awaiting what he knew was coming.

"If you can't cast Blessing Runes," Gardain said, "then who made these?"

Will knew this was a question on the minds of many, both rebels and loyal Rhethosians alike. But Gardain had unknowingly given Will some knowledge: rumors about an Armellan girl with the Goddess' Touch were spreading among the rebels, but Will didn't know if the locals had gotten wind of what Devaki looked like or where she might be located. Now seemed like the time to begin telling the tale he knew would most benefit his people, despite the untruths he'd have to weave into it.

"You're very smart, Gardain," Will began, though he didn't expect the flattery to have much of an effect. "And because I like you, and we have much in common, I won't lie to you. The truth is I do have a Goddess Touched from Armelle working for me. They are very loyal to Cybarys, and if you know as much as you say you do about the Goddess' people, you'll know this person is capable of feats much greater than breaking the gates of your home."

Gardain licked his lips, his gaze dancing across the glowing bits of magic. "Your rebellion doesn't have Armelle's support," he began, his tone uncertain for the first time.

"No," Will agreed, "but things change. Your father is right about one thing: I don't have a lot of time at this stage in 'the game,' as you call it. I'm at the point where I'll use any tools I can to win this war. If your family chooses not to be on the winning side, I hope that you, at least, will be."

He had to take a breath and realize why his tone had shifted to threatening; just the idea of someone being able to find and interrogate Devaki set his blood boiling. He was thankful that Rowlann had her somewhere safe.

Will cleared his throat, leaned over the table, and put the magic remnants he held back in Gardain's hand. It was time to play another card to gain this young man's loyalty, and Will put on his most convincing, sincere expression despite how it hurt to lie.

"Would you like to meet the person who made these?" Will asked quietly.

Gardain snapped his gaze to Will's, clearly unable to hide his excitement. "You'd really let the son of your enemy see your greatest weapon?" he asked.

"I told you," Will replied, "I don't want any enemies within these walls, including you and your family. I have a feeling you never thought you'd meet an Armellan, let alone someone Goddess Touched."

Gardain failed to hide a genuine smile. "And in exchange," he began, "you think I have the ability to make peace between your people and mine?"

Will smiled. "That sounds childishly naive," he said. "But I do believe that if we all have a voice and speak without fear to help one another, anything is possible."

Gardain seemed to be thinking intently, his eyebrows narrowed. He quietly collected the magic remnants in his gloved hand and stored them away with a reverent touch. The silence stretched out before them.

"I'll let you think on it," began Will. "You understand, of course, that in the meantime I'll be placing you back in the dungeon with your family." He stood and adjusted his coat after slipping his gloves back on. "If you want to discuss how we can further help one another, bring those with you. My Goddess Touched friend can do something beautiful with those Bloodgems."

A slight smile rose to Gardain's lips, and Will was surprised he recognized the outdated term. *Whatever "resources" he has in this towne are close to ancient if he knows that one.*

"Your efforts here might be wasted, you know," Gardain began, suppressing his interest once more. "I don't have any influence over Adlar or my father."

Will shrugged. "You are your own person, Gardain Moore," he said, and put a hand on the young man's shoulder briefly as he stepped toward the door. "What you choose to do and say are entirely up to you."

CHAPTER NINE

LORINGTON'S FORGOTTEN WOMEN

Angelyn felt like she'd just collapsed on the bed when Marselle shook her awake. She threw off the three layers of blankets needed to keep her warm in the cold city and pressed wild locks of hair out of her eyes. Disorientation in an unfamiliar place made every muscle in her body tense until she focused on Marselle's thin smile.

"What is it?" Angelyn asked, sitting up. "Don't you ever sleep?"

Marselle laughed, then threw a heavy cloak on top of Angelyn. "I did," she returned. "But not for twelve full hours, like you did."

"Half a day?" Angelyn repeated. Had she really been that exhausted?

"I have better things to lie about, McKinlee," Marselle said. "The truth is since we arrived, I've been busy in the city, and I think I've found a potential solution to our problem."

Angelyn stood, smoothing out the layers of the new black dress she wore. Someone had taken away the garment that was stained with the blood of Sarrett's guardsmen and the dying Belka, and given Angelyn something more plain yet in the same somber color. She gathered the rich velvet cloak Marselle had thrown at her.

"What do you mean?" Angelyn asked, marveling at the quality of the cloak; it was edged with a fine pink satin ribbon, and the material's deep blue color shone. It smelled strongly of perfume, a brilliant bouquet of lilac overtaking her senses. *Best not to ask where she got this.*

"You'll see," Marselle replied with a cryptic smirk. "If this connection pans out, we may be able to get Lorington flying rebel banners before the Insane Captain gets to your old towne within the month."

Angelyn's hands, which were struggling with the ornate clasp of the cloak at her collarbone, froze. *"What?"*

Marselle rolled her tongue along her teeth. "Ah, I assumed Will would have told you about that little deadline of ours."

"He doesn't tell me everything," Angelyn snapped. "Did you say the Rhethosian Captain is marching north?"

Marselle put a hand on Angelyn's shoulder, guiding her firmly toward the door. "He'll be planning to garrison Kaylyn, no doubt, what with the place without leadership and its proximity to us. But don't worry! Big armies move slowly, and that man's a true basket case; with this towne on our side, we can withstand him."

It was barely detectable, but Angelyn heard an unsure weight in Marselle's confident voice as they left. *I am already worried about being away from Josh,* she thought, *not to mention whoever "Devaki" is that Will seemed so troubled about. . . and now this?*

Angelyn couldn't help staring down the streets of the market district of Lorington, aware of the heavy silence. Though they'd walked by the majority of the rebel guards back at the edge of the barracks, there were still at least two men in violet on every corner, stationed under the Rhethosian Blue awnings.

Their authoritative presence in the streets brought back an unpleasant feeling from Kaylyn that made Angelyn shiver. It was too similar to her old home.

"This doesn't feel right," she murmured to Marselle. "How will these people see our soldiers as any different than the men who stood here before?"

"Oh, it's not that bad," Marselle dismissed, flashing bright smiles at the rebels. "They're not Rhethosian guardsmen." She put her shoulders back for emphasis, pressing back the folds of her cloak to show off her fitted gown.

Angelyn noticed that Marselle wore the deep black color she favored while making runs. Now within the walls of a towne where she felt confident, there were bright violet ribbons along the neckline and down the bodice. No doubt the decoration was a bold statement to any of the locals who saw her as they went by.

The block they traversed was slowly changing from storefronts and upper level housing to larger buildings that dominated intimidating chunks of real estate. They took up the bulk of the streets and adjoining pathways, rising in great gray stacks with their windows closed to the afternoon light.

Despite the more modern, clean layout of this city compared to her old home, Angelyn still felt a wave of nostalgia when she realized what these structures were: Lorington's inns and taverns.

She took in the aroma of musky fire smoke, warm bread, and sharp ale. Despite the subdued streets, inside each building were light and noise that brought back bittersweet memories. Angelyn knew that these people were doing exactly what those in Kaylyn did when Sarrett brought harsher laws with him: they kept living their lives as best as they could. The same was happening here even though the armed men on the street now bore rebel violet.

"Where exactly are we going?" Angelyn asked, nervousness creeping into her tone. The few townesfolk they saw on the street stared at them, some with fascination and others with clear malice.

"Spies are hard to come by in places full of Loyals," Marselle explained, leaning close to Angelyn. "An old friend of mine lives down here. We've been in contact sparingly over the last few years because things ended badly between us back in Clancy. But she's going to help us."

"How's that?" Angelyn questioned disbelievingly.

"She merely needs to meet you, darling. The two of you have something in common."

"I'd love to know what that is," Angelyn replied. She craned her neck up at the curtained windows, then down the sparsely populated walkways between buildings.

"You're both bridges," Marselle replied shortly. She halted at the next set of tavern doors, a huge slab of oak held up by six enormous hinges. Instead of knocking, however, Marselle turned down the side street, toward a narrow set of metal stairs that climbed up to a much smaller door on the side of the building.

"Marselle. . .?" Angelyn began.

"Lady Remora came from the south, where I used to live," Marselle continued in a low tone. "She's been on both sides of our kingdom: the upper class of The Bradford's home itself, surrounded by those with the highest influence, and she's been here, at the bottom of the barrel." She jerked her head up the rusted steps, as if that was supposed to explain everything. "And *you*, McKinlee, are another bridge. You've suffered in silence, alone, in a dying towne, beaten down by our Lord and every other man above you."

"Such kind words," Angelyn interjected dryly. She still wasn't used to people describing her "old life" in those words; the wounds were very fresh.

"But now you're on the other side," Marselle continued, determination glinting in her eyes. "You bridge that cage of a typical Rhethosian woman to this idea of freedom." She held out her hands, demonstrating an arc across her chest. "*And,* most importantly, you have Will's ear. If anyone can win a woman like Remora to our cause and all of those who trust her. . .it's you."

With that, Marselle ascended the steps. When she knocked on the door, Angelyn caught up and stood behind her. Her mind spun with Marselle's plan and the entire concept of "bridging" freedom to another area of Rhethos.

"Remora," Marselle began, "It's the Lady Marselle. I'm here to help."

A heavy lock withdrew. A short, middle-aged woman stuck her head through a crack in the door, her brown eyes wide. "Lord save us!" she scoffed, looking Marselle up and down. "I should have known you'd be here with these rebel monsters."

"We're not monsters," Angelyn spoke up. There was barely any room on the raised landing for her to look around Marselle's shoulders. "We just want to talk."

Marselle's hand darted forward and grabbed the edge of the door. "Things are different this time, dear," she added seriously. "Please, hear us out, for your sake, and the sake of anyone with you."

Grumbling, Remora snapped the door open. Inside, the long stretch of attic at the tavern's top floor was dimly lit and poorly ventilated. Though it was hard to see, Angelyn noticed many people were living up here.

This isn't a space meant for living. It looks like they're hiding up here, Angelyn thought, noticing how, despite the many windows on the east-facing stretch of the room, everything was shut in with heavy swatches of suffocating fabric. Beds lined most of the floor, separated by trunks and crates of meager belongings, food, and a few tables where many women and young girls sat quietly. The air stung with the bitter smells of sweat, tears, and mold.

"Sit," Remora said, gesturing at a table in the nearest corner that was unoccupied. She was, Angelyn could now see, about the same age as Marselle, though considerably shorter and rough around the edges.

Most heads turned toward them as they entered, and the attention locked onto Marselle in her violet-accented dress. Angelyn had barely made her way over to sit when she noticed something:

"Remora . . ." she began, unable to take her eyes off of dozens of the young girls in the room, "I'm sorry, but are all of these girls pregnant?"

The more she squinted in the poor light, the more swollen bellies she saw on those sitting at tables, curled on beds, or slowly pacing around the edges of the cramped attic space.

"All? No. About half," Remora corrected bitterly, keeping her voice low. "And not by choice."

"And the other half?" Angelyn breathed.

"Digsite widows," Remora replied, earning some harsh stares from the women closest to her. "Unnecessary death combined with shameful new life. They'd be outcast or even killed by most in Lorington because of their current 'states,' no matter what district they come from, especially if Moore's Towne Masters found them. But they're safe here."

She set her hands on the tiny circular table between them. Angelyn took the time to see the finely tailored lines of her satin bodice and the clean, white lace around her sleeves.

"You mean you house them and feed them and help them give birth, all on your own?" Angelyn asked in awe.

"I was already on my own too," Remora scoffed. "My husband is dead, thanks to that cursed hole in the western district."

Digsite? Angelyn thought, confused. *Cursed hole? What is she talking about?* She was about to ask some of these questions, but Marselle spoke. "I'm sorry to hear about Coyle."

"No, you're not," Remora replied. "You abandoned all of us in Clancy so quickly that you didn't see the consequences of your choices. How much pity can you have for my husband when yours, and your son are dead because of your rebel mischief?"

Angelyn stared at Marselle, whose face was expressionless.

"How little you tell your new girls," Remora commented at Marselle. "But I won't ruin it for Miss . . .?"

"McKinlee," Angelyn finished, noticing how Remora automatically gave her the lowborn title of "Miss" compared to Marselle's illustrious "Lady."

She took a breath, remembering why she was here. Remora gave shamed and abandoned women, despite their class, a safe place to live, away from judgment or violence.

Like Marselle mentioned, Remora was a bridge for all women in this towne and likely had their trust. But how could her foothold be strengthened if she embraced rebel violet? What brighter future could these unborn children have if their mothers supported Will? And what brighter opportunities could these widows undertake without The Bradford's rule holding them back?

"Marselle and I believe in the benefits of the rebel cause, regardless of where we come from," Angelyn began quietly to Remora. "There's no need to pick apart Marselle's old motivations or yours or mine."

Remora sighed. "As I'm sure Marselle *hasn't* told you, I used to work with her, alongside my husband, when whispers of the rebellion reached Clancy years ago. It is not your cause that I hate, Miss McKinlee; the Lord knows it could be better than what we have now. . . anything would, really. It's Marselle's motives that leave a bitter taste in my mouth. I won't let her hurt the women of Lorington like she's done to others."

Several heads turned toward them at those words, and the energy in the room shifted to an even more dangerous low. It felt as though rape and shame were nothing compared to what could be inflicted upon women like this if the powerful men of Lorington found them up here. Angelyn felt terrified eyes on her, weighing down her newfound freedom with the cage-like elements of her old life.

"Then don't worry about Marselle," Angelyn insisted. "She's only here to introduce us."

"She doesn't like to admit it," Marselle muttered, "but I've done what I can to help you from a distance since we left Clancy. I know how important it is that all of you are kept hidden here."

"You only occasionally do so out of guilt," Remora snapped back. "And there are other women in towne who help me, a lot more efficiently than you have. Though they'd never want anyone to know they stoop to such levels."

Angelyn cleared her throat, trying to bring Remora's focus back to her. "You and I have more in common than you think," she said. "I also lost my husband and had to learn how to survive on my own, without having my son conscripted to the military, even when Sarrett himself tried to hurt me."

Remora's eyebrows narrowed in the gloom. "You're from Kaylyn, then?"

Angelyn nodded. "There were many men who came to my home over the years, offering me their family name, their protection, their money, but I knew the price involved. I'd been punished enough by my husband for having a voice to know that. . ." She faded off, suddenly feeling her throat constrict.

What did she know now? Had she ever really vocalized it before this moment? She felt Marselle's hand rest on her shoulder. It felt genuine, and so did the rest of her thought when she finally was able to say it, looking directly into Remora's eyes.

"I will never have another person rule me again."

With a grimace, Remora gave her a subtle nod.

Angelyn blinked back a few tears. "First, can you tell me more about what happened in this towne since you arrived?"

Sighing, Remora leaned against the table. Her relaxed body language gave Angelyn hope that what she'd shared about herself made her worthy of some trust. Remora lowered her voice, as if her explanation might set the very air in the room on fire. "A year ago, Caldrell and his men were already here in Lorington."

Angelyn felt herself pressing forward, too, her gaze glued to Remora's round, brown eyes. She could practically see memories of pain emerging across the Rhethosian woman's features, knitted like dark shadows in the lines of her face.

"An entire battalion of the Captain's men, the cruelest, hardest soldiers in this damned kingdom, were ordered to tear into the western district," Remora continued. "We were given no explanation; we only watched as they turned the slums into a huge, mysterious digsite. When The Bradford himself demanded faster results, the soldiers made the locals dig without pay, even folk from the northern district. They forced my husband and his friends into that damned hole, too."

"And what did they find in the digsite?" Marselle asked.

"I'd rather not speak of anything below the surface of that cursed land," Remora snapped. Her anger at the recollection of her recent suffering honed in on Marselle. "We had established ourselves here after fleeing from Clancy, thanks to the generosity of Coyle's brother and their Loyal status, but the Captain's men destroyed our lives once more."

"So these unwanted pregnancies," Angelyn whispered, "are a result of the soldiers who came into Lorington to dig that hole?"

Remora grimaced and nodded.

"And you give shelter to these girls, along with anyone who lost family in that digsite, no matter what district they come from," Angelyn said, earning another silent confirmation from Remora. "That isn't something most Rhethosian women, let alone a wealthy Loyal from Clancy, would think to be proper."

"And you should note," Marselle added evenly, "that since Master Will's men have entered this city, no one has come looking for you here. No one has been assaulted on the streets either."

With hesitancy in her eyes, Angelyn watched Remora concede to this point.

"None of that behavior is tolerated in Master Will's ranks," Marselle pressed on. "Things may be bad for you here, but the rebels have not made it worse. There is control and respect amongst our people."

Angelyn nodded in support, though she could see Remora wasn't entirely convinced. With the way Marselle and Remora were at odds, it was up to Angelyn to find agreeable, common ground, to be the bridge between these women. To be the bridge between the fearful rule of The Bradford and the endless possibilities within Will's cause.

She straightened her back in her chair and met the Lorington woman's eyes once more, this time with the same amount of calm confidence that Will always demonstrated.

"What do you want, Remora?" she asked. When the woman stared blankly at her, Angelyn continued, "What would you do for these women if you had any option in your power?"

"Easy. For you and this other troublemaker to leave," Remora returned dismissively.

Angelyn smiled, then settled back in her chair. "We'll leave soon," she replied. "But first, tell me what you'd do if every possibility was open to you."

Remora looked away, glancing at everyone in the tiny attic-shaped sanctuary. From the poorly lit shadows, Angelyn saw that the murmurs of noise, stifled tears, and movement had stopped.

Everyone who had first tried to ignore Angelyn and Marselle was now waiting to see how their protector would respond to such a question. Whether they wore fine dresses stretched thin by pregnant bellies or tattered rags, all of the women watched Remora as the woman struggled for words.

"I know," Angelyn added, lowering her tone to a sympathetic one. "Before I met Will Tarran, no one had ever asked me that either. I was always pushed under the heels of the men above me. It's been terrifying knowing the answer to that question and working toward it, but I can promise you that 'freedom' can be whatever you want . . . if you're willing to fight."

A couple of the girls on cots nearby covered their mouths and burst into tears. One of the digsite widows around Remora's age stepped over to them, whispering softly. Remora kept her expression neutral before finally speaking her answer:

"I want nothing like this to happen again."

Angelyn reached a hand across the table, palm up. "I feel the same, and even if Marselle has made mistakes, she does, too. Here is the truth, as I understand it: you have helped people from every part of Lorington, yes? The slums in the western district to the families inside Towne Centre itself?"

"I have," Remora replied, without a trace of pride.

"Then they all trust you, and all may possibly owe you something. Now, here is the truth from my side." She swallowed, gathering courage for what Marselle no doubt saw as the vital connecting piece. "I have the rebel leader's ear. You've told me what you want and I promise you that I can speak to Will as his equal and we can have a discussion together. For you and for every one of these women."

She paused, a little uncomfortable seeing that almost everyone was listening to her, too. There were murmurs spreading throughout the space that someone like them, a woman with no voice or place in Rhethos, now was held in the high esteem of a man as powerful as Will.

When Angelyn held Remora's gaze, she thought she caught a glint of something, the beginnings of that bridge solidifying. She observed the changes in the faces of those around her, remembering the glimmers she'd seen in her patrons' eyes the first night the rebel leader spoke in The Hamond. That same light was now reflected in many around her.

Marselle was right. If Remora can trust me enough with this next step, together Will and I can build a real foundation, different from the northern townes. This is a pivotal point for me and for him and for Rhethos.

"The rebellion may be about fighting those against us," Angelyn continued, "but it's also about changing hearts. Gather everyone connected to those you've helped here, from all four corners of Lorington. We're going to begin shattering the stigmas around being equal to our partners or taking on a business in a husband's or father's stead. Or mothering a bastard or being forced to bow underneath Towne Masters who would force anyone to live like this."

Remora's expression remained tight-lipped, though Angelyn noticed, out of the corner of her eye, that some of the women were nodding at one another.

"If you can get everyone in one place," Angelyn pressed, "I promise it will be like nothing Rhethos has ever seen."

"You're quick to deal out promises, Miss McKinlee," Remora began, with cold practicality and protection for the people around her. When she spoke again, her voice was a whisper. "You really think you can make peace and have us following your cause before the Rhethosian military retaliates?"

Angelyn gave the woman a reassuring smile. "Yes."

Remora's gaze shot to Marselle for a mere second. "Fine," she agreed. "There's a tavern in the center of Farring Street, four blocks south of here called The Butterfly's Breath. My former brother-in-law owns it, and he's a good man. Everyone we can gather will be there when the sun goes down. I have a feeling we don't have much time, do we?"

"No," Angelyn said, and reached across the table to grab Remora's hand. "But we're going to make the most of it."

Angelyn waited by the door while Marselle murmured a few quiet words to some of the women. Not long after they took their leave, Remora headed back to her home in the northern district, mentioning that she regularly met with women from Loyal families who helped support her work here, in secret. That, Angelyn thought, was another key piece to remember.

Though it wasn't bright outside, it felt blinding after being in the dark attic. She shielded her eyes down the stairs, keeping her attention on her boots until the world was back to normal.

She took a cleansing breath of fresh air. All of a sudden, fresh adrenaline ran through her veins, setting her entire body on a trembling, thrilling high. Was this what Will felt like every time he spoke? She honed all of that energy, because, before anything else happened, there was something she had to know.

"Wait," Angelyn said. She grabbed Marselle's arm, forcing her to stop at the nearest corner. The two rebels stationed a few feet away glanced in their direction.

"What's the matter, McKinlee?" Marselle laughed, giving her an odd look. "You should be proud. I couldn't have done it without you."

Angelyn tightened her grip on Marselle's black satin sleeve. There were too many questions, and too much she was neck-deep in right now. "I need you to tell me the truth about Clancy," she insisted. "All of it. Now."

Marselle raised an eyebrow, a dangerous glint appearing in her green eyes. "I hardly think this is the time or place for you to demand things of me, dear."

She almost let go when Marselle took a step back toward the barracks, but Angelyn held her ground. "No," she insisted. "You put me in that situation with minimal information, and yet I still convinced her to meet with us. And you're right: Will listens to me more than anyone else, so if we're going to keep working together, I can't have mysteries from your past thrown in my face, making me look bad."

A surprised expression appeared on Marselle's face. "I'll be damned," she scoffed. "Didn't think you had *that* in you, darling." After a moment, Marselle sighed, then waved her back into the privacy of the alley. She leaned against the wall underneath the stairs that climbed to the attic's entrance.

"You probably think of Clancy as the perfect picture of Rhethosian peace," she began quietly, "and it is . . . for many. The cage I lived in wasn't as physical as what those girls have endured, but I still was constrained, viewed as less than any man around me. But planting seeds for the rebellion in The Bradford's city was impossible. I failed. People died. Can we go now?"

"What happened to your family?" Angelyn insisted.

Marselle winced, tilting her head back toward the gray sky. "You do know that if a traitor to our Lord is caught, their families are executed, too? In Clancy, Caldrell likes to do it in public. A weekly ritual, even if he had to kill innocents to keep his insanity on schedule. They came to my home one night, but I wasn't there. The guardsmen arrested my husband and my twenty-year-old son. Remora and Coyle ran, and. . . so did I. I left them all behind, without a damned glance backward because I was that afraid of shame, torture, and public execution."

Angelyn swallowed dryly. "Marselle," she whispered. "I . . ."

Marselle glanced her way, and Angelyn saw, for the first time, a sheen of tears in her eyes. "My husband was a good man, but he was always so afraid," she murmured. "Comfortable, lazy, even, with our status. He never dared risk the benefits of Will's cause even to give me a better life. So I took on the task myself and I failed.

"I was already fleeing up the coast on a friend's ship when they put the nooses around my family's necks. The worst part is that, unlike Coyle, my husband did nothing 'wrong.' Yet he and our son Ascot died that day, along with ten others, including the Captain's wife! I even had Selise Caldrell herself on our side, then someone wrote a confession letter, and it all fell apart."

"I can understand Remora being bitter about the rebel cause," Angelyn began, "but why did she keep mentioning 'dead girls' as if she meant women who've worked with you *after* you left Clancy?"

Marselle flicked an errant tear from her cheek, then glared matter-of-factly at Angelyn. "Rebellion can mean death for anyone," she snapped. "Running supplies across enemy lines, by land and on dangerous seas? Bribing and blackmailing tradesmen in loyal Rhethosian townes? Making runs to supply drops that could or could not be flooded by unexpected storms? Of course girls have died, McKinlee. What Remora was implying was *I don't care about them.*"

"That's. . . not true," Angelyn replied, finding her voice unsteady.

"You know what I liked about you right away, McKinlee?" Marselle said, clearing her throat. "How much you care about your child. I didn't know real love, gut-wrenching, heart-bursting love until I held my son. At first, I let many girls die to get closer to destroying Mercer Caldrell and his master for what they did to Ascot. I hope you can believe that I'm not actually that heartless; I'll stoop low enough to do things that Will wouldn't approve of, yes. If that comes across as being a cold bitch, then so be it."

Angelyn shook her head. She hadn't seen Marselle do anything that Will wouldn't think aligned with the rebellion's ideals. . . but she didn't see everything. "We're creating something new here, together," she said pointedly.

Marselle smiled, and just like that, her confident grin was back in place. She fixed the curls on the sides of her face and straightened her bodice under her cloak. "Then we'd better get going. It'll be night before we know it, and *you* still have to ask our leader to show his pretty face at this world-changing meeting."

CHAPTER TEN

A MOTHER'S CALL

Devaki told herself she wouldn't cry. After being abused for sixteen years in Valsara, and now bleeding for Rhethos, she would *not* cry because of the way her father had treated her. Yet, when she was finally alone and the adrenaline wore down and everything that had occurred over the last forty-eight hours crashed down on her shoulders, the tears were unstoppable.

Did I really expect him to welcome me with open arms and tell me how much he loves me, like he did in his letters for five years? she thought, cursing her childish notions.

Instead, she was now hidden away in a small room at the back of Lorington's barracks behind a locked door. The message from Rowlann was clear that she wasn't allowed to go anywhere. The room's only windows were a bay of open rectangles cut into the granite that ran along the ceiling, too high and too miniscule for her to reach.

Next to the door was a wooden chest that had been emptied by Rowlann's men before her arrival. The commander of her father's elite forces had left her a pile of clean clothes to choose from in different sizes, ranging from shades of gray to duller shades of tan, stacked on top of the chest's iron-studded lid.

"They're meant to be discreet, Princess," Rowlann had muttered when he saw the look on her face. "And they're clean. I will make someone bring you hot water to wash yourself as soon as I can."

Discarding her traditional Armellan garments hurt, but they had been destroyed beyond repair. The heavy, itchy Rhethosian wool grated against her skin, so foreign compared to the light silk and smooth leather she was used to. At least it kept her warm. Her frustration burned bright when she had to scrub the remains of other people's blood off of her body, especially where it was caked on old Rune Scars that ran up and down her arms and shoulders.

Just as Devaki had stubbornly fought her tears, she also fought sleep. She thought back to the fact that the last time she'd slept had been in the belly of *The Blue Memory,* stowed away before the storm hit on her way to Rhethos three days ago. That fact reminded her of what the recent battle and her ride to Lorington's digsite had pushed to the back of her exhausted mind.

We were going to drown, but I pleaded for help and gave blood . . . more blood than I've ever given before, dangerously close to what would kill me. Rowlann helped, too, and then . . .

The little bed in the corner beckoned her as her legs refused to support her any longer. Stubbornly, Devaki only sat on its edge. She touched her collar and pulled it back to glance down at the mysterious rune above her heart. She hadn't cut the shape, and couldn't have even if she wanted to; it was a mark from a language she didn't know, and every time she tried to focus on the symbol, her vision blurred uncontrollably.

All she knew was that after some unseen force had cut that mark into her chest, her prayer for the storm to calm was answered. There were no answers to all the questions it brought up. Will may have been able to understand, but he certainly didn't want to, and that hurt her enough to remain silent.

And he's too afraid, I think, to be around me under "calm" circumstances.

Her head spun, and Devaki could no longer stay conscious. After she collapsed, she slept for an entire day. When she opened her eyes, her body insisted it was night again, but it was confused even further by Lorington's huge outer wall that hid the sun and made daylight show itself at a later time.

She did one loop around the room, anxiousness skittering across her skin. Devaki balled her hands in fists, refusing to accept that she was put away like a weapon until she was deemed worthy of shining. *I'm more than this,* she thought. *The Goddess sent me here for a reason.*

Her hand went to the mysterious rune over her heart, wondering what it would do for her now, or if she was even capable of bleeding that much again without actually dying. She reached instinctively for her rune ring but remembered that one of Rowlann's men had taken it. There were no sharp objects around, nothing she could use to make an offering to Cybarys. A bit of Strength would break the door, and some Guidance would lead her back to that place she couldn't stop thinking about.

"Armellan curses," she murmured aloud, pacing to a wall and touching its cool stone. That was what one of the rebels had said when she and Will had ridden through the neighborhood dug apart with precise depth. She wanted to ask Will what that word "curses" meant because no one in her home used a term like that to describe the Goddess' energy.

Beneath all that magic was something I've never felt around Blessing Runes before: an older strength. I have to go back and find out what it is.

The lock on the room's door shifted. Rowlann stood there with fresh bread, dried meat, and a jug of water. He set these items down on her bed, the only flat surface in the room. "You're awake now," Rowlann grunted, telling Devaki that he had probably stopped by in the last full day.

"That looks awful," Devaki teased, making a sour face at the meal, but Rowlann gave her a hard frown.

"We need to be careful with food," he replied coldly. "Until we receive more from our suppliers or make headway with the locals, things are rationed severely."

Devaki swallowed her playfully contemptuous attitude. She'd found the best way to get Rowlann to talk with her was with a joke that got on his nerves, but he didn't seem in the mood today. When she looked more closely, she noticed how disheveled the Rhethosian man was. His short, graying hair was not combed, and his beard was coming in unkempt. The pale blue of his eyes was ringed with red, as if he hadn't slept since breaking open Lorington's gates two nights ago.

"Do I really have to stay here?" she asked, picking up the mug and pouring herself a full glass of water. "I could help, you know."

Rowlann shook his head. "Master Will said you must stay hidden for your own safety. Your skin and your Touch will only make things worse."

"I did you a favor," she began hotly, deciding to play a different card. "The entire rebel army, really."

Rowlann gave her an exasperated look. "I know, Princess," he said. "And you did the right thing."

"I know," Devaki lied, hoping it didn't show on her face. "And now you owe me."

"What is your point?" Rowlann asked, though Devaki didn't sense any impatience in his voice. He knew what she was capable of. He was a military man, and she was a tool that shouldn't be locked up in a time of need. She could use that to her advantage, she was sure, even if in her heart she wanted to avoid ever being connected to battle again.

Devaki smiled, sat on the edge of her bed, and sipped her cup of water. She noticed the amount of food on the tray seemed like a lot for a stringent army ration, and part of her guessed Rowlann had added some of his meal to her share.

"We would be even, for your armor's Blessing Runes and for breaking open the gate," she said slowly, "if you give me my ring back and leave that door unlocked."

Rowlann shook his head. "Your father—"

"You know he wrote to me for years?" Devaki cut in. "He told me about his plan to make a place where we could be together. He wrote about how it broke his heart to leave me as a baby. But last night, he could barely look in my eyes once we stood in the quiet, face to face."

"You put yourself in this situation because you didn't listen to him," Rowlann pointed out. "He didn't want you here . . . not yet."

"You're right," Devaki admitted, setting her cup down. "I listened to my Goddess instead. And I won't stop moving forward." *Even if Will keeps me at arm's length.*

"It's dangerous for you in this city," Rowlann countered, and Devaki saw a flinch in the corners of his pale blue eyes that showed he knew how weak that argument sounded. After all, he'd grudgingly bled next to her on the ship's deck during the storm and knew what she could do if she had to.

"Give me my ring back," Devaki repeated strongly, "and leave the door open. I need to go back to the western district. The people there are sick, and they're blaming it on the Goddess. I think she's calling me there to help them."

Rowlann gave her a worried look, his thick brows furrowing on his square forehead. "What exactly are you going to do?"

"A lot more than you or Will could," Devaki countered. "Let me help. Then you can take the credit and win their hearts like Will wants."

Rowlann was silent, standing his ground in the center of the room. Devaki casually picked up the thick piece of bread from its tray, tearing off the edge of it and letting it cool in her palm. She glanced at Rowlann, watching the emotions twitch in the muscles of his jaw. One time, Devaki challenged herself, she would be able to tell what he was thinking.

As the silence held, Devaki found herself squeezing the bread in her hand, flattening its fluffy inside. *I can't stay trapped in this room,* she thought, fighting back panic. *In Valsara I was locked up, and they didn't need shackles or bolted doors to do it. This kingdom is supposed to be different!*

Rowlann muttered something under his breath, then reached into his pocket. He pulled out her rune ring, and as he held it up, the afternoon sun fell into the room. Bright orange flashed across the deep red stone and glinted on its purposefully sharp outer edge.

"You use that Protection Rune often," he warned her, and tossed the ring to Devaki, who caught it deftly. "Understood?"

Devaki nodded, slipping her ring back onto its proper finger over the band of lighter brown skin. She hopped to her feet, shoving the rest of her food hastily in her mouth.

"And Princess?" Rowlann added. "You need to tell me everything you see: what the people say, what you find down there."

Devaki nodded, expecting this, though she couldn't stop her lips from tightening into a grimace. "I'd rather be telling my father what I find."

"I know," Rowlann replied, and Devaki heard an uncommon touch of sympathy in the two words. "But he is trying to reason with the Towne Masters right now, and that is an all-consuming feat. I also have duties I'm neglecting, being here."

Even though she knew this was true, Devaki still felt ignored.

"And be careful," Rowlann insisted. "You don't know your father, but he will hang me if he finds out something's happened to you."

Devaki waited a few minutes after Rowlann left to set out on her own, grabbing a spare scarf from the trunk in her room to tie over her head and hide all of her hair. Though it was toward the day's end, the rebels in the hallways of the barracks were still moving about in organized groups. Many of them had arms full of ration boxes, some of them singed by fire. Devaki noticed that these men were walking the fastest and in the most deliberate paths toward the center of the barracks.

She looked around to find the easiest exit, and her attention focused on the covered paths that ran around the edge of each rectangular stone building.

Rhethosian Blue cloths spanned over the sides, giving privacy and protection to the buildings' doorways. Right now, the shadows under them were minimal because of the setting sun.

The sun, Devaki thought, and smiled. It currently lit the west sides of the gray stone pathways with blinding light as evening's chill embraced the city. Almost all of the rebels chose to march on the eastern, shady sides. Those who needed to travel along the glaring pathways covered their eyes, barely paying attention.

Devaki waited for a large group of violet-clad men to pass by her door, then turned her ring toward the scar of a Protection Rune. She barely broke the surface of her skin, sighing at the familiar heat that bloomed across her body as a bit of blood ran down her arm. *Cybarys,* she prayed, *I know where you want me to go, and even though I'm afraid, I'll still follow wherever you lead. Help me get there in one piece.*

She crossed out into the sunshine, hand pressed firmly over her Blessing Rune. In the orange light, everything around Devaki was a mess of stone, clumps of grass, and flashes of rebel violet. She ducked under the next building's awning, forcing herself to not run and draw more attention to herself.

The digsite is northwest of here, Devaki remembered, trying to maintain her sense of direction from the chaos of two nights before.

She found herself darting around corners and pressing herself against the stone walls to avoid larger gatherings of rebels. The lines of barracks got smaller as she went, though she did notice that a large stretch of the military housing was guarded by many rebel soldiers, indicating where the large portion of Lorington's fighters were being kept under lock and key until they were commanded to fall in line with the rebel cause.

It seemed like, as she stayed along the sun-blinded western paths, no one paid much attention to her. Part of her wanted to give credit to the busy energy or the setting sun, but she also knew it had to do with her magic.

On the outskirts was another iron archway, similar to the decorative structure that she and Will had ridden under to reach the main courtyard. She noticed there were not many entrances and exits cut in the pale stone that encompassed most of Lorington, and she knew this narrow gateway, guarded by several of Will's men, was her only option.

Devaki squeezed the cut on her arm in reverence and nervousness. *I should wait for the next group of people who are coming or going,* she thought, *so I won't be as noticeable.* It made her think of the night she'd given enough blood to sneak onto Rowlann's ship leaving Valsara.

Her heart pounded as she thought on Rowlann's words and the danger she was putting herself in. She rolled her shoulders resolutely when she saw a large group of men heading toward the archway in her path.

She fell in step with the end of the bunch, keeping pressure on her Protection Rune. Her heart only left her throat after she walked underneath the twisted iron design that ranged between the two walls. Devaki dug her heel in, ready to take off, when someone clamped a hand on her shoulder.

"Miss Tarran," said a quiet voice, and Devaki barely stifled a scream as she spun to look at a short, young Rhethosian man, not much taller than her. She had been so set on moving through the exit that she didn't notice one of the rebels guarding it had followed her several steps. His grip rooted her in place.

"Let me go," Devaki insisted as calmly as she could.

"I will," he said with a small nod. "But not like that."

Devaki felt the tension in her jaw loosen, confused as the man reached up with his free hand and released the clasp on his cloak. As he offered it to her, Devaki realized she recognized him as one of Rowlann's company. She spotted the familiar Protection Rune she'd carved on his chest plate, a tiny scrawl stained in her dried blood.

"Not sure where you think you're headed, but you'll need to cover up more," the rebel continued, and Devaki took his cloak silently. "And watch where you drop these. You might've gone right past us if I didn't notice them."

Devaki glanced at the ground, where the rebel was shuffling his feet. Along the stretch of dirty stone pathway, she made out some magic remnants even though this man had tried to kick them over in the dust. She ground her teeth, upset with herself for not realizing that here, across the sea, scatterings of the tiny red gems were not commonplace like they were in Valsara.

"Thank you," she murmured, shocked that this man was helping her. She assumed Rowlann's company was inconvenienced by her on their voyage and frightened by what had happened during the storm. Even though she'd helped them, she thought they still hated her for what she was.

As if knowing her thoughts, the young rebel gave her a quick smile. He tugged at the collar of his jerkin, just visible under his chest plate, and pulled out a couple inches of a leather Armellan prayer necklace.

No, Devaki thought as the man went back to his post. *Someone here in Rhethos loves our Mother? Goddess, you really have led me to the right place.*

As she moved through the city blocks, Devaki noticed that every dozen or so there was a large wagon decorated with violet banners. In the wagon's beds were baskets full of supplies, ranging from food to blankets to firewood, most of the containers wide enough for two grown men to carry.

She slowed as she continued westward, squinting in the torchlight as the structures around her towered higher and grew dingier. The rebel soldiers around each wagon in this district were on high alert, their pale faces lined with hard, sharp shadows. Devaki saw their hands on their weapons as they talked quietly to a few locals in their doorways.

"Why wait till dawn to distribute those?" one man spoke to the rebel soldiers. Around his thin frame, Devaki spotted several children filed back into the home.

"Master Will and Master Colwell are speaking with the Trade Master now," replied one of the rebels, and from the edge in his voice, Devaki guessed he'd already explained himself many times. "The rations will be given to each household with a representative from our cause and from your people. To show unity moving forward."

"Unity?" repeated the townesman, shaking his head. "Wouldn't that be nice? Who's idea was that?"

The rebels glanced at one another, shrugging. Then, one who sat on the edge of the supply wagon spoke up. "New rebel woman," he commented. "One of Marselle's girls. McKinlee, I think, from Kaylyn. Got to admit it's a good idea."

"But it's not gonna happen," scoffed another local, this one an older man from the home next door. Devaki could hardly make out the outline of his body, but his high voice was loud and strong. "Master Torald used to care for us . . . used to be like us. But with the city full of violet-wearing traitors, it's a great excuse for him to let us starve."

The rebel soldiers grimaced, and Devaki thought their faces said they knew the struggle of Lorington's people well. "You'd be surprised how well Master

Will can make people see reason in change," replied the same man on the wagon's edge. "We're waiting till morning, like he said, but if Torald's people don't show, we'll still give out what we have. No one's starvin' if we can help it."

The kindness in this man's voice made Devaki smile as she walked on, keeping the cloak of Rowlann's man tight around her shoulders. It was good to see that her father's followers were not here to torture the townesfolk by keeping much-needed supplies from them, though she could tell, from the wary looks on the shadowed faces she passed by, the same thought was on everyone's mind: there wasn't much in the wagons, and what they had wouldn't last long.

Dear Goddess, Devaki prayed silently, *please let us help these people, and show them that peace, without bloodshed, will give them many blessings moving forward.*

As she thought the words, she traced the scar of a Guidance Rune along the side of her wrist, remembering how Will had thought it was odd she could reach her Mother by merely touching her scars. She assumed it was because her faith was strong. Even though she'd never seen any of the Goddess Touched in Valsara do the same, to figure out the reason why didn't matter much to her.

She began to feel a soft pull inside of her chest, like the rising of her lungs with each breath was being created by an unseen force. That pull anchored behind her heart and physically moved her down the nearest alleyway that was not lit by any torches like the main roads were.

"Follow the call of your Mother, child."

Devaki gasped as she felt her feet move faster, her shoulders dusting against the cracked siding of the intimidating structures on either side of her. She'd felt this pull before, especially two nights ago, but this was stronger. The voice in her head, as clear and deep as the tones of the temple bells in Valsara, was something she rarely heard.

Sometimes, deep in a meditative Sahma trance, the Goddess' words would comfort her as if someone was right next to her speaking in her ear, a real mother who Devaki had never had. How was it that Cybarys could reach her so easily and speak to her so strongly in the middle of Rhethos?

"Dear child, full of faith. You shine as your Mother's beacon in this lost kingdom. Come here. Be the balancing point between those who would shed unholy blood. Heal them and lead them back home."

Devaki winced as the words in her head echoed with stinging reverbera-tion. The pull in her chest tightened, making it hard to breathe. She noticed the shacks on either side of her were abandoned; there were no townesfolk living here, and no rebel soldiers nearby. Everything outside of her was dark and quiet, while the inside of her boomed with sound and dry heat.

She wanted to slow her steps, to be more cautious, and contemplate the meaning of the words delivered to her, but she had arrived. Devaki found herself once again at the mouth of the hole in Lorington's western district. The ground opened up before her, lined with precise walkways that slanted farther than she could see.

I'm here, Devaki thought. *What is this place?*

Terrific pain split across her skull, and Devaki shrieked.

"You didn't heed our warning! Stay away from here!"

These words were powerful stabs of lightning-like pain that echoed as if they were spoken simultaneously by ten different people. Exactly like when she and Will had been here before, the agony made her lose her sight. Moments before, it had only been the Goddess' voice all around her, but this . . . this was pure pain.

"Come down here, to the old bones of this place where many ancient spir-its lie. Save these people with me. Bleed for your Mother."

Devaki whimpered, fear clawing at her throat: *this* voice was different. Different from the bell-like tone of Cybarys she was used to. Different from the pain-inducing cacophony that struck her like a visible weapon. This was another powerful, feminine voice, darker and distorted, filled with a demand for immediate obedience.

She reached both hands out on the cracked road, her trembling fingers sifting blindly through split cobblestones and fine dirt. As tears rolled down her cheeks, Devaki finally found the edge of the digsite. Why was she getting conflicting messages, in different voices? What was she supposed to do? Die here, in a foreign land, alone, filled with unanswered questions?

There's only one thing I can do, she thought resolutely. *Before this pain kills me.*

She turned her ring toward a Strength Rune on her shoulder, then against a Guidance Rune below her collarbone. Finally, she cut open a Protection Rune above her elbow, all fresh offerings she made with expert ease; there was no need for sight. Her faith in her Mother was all she needed to summon every bit of magic in her Goddess Touched blood.

Devaki made the cuts deeper than usual, knowing that the more intense the offering, the more fervent her prayer, the more powerful magic would be given to her.

Making her left hand into a fist, Devaki felt hot lines of blood course down her entire arm. She threw off her borrowed cloak and shakily got to her feet. Desert heat engulfed her body, and she fought back the choir of angry voices in her head. The sudden, intense blood loss made her sway, but she held her ground.

Slowly, her vision returned, though it was still blurred with tears. Her magic pressed back the agony that assaulted her brain. One thing seemed to be clear: her Goddess wanted her here, but something else didn't.

Whatever that "something else" was did not like Blessing Runes.

As she blinked to clear her eyes, Devaki heard movement on either side of her. She whipped her head to the left, then the right, and saw several figures emerging from the darkness. Her throat went dry when almost a dozen townesfolk stalked toward her.

"Lord save us!" exclaimed one of them. "This one can make magic!"

"They've never come out of the site before!"

"Kill it before it takes more blood!"

Devaki spun, ducking underneath the outstretched arm of the woman nearest her. She cried out when fingers grasped her hair, and she kicked until she connected hard with someone's gut. Her heels slipped, but she ran away from the crowd and back into the tight-knit buildings. They were right behind her, and she was weak from the mental struggle she'd faced and the large amount of blood she'd given.

Where could she go? And how long should she keep up this pace?

Mother, give me strength, she prayed, wheeling around the nearest corner. As she ran, her body protesting despite the burst of magic energy that ran through her, Devaki had a thought that brought forth fresh anger and shame: *Will was right. I shouldn't have gone back there alone.*

A pair of hands dug into her tunic, almost dragging her to the ground. She stumbled, then was spun around, and came face to face with a tall, sickly thin man. "Why?" he shrieked. "Why are you cursing us? Go back in your hole and leave us alone!"

Devaki cried out, the world a blur of swarming colors. She jerked herself free as the rest of the mob from the western district caught up to them. Magic remnants blossomed around her, and everyone stepped back. Now, she ran slower. She'd used too much magic, lost too much blood, and couldn't move much longer.

Ahead of her, down the latest stretch of alleys, she saw a pair of rebel soldiers on the corner. A bit of hope leapt in her chest. She raised a hand, too exhausted to cry out, but when the violet-clad men saw her brown, blood-soaked skin, their expressions hardened and their hands went to their swords. Devaki stumbled, whipped her head back, and saw that the mob had slowed when they, too, saw Will's men ahead.

She spotted two women down the alley across the street. They stood very close together, wearing fine velvet cloaks and talking quietly. Devaki looked at the rebel soldiers, then the women, and forced her last steps toward the latter, saying a silent prayer to Cybarys that she wasn't walking into the arms of death.

"Good Lord!" exclaimed one of the women as Devaki staggered into the street and toward them. Devaki fell at her feet at the same moment that the two rebel soldiers drew their weapons and moved toward her. "She's just a child!" the woman snapped. She pointed back in the direction Devaki had come from. "Go take care of the monsters who were chasing her!"

Devaki, head still spinning, only saw the cobblestones under her knees and the pale hands that rested gently on her arms. When she managed to look up, she saw a pair of beautiful Rhethosian Blue eyes, framed by a round face and long, dirty blonde hair.

The woman smiled unsurely at her, while the second woman with curled red hair stood a step back. Devaki looked over her shoulder, aware that the people from the western district were already several blocks away, Will's men behind them.

"Are you all right?" the woman asked her. "Can you stand?"

Devaki shook her head. "I . . . not on my own." She barely said the words before the Rhethosian woman tightened her grip on Devaki's elbows and supported her full weight. Her touch was kind and protective, as if she was used to helping someone younger than her. *She must be a mother,* Devaki thought.

"She's Armellan *and* Goddess Touched!" snapped the woman who stood back a couple paces. Her voice was low and smooth, but filled with disbelief. "Where did you come from? Are *you* the one who broke the gates open the night of the siege?"

Devaki opened her mouth, but she found she didn't have the strength to speak. Part of her was terrified that the answers to questions like those could put her back in the same situation she'd run from; just because these women didn't look like monsters didn't mean they weren't capable of horrible things that her people had taught her all Rhethosians would do given the chance.

The blonde woman led her to the covered patios that ranged along the edges of the streets in the beginnings of the eastern district. She gathered the velvet of her cloak and draped it over Devaki, gingerly wiping the blood from the three different runes she'd cut into her left shoulder, collarbone, and forearm.

She's ruining that cloak, Devaki thought, her racing heart starting to slow as sweat dried on her skin. *Shouldn't she be afraid of me, or hate me now that she's seen my Rune Scars?*

Instead, the woman was hushing the redhead who had come to stand over them. That woman, the one who stood like a man but dressed in an elaborate gown, seemed to be in charge and had a lot of questions. The blonde woman, however, made Devaki jump when she put a hand over the Protection Rune above her elbow. Devaki glanced down and was shocked at the sight of the woman's long, white fingers staunching the last bits of blood from her cut.

"It's all right," she said. "My name's Angelyn McKinlee. You're safe now. Those are deep cuts."

Devaki felt her breath steady and couldn't help leaning against the woman named Angelyn. She had no idea if she was running from one danger into another, from the dark alley full of people screaming at her to rebel strangers who hated her kingdom and her faith. *But she said I'm safe. I . . . I don't think anyone's ever said that to me before.*

"What's your name?" Angelyn asked gently.

"Devaki," she replied. "Devaki Tarran."

She was surprised when the Rhethosian woman's eyes immediately went wide. Devaki waited as Angelyn searched her face, oddly scrutinizing her cheekbones, jawline, and mouth. Then Angelyn seemed to break free of whatever was happening in her head, and a knowing smile touched her thin lips.

"Devaki," Angelyn began, "something tells me you know Master Will."

She nodded, not sure what that meant to this woman, or her friend who was still analyzing her from a distance. "I do. But he wouldn't be happy if he knew I was out here."

"Are you in some kind of trouble?" Angelyn asked.

"I've got a million more questions besides that!" the other woman demanded. She raised her thin eyebrows at Devaki when the Armellan girl looked at her, and something told Devaki this woman was used to getting unequivocal answers.

Devaki squared her shoulders, shrugging off some of Angelyn's cloak. "The Goddess sent me here, to help all of you with something you can't do yourselves," she began, determined to stand up for herself with her words even if she couldn't find her feet yet. "That digsite out there has some incredible magic in it. It calls to me, but it also hurts me. It tells me to come closer, but then it tries to split my head in two."

"She doesn't make any sense, McKinlee," said Angelyn's friend, rolling her dark green eyes.

"She's lost a lot of blood," Angelyn replied, giving the other woman a concerned look and pointedly eyeing Devaki's clotting Rune Scars. "And obviously the streets aren't safe for someone like her. We need to—"

"Miss McKinlee."

Devaki and the two Rhethosian women turned when someone said Angelyn's name. Three rebel soldiers approached from the south. One of them looked at Angelyn directly, who stood up and placed herself in front of Devaki, flaring her cloak and blocking her from view.

Is she ashamed to be seen with me? Devaki thought. *Or is she protecting me?*

"Miss McKinlee, Master Will has asked for you to attend an important meeting in the barracks," Devaki heard the rebel say.

Devaki glanced at Angelyn's friend, who raised her eyebrows and had a clear, "I told you so" expression on her face. "Interesting timing, though," the woman murmured.

"Now?" Angelyn asked, and Devaki assumed the rebel nodded because Angelyn turned to her friend.

"Marselle, can you make sure she's safe? She still looks frightened and ill."

"You think I don't stand out enough already?" said the woman named Marselle, then sighed. "Of course I will." She made eye contact with Devaki, who realized that this woman had the same color eyes as her father. *Maybe they are related,* she thought, *or from the same place?* Marselle seemed harsh compared to Angelyn, and in her current state, that made Devaki nervous.

"Devaki," Angelyn said, lowering her voice as she turned back toward her, away from the waiting rebels. "I have an idea about who you are, and I'd like to talk with you again sometime. Marselle can make sure you're safe for now, but be careful when you're out here on your own."

Devaki blinked, not sure how to respond. Clearly, this woman was important if Will was summoning her. "Don't tell him you saw me," Devaki insisted as Angelyn turned to leave. The Rhethosian woman nodded. When Angelyn and one of the rebels disappeared around the corner, the remaining two soldiers took up the empty post.

"Well, little Armellan girl," began Marselle, and Devaki glanced at her. "You're quite the mystery on top of everything else, aren't you?"

Devaki held her head high, and this time the world only spun a little bit. She paused, rethinking how to interact with this woman, who was clearly the complete opposite of her in every way. "I think right now," she began honestly, "I just need a bath." After that, she was positive she'd need to be back in her room, to avoid further risking Rowlann's punishment from her father for letting her out.

Marselle laughed and the sound broke apart some of Devaki's trepidation. "Come with me, darling, and I'll show you the best Rhethosian hospitality this place can offer."

CHAPTER ELEVEN

A BULLY FROM THE PAST

"**Y**ou must think I'm an idiot."

Joshua glanced up at Orton. They stood in the training yard right after dawn, both of them draped in heavy furs against the harsh chill at the foot of the mountains. Today, at least there wasn't a fresh coating of snow.

"What?" Joshua questioned. He'd barely arrived, so he wasn't sure what had irritated the giant rebel Master.

"Those gloves," Orton clarified, and his mouth twisted in an unimpressed grimace. "How cut up are your hands today?"

Joshua scoffed, leaning back against the fence that wrapped around the cleared area. Flakes of frost dusted his arms and sprinkled the sandy earth. He watched the cloud from his lips dissipate. Matching puffs of smoke rose from the fires nearby. Not many were traversing the elevated causeways that ranged between the buildings yet. Josh liked it this early, when things were quiet, and no one stared at him with increasing distrust.

Orton's right, as usual, he thought, refusing to meet the man's gaze. *I can't hold a weapon if my knuckles are swollen. They need time to heal if I'm going to keep this up.*

"The last thing I think is that you're stupid," Joshua finally replied. He shrugged off his warm furs, then removed the thick leather gloves.

"What a relief," Orton droned. "Will was the idiot, then, leaving you with those markings. Like giving a set of knives to an untrained child."

"I'm not a child!" Joshua insisted, then checked the petulance that rose in his voice. He cleared his throat, made a fist, and held out his hand toward Orton. The scabs on his knuckles were small and barely healed, the Strength and Protection Runes ringed with bright red skin. "Will trusted me with these so I could choose how to use them. I practice out there every day to make the most of this Goddess' Touch. I'm doing it to help you and the cause, you know."

"You really *do* think I'm an idiot," Orton said, rolling his eyes. He'd barely finished the gesture when, in a flash, his hand went to his sword belt, drew his weapon, and without any effort flicked the tip of his broadsword up to Joshua's throat. "What good is your pagan magic now?"

"I wasn't ready!" Joshua snapped, though the words had little meaning when he had to hold absolutely still.

"You never will be if you think you can play both sides," Orton replied. He let the tip of his weapon lower, took a sidestep, and raised it for another attack. Joshua ducked underneath the wide swing and drew one of his daggers.

In his crouched position, he ground the knuckles of his right hand into his left palm, breaking the scabs of the runes and sending blood down his fingertips. The pain of the open cuts made him wince, but he was starting to get used to it.

A pleasant heat flashed along his arm as he thought a quick prayer to Cybarys, asking her to keep him safe and give him strength. From his hunched spot at Orton's waist, Joshua saw the rebel Master's feet pivot, then plant themselves in the frosted earth, toes pointed slightly outward.

He always does that before an overhead swing, Josh thought. He dropped his blade and held his bleeding hand above his head, just in time to catch Orton's wrist. His fingers could barely wrap halfway around the man's arm. A brilliant flash of red sparks burst between them.

Joshua found himself able to press the man's heavy weapon up and away from him. Sweat broke out on Orton's forehead, dripping past the dark curls on either side of his square face. Finally, he swore under his breath and stepped back from Joshua, who let go of the man's wrist.

"You know . . ." Joshua began, picking up his blade and straightening. He balanced the weight of the dagger in his hand, letting the tip fall straight up and then down without looking. "If you could help me figure out ways to use this magic instead of fighting me on it, I could be of better use to you."

Orton scowled. "I don't see that happening." He raised his weapon. "Again."

Joshua dodged Orton's next swing and drew his second dagger, a new addition he wasn't used to fighting with yet. He held the blades perpendicular to the ground and turned protectively sideways, like Orton had taught him.

He knew better than to push Orton too hard when it came to his Touch, especially because the brutish man was one of his only friends. Mistress Merheene did not leave her quarters often, and the charred bundle of Sahma she'd given Joshua sat unused under his pallet bed. He was too frightened to commune with the Goddess again, and part of him understood how Orton felt.

This is simple. Attack your enemy, memorize his stances, anticipate his next moves. Kill or be killed. No riddled prophecies, no questioning your beliefs of the entire world and what your purpose is in it.

Suddenly, Joshua and Orton froze at the same moment. Orton was mid-swing, and his sword halted as if it had met an invisible wall. Joshua's crossed daggers stayed still level with his forehead, his elbows locked and knees bent. Even though his muscles burned, his heart was instant ice.

The bellow of a horn blasted down from the watchtower. Such a sound only meant two things: either a much-needed resupply from the nearby rebel townes or rebel scouts with some news.

"Head up to the tower," Orton ordered as he strode across the practice yard to meet some men already gathering. "Get a report from Master Lackman."

Joshua nodded, excitedly putting his dagger away and running out of the training area. He only felt a little lightheaded from the blood loss required for his magic use.

One thing Will hadn't cared to mention before leaving him with copies of the Blessing Runes was how much one had to bleed to get a stronger result. The Goddess pulled what she wanted from his body once the rune was cut, and, apparently, stopping an attack from a man like Orton took quite a bit of blood. *Not a pleasant thing to figure out on my own.*

As the horn's echoes faded, dozens emerged from the lower levels of the camp. The voices of women, crying children, and older men blew past Joshua on the cold air. Above him, Joshua saw people marching across the slanted walkways, their boots cracking the fresh ice in uneven bursts.

He was up the watchtower ladder in less than ten seconds, banging the trap door open with his fist.

"A troop of men coming our way," Master Lackman said immediately, his frosted beard hanging down in Josh's face. "About forty. They've got several wagons with them, though they're not Lady Marselle's usual girls driving."

Joshua wasn't sure if that made him feel relieved or disappointed, knowing that the chance of his mother returning with the anticipated supplies had just been eliminated. He thanked Lackman and headed back down to tell Orton what to expect.

At the central common hall, many had gathered, huddled together, eager for news. Joshua noticed Orton, Lackman, and a few others were already greeting the newcomers as they cautiously navigated the heavy wagons over the trench at the camp's edge.

Josh spotted Ada nearby, though the tall, slim bargirl only gave him a brief smile. Her eyes darted to the clotting Rune Scars on his knuckles with clear distaste. She pushed her way slowly through the crowd to stand at its front while Orton and the leader of the resupply group approached.

Something in the back of Joshua's mind told him to pull down his tunic sleeves and put his gloves tightly on his hands. He did so, focusing on the stranger in the lead smiling easily at Lackman.

For some reason, an odd feeling touched the bottom of Joshua's stomach, like he'd eaten something sour the night before. He tried to shake it off, telling himself it had nothing to do with the person he was looking at. After all, if these men bore rebel violet and were delivering Lady Marselle's supplies, what was there to be nervous about?

"Her latest run had to be redirected down to Lorington," the newcomer was explaining. Joshua practically felt the crowd lean forward to hear his news. "Master Yarwell across the forest in Morely got orders to have all this sent to you. Said you were stretched thin and could use it."

Dozens of women stepped forward to help lead the wagons back to the storehouses to be organized. Joshua was shoved aside by several of the young boys in camp, eager to follow where the food was going. But his eyes remained glued to the man speaking to Orton.

"Only been here a few times over the years. . ." the man began. He raised his eyebrows, two thick, coarse knots of light brown hair that disappeared into his messy bangs as he stared up at the interwoven walkways. "It's all ropes, isn't it?"

Lackman chuckled, and Joshua guessed he was familiar with this man. Orton, however, had a more determined look on his face. "We would welcome all your reports regarding Master Will's advance. Let's step inside, where it's warmer."

The remainder of the crowd that hadn't followed the supply wagons began to filter into the common hall. Joshua let everyone flow past him. The newcomer was giving Lackman a lopsided grin as he muttered something quietly, then Joshua heard Orton ask, "What was your name, brother?"

"Oh, I've had a few over the years," the man replied, "what with going in and out of townes still flying The Bradford's sigil. But we're among friends, yes? Best to use my real name: McKinlee. Travok McKinlee."

Joshua's throat constricted. He found that air wouldn't move through his lungs. Unable to stop himself, he stared harder, mouth open, just noticing the sandy blond color of his hair and his frighteningly similar deep brown eyes.

"McKinlee," Orton repeated, his gaze snapping across the now-empty entryway toward Joshua. "From Kaylyn Towne?"

The man shrugged, as if the place was of little consequence to him. "Yes. Haven't been there for many years, though. Too busy fighting for the cause up here in the north where people have more sense! Much more rewarding than a life in a dying seaside towne."

Joshua nearly screamed when he felt a hand on his shoulder. He reached toward one of his daggers, but Ada's other hand stopped him. "Little Josh . . ." she began, falling back into the nickname she'd always used for him in their old lives.

He can't be . . . Joshua thought, the words ringing with an unstable echo in his head. The rest of the camp seemed to blur around him, like in the haze of the Sahma plant, but with an unsettling blur of dull, nauseating colors. This wasn't right.

Mum said my father left sixteen years ago when I was born, but the rebellion has only been massing for a decade. That doesn't add up. He can't *be my father.*

"Josh!" Ada snapped when he took a step forward.

"Let go," he insisted, and ripped his shoulder out of her reach. "*McKinlee.*"

He raised his voice when he said the family name, not loud enough to shout but at a volume that ranged over the open space. Travok turned. His eyes, reflections of Joshua's, narrowed immediately. For a moment Joshua saw recognition and then anger spark, crackle, and die.

"Well, I'll be damned," he laughed. A grin lit up the man's face, stretching from one corner of his square jaw to the other. "I heard a rumor that my wife's family business was burned down in Kaylyn. I had no idea if Angelyn or you survived. Glad you made it to the right side of the fight, my boy!"

Joshua stiffened when Travok put a hearty arm around his shoulder. There were many things he wanted to blurt out in response, sixteen years of questions denied by his mother that demanded answers. Yet they all remained crammed in his head when his father took a step back.

"Why do you look so upset, son?" Travok asked, a smooth grin plastered on his face. "This should be a happy reunion, with both of us wearing rebel violet."

Joshua glanced at Orton, who still seemed surprised but not worried. Lackman was grinning as widely as Travok, insisting they celebrate inside while news was shared.

"Wait a minute," Joshua insisted. He planted his feet in the open doorway to the common hall as his heart raced. "You don't have anything to celebrate. You abandoned us. My mother suffered because of you!"

Travok glanced sideways at Orton and Lackman, bemused, as if he were slightly embarrassed by a child's outburst. "Now, now," he began with patience. "Your old man has been bleeding for Rhethos' freedom—"

"How's that?" Joshua demanded. The sudden fire in his chest was growing uncontrollably, and even though he felt Ada try to touch his arm again, he shook her off angrily. Hot indignation blinded him. "Ten years, you said? You left us when I was born, sixteen years ago! Where were you all *that* time? First you hurt her when you were at home, then you hurt her by leaving!"

"Josh, I'm sure your father can speak with you privately, after he gives his reports," Orton said. He stepped into the space between Joshua and Travok, his broad shoulders almost blocking Joshua's view of the man he thought had been either a monster or a dead man his whole life.

Out of the corner of his eye, he noticed people glancing back outside the common hall with curious expressions. He knew he should lower his voice, take a deep breath, but no. His hands balled into tight fists that demanded immediate answers he felt he deserved.

He stands like the guardsmen did in Kaylyn, with their shoulders back and their guts out, and that stupidly confident smirk on their faces that said they knew their words could hold as much hurt as their weapons, without any consequences.

"No, you're going to tell me the truth, now!" Joshua shouted. "If you've been working with the rebellion for so long, you must be a good liar, huh? Where did you go when Mum had to hide me when I was born during the Blood Moon? That was *your* fault, too, you know. And you were just *gone!*"

Orton shifted his attention back toward Travok, dark eyebrows raised. That particular question, it seemed, got the rebel Master's attention. For the first time, Travok's lips warped into a dangerous grimace.

"If you are my father," Joshua seethed, "my mother told me the truth about you. You're a bully and a coward. You don't belong here with these people!"

Travok's demeanor darkened. He reached an arm around Orton and grabbed the overgrown hair at the back of Joshua's head. "Respect," Travok demanded, "can only be beaten into a boy! It's time for an overdue lashing!"

Joshua writhed, trying to break free of the fingers digging into his scalp and tearing out his hair. Even though Orton started speaking some placating words, Josh noticed the rebel families retreating further into the building. A rude child being punished by a parent was commonplace, and not something another Rhethosian interfered with.

But I'm not a child, Joshua thought, quickly recalling Orton's words. *I have to be smart.*

Joshua let his knees buckle, using his body weight to pull himself to the ground. Blood trickled down the sides of his face, but he gritted his teeth: bleeding was something he did often lately. When his hands and knees met the frozen earth, Joshua tore off his gloves and raked his nails across the knuckles of his right hand. The warmth of a dry, desert sun rose around him, and the Strength and Protection Runes scabs he'd freshly opened glowed with a deep red light.

Travok's grip loosened, and Joshua pivoted on his knees. Halfway through the motion, he stood, pulled back his fist, and connected with his father's gut. Magical energy blossomed out in a visible arc, knocking Travok, Orton, and everyone near the common hall's entrance to the ground.

The rickety walls shuddered, and splinters of planks and loose ropes rained down. Frightened cries rose from the rebel families and shouts of distress echoed through the men who'd arrived with Travok. Joshua did *not* use magic anywhere in the camp, except for the training grounds when most were asleep.

"Pagan magic!" gasped one member of Travok's group.

"Cybarys' slave!" cried another, and further curses echoed back and forth.

"Stand down," Orton commanded, getting to his feet before the rest. He put out his arms to try and calm Travok's men. "We know Joshua, and Master Will trusts him. There's no need to fear—"

"You disobedient little bastard!" Travok growled. His words were distorted with pain and a rough cough as he tried to stand. He clutched at his stomach, his oversized, stained tunic bunched between his large fingers. "I *knew* there was something wrong with you the night you were born." His gaze snapped to his men, who were glaring at Joshua and the radiating, gemlike stones that were scattered on the ground at his feet.

Now, he was in trouble.

"Being close to these trees is like poison!" Travok shouted. "Anyone who truly stands for the rebellion will execute those cursed with magic."

Joshua ground his teeth nervously, feeling the cuts on his fingers start to dry, slowing the minimal blood flow. Would Orton really let this man hurt him? A beating for being disrespectful was one thing. . .death for his Goddess Touched blood (the same type of blood that ran through their leader's veins) seemed extreme.

"Get that Goddess Touched brat!" Travok barked, clinging to one of the nearest support beams. "I'm going to burn every pagan mark off his skin!"

Joshua spun, ducking under several outstretched arms. Orton's voice disappeared in the chaos Joshua had created. He cried out when the edge of a blade met with his back, slicing through his tunic and his left shoulder blade.

Stumbling around the bend at the edge of The Forts, Joshua yanked his right dagger from its sheath. Hot pain dripped down his back, and he decided the next man who touched him would at least lose a finger.

Something hard bounced off the back of Joshua's head. *Was that a rock?* he thought incredulously, ducking. All he could do was keep running, barely out of their range.

Where to? he realized, panic rising in his throat.

The only real answer came to him: the trees.

If his father's men hated magic so much, and they feared the Goddess' Woods just as equally, he had to make it across the camp's spike-filled trench and under the cover of the ancient oaks. From experience, he knew there were only a few places where the gap was narrow enough to jump, and Joshua frantically got his bearings. The western watchtower was over his left shoulder, so if he kept going, it wouldn't be far—

"Got him!" someone cried, and Joshua felt arms wrap around his waist.

He struggled forward one more step but was pulled to the ground. His forearms skidded on the rocky earth. More hands piled onto his legs and his back, pinning him down. Joshua couldn't see, couldn't move, and barely managed to keep his right hand with his dagger raised above his head to ward off a fresh rain of blows.

Someone tried to pull him up, but Joshua lashed out and felt his blade meet flesh. When his assailant cried out and let go, part of the pressure on his body lessened, but his heart tensed with fear: without seeing who he was attacking and where, he could seriously injure someone, possibly kill them.

Even though Travok had ordered his men to only capture Joshua, he knew that he could easily be killed by "accident." As he tried to scramble away, the crowd pressed in on him again. Another pair of hands seized the back of his neck, forcing his face against the jagged ground, squeezing all the air out of his throat.

"Let the boy be!" Joshua heard Orton's voice, but it was quickly overcome by the shouts of dozens of other men.

"This place needs to be cleansed of the Blood Goddess' slaves!" a voice shouted above the cacophony. He barely recognized it as his father's as his vision darkened. "If the leadership here can't see that, maybe it's time for a change for Rhethos."

Joshua opened his mouth, desperate to stand up for himself, but he couldn't take in any air. He wanted to lash out with his dagger, to blindly attack whoever was suffocating him, but Mistress Merheene's words came back to him: "Do not cause unnecessary pain in a necessarily painful life. Trust in your Mother."

Cybarys, he thought desperately, *help me get away from these people, and I promise I'll do whatever you want. I trust you. Just let me live to figure this all out!*

Joshua felt his eyes close against his will, and he used his remaining strength to scrape his knuckles, fresh with blood and the power of his prayer, against the earth. A red glow tinged the blackness around him, and the dozens of hands on his arms and legs suddenly let go. Last to release was the grip around his neck, and Joshua hacked as he fought to blink light and life back into his world.

"Josh! Go, now!"

He wasn't sure who shouted at him, but hearing his name in the icy morning air gave him courage to scramble to his feet. He ground fresh magic remnants under his boots, launching himself toward the narrowest point in the camp's defenses. With a desperate shout, Joshua jumped over the trench and landed shakily on the other side. There was only a thin strip of bare land between the camp's edge and the beginning of the woods. Sharp air burning his lungs, he forced himself under the freezing shade of the oak's branches.

Without daring to look back, Joshua kept stumbling on. He brushed his bare fingers against the trees around him, both for balance and reassurance. The Goddess' presence, something he always felt at the back of his mind nowadays, was amplified here. At first, he heard footfalls in the underbrush behind him, but the deeper he went, the stronger Cybarys' Touch settled in . . . and so did the silence.

Finally, he was alone. He'd sought the solitude of these trees many times lately, but today there was a sinister heaviness to being here; he could not leave this place without his life being threatened, by a man his mother had hoped was dead. Frustrated and alone, Joshua ground his teeth. He was the only one in the rebel camp who knew of the discrepancy in Travok's timeline.

What was he doing for those six unaccounted years? Who was he working for then? And what does he want now?

Even if he was lying, and Joshua was sure he was, there was one thing he couldn't deny because he knew it in his blood: that man was his father.

More questions plagued his mind as he sank to the ground at the base of the nearest oak, catching his breath. *How do I get word to Will about this?* He thought of trying to make his way through the woods to the other side to the Brother Townes of Patten and Morely.

Then he thought of Orton. The rebel Master was only one man, and if Travok and his forty men could subdue Orton to take charge on their own.

There was Ada, too, and Mistress Merheene whom Joshua couldn't imagine leaving behind even in search of the truth. *I can't leave,* he decided, gingerly reaching back to touch the cut on his shoulder blade. It felt shallow, but burned at the slightest pressure. *I have to figure this out on my own.*

"Not on your own, little one. I am here."

Joshua jumped, snapping his head from side to side. He saw no one amongst the cool gray and green shadows of the tight-knit oaks. It took him a moment to realize that the voice had spoken in his head. He really was deep in the woods, he thought, if that feminine tone full of power and reassurance could enter his mind so seamlessly.

He shivered and thought of how, a few hours ago, his biggest problem was facing another cold round of training with Orton. Part of him thought that he'd asked for this dilemma, praying every time he went into these woods for an understanding of his higher purpose, his place in the world, or a way to find the balance of life and how to fight for it.

Okay, Joshua thought back, crossing his arms over his chest in a gesture very similar to his mother. *Well, what am I supposed to do now?*

CHAPTER TWELVE

BITTER WINE'S BURIED SECRETS

Sarrett prayed for the relief of a physical confrontation instead of the mental one he faced whether he was awake or asleep. When his eyes were open, he threw up blocks in his mind to ward off the memories that returned with his sobriety. When he passed out on the earth-crusted floor, he retreated from the unending demand for Sahma wine that battered the confines of his soul.

Every time he thought he'd break and slip into the sweet, dark depths of insanity, his sister would appear opposite him and offer him her open arms. First, he'd hear the lapping of river water against an unseen bank, little ripples that met a deceptively stable shoreline.

Then that smoky glow would encompass his cell and illuminate the remains of his Rhethosian Blue lieutenant's jacket. In between his meager meals and fitful sleep, Sarrett couldn't help looking at Lily.

"Stop fighting. Let it all in. Remember what you've done to face what you can now do."

She was so young when she died, yet when she appeared to him she spoke tempting wisdom beyond her nine years. Lily took two steps forward, her bloated, bare feet shuffling into the space between them. Even when she stopped an inch from him and he could touch her damp hair if he dared, he knew it wasn't real. Then Lily's fingers rested on his chest. The push of her hand against his bloodstained tunic had weight behind it.

"I know it hurts, Jon. It's time to open yourself to what you've buried with bitter wine and military brutality. Do it . . . or perish."

Sarrett swore. This manifestation was trying to give him what he wanted: the touch of another human being. Instead of lashing out, he took a deep breath, and finally let go.

Enough was enough.

Sarrett wrapped his arms around Lily's shoulders. A piece of his painfully sober mind almost expected to feel her, to give him the moment he'd wanted for fifteen years, to apologize to the one person he wished he could have saved. Instead, he only hugged himself, and that physical connection in the dark of Lorington's dungeons triggered the first memory that the Sahma wine had drowned:

The day Lily died. But no. He would not relive that. Instead, he let himself feel everything that happened two days later.

Clancy shone with immeasurable beauty. Every Loyal dreamed of living in Rhethos' capitol. Pristine shipping yards, luxurious seaside homes, and intricately gardened fields ranged along the cliffsides that skirted the southern coast. Even the poorest in Clancy, further inland on the edges of the city, were blissful in the knowledge that they were close to the one person capable of keeping them safe from the Blood Goddess and her pagan children.

Clear waterways ran into the city in dozens of small tributaries full of rich silt. As the nexus for southern Rhethos' rivers, both people and trade sailed in and out of the beautiful port. Outside the city walls and under the eye of The Bradford's Pure Palace, many children played in the warm sun and cool river waters across the open, green countryside. Even the children of Loyals and lesser families mingled and enjoyed the pleasant afternoons while their parents were occupied.

That day, however, fifteen years in the past, the boy who walked with the river's flow toward Clancy did not smile. The joyful splashes did not meet his ears. He walked with the heavy weight of one who bore tragedy on his slim, teenage shoulders. Yet his steps were unwavering along the riverside that had claimed the life of his only sibling two days ago.

Anyone who did see him steered clear. Whether out of respect for his family's loss or out of fear of his cold, driven glare, he didn't know. His eyes glazed over the ancient beauty of the stone wall and its gilded entrances. The pleasant sounds that echoed down the idyllic streets made him want to scream with raw fury.

The world around him was blinded by the shards of his broken heart as he made his way uphill through the city, past the armed guardsmen on the corners, toward the buildings that wrapped like armor around their Lord's castle: this was the only thing that made sense right now, and he would not stop until the doors of The Academy where future Bradfords were trained were opened before him.

"I need to see Master Boward."

His voice cracked harshly, and he realized he hadn't spoken since the screaming that had happened in his house two nights ago when he carried Lily's small, waterlogged body back to their parents.

One of the guardsmen, dressed in brilliantly polished iron armor, glanced down at him. "The Academy's Master? What in the Lord's name would he talk to you about?"

"He needs to let me in," Sarrett explained, straight-faced. "I'm supposed to be here."

"Bullshit," the man laughed, his disbelief mirrored on the faces of the rest of the guardsmen nearby.

"I . . ." Sarrett faltered, a bit of clarity coming into his haze of grief when he realized how stupid he was behaving; only a few, elite children, no older than ten, from Loyal families were accepted into The Bradford's private academy every year. "Please," he tried now. "This is where I belong."

The guardsmen sighed, reluctant pity on his face. "Family name?" he asked.

"Sarrett."

Another soldier briefly checked several papers. "Not even mentioned in the new Loyals," he muttered, with less patience than the first. "Get off this hill, boy. We'll even let you do it in one piece."

Sarrett balled his hands into fists. Nothing in the world made sense except the overwhelming guilt inside of him, and the need to do something to prove he was worth more than that consuming feeling was all he could think of. "Either you let me into the next Academy class," he began bravely, "or I will come back here every day till you do. Or until you kill me. I have nowhere else to go."

"Who do you think you are?" snapped the guardsmen with the papers, his hand touching his sword. "Rude little shit—"

"Relax," the first cut in. He gestured at Sarrett, like one pointing at a stray dog that shouldn't be touched. "Look at his eyes. You're wrong, Sarrett; there is somewhere else you can go, and I think you'll do better there."

The guardsman walked him down to the outer ring of buildings inside the city wall, decorated in Rhethosian Blue stones and flowing sigil banners. He found himself in front of the command center of the military barracks. Sarrett glanced around, confused; what would the military want with him?

"Captain Caldrell!" the guardsman next to Sarrett said suddenly. Sarrett halted, looking at the man who had turned the nearest corner. He had not expected to run into Rhethos' military leader, and now he couldn't help but stare.

There was nothing physically exceptional about him, but the way he stood and the energy he exuded in his full uniform was remarkable. Barely in his forties with touches of gray in his short brown hair, Mercer Caldrell adjusted his jacket and looked silently at the guardsman he'd nearly run into, eyebrows raised.

Sarrett gazed at the man's shoulders, cased in plates of iron that were studded into his Rhethosian Blue coat. Rows of carved gemstones on his chest gleamed in the sunshine, and the pressed, perfect seams of every line of the thick, spotless fabric were awe-inspiring.

Sarrett assumed any other boy his age would be staring at the gold-embossed, single-handed sword at the Captain's waist that must have cost several fortunes, but Sarrett couldn't take his eyes off the military jacket, and the way it seemed to turn this man into an instantly respectable, formidable leader.

"Forgive us, Captain," the guardsman was saying, eyes cast to the dirt walkway. "I was taking this boy to the assignment barracks."

"Why?" Caldrell didn't bark the word, but Sarrett still saw the guardsman flinch. The man who'd led Sarrett here stammered, uttering jumbled explanations, till Caldrell held up a hand. "Go back to your station," he commanded shortly. Once the guardsman had scurried away, Caldrell's face broke into a sharp smile, one that gave Sarrett an unpleasant tightness in the pit of his stomach.

"So you just walked up to Bradford's Academy?" he questioned, tilting his head to the right at a severe angle, eyebrows narrowed.

Sarrett nodded wordlessly.

"You realize you're too old to be accepted up there? And you're too young to enlist down here. What a fantastic piece of shit life has dealt you, boy!"

Caldrell laughed, an uneven, erratic sound, like mice skittering on glass, and Sarrett felt his rage rekindle in his chest. It took all of his courage to hold the Captain's gaze, glaring at the man's dark brown eyes.

"I'm giving you my admiration for your ambition, you know," Caldrell snapped. Now, his smile was gone and his stance suddenly rigid. "Every boy who goes into the Academy has the sole purpose of training for the greatest potential honor in Rhethos: becoming our next Lord. You think you're worthy of that?"

Sarrett blinked, made uneasy by the Captain's sharp, unexpected changes in expression and body language. "I could do it," he insisted. "Given the chance, I could—"

"This is the only chance you'll get to be worth a damn in this lifetime," Caldrell cut in, gesturing around at the bustling barracks. "If you go up there again, they'll kill you. Unwanted attention at a place where every door has ten locks is a death sentence. If that's what you want, go get it done. But do you want revenge on whoever or whatever put that nasty glint in your eye? You want to make your family worthy of being a Loyal? The Rhethosian military is your only option to serve your Lord. . . and yourself."

Sarrett flinched, still finding it hard to believe he was having this conversation with Captain Mercer Caldrell himself. He let the anger and the helplessness and the guilt flood over him again, numbing everything. "I'm ready."

"You're sixteen, yes?" the Captain asked pointedly.

"Yes."

"Family?"

"Doesn't want me anymore."

"Pity," Caldrell sighed, and the traces of that unstable smile bubbled across the corners of his lips again. "Because, after five years under my command, they'll change that tune. Ten, and I'll have taken that sweet, raw emptiness inside of you and turned it into a weapon the entire kingdom will fear."

Something in the back of Sarrett's mind told him to turn around, run, and never come back to this city. There was a sick, twisted piece of this man that, even in his sorrow, he didn't want infecting any part of himself. Instead, he eyed the Rhethosian Captain's jacket and everything it stood for. He followed Caldrell farther into the barracks, thinking about what he actually knew about this man. He was relatively new to his post, being instated by the newest Lord Bradford who had come to power three years ago.

Caldrell was from a long line of Loyals, though amongst Sarrett's community, his family name had always been clouded in dark secrets and violent rumors. Even at fourteen, Sarrett understood what words like "blackmail," "incest," and "insanity" meant. According to his mother, such dealings always simmered under the surface of The Bradford's society, particularly in the Caldrells.

"It has escalated to a point of it being noticeable*," she had said with disgust, not a week before Lily stumbled into the deep part of the river. "Even people like us have seen things turn for the worse. Why our Lord wants a man like Mercer wielding the entire military we'll never know."*

"We're not meant to know," his father had barked back, ever in his cold, crushing voice. "Caldrell deals Rhethosian Justice with pride, and we should be grateful the Lord chose him to keep us safe. You heard The Bradford: the Blood Goddess and her slaves could make real on their threats to invade any day. Keep quiet and be thankful for who rules over you."

Whatever Caldrell saw in Sarrett that day, he never spoke of it aloud. He placed him in a barrack, under a commanding Master, and when the next training began, he lined up with the other boys, all at least two years older than him. The brutal physical and mental challenges that ensued for the next year were exactly what his heart and mind needed in the wake of losing his little sister. The complicated emotions of grief, guilt, and revenge all melded together into a simplified task: follow orders. . . faster and smarter than everyone else.

Which he did.

He ran extra miles during drills, without shoes, as was the tradition for new guardsmen. He memorized formations while the others stumbled and were beaten. He carried full armor and weaponry along the very riverside where he'd lost Lily, back and forth all day, while the training Masters watched and the local children scattered.

And each day, it hurt a little less. Or maybe he just buried the hurt deeper with increasing expertise.

Since the pressure of his promotion to lieutenant years later and his assignment to Kaylyn, and his discovery of the Sahma wine, he'd blocked it all out. Now, however, every detail came back and repeated itself with lifelike clarity in his mind's eye.

The bright whitewashed stone streets of Clancy under his feet as he tried to find a place in the world . . .

The look in Caldrell's eye when he took advantage of his brokenness . . .

The crash of harsh fists against his stomach when he let his arrogance get the better of him . . .

The cuts along his neck, elbows, and wrists from the excruciating weight of heavy armor . . .

The smell of sweaty, bloodied young men packed into the barracks at night, only to be woken for midnight drills . . .

The taste of pride, like a sweet, bitter liquor coursing through his whole body when he excelled beyond the rest . . .

But for what? Where was he *now*, after everything he'd done in his youth? What was the point of letting his sober, aching head bring back what he had chosen to forget? Sarrett groaned, let go of his grip around his torso, and sunk back to his cell's floor at the back of Lorington's dungeons. One final truth hit him in that moment of clarity: no one was going to come save him, especially not Mercer Caldrell.

He only had himself.

"Lieutenant Sarrett. You *are* a mess."

Sarrett winced, not sure if the words had come from his mind. He blinked against the darkness, then heard the clink of metal on metal. The sound echoed in a succinct beat until sparks flew and created glorious bits of light. Flames grew at the end of a torch, and Sarrett leaned forward despite the pain in his eyes.

"Who's there?" he asked.

The voice chuckled, clearly a man, and a stranger knelt on the other side of the bars. He held the torch at eye's level between them so the light kept Sarrett blind. "Oh, we haven't officially met," the man said, "but we do know of each other."

"If we're *officially* meeting in this nasty place, I doubt it," Sarrett returned, surprised at his own sudden response.

A flicker of a grin caught Sarrett's eye, and for a moment he saw the light highlight high, pale cheekbones on the other side of the bars. He squinted harder, trying to see another part of the stranger's face.

"Well, I know who you are well enough," the man said. "I know that Mercer Caldrell made you. He promised you everything you wanted in exchange for your devotion to the Rhethosian military and its Lord. After all, who else can keep Rhethos safe from the pagan Goddess? It's your duty to help common folk resist the temptation of the old religion."

Sarrett frowned suspiciously. There were too many possibilities running through his exhausted mind: was this stranger even real? Was he a spy of Caldrell's come to test his loyalty? Was he a rebel here to taunt him? There was comfort in hearing the ideals he'd believed in his entire life, but the way this man said them was odd, like hearing heartfelt poetry from a scorned lover.

"Who *are* you?" Sarrett demanded. He inched closer to the bars on his knees.

"Someone who used to believe in such things. But I know better now."

"You're rebel trash," Sarrett said, losing all hope of comradery created by the man's Rhethosian words. He found it so easy to let go when he barely had a handhold on hope to begin with. "You're wasting your time here."

The stranger shrugged, moving the torchlight up and down in the process, making Sarrett nauseous. "I agree. If I had *my* way, you would have lost your head on the field the night of the siege. Would have done it myself, to save Will the trouble. Instead, here we are. Things have changed, and I'd like to know if you want to make something of your life, or if you'd like it to be cut short as it already should have been."

Sarrett clutched at the remains of his lieutenant's jacket, feeling the fabric as if it represented his fraying nerves. He almost laughed at the idea of complying with this rebel who thought he could . . . what? Redeem his soul?

His jaw trembled with a combination of unstable laughter and despair. As always, when his mind teetered, he heard Clancy's river water splash gently against the other side of his cell and a soft blue glow crept across the floor toward him. He blinked furiously, and it all went away.

"I don't care if 'things have changed,'" Sarrett spat. "I don't need you tormenting me, and I don't need your cause to save me."

"But someone needs to save your mistress," the stranger replied smoothly. "The one who cares for your two children. Her name is . . . Mayra?"

Sarrett froze. Time seemed to stop for one breathless moment, in which he recalled the last time he'd seen Mayra before heading to Kaylyn. Then there was the painful stab of that last letter she'd sent him, explaining how he wasn't "excelling" fast enough for her. She was taking the children away, to a place with, assumedly, more successful men.

"What do you mean *save* her?" he whispered.

"All I'm saying is you really should throw away that disgusting Rhethosian jacket and try on some rebel violet. Who knows? You might like the color. But there are other ways to get you to share what might be helpful to me." The man moved the torch down enough so Sarrett could see his friendly smile. "Oh, don't worry; I don't have her or your bastards here yet. Whether they'll need saving from someone stronger and smarter than you is to be determined."

The irony was not lost on Sarrett that, not long ago, his situation had been reversed in the tiny, dingy dungeons of Kaylyn's Towne Centre. With a sour taste in his mouth, to prove his "heartlessness" to his new officers, he'd tortured and blackmailed and strung up guilty and innocent men and women, and here he was, at this stranger's mercy.

"I'm not wasting my breath on you," Sarrett growled defiantly.

"Not the response I was expecting," the man said, with a hint of surprise. "But I'll let you think on it. What else do you have to do down here?" He rose, and Sarrett caught a glimpse of the hilt of a beautiful sword at the man's waist.

Sarrett resisted the urge to grab the bars and beg the rebel bastard to stay. But his pride, as Lily kept telling him, made him stay seated and silent. There had to be another way, one where he didn't give up what was left of his self-respect.

The stranger laughed at the dungeon's exit, as if he knew what was going through Sarrett's mind. He extinguished his torch, plunging the dungeon into a hopeless shade of black. "Enjoy the darkness, Lieutenant."

CHAPTER THIRTEEN

CRACKING OPEN THE DETAILS

Public settings were a place where Will thrived. He had found accountability and transparency were powerful tools throughout the last decade. Despite the different circumstances in Lorington, his core tactics remained the same. Now . . .he just needed Angelyn.

He waited patiently, observing the outdoor space he'd created as soon as the pieces fell into place. As soon as Irvin informed him that Master Torald was ready to negotiate outside of Jeras Moore's influence, Will sent word to the northern townes. Over the last day, Master Greggor from Morely and several other rebels had traveled to Lorington, ready to open trade lines into the southernmost towne facing the rebellion.

"Interesting choice of location," Angelyn commented when she arrived.

Will smirked as her rebel escorts stepped to the side. At the back of one of the central barracks was an open space covered by a Rhethosian Blue awning. Along it he'd set up a narrow table with eight chairs, underneath the calm, cool shadows. On each corner was a large iron sconce, full of hot flames that chased back the prewinter chill.

"Not like meetings in the private parlor of your inn, I know," he commented. "Then, we had to meet in secret. But today is meant to be inviting and open, a place for change. Now," he added, "I'm in need of your expertise, Miss McKinlee. The military matters of this towne I can handle, but I have no skills when it comes to supply rationing."

"So they're ready to work with us, then?" Angelyn asked, stepping under the awning and up to one of the empty chairs.

"Lorington's Trade Master is," Will clarified. "They'll be here shortly."

"Then I'll help however I can," Angelyn said. He noticed how she carefully chose a seat in one of the center chairs, her back to the building, facing the walkways that were teeming with the traffic of countless violet-bearing rebels. Having her here calmed his nerves.

When Torald, Greggor, and two other northern towne representatives arrived, they took their seats, each one glancing a bit longer at Angelyn, who introduced herself. Will noticed that Angelyn observed Lorington's Trade Master more closely. He remembered that the man who held the title in her old towne had been ancient and forgetful, ruled by military men like Sarrett.

Yet Torald was a fit, middle-aged man with a calculative gaze. Will could already see the difference in his demeanor without Jeras present. When each of them were seated, Will offered wine to everyone. The sounds of rebels reinforcing buildings, sharpening weapons, and conversing as they passed faded into the background as he focused on the group before him.

"Master Will," Torald began, "I am sure Master Colwell has already told you that I am in favor of all the trade opportunities your cause offers. They are vital to Lorington's survival. . . even more so, its ability to recover from that damned digsite and our sufferings because of the war. Bearing rebel violet is no burden for me."

Will nodded, satisfied with this opening. He stood at the head of the table, his arms resting on the back of the high, wooden chair before him.

"But," Torald added sharply, "as much as I love this towne, I cannot move forward alongside you without a reassurance of my family's safety from Moore."

Everyone at the table shifted their attention from Torald to Will, who finally took his seat. Will inhaled deeply, taking in the smells of acrid stone, campfire dust, and freshly cut wood. He was expecting this and was ready with this response.

"I wanted to discuss your family today," he began. "From my recent studying of the Towne Master's ledgers, you aren't from a line of Loyals. Your family name actually comes from outside these walls, farming a large area of the countryside for . . .five generations, yes?"

Torald's salt and pepper eyebrows shot up in surprise, then he relaxed, as if ready to share more himself. "Yes. And we're quite proud of our history. I. . .I helped settle some disputes between the farmers and the Masters of Lorington years ago. Moore saw my worth and brought me back to the city, gave me a title I never could have dreamed of, but I haven't been allowed to go back to my land. I'm too 'useful' to Jeras and increasing profits for him and other Loyals."

"Yet you *do* go see your people, in secret," Will replied smoothly. "Moore knows this and I'm sure feels threatened by your disobedience. That's why he would harm them if you helped us, correct?"

"How did you . . .?" Torald stuttered.

"It's your hands that helped give me the idea, when we met the other night," Will commented. "No one else in the northern district has calluses like that."

Torald scoffed and wrapped his arms around himself, as if warding off the chill of the shade despite the burning sconces. "Outside Lorington," he began with passion in his tone, "we don't hide behind false faces and stab neighbors in the back. We're hard, honest workers, Master Will. It didn't take me long to see the glaring corruption in this city, where Moore and his folk benefit while others, like those on my farmland, are stripped of their resources and people in the western district here are left to starve. It's not right, and something has to change."

Will let the silence hold, the northern Towne Masters nodding subtly with clear understanding at Torald's words. They had faced similar situations while under the rule of The Bradford, and Will knew they'd share such things in time. For now, the silent bond was enough.

Torald glanced beyond the shaded area, into the afternoon sun that graced the squat, stone structures surrounding them. He sighed, then folded his workman's hands gently on the table's edge. "I go outside these walls so I can still feel alive. You must understand that I've been terrified to side with you. Somehow, Moore would find a way to reach my family, so the next time I go see them, I'll find nothing more than burned fields and corpses."

Angelyn cleared her throat. "Coming from Kaylyn, Master, I can understand the threat of losing family by fire more than most."

Torald nodded wordlessly.

"We can go to your family's farm personally," Angelyn added, "and ensure their safety, with any guardsmen you trust." She caught Will's eye as she spoke and he inclined his head in agreement.

He watched, however, as Torald opened his mouth, then seemed to think better and closed it. He'd seen the man do that several times in their previous encounters, when Moore had been present to stop him from speaking his mind with a silent threat.

"There's something else you're not telling us, I think," Will began. "What else haven't you shared?"

Torald grimaced, shifting uncomfortably in his seat.

"If we are to work together," Will continued, "you have to tell us what remains on your mind. For your family's sake."

Will watched as Torald's expression changed from one of resolute honesty he'd witnessed so far to a more cold, vindictive expression. The lines around his eyes bunched as if he were wrestling with how to open up further.

"Over the years, while I worked for him, practically imprisoned in this towne, I found out a secret about Jeras' family that could destroy him." Torald paused once more, his throat working. "Use this, if you must, to keep my family safe while we feed these people. Adlar Moore is a bastard. That sycophant of a son isn't legitimate."

Everyone around the table tensed, though none more so than Will. "So Gardain. . .?" he began slowly.

"Yes, the child Jeras hates is the real heir to this city," Torald sneered, clearly delighted in the truth of it. "Imagine how Jeras would feel if you told him you could prove that Adlar, so desperate to be like his father, was the queen's child by another man? How furious would he be, if you forced him to have a Goddess-loving pagan like Gardain take his seat instead?"

Will ran a hand along his jaw, taking in this information. Rhethosian inheritance was simple enough: the eldest son took on the father's role when the father either retired or passed. Second sons, like himself and Gardain, were as present but equally unimportant as shadows. Showing the world that Adlar did not have his father's blood, no matter how well Jeras had trained him, would certainly upset the Towne Master greatly.

In his mind, he made notes to ask both Irvin and Marselle to find out if what Torald said was true. If so, it could be a powerful tool, to not only ensure the safety of Torald's family but also Moore's compliance to the rebel's cause.

"Thank you," he said aloud, earning a relieved sigh from Torald, who clearly felt better sharing his secret. Will rose from his seat. Picking up the nearest pitcher on the table, he refilled each cup he walked by. "Now, if you are ready, I would like you to work closely with everyone at this table, Master Torald. Connecting these Towne Masters, as well as Miss McKinlee, with your tradesmen and farmers will open immediate lines of supplies that Lorington desperately needs all under violet banners."

Torald's demeanor shifted back to his previous likeness at the idea of dealing business instead of discussing personal matters. When Will took his seat again, he watched as Torald, the northern Towne Masters, and Angelyn shifted their chairs to face one another, ready to discuss logistics.

"Can you help us determine numbers first?" Angelyn asked. "So we know where the needs are strongest in the city?"

"Of course," Torald replied. Will motioned to one of the waiting rebel guards, who brought forward the Trade Master's ledgers he had brought over.

Angelyn leaned in, her forearms resting on the tops of her legs as she listened intently to Torald's descriptions. Dividing and rationing what the northern townes could have sent to Lorington's gates was key. Will smiled when the rest of the men heard Angelyn propose the idea of each set of rations being distributed by a representative of both the rebel cause and Lorington itself. Feeding people on a budget was a skill set of hers, yet the way the vital supplies were given to the city was just as important.

The five spoke for some time while Will merely listened, then made sure Torald was escorted back to his family home to conduct business, nowhere near the barrack prison where he'd previously been housed with the Moore family.

The northern Towne Masters were eager to begin putting their plan into action, each of them thanking Angelyn before they left. When she glanced back at him, Will noticed how fresh sparks of hope were alight in her deep blue eyes. That determination in her gaze, the confidence in her demeanor, seemed to chase away every cool shadow under the awning. A fierce pride rose in his chest when he grinned at her.

"Well done," he managed to say.

A blush rose on her cheeks. "I. . .I actually have something else I need to speak with you about, if you have the time."

"Of course, Miss McKinlee." He motioned to the back door that led into the barrack, where he began to work the remains of the smoldering fireplace back to life. Inviting flames lit the stone room with red and orange tones. Will indicated one of the chairs nearest the fire and Angelyn sat.

He slumped into the seat next to her and motioned for a small bottle of wine on a nearby bookshelf. Angelyn passed it to him, and after he took a drink, Will gave it back, letting relief and silence wash over him.

"Marselle and I have found some people you really should speak to, this evening, in the market district," Angelyn explained.

Will flashed a smile at her, some of the tiredness leaving his green eyes. "Two incredible women like you need *me*? How can I be of service?"

He listened with increasing interest as Angelyn told him about Remora's operation. Torald had shared how the lower class of Lorington suffered while the high Loyals benefitted, and now he was hearing a similar story from the women of the city. If he could hear them out, make promises, present change. . .everything could move forward without further bloodshed. *Even without Moore himself.*

"I will be there, Angelyn," Will replied when she finished her story. "For anything you need."

She handed the bottle back to him, and he let his fingers brush against hers, pressing his thumb against the top of her hand longer than necessary. He could tell, by the way her fingers shook ever so slightly, that the details of it all weighed heavily on her mind, too.

He knew there was one piece that tipped the scales. "Do you miss Joshua?" Will asked.

Angelyn blinked, as if she didn't expect the question. "More than anything," she answered. "Though, it's not as hard as I thought."

"What isn't?" Will asked. He shifted in his seat, turning the chair so he could look straight at her.

"Being away from him is less painful each day," Angelyn admitted. "At first, it was a nightmare come true, not knowing where he was and if he was safe. It's still difficult, but I know it's good for him. And me."

Will nodded, his mind immediately going to Devaki. He wanted to go see her; in fact, he'd tried several times in the last day, but there was always something or someone who needed his attention. Guilt wormed its way up his throat from his heart, but a large portion of that emotion was laced with relief.

Maybe, if he spoke to Angelyn about the girl, it would help ease the tension he constantly felt.

"When you arrived," he began slowly, his tone guarded, "I mentioned a girl named Devaki."

"Yes, you did," she said with a smile. "I could tell when you said her name that she was someone important . . . your daughter?"

Will worked his jaw silently. "Well, that was unexpectedly impressive."

Angelyn inclined her head. He could tell she was trying to tread lightly as he needed her to. "You don't have to explain her to me," she said quietly.

"Thank you," Will muttered, and he took several long draws from the wine. "Even though we wrote to each other for years, I have no idea how to treat her in person or talk about her mother as she clearly wants me to."

"Will," Angelyn began, "have you . . .never met her before?"

He shook his head. "No. She doesn't belong in Rhethos, not yet," he said. "And now she's in over her head." He rotated to lean against his chair's armrest, favoring his healing injury on his right side. "You didn't see the look in her eyes after Rowlann used her magic to break open the gates. It was heartbreaking, and somehow I know it's my fault."

"Why is that?"

"Because she's my child, Angelyn," Will replied. "And I had to flee Valsara the night she was born or risk being executed for an unspeakable crime I didn't commit."

Angelyn sat up, her back rigid. "I . . ." she began, then cleared her throat when her voice was uneasy. "I thought they didn't shed blood across the sea unless it was in service of Cybarys."

Will met her eyes, self-hatred churning in his stomach. "After what happened, they would have found a way to justify draining every drop of blood in my body to that ancient bitch."

"I'm . . ." Angelyn began, but he dismissively handed the wine to her.

"I was young and stupid when she was born, so Devaki has always been a distant dream for me," Will continued, changing the subject slightly. He could tell from the compassion in her eyes that she wanted to know more, but he refused to delve any deeper in that direction. "She's here now because the damned Goddess and her magic make her think she *has* to be."

"What can I do to help?" she asked.

Will ran a hand through his hair, sighing. "I actually have the solution, if she would be open to receiving it." He paused. "I write about the difficult things just fine," he finished and reached into an inner pocket of his coat. "I've been writing this for years, hoping to give it to her one day to help her understand what I have a hard time speaking."

He watched her eyes grow wide at the journal he produced, a beaten little thing wrapped in wrinkled leather.

"Why do you still have it, then?" Angelyn asked.

"Devaki was upset. I'm sure she still is," Will explained, taking the spine of the journal in his palm and flexing it back and forth. "Because I won't let her go near that giant hole in the western district. It didn't seem like the right time to give her something I've been spilling my heart into for twenty years."

"I'll take it off your hands, then," Angelyn joked. He snapped his calculating gaze to hers and her grin faltered.

"Here," he said, and tossed the journal to her.

Angelyn caught it in her free hand, then held it gingerly, as if she were aware of the emotional importance of the pages. "I didn't mean it," she began softly.

"Yes, you did," Will said with a wry smile.

Angelyn stood, leaving the wine bottle in her chair. She set the journal down on a crate against the wall, unopened, then reached out a hand to Will, palm up. His brow furrowed before he stood and extended his right arm till his fingers wrapped around hers.

"I don't know much about Devaki," Angelyn said, "but I can tell you what *not* to do, based on mistakes I've made with my child: don't lie to her, don't keep things from her, and don't make her feel small."

Will nodded, squeezing her hand. He raised her fingers to his lips and kissed her knuckles gently. Angelyn smiled as he let his mouth linger on her skin. One heartbeat later, he pulled on her arm and closed the space between them.

It was similar to the gesture he'd made in The Hamond's cellar when he'd kissed her, except this time he didn't feel like he had anything to prove. There was no haughtiness or superiority behind the movement, and, unlike that night that felt like a lifetime ago, now Angelyn didn't push him away.

He felt her shiver as he ran his hands up her arms till they rested on either side of her jaw. Despite their closeness, he made sure there wasn't any strength behind his touch. His fingers only rested lightly on her skin, with plenty of room for her to step back, knowing something like this was not easy for her.

"What are you doing?" she asked, her voice coming out in a whisper. She kept her eyes on his chest, not looking up.

"Waiting," Will replied, running his thumbs along her cheeks. He brushed his forehead against hers, and everything in the room seemed very warm. "For you."

Will could only guess what was running through her mind. He at least knew how she felt about men. They had always equaled fear, pain, and authority. But he hoped, more than anything else, that she could see the space he created for her, where she could stand beside him and change everything.

Angelyn leaned in, tilted her head, and pressed her lips against his. He folded his arms around her, crushing the velvet of her cloak. She gasped and clung to his neck to keep her balance. Heat rose all over his body, focused on Angelyn's mouth and the way her lips felt on his. Everything swirled in a pleasant bubble as desire rose in his chest.

"I . . ." Angelyn began after several moments, pulling back and running her tongue along her lower lip. He was mere moments away from reaching down toward the hem of her skirt to gather it in his grip. He stopped, however, when he heard her speak. "I can't. Not right now."

He met her eyes, and, with some effort, Will nodded and let her go. Angelyn cleared her throat, then bent to pick up Will's journal and handed it back to him.

"Go give that to your daughter," she said. "And maybe," she added, "one of these nights you can tell me a story from that book."

"Unfortunately," Will began, "that is something I'll have to work up to."

CHAPTER FOURTEEN

THE BUTTERFLY'S BREATH

Will paused outside the massive inn on a corner of Lorington's market district, Rowlann standing behind him. The man was giving out final orders to his soldiers, who were stationed alongside the regular guards on the adjoining roads. The chill itched up Will's spine. Though he could barely make out the Rhethosian Mountains in the distance, it was as if he could see the change in season plummeting down toward them.

"The men will be ready when we need them?" Will asked, not looking at the seasoned soldier. He gazed at the white brick structure with large, vertical windows filled with light. He didn't expect The Butterfly's Breath to be so grand, with carved stone balconies on its three levels, decorated with flower baskets and Rhethosian Blue ribbons.

"Of course," Rowlann replied. He adjusted the gauntlets on his forearms, pale moonlight gleaming off the metal that he rarely removed from his body. "It's an . . .unusual order, but not one any of them are against following."

"Good," Will sighed, solidifying his plan in his mind. The inn had a set of wooden double doors in the middle of its curved streetside wall. As he approached them, Will unfastened his sword and knife belt and handed it to the closest rebel soldier. There were many other weapons on him, but he knew that he should appear here, surrounded by women who had experienced violent men, with no visible forms of harm.

Inside, the main floor of the inn was spacious and clean, with a bar on the far wall and the open floor covered in tables and chairs. An instant flood of cinnamon-scented warmth and gold candlelight engulfed him. He had feared that there would only be a small, reluctant group here.

Instead, Will was pleased to see every spot full, including the chairs, tables, barstools, and floor space. The women ranged before him were speaking quietly. There was a clear distinction between the people who came from different districts; despite the fully occupied space, each group was separated, with wary glances being thrown from one gathering to another.

He looked up and saw that the top two floors of the inn were open with balconies that curved around the walls. The ceiling three stories above was covered in an elaborate work of art, decorated in dazzling blue and yellow butterflies.

"You could smile, you know," said a voice behind him, and Will felt a hand on his elbow.

He turned and grinned, a bit forcefully, as he recognized the voice. "Lady Marselle," Will began. "When was the last time we saw each other in a nice place like this?"

Marselle shrugged as if the time was insignificant to her. Her red curls were pinned delicately around the oval shape of her face. The cream-colored dress she wore complimented her pale skin, as did the delicate gold chains around her neck. "I know it's been a little while," she replied, "but there's no need to stare."

Will laughed politely. His gaze was actually drawn behind the former southern Rhethosian lady to where Angelyn stood, not far behind her. Turning from Marselle, Will caught Angelyn's eye. His smile settled into one more genuine, but she only returned it briefly.

Is she nervous about this? he thought. *Or does that expression have something to do with this afternoon?*

The noise on the main floor, meanwhile, had almost quieted. The women at the ornate stools along the bar and situated in the comfortable, high-backed chairs eyed him suspiciously. They were dressed in the finest clothes, and Will guessed them to be the wives and sisters of Loyals from the northern district and tradesmen families in the eastern market district. It was subtle, but he still saw them shoot looks of disdain toward the women they saw as below themselves, all clothed more plainly and not being offered seats.

"You did say Irvin was coming, yes?" Angelyn asked as she stepped over to him, her voice low as she glanced at the clock above the door.

"He should be here already," Will replied. He knew his old friend was handling many other tasks Will had assigned him, but he had made a point to tell Irvin to be on time. Presenting a united front at his meetings was important to him.

"We can manage without him, if need be," Will added. "First, I'd like to—"

"Don't worry! I'm here."

Will looked back toward the door as it shut behind Irvin. "Can you believe," Irvin began in an incredulous tone, "that Rowlann had the nerve to take my sword? Who takes a Towne Master's. . . well, *former* Towne Master's sword from him? As if I'd use it in a place like this. Now I feel naked in front of all of these women."

"A charming prospect for us all. You look like you could use a glass of wine," Marselle spoke up, and took Irvin's arm, drawing him out of the entry-way. "Let our leader do what he does best."

Will cleared his throat as Marselle led Irvin toward the bar, earning a few wary looks from the women seated there as they took in his bright violet tunic. Irvin didn't have to ask for a seat; several people moved as far away as possible.

"Remora worked a miracle getting them all here," Angelyn commented in Will's ear. "Her Loyal friends and the girls from the attic have never been under the same roof. Now it's up to you."

Will grasped her hand, glad when she didn't immediately pull away, especially with everyone seeing the physical contact between them. "I think," he said, giving her fingers one more squeeze before letting them go, "it's up to all of us." He walked to a table close to the center of the great room and sat on its polished edge.

"This is a pleasant change of pace for me," Will began, raising his voice. "Instead of sitting here and addressing you, I'd like to be a listener for the first part of this evening."

His gaze swept over the rest of the women, focusing on those who weren't seated comfortably. His attention went to those who were standing against the banisters, looking down at him warily. Many of them were young and pregnant, and no one offered them seats.

"I would like to say something first, then, Master," began a woman seated by the door with fine furs draped around her neck, "if you will permit it."

Will inclined his head. "Your name?"

The woman pressed several lengths of gray hair away from her wrinkled face. "Lady Ratley," she sighed. "My husband is a cousin of Jeras Moore."

Will gave her a respectful nod, though he noticed others roll their eyes at the mention of Moore.

"What the Lady Remora does is commendable," Lady Ratley began. She nodded in the direction of a woman across the hall with black and silver curls. "Though it isn't acceptable for us to publicly associate with her cause, we have done our best to provide her charges with resources in any way we can."

One of the older women on the staircase scoffed, as if she didn't believe this statement. "*You* and your friends support Remora?" the woman asked disbelievingly. "How could you do such a thing when we're so 'shameful'? And how do your husbands let you spend their money on outcasts?"

Will caught Angelyn's eye, knowing from what she'd told her that as a Loyal herself, Remora was able to get money and supplies from her fellow upper-class women in secret, even though such a thing wasn't openly allowed. Though she was a bridge, neither group of women had ever crossed that gap to either side.

"Lady Ratley is telling you the truth," Remora said. "The food we have, the blankets I bring in, the healers who show up for the births of babies . . . Loyal women near my home make that possible." She put a hand on the wall next to her, under the archway that led up the main staircase. "Though one of the points we're making here tonight is that all of us have suffered equally no matter where we come from in this towne."

Many heads shook against that statement, and Will watched in silence as Remora and Angelyn gave each other a pointed look across the hall. "All of us know," Remora began, "that every man in this towne isn't evil. But the worst of them are always in charge. When the captain's men came, my husband helped me make a home for the girls assaulted by his soldiers. When he spoke against the Towne Masters, they put Coyle in that digsite."

Murmurs of pity and anger floated through the inn. Will doubted that anyone ever spoke so clearly about the awful losses they experienced in a public place. Will waited; they had opened the door, one any sane person would be frightened to step through, but someone, someone else would speak. He had to be the kind of man who would listen.

"I lost my brother to the military."

Everyone looked around to find the woman who'd spoken, and Will caught the eye of a girl at least ten years younger than Angelyn on the staircase behind Remora.

"He was a good man, always kept me safe. But when he tried to stop a Rhethosian officer from hurting me, they conscripted him the next day. I haven't seen or heard from him since, but I see those officers all the time and there's nothing I can do to stop them."

"Every day I watch my father run our family's business into the ground," said one of the women at the bar. She touched a string of pearls at her neck as she spoke. Will saw her fingers trembling. "He just never stops drinking. I could save it, and save my entire family so much stress and heartache, if I could speak up and take charge."

"My brother-in-law does unspeakable things to me that my husband is well aware of. But furious as my husband is, he cannot say a word," an older woman next to Lady Ratley said, her voice shaky, "because my father already tried. Moore had him executed for 'disturbing the peace.' So I've endured the abuse for the last twenty years."

"The same thing happened to my mother," said a younger woman seated at the table next to Will. "But she never let my father know because she was so afraid to have him taken from her if he tried to save her."

"The soldiers in this towne raped my little sister," shared a girl on the second balcony. Her voice was barely strong enough to be heard on the main floor. "She was so shamed for her bastard child that she killed herself. I'm naming this baby of mine after her so she's not entirely forgotten."

Will felt Angelyn's grip on his and looked down at her fingers. He realized that his own hand was shaking. When had that started? Swallowing deliberately, he sat up straighter in his seat.

The stories around him were powerful albeit immensely frustrating. They made him think of difficulties Devaki had mentioned in her more recent letters, about the verbal and emotional abuse her Temple Leader inflicted on her for merely existing. The men of Lorington had to endure the abuse of family members they cared for or risk banishment, conscription, or even execution.

What would I have done to those who hurt my child if I'd been there? Could I have been in a similar, powerless situation in a place like

Valsara? It has to stop now. Protection and respect should be the norm, not privileges.

Every beat of his heart that reflected back to Devaki reminded him of the journal he had not yet given her. It felt too much like a letdown, another hurt in her wounded eyes that he didn't think he could take. But these women and their families. . .he could help them.

"How many of you have had similar experiences but haven't spoken yet?" Will asked quietly. Slowly, almost every hand in the room raised. "Hold them up for a moment longer. Look around. . .look up."

Tears and sniffles filled the silent space of The Butterfly's Breath, then Will decided it was time.

"Ladies," he began, "I have to share something that I've never told anyone else." He paused, making eye contact slowly with those near him. "My mother died when I was very young. She worked with crude seatraders and never fought back when they shouted at her, slapped her, or worse. There was no room, she was taught, in a woman's life for much else besides the care of her children and the serving of the kingdom's leaders above her. But every night, she told my brother and me how we could be different from other men. She taught us ideas of freedom for everyone, but more distinctly for ladies like you.

"Now, her dreams died with her and my brother, leaving me to carry them forward. I have succeeded in this cause so far, and you can play the biggest role of any group in Rhethos. I've seen the Towne Master's ledgers; there are many more women in Lorington than men. If you step forward with us, and the men in your lives who love you, you will bring the power of choice to yourselves and the generations after you."

"How, exactly?" Lady Ratley inquired, one eyebrow raised skeptically.

Will glanced down at Angelyn, and gave her a nod to explain, as they'd discussed earlier.

"We will make a list tonight," Angelyn replied, her voice carrying up to the high ceiling and the lines of women staring down at them. "Rebel soldiers will arrest and imprison those who've hurt you, so you can begin to feel some justice. Tell your fathers and brothers and husbands that they don't need to be afraid anymore. Even if you're sharing your abuse with them for the first time, let them know that we are here to stand with them and stop such awful acts from ever happening again."

She paused, looking at Will for a moment. He gave her a small, encouraging smile. "Next," Angelyn continued, "we can promise you protection within these walls against anyone who would still dare to harm you. You'll also be given every right a man has. Then, when you begin to reap the benefits of these arrangements with your families at your sides, we believe the towne's leadership will have no choice but to fly violet banners and unite against The Bradford."

"Regretfully, without heads flying or ropes swinging," Irvin muttered, and when Will glanced his way, he saw Marselle elbow him. Irvin chuckled awkwardly, as if his words were a joke taken the wrong way.

"But what if we want those things?" Remora asked.

"Then you came to the wrong bar, beautiful," Irvin returned.

Will rotated atop the table, turning his gaze back toward Remora, letting the truth of Irvin's words sit. He raised his eyebrows, inviting her to speak further. As far as he knew, Remora was on their side, so to hear some dissension from her was unexpected.

"There are heads that *should* fly, I mean," Remora clarified, and she blew an errant black curl out of her eyes. "I'd personally like to see several Loyal men marched to a headsman for what they've done to girls far too young. From what I've heard, *you* have The Bradford's best executioner wearing violet now. Why can't we use him?"

From the bar, Will heard Irvin choke on his wine, then cough in the abrupt silence. "I'm surprised," Will said smoothly, "that you know of Master Orton. Lady Marselle did say you were from Clancy. I can assure you, though, that Lander Orton does *not* cut off heads on anyone's orders anymore, no matter how good he was at it."

"Orton?" Angelyn clarified, a look of incredulity on her face. Will knew she was shocked to hear the man he'd left at The Forts to teach her son used to be employed in such a way, but he'd never thought to bring it up. It was, after all, the man's past, and not Will's to share.

Will nodded at her briefly. "I can't tell you how many men are in my ranks who are like Orton," he spoke, trying to steer the conversation back to his goals. "They have made many horrible choices, in the service of fear and greed and tyranny. But again, we are here tonight to put those to rest."

"Even though plenty of them *should* lose their heads," Remora insisted. She leaned against the post at the bottom of the staircase, her brown, satin-lined dress wrinkling. "Or hang slowly till they piss themselves in front of people they've done unspeakable things to. Have you ever been raped, Master Will? Have you ever been shamed for loving an innocent newborn bastard?"

"No," Will replied, "I'm here to give you a long-overdue opportunity to witness the power we hold standing together. It doesn't matter if you were abused by one of Moore's closest associates in the nicest villa or shoved to the ground by one of Caldrell's soldiers in the western slums. It was *wrong*."

Remora glanced up at her girls, who stared hopefully at her from the balconies, then to the sympathetic eyes of the finely dressed women at the bar and tables.

"You are right, Remora," Will continued, ready to drive his point home. He stood from the table, his boots landing softly on the polished floor. "I don't know what rape feels like. But I do know what it feels like to want someone to suffer for what they've done. To watch them cry and bleed like I have until I'm the one left standing for a change, and they are coughing up their life's blood in the dirt."

Remora's lips tightened into a thin line, and her grimace was reflected on the faces of many around her. Some shook their heads, clearly not as vengeful, while others seemed to find his last sentence chillingly appealing.

"It kills you inside," Will said softly, "if you let it."

He paced in the narrow space between tables and observed the hall, then the faces above him. "Tonight," he added, making his way back to where Angelyn stood and adjusting his coat, "I have an offering of peace and respect I'd like to present each of you with. Know that, whether you accept it or not, you will always be protected by my men in this towne." He paused again, letting the gravity of this promise solidify in the air. "I do not expect change overnight, but I will openly offer it to this kingdom, one person at a time."

He gestured to Rowlann, who still stood by the double doors. The man opened the left side and let in the night's sharp chill. He spoke a few words to the guards on the steps. Will let the silence hold, feeling like he'd spoken more than enough. There were small ripples of sound that coursed through the women, back and forth across the inn's floor and up its stairs like the turning of a tide.

The noise quieted once more, however, when Rowlann let in a line of rebel soldiers. Though the six of them were all disarmed and stood nonthreateningly, several of the women gasped and stepped backward. A few of the pregnant girls on the balconies clung to each other with trembling arms. All eyes in The Butterfly's Breath, however, ended up focusing on what the rebels carried in their arms:

Purple irises.

One rebel stepped forward, a shorter man with long, white hair and old scars across the backs of his hands. He stopped in front of the nearest table of women, all of whom stared at him with wide eyes. With a quiet smile, he pulled five flowers from the bunch and offered one to each woman.

"For you," he said, extending his worn hand that held the bright violet bloom. "And for Rhethos."

Will watched as his men slowly moved across the crowded floor, the only sounds the murmurs of words that they each said as they made their offerings. It took time, but eventually they arrived at the stairs to make their way to the balconies above. Remora, however, blocked their path.

"Not them," she said, soft but firm. "The young ones with child can't be near a man, even with your good intentions."

Will nodded when the rebel glanced back at him, then made his way to the base of the stairs himself. He took the irises from the rebel's hands, pulled one from the bunch, and held it out to Remora.

"You deserve much more," he began quietly, "for what you've endured, and what you do for others. Let this be a start."

She smiled thinly and snatched the flower out of his gloved hands. "Give me the rest of those," she said grudgingly, then jerked her head at a couple women nearby. Remora gave Will a small nod before going up the stairs with the remainder of the flowers.

Will shouldered his way over to the bar, where Marselle and Irvin stood. Irvin was murmuring something to the woman behind the stretch of walnut wood, who was nodding and handing trays of mulled wine out by the dozen to be distributed amongst the women. The soothing scents of cloves, berries, and peaceful cardamom in the glasses blanketed the space around them.

When Will glanced back, he noticed that Angelyn had moved into the crowd on the main floor, speaking quietly with a group of women who'd approached her with questions. Will felt something he couldn't quite name when he watched her, wearing his mother's necklace, speaking about his cause to those who had more power than they knew.

"Well done," Irvin commented. "Not a typical use of your time, but . . ."

"But you're glad you came, I know," Will finished for him. Irvin grinned.

"I wasn't aware of this last bit," Marselle spoke up, inclining her head toward the women holding their flowers. "I knew there was a reason I liked you so much."

Will smirked. "Marselle," he began, "I know that things are complicated between you and Remora, but the two of you can build on what we've started tonight. We'll have this place covered in violet long before Caldrell sets up a single tent."

Marselle flashed him a bright smile. "Of course we will." She lowered her voice, and leaned an elbow on the bar before adding, "The more vengeful women here can find a place working with my girls doing supply runs on the coast."

Irvin seemed pleased at that idea. "Lucky them," he said, then finished his glass of wine and set it on the bar's edge. "Speaking of that delightful treat we call vengeance, I need a private word with you, Lady Marselle. I need your skills to find someone. . ."

Marselle raised an eyebrow at Irvin, but she followed him into a quieter corner of the inn, giving Will a shrug as they left. Angelyn made her way over to Will, and he saw her watching Irvin and Marselle as well. "What's going on there?" she asked.

Will shook his head. "I've no idea," he replied, watching Irvin whisper quietly at Marselle, gesturing emphatically to either side. The former southern Rhethosian lady kept her face completely neutral, but that did not surprise Will; he knew full-well that Irvin and Marselle took care of "problems" that he couldn't resolve easily on his own.

Some of their actions stooped to levels that didn't align with his image as a just leader, and his throat dried as he made a mental note to confront Irvin later about whatever he was planning. The success they hoped to achieve with tonight's meeting could not be jeopardized in any way.

He knew this victory was contingent on follow-through and the last remaining, frustrating piece. The digsite widows had mentioned losing their husbands inside that mysterious excavation. Whatever was in that hole in the western district was full of the Armellan Goddess' energy, and it was no small occurrence for an entire troop of Rhethosian soldiers to be lost to it.

Will needed answers because Lorington could not entirely be his with that secret in his way. Unfortunately, he knew someone more than willing to help him solve his next biggest challenge. He touched the journal inside his jacket, back in its pocket since showing it to Angelyn that afternoon. It was time to speak with his daughter.

CHAPTER FIFTEEN

DETERMINED DIGGING

Devaki's most recent Rune Scars, deeper and more painful than others, took several days to heal. That time, locked in her room, hiding her ring from any of Rowlann's men who came by, she gathered the courage to ask enough questions to move forward.

Though their words were full of distrust, the rebel soldiers told her who the young man was who wore the Armellan prayer necklace under his armor. His name was Sutton, he was a few years older than Devaki, and she intended to find him tonight. Someone, anyone, had to treat her like more than a locked away weapon.

A small Strength Rune turned the lock open on her room's door. A bit of blood from a Protection Rune kept her hidden in the night's shadows between the barracks. And a Guidance Rune led her to the soldier she was looking for, walking down one of the stone pathways.

"Miss Tarran?" he asked, seemingly surprised to see her. He wore the same iron plate armor, and she noticed now that it wasn't damaged at all. She hoped that meant that he hadn't spilled blood in the name of freedom. If he really believed in their Mother, he wouldn't do such a thing.

"I lost your cloak," Devaki began when he reached her. "I meant to give it back to you."

He shrugged, tilting his head to one side. "I can get another one. Seems like you're a little more cautious tonight than the other day, if you're worried about a cloak now."

Devaki smiled grimly. He didn't know she'd had plenty of time lately to contemplate her mistakes. "Our Mother teaches us that moving at a steady pace—"

"—leads to less falls," Sutton cut in, then seemed to catch himself. A blush rose on the round cheekbones underneath his pale green eyes. "Sorry. I don't get to say things like that aloud. . . ever, really. What can I help you with?"

"I realize," Devaki began after a sigh, "that I need someone to watch my back. Can you help me? And get rid of the magic remnants around me?"

Sutton blinked, his jaw dropping a little. He laughed nervously, as if she'd asked him to do something much more intimate. "I-I'm sorry," he stuttered, the professional rebel demeanor he tried to hold falling away. "It's just, before the siege, I'd only heard stories about Goddess Touched. When Master Rowlann told us how you could Bless us, I was speechless. My great-great-uncle had prayer books and drawings of Blessing Runes hidden in his fishery's basement. This necklace was his. I loved the stories about Cybarys he shared when no one else could hear."

Devaki raised her eyebrows. When she'd met the young man, he'd been on duty in broad daylight and was much more serious and short with his words. She couldn't understand what it was like to *hide* one's faith or casually collect prayer books like it was a hobby. It baffled her for a moment.

"Well, let's see if we can make a real difference in this fight," Devaki said, giving Sutton a reassuring smile. "Just keep watch and let me know if you see anyone coming."

"I can do that," Sutton agreed and put a hand to his sword's hilt. "My next shift isn't for a little while." He glanced around the barrack's corner, squinting in both directions in the increasing shadows. Now that he had an assignment, the young man seemed to fall back into his soldier's mentality.

I need to be quiet and cautious about this, she told herself as she turned the sharp edge of her rune ring inward. She knew her Goddess was teaching her an important lesson about patience and adaptation to her circumstances. Pressing the ring against her skin, Devaki gritted her teeth against the pain that quickly went away as magic flowed through her.

The Guidance Rune on her arm leaked fresh heat in every direction, like the spark of a much-needed fire on a freezing night. Devaki breathed deep and her eyes closed. *Take my feet, Mother,* she prayed, her lips relaxed as her mind worked fervently. *Lead them where I'll find help for your people and answers. . .and acceptance. I am yours, so guide me.*

Devaki smiled as she felt unseen hands on her back. The touch was light, soft as a breeze, but it increased as she tightened her grip around her Blessing Rune. She started forward, then halted abruptly; the feeling of blood dripping down her arm reminded her of the night at the digsite where she'd bled almost to the point of passing out. Everything near that pit had been jumbled, conflicted, and dark.

She'd never felt any of those negative emotions toward her faith before, and they haunted her again now.

"Everything all right, Miss Tarran?" Sutton asked behind her. She saw the young man had pulled his sword halfway from its sheath, as if he could combat whatever had stopped her progress.

"I'm fine," Devaki insisted and gathered her determination. She let the magic pull her forward, down the barrack streets, back and forth between the tracks that ran in strict, militaristic patterns. She heard Sutton's steady footsteps behind her, breaking every so often to sweep the solidified sparks of magic remnants into the dirt.

The push against her shoulder blades stopped when they reached one of the largest structures at the northernmost point of the barracks. She stared at a long, rectangular building that stood out from the square units covered in granite. Devaki put a hand to the wall, and the heat on her palm almost seared in comparison to the chilled stone.

This place is important. Something or someone in it can help answer my prayers.

"Umm," Sutton began uncertainly. "Those are the dungeons . . . where they're keeping the Moores and Sarrett."

Devaki raised her eyebrows. Why would Cybarys lead her here?

"Can you get in?" she asked.

He put a hand to the back of his neck, rubbing nervously at his short hair as he glanced around. "Yes. But people will want to know why if we're here too long."

"We're here for Rhethos, of course," Devaki replied, and he smiled at the familiar rebel phrase.

Sutton touched the prayer necklace he wore, murmuring something too quiet for her to hear. He walked around the corner and spoke to the men stationed at its only entrance and exit. As a member of Rowlann's elite group of fighters, he had some pull compared to her father's typical soldiers. A moment later, Sutton motioned for Devaki to follow him.

"These are dangerous people Master Will has kept down here," he said as he worked the locks open. "So do what you must, Goddess willing, but keep your distance."

There were only a few candles lit in the main hall, which was bare of most furniture, leaving the walls and exposed, wooden rafters in deep shadow. Devaki glanced around, feeling the evening's draft tickle her skin through the gaps in the stone. The empty space was, she assumed, used to receive and release prisoners, but not much else.

A huge doorway consumed most of the wall on the opposite end of the rectangular hall, full of dark iron bars and two imposing handles that ran along its entire height. Devaki took a step toward it, but Sutton put a hand on her shoulder. When she glanced sideways at him, he shook his head.

"Who are you looking for, exactly? If it's the Moores, we aren't keeping them down there," he said, his voice soft due to the sharp echo in the vacant space. "Sarrett's the one in the dungeons below, and if we're going down there, you'll have to cut a Strength Rune into my armor, my lady, because that hole terrifies me."

Devaki found her gaze drawn to the small Protection Rune already on the left side of his breastplate, barely any specks of her dried blood left on it. She shivered and wrapped her arms around herself when the memory of the night of the siege hit her.

"Where are the Moores?" she asked.

Sutton jerked his head to the right, into the only other hallway of the prison's main floor. When Devaki craned her neck, she saw brighter flickers of firelight and heard the faintest echo of voices. "Back there are the old Rhethosian officers' quarters," Sutton explained. "Many of them lived here before we came, and because Master Will wanted to honor the Towne Master and his family, we fashioned the space into a confinement of sorts. It's probably horrible compared to what they were used to up in that castle, but. . ." Sutton shrugged, as if indicating it could be worse, and Devaki knew he was right: they could have been executed instead.

She twisted her Guidance Rune again, murmuring a prayer to help her see where she was supposed to go: down that hall, or down the black staircase behind the thick bars. Gem-like sparks tapped lightly on the stone floor around her, sprinkling red against pale gray. It only took a moment for her to point down the main floor's hall, and Sutton nodded.

"It's a straight path," he said, "so I think it'd be best if I stay here, near the entrance. I suggest getting this done quickly, since I have to be back on duty in less than an hour. I. . .I don't mean to be rude, but. . ."

Devaki nodded. "I understand." She didn't want him getting in trouble on her behalf, so she broke the surface of her skin on a healing Protection Rune. As she'd used its power while walking along the barrack's roads outside, she hoped it would keep her safe from danger now. Sutton positioned himself at the entrance, one shoulder facing the Moore's confinement area, the other toward the exit. His hand never left his weapon.

Without knowing what to expect, Devaki started down the hallway. She didn't know if she'd have to speak to these people, merely listen to them, or try something else. Her gut, however, told her to keep being cautious, and she consciously made her steps as light as possible. Now she missed the silk slippers she wore with her traditional Armellan clothing. The Rhethosian boots she wore were loud and imposing.

Sutton had been right; there wasn't a lot of variation on this floor of the building, and she followed the poorly lit hall to its end. She stepped into a shadowed alcove and pressed her hands against the heavy door before her. It looked like it had been recently fitted with several padlocks, all of which were shut tight. The door's top was a pane of thick glass, and Devaki stood on her toes to peer through it.

In the chamber beyond, she saw a windowless room with one decent bed and two small cots. A makeshift table and chairs had been crafted from old supply crates, all of which were situated close to the fireplace that fought to maintain its meager flames. Her eyes narrowed when she recognized the people here from the night of the siege, when Will had tried to negotiate immediate peace.

Jeras Moore sat on the crate closest to the fire, still wrapped in his deep blue and orange robes. His beard was longer now, and his white hair was less presentable, though Devaki noticed his wife, who sat on the largest bed silently, still had her hair up and her gown wrinkleless.

"You must be patient," Jeras Moore was saying, and Devaki noticed him looking pointedly at both of his sons, who stood with as much distance between them as possible. "Do not negotiate. I'll hear no more of it, Gardain."

Devaki adjusted her stance so she could look over at the younger of the brothers, the one with ashy blond curls and gray eyes. He wore the same fine clothes as his father, though his shoulders were not held nearly as high, and his chin pointed toward the floor.

"You must see my point, though, Father," Gardain began, his voice low and apologetic. He tugged at the green fabric of his tunic as he spoke. "It would be better for all of us if we spoke to him openly about the ruins."

Devaki felt all of her muscles tense, and her throat went dry. She renewed her grip on the edges of the door's glass pane, straining her ears.

"Master Will seems to be a fair man, once given all the details. And we should assume that the rebels are winning over the people by now. I've even heard that they are treating our imprisoned soldiers with the utmost respect within the barracks." Gardain's voice was hesitant, but Devaki caught a bright flash of intelligence in his round eyes.

"The ignorant masses might be fooled," Adlar muttered, "but not the army. They respond to Father alone. The rebels can't hope to hold this city, let alone lead an offensive attack against Caldrell without our men on their side. Of course they want twenty-five thousand added to their ranks!"

"And Torald is, no doubt, won over," spat Moore. "It was stupid of him to accept their terms. The people only stay in line because they need things from us. Giving them better trade, safe streets, and every freedom they can dream of? It'll only lead to bankruptcy for us, and more laziness from the poor. The Bradford's wrath is coming. We just have to wait."

"The Captain will reward our patience, little brother," Adlar Moore contributed, in the same line as his father. Devaki watched the older son, who was almost exactly like his father, both in his mannerisms and speech. "Caldrell is a genius; he knows when to attack his enemy at their weakest, and those rebels are slowly digging their own graves."

That last comment was clearly intended to upset Gardain, and some of his shyness gave way to irritation. "There's been enough *digging* in Lorington!" Gardain insisted, his voice rising.

Devaki blinked. Was he, the son of a Towne Master, really concerned about the people around the digsite? And why did he sound offended when his family refused discussing whatever the Rhethosian military had unearthed in their city?

"Our people *do* need things from us," Gardain was continuing, "and one we've never given them is protection."

"Gardain," Moore's wife cautioned.

"We let Caldrell come here and kill local men, mistreat local women, and destroy our western district," Gardain continued anyway, and Devaki was both impressed by and surprised by his courage. "And for what? Now the Goddess is angry; we've displaced the remains of her blessed city and touched what should have been left—"

"Silence!" Moore boomed. Devaki flinched, and she watched as Gardain did the same, almost like a child. "You offend your Lord with words like that. And look at your mother's face! How dare you spill pagan blaspheme in her presence?"

"Father, I . . ." Gardain started, his cheeks flushed.

"You're disgusting," Adlar scoffed. He took several aggressive steps toward his brother, who pressed himself back into the corner. "And you still won't tell us what you told the rebel leader. He *liked* you, didn't he?" Adlar sneered, and his demeaning laugh echoed around the chamber. "He poisoned you easily, I'm sure. So why are you even here with us? Call the guard and go lick Will's boots. You can bow under the Blood Goddess' chains together."

"Please," Moore's wife began, though she didn't seem to have the strength to say much more.

Gardain sighed, rubbing his temples on either side of his strained, gray eyes. Devaki thought he might fight back, or at least bristle at Adlar's comments, but instead his body language was rather passive. "I do want to speak with him again," he began in a quiet, matter-of-fact tone, "for our family. For our city. That digsite has been a plague, literally, on our legacy. But Will is Goddess Touched! Maybe, with his magic and my knowledge, we can go down there and put to rest whatever the military dug up."

Devaki felt her throat constrict. "Knowledge"? What could this young man know about her people? It sounded like this city her Goddess had led her to was much older than she'd thought, and it still contained remnants of a time when both kingdoms were one and worshiped Cybarys as a whole. Both

Rhethos and Armelle had created their own versions of "history" regarding what happened back then.

What didn't make sense to her, however, was how the digsite was so contradictory to her Mother's faith. *Why would she hurt anyone who came across those ruins? Even if they were men loyal to The Bradford, she wouldn't attack them, let alone harm the innocents living nearby. It doesn't make sense, not based on any teachings from Brother Sehran and the monks in Valsara.*

"Let them all burn," Adlar spat, and Devaki watched as tears filled his mother's eyes before she blinked them away and reset her blank expression. "Let the Blood Goddess' disease spread and consume the rebels and the city. Caldrell can't blame us for that; he'll let us rebuild in our Lord's name. Those ancient souls can drain every drop of blood from them all."

Devaki glanced back down the hall toward Sutton, curious if he could hear any of this. "Ancient souls"? Souls didn't stay in this realm after death; they went home to their Mother. And Cybarys didn't drain blood; it was willingly given in devotion.

"And what keeps you safe in that scenario?" Gardain began. His hands clenched into fists, as if the illogic of his brother's words had finally driven him to the edge. "*If* they can come down here, what'll stop them from doing the same to you?"

"You're the brilliant one, little brother," Adlar returned wryly. "You've wasted your life studying that useless, pagan history in those forbidden tomes of Father's private libraries. Now maybe you should leave us and go die with those traitors."

Jeras reached out and slapped Adlar across the face. It was a quick, swift movement that seemed to require little effort. Adlar shrieked in surprise and pain and cowered before his father with his fingers trembling on his cheek. Devaki hardly had a chance to register the motion or blink before Moore turned on his younger son.

Gardain didn't move a muscle when the back of his father's hand struck his cheekbone. One of Moore's rings brought blood, sending droplets spraying to the dungeon's floor. Devaki herself ducked instinctively, on both swings, but she watched as Adlar whimpered while Gardain only let his shoulders slump and his chin lower to his chest in simple defeat. It almost, she thought, seemed like a subconscious, memorized movement in reaction to his father's violence, one he didn't have to think of doing but merely accepted as the norm.

And just like that, the conversation was over.

Devaki let her heels hit the ground as she turned and leaned back against the door. Pity filled her heart, but at the same time, she felt hope spark at her core; since arriving in Rhethos, everything about the rebellion and the presence of her Goddess was confusing and raised doubts.

This, though . . . *I asked for guidance, and the Goddess led me here, to someone who could have the answers to the biggest threat Will faces in this war. But Gardain Moore is in a cell with the rest of his family, and I can tell he's torn between staying loyal to his blood and exploring what clearly means a lot to him.*

"Miss Tarran," Sutton whispered, and Devaki made her way back down the hall. "We shouldn't stay much longer. The guard is changing, and I've got to be posted back at the main gate soon."

Devaki frowned. Part of her wanted to go back and talk to Gardain, or demand that Sutton open the padlocks and take him out. But that also felt like reaching too far; this was a complicated family situation, and a nest of political tangles that she didn't fully understand. Did she really have the right to step into all of that?

She reluctantly followed the young rebel toward the exit of the prison's main floor, back toward the moonlight and fresh air. Sutton was looking around with a nervous jitter, as if they'd gone too far, and he would surely be punished.

"Thank you," she murmured, which earned her a nervous grin from the young man. "Now, take me to Master Will."

Sutton's grin died. "I . . . right now?"

"Just show me where he is, please," Devaki insisted. She had to tell him what she'd discovered, and everything else, if he'd let her. Taking no for an answer, she decided, was stopping tonight. When Sutton marched down the path, Devaki followed at his heels. He stopped at the door to a particular barrack, then froze.

When Devaki peeked around him, she saw the Lady Marselle outside the entrance. The Rhethosian woman stopped smoothing her dark skirts when she spotted them.

"Well, what are you two doing out in the dark?" she questioned.

Sutton's face and neck turned red and blotchy. After stuttering for a moment, he muttered an excuse about his upcoming stationing and a quick goodnight to Devaki as he left.

"I need to see Will," Devaki began. She held her chin high, knowing from her brief interaction with this woman that she was very distrustful of someone like her.

Marselle gave her a skeptical look, put her ear to the door next to her, then bit her lower lip. She smiled and beckoned Devaki forward. Listening as well, Devaki immediately recognized several voices in the room beyond: Will's, Angelyn's, and Rowlann's.

"Our food crisis is on its way to being well managed, then," Will was saying. "Torald has begun working with our northern Towne Masters, and I've spent time out at his family's farm today. Goods are beginning to flow like they used to into Lorington but under much more beneficial terms."

"Excellent. And those arrests have been placed from the list you collected at the inn," came a response from a voice Devaki didn't know. "The remaining elite in the northern district aren't happy, but I have those families under control, brother."

Rowlann's voice echoed toward Devaki next. "The men have been reporting cooperation between the locals and the rebels on the streets throughout most of the city, particularly in the eastern market district. Progress is spreading. And the proper resupplies have been sent to The Forts after emergency wagons were utilized here."

"Good," came Will's response. "And where are the reports from scouts along the southern roads? How close is Caldrell?"

"At least two weeks away. An army like that, fifty-thousand strong, is moving slowly, but people in the city are well aware of his progress. Some are excited, and some are afraid. That news from messengers has been hard to hide and harder to manage."

Devaki heard Angelyn next, but her voice, quieter than the others, was hard to make out.

"Now's as good a time as any, dear girl," Marselle whispered. Before Devaki had a chance to even nod, Marselle twisted the handle and marched into the room, pulling Devaki along.

CHAPTER SIXTEEN

WHEN THE FLOODGATES OPEN

All conversation stopped, cut off mid-sentence as everyone turned toward Devaki and Marselle. Will sat behind a desk on the far side of the room, with a thin, blond man in a violet tunic perched on its corner. Angelyn was in a chair by the fire, and Rowlann stood directly to Devaki's left near the entrance. There were several other men Devaki didn't recognize situated around the square space, and expressions of shock and hostility ranged across their faces as they stared at her dark skin and freshly clotted Blessing Runes.

"Marselle. . .?" Angelyn began, her wide, dark blue eyes on Devaki.

Devaki, however, was looking at Will. The last time she'd seen him, he'd been so different. He'd just killed his enemies, ordered his men to peacefully take the city, and rode with her to the digsite. He'd been covered in blood, clothes burned, shoulders weary.

Now he was clean-shaven, well-dressed, and comfortably seated in his leadership role. She was almost seeing another person, one closer to the man who'd written her honest, open letters for years. He sat up, and she watched his throat tighten above the woven collar of his black tunic.

"You seemed to be missing one latecomer," Marselle announced in the taut silence. She shut the door behind her, keeping the fireplace's warmth inside the stone walls.

The man seated on the corner of Will's desk chuckled, shaking his head at Marselle. From the appreciative look he gave the Rhethosian woman, Devaki assumed they knew each other well. "If I didn't know any better, I'd say you've got quite the pair of balls under that skirt, my lady."

Marselle tilted her head, as if thinking hard on how to respond to this man about "knowing any better." Devaki assumed, if the rebel *actually* knew any better, he wouldn't provoke Marselle. "Master Colwell, I'd remind you that it doesn't take balls to accomplish tasks. Why not give Miss Tarran the floor instead of locking her up, if no one objects?"

Devaki bit her lip. Standing in the center of the room with all of these people intent on her wasn't what she had in mind; she'd only wanted her father to pay attention to her. Not this. She could see questions flash across Will's eyes, and she knew, if she looked to the side, she'd see the same wordless expressions from Rowlann.

"Why are you not locked safe in your room?" "What made you think it was a good idea to barge in here?" "Who do you think you are?"

"Umm, I object," said the man Marselle named as Master Colwell. He raised his hand above his head, then hopped off the edge of the desk in a graceful motion. "This is exactly what I've been telling Will is a *bad* idea. You seem nice enough, young lady, but why don't you girls head back—"

Rowlann reached out in the middle of Master Colwell's sentence and put a hand on Devaki's shoulder, as if to turn her back toward the door in silent agreement.

"Just a moment," spoke one of the men Devaki didn't recognize. Everyone looked to a short, plump man on the other side of the room. He stared at Devaki as if speaking of an untrained dog that might attack. "Is this the pagan weapon people are talking about in the barracks? The thing that broke the gates open and cursed Rowlann's armor?"

"Not *quite* the right choice of words," Rowlann growled.

"I don't appreciate being kept in the dark on this, Master Will," the other man continued. "The men under my command want nothing to do with the Blood Goddess."

"Don't call her that," Devaki snapped. She hated the Rhethosian slang "Blood Goddess," reducing her Mother to something so . . .simple and sinister-sounding.

The man, however, didn't seem to hear her. "When they heard the rumors of a Goddess Touched rebel, they questioned everything. If they see an Armellan soldier, I can't guarantee—"

"You can't control your own charges?" Marselle interrupted. She took a step forward, brushed Rowlann's hand off Devaki's shoulder, and turned to Will.

Devaki cleared her throat and strode to the very middle of the room. Every eye on her made her feel very exposed. "I'm not a weapon," she began quietly. "I'm not a soldier, either. I want to help you, Will."

"Kid, we don't need your outlawed foreign magic to put The Bradford down," Master Colwell emphasized, the tightened muscles of his sharp jawline barely letting out the words.

The other rebel Masters present nodded. "From the beginning, Master Will," began one of them, "you've been honest about your history with Armelle. You've also been clear that the kingdom across the sea and its faith will have *no* part in this cause."

One of the others added, "We all know that fearing the Blood Goddess' chains is the one thing The Bradford has right—"

Will stood violently from his chair, slamming it back against the wall behind him. Everyone froze, and Devaki jumped back a step. She saw Angelyn put a hand over her mouth and swallow with some effort.

"Out, now." Will hissed the words. His eyes were cast down at the stacks of books and papers on the desk. "Irvin, Marselle, the rest of you leave."

"Will," Angelyn began, standing from her chair.

"Miss McKinlee, you are welcome to stay." Will's words were controlled, as if it took most of his effort to not scream them. "But I would prefer, as the situation lies, to speak with Miss Tarran alone."

Angelyn looked back to Devaki, who saw a clear question in her eyes: *"Do you want me to stay?"* Devaki shook her head, indicating that she was fine. After all, Devaki assumed that Angelyn had kept her word and hadn't told Will about her narrow escape from the sick locals near the digsite. Therefore, she and Angelyn had never met before.

The room cleared, with a few men murmuring apologies as they left. Master Colwell put a hand on Will's desk, leaned toward him, and whispered. Will smiled thinly and patted Colwell on the shoulder. Marselle eyed Will and Angelyn for a moment as she stepped toward the door, and Devaki was confused when she thought she saw a tinge of jealousy in the red-head's eyes.

But that didn't matter. For the first time, outside of the necessity of battle and survival, Devaki had her father's undivided attention.

"Isaka used to do that, too," Will began in the silence.

"My . . .mother?" Shock slowed Devaki's speech. She did not expect *that* after the aggressive display she'd just seen.

Will nodded. He made his way around the desk, then sat by the fire, and held his hand out toward the opposite chair. Devaki shook her head, preferring to stand. She didn't think it was out of fear, but all the same, she felt she needed her space.

"I met her when she was about your age," Will continued. "And every time we could see each other, we were breaking a dozen different Valsaran Royal codes. She didn't like getting in trouble, so when she was nervous, she'd fidget with her prayer bracelets . . .and tap her left heel, like that."

Devaki suddenly held still, unaware she'd been doing either of those things. No one spoke of her mother or her aunt, who'd both been murdered the night Devaki was born. All of Armelle believed that the Rhethosian boy who dishonored their princess was responsible for this crime, but Devaki knew in her heart her father would never do such a thing.

It had been the first violent act in Armellan society in a hundred years, and the shame of it all was placed on her shoulders: bloodshed not in service to her Goddess, the ultimate blaspheme, was her birthright.

A heavy, dismal energy suffocated the memory of the mother she always craved, sealing the lips of any who knew Isaka, forcing them to despise her child as if she were at fault. This was the first time anyone had casually mentioned something positive to Devaki about Isaka Tarran.

"Does it upset you?" she asked Will. "To talk about her?"

Will sat back in his seat, and a shadow passed over his face that didn't come from the flickers of the fireplace. "Not as much as it upsets me to know you haven't been safe. You haven't been staying in that room." When he looked at her, she didn't see any of the anger from before: she only saw worry for her safety. *He loves me enough to feel that?*

And just like that, everything she wanted to tell him flooded to the forefront of her mind. Devaki put out a hand, steadying herself on the warm arm of the chair opposite Will's. She wanted to tell him that she'd heard conflicting voices at the digsite, one that warned them away from hidden secrets, one that begged her to come forward and help her Goddess, and one that dripped in darkness and power that terrified her to the core.

On top of that, he had to open the door of her mother? He'd only known Isaka for a short time, in her youth, but he could tell her so much that she longed for.

Devaki sank into the chair and put her head in her hands. Why was this so hard? She had a plan of what she'd say, once she finally got her father to face her. But she'd never thought of how it would make *him* feel. Any judgment or foreign objection she could combat with the conviction of her faith. But the weary, worried expression Will bore washed everything away.

"Devaki?" Will began. "What's wrong? What happened?"

She gripped her head tighter, sudden tears clogging her throat. A short, frustrated sigh escaped her lips. "I don't know how to do this either, you know," she snapped. "I need to tell you things, but you can't ignore me anymore. I know you didn't expect to have me here and I know it complicates your plans and I know it isn't safe. But we have to do this together." It took all of her courage, but she pushed back her masses of tight curls and looked up at Will.

He met her eyes and wordlessly nodded.

Devaki took a deep breath, inhaling the scents of firewood and old papers. Finally, she let the dam open: she told him about what she'd experienced at the digsite, about meeting Angelyn and Marselle, about being led to where the Moores were kept, and about Gardain's knowledge he'd gained in his father's private libraries.

For a moment, Will's eyes flashed dangerously. That anger Devaki had seen right before he'd dismissed everyone crossed his face. "You went down into that pit, alone?" he repeated shortly. "And you . . .spied on Jeras Moore and his family?"

Devaki put up a finger. "Not exactly," she corrected. "I only got to the *edge* of the digsite, and I wasn't *spying*, only following the Goddess' lead." She smiled innocently.

Will smirked, then looked away as if he was still processing everything she'd confessed. "You've given me a lot to think about," he muttered.

"Well, you should know about what I saw before I left Armelle, too," Devaki added. She felt that she needed to share her vision in the Valsara Temple that had told her she had to sail to Rhethos immediately. Somehow, she felt this last detail would justify everything she'd done so far.

"There were flames in the Goddess' Woods," she said. "If you know anything about what they teach across the sea, those trees are Cybarys' most sacred place, and we tend to idolize them since we cannot journey to them anymore. The Goddess' first temple used to sit at its center, and seeing its remains on fire was the ultimate warning sign. Especially because in the vision she gave me of those burning trees, I held the power to put it out. I'm the only one who can save it . . .and somehow save her."

Will's eyebrows narrowed and he propped his elbows on his knees, hands extended out before him with his fingers laced. "I don't understand."

"What's crazy is I don't, either!" Devaki sighed, frustrated. "But at the same time, somehow I do. It's like the Goddess put the knowledge I need inside of me, but I can't access it until the right time. All I know is it's true, and it's where my Fate's String will lead me. I have to help you help these people, and that will lead me closer to saving everyone."

Will's face contorted as if he was truly trying to comprehend what she was sharing. A large group of men passed by the window on the far wall, speaking loudly, but Devaki noticed that Will's attention wasn't drawn away. Despite how uncomfortable he seemed, he wasn't distracted by anything outside of where they sat.

"And what did Sehran say?" Will asked her. "When you spoke to him? Aren't all Sahma visions supposed to be reported to the Temple Leader immediately?"

Devaki felt a harsh chill at the mention of her cousin's name, and she leaned closer to the fire's warmth. Even as sweat broke out on her rune-covered skin, she didn't feel any comfort. "Sehran *hates* me," she whispered. "He orchestrated the way society shunned me. Whenever I tried to come to him for religious guidance or as a family member, he was not kind. I forced my way into his audience chamber the night before I left, and he made it clear he would never tolerate being in my presence again."

"That isn't right," Will said, indignation in his voice. "I heard rumors about his behavior, after he took the place of . . ."

Devaki snapped her gaze up to him, a tear leaking down her cheek. Sehran never should have been Temple Leader as the son of her mother's sister, but the role had been put on his shoulders after the untimely deaths of so many members of the royal family. "He does a lot of things differently," Devaki said, clearing her throat. "But because of what happened, he can justify anything to keep us safe from other violent Rhethosians."

"Isn't it horrible what our kingdoms' leaders say about each other?" Will commented. He sat back and pressed a hand slowly through his hair. "I wish you could have seen your kingdom as it was before. It wasn't perfect, because nothing is, but I fell in love with Valsara the minute I set foot on its streets when I was eight."

"Will," she began, and saw his eyebrows raise.

"Not 'Father'?" he said, a thin smile barely raising the corners of his lips. "I suppose I should earn that."

She winced, not comfortable explaining that she wanted to call him that, but every time she tried, the word stuck painfully in her throat like it wasn't meant to be there. "You could start," she tried slowly, "by telling me a few things. I feel like I've talked enough." She leaned forward, aware she was treading on dangerous, emotional territory. Her hands gripped the cloth of her chair's arms.

"What happened between you and my mother, exactly? How did things go so wrong that so many people were killed when I was born? You say you loved Valsara, but when you and your brother were orphaned and raised there, it seemed like only disaster came out of it. How did he die?"

Will shut his eyes, tension showing on every line of his face. He opened his mouth as if to speak, then closed it. His hand trailed along his jawline while his throat worked silently, as if fighting back tears. Leaning back in his seat, he reached inside his coat and pulled a small journal from an inner pocket. He ran a thumb along the spine, then held it out in the space between them.

"I know you can't forgive me for this, but I will not speak about those things," he murmured. "I hope what you are looking for is in here instead. I've been writing in it for you."

Devaki took the journal with a respectful touch, but somehow her heart felt cheated. She didn't want his writing; she wanted his words, spoken to her face, explaining away at least some of the shame and judgment she'd carried all of her life. He left Armelle, but she had grown up not knowing a thing about why she suffered in society but was Blessed by her Goddess.

"I just have to know—"

"Please," Will cut in. "This has been more than enough, Devaki." He stood from his seat, a finality in his stance. "You need to respect that."

Devaki stood as well, holding the worn journal at her side. She understood, even though it hurt to be shut out yet again. There was one thing she was still holding back, one thing she was terrified to speak of because it was the greatest mystery she experienced. Maybe, if Will could listen for five more minutes and make her feel safe enough to share, this was a subject he could help her understand. *Or, at least,* she thought, *make me feel less alone.*

"You should know one more thing," Devaki insisted. "The night I sailed here, with Rowlann—"

Will put up a hand. "I'm sorry. It will have to wait. I still have a lot to work through this evening. *Please*, for the love of the Goddess, do not go near that digsite or Gardain Moore for now."

Devaki bit her lower lip, holding back several retorts. For the last hour, she'd had a rare glimpse into the bright, kind young man who'd fallen in love with Isaka Tarran at fifteen, but now Master Will, the leader of Rhethos' rebellion, stood before her. She could tell that persona was much easier for him because everything was clear and didn't involve the muddied, uncomfortable past.

"We'll speak again, soon," he added, but there wasn't much conviction behind the words. "I'll have someone show you to those libraries in Towne Centre that Master Moore mentioned tomorrow. I'm sure you'd like to look for those books and read them."

"Right. Thanks," Devaki said shortly, trying to keep the disappointment out of her voice. Almost against her own will, she touched the spot under her tunic above her heart, where the Goddess had cut a rune she couldn't read.

She never felt it heat up like her Blessing Rune scars when she used magic. It just sat on her chest, a reminder that the powerful deity she loved was capable of more than she knew . . .or more than she was allowed to know.

CHAPTER SEVENTEEN

BE SMART, STAY ALIVE

Joshua ran through the streets of Kaylyn with death behind him. The left shoulder of his tunic was plastered to his skin, wet with blood and sweat. Local guardsmen were waiting on the corner of every shipping yard block, every back alley stable, and every seaside square. There was nowhere safe from arrest, torture, and public execution, yet his feet pounded the cobblestones, drenched in unforgiving rain puddles.

Every Blessing Rune he'd ever cut into his skin blazed with red light, drawing attention to him like a lighthouse beacon. It didn't make sense. His magic didn't do that; after all, a tiny bit of magic was how his mother hid his Goddess' Touch for sixteen years. Blessing Runes didn't *shine*.

Shouts of disdain against the Goddess sprang at him from every sharp corner, but Joshua swore he heard his family and friends calling to him from behind, too. No matter what, he couldn't stop, couldn't turn, or someone would finish what they'd started with the bleeding injury on his shoulder.

"You must think I'm an idiot!" Orton's voice shot out from the nearest alley, a narrow strip of darkness between two towering shipping houses. Joshua flinched, but kept going.

"I'm so proud of you, little Josh." His mother's words came next, soothing him, begging him to slow down and wait for her. Joshua heaved a labored breath and ran on.

"I don't live with the fire, Josh. I do something about it!" Will's voice didn't come from around Joshua. Unlike the others, it echoed from within his chest. That meant that it was safe, right? Josh's legs shrieked. His lungs were pain-ridden weights, and he knew he couldn't run much longer.

Ahead of him was Kaylyn's Towne Centre, its spire with The Bradford's statue atop it covered in a thick blanket of rainy fog. Bodies hung from the walls, in varying states of decay. Joshua felt his feet slow from exhaustion. He hoped that this time, compared to when he'd dared to look up at the corpses the day before his home burned, he would have the courage to stand up for himself.

Bright pain exploded at the back of his head, as if someone had hit him with a rock. When he blinked, Joshua was back at The Forts, lying in the dirt and being beaten by the people who were afraid of his Goddess Touched blood. This time, no one let their grip slip long enough for him to scramble away, and no air made it into his lungs.

Everything was a suffocating haze of panic and death.

"Josh . . . Josh? Where are you?"

He peeled himself awake, painful layer by painful layer. Sitting up, he found himself in the shade of several massive oaks, protected by their encompassing, overhanging branches. He breathed shakily, then touched his tender shoulder.

"Joshua!"

So that wasn't part of the dream, he thought. *Nightmare, actually.* It had been a few days since Travok's men had driven him into the woods, and he'd heard nothing but the sounds of the trees around him, till now.

"Do you have any idea how cold and wet it is out here? Where *are* you?"

"Ada," Joshua muttered. His muscles were stiff from sleeping on the forest floor, and it took a moment for him to walk a steady line through the under-brush toward where he'd heard her voice.

Judging by the way the tree branches above were beginning to brighten with a hazy silver color, it was sometime before dawn. It only took a moment for Joshua to make out Ada's outline in the trees ahead, her slim arm steady-ing herself on the trunk of the nearest oak.

"I'm here," Josh said, and he heard her sigh with relief.

"Finally!" She waved at him. "I thought I was lost and would freeze out here."

"By the Goddess," sighed a new voice. "You are quite dramatic, young lady."

Joshua craned his neck to see around Ada in the gloom, and smiled when he saw Mistress Merheene. He had been worried about the Armellan woman and what Travok's men might do to her. She looked well enough, wrapped in a thick woolen coat the shade of deep ocean waters. It had been a while since Joshua had seen something so close to Rhethosian Blue, but he assumed, because the woman couldn't see, that it didn't matter much to her what she wore to stay warm.

"What are you two doing out here?" Joshua asked.

Ada set down a sack she'd been carrying over her shoulder. The loud thump sent an echo through the open space between the trees, scattering birds and disrupting thick coatings of old leaves. "Those new men have turned everything upside down. You two can't go back there."

"Really?" Joshua balked, watching as Ada unpacked several baskets of food, jugs of water, and what appeared to be materials for a salve for his wounds.

Mistress Merheene felt for and then took the latter before sitting in the underbrush. His starving stomach growled, though it didn't seem as important as the weight of a new responsibility. Was he supposed to help care for the old, blind woman now out in the woods?

"It's a nightmare, Josh," Ada said angrily. She handed him some of the water, then brushed back a few strands of her straight brown hair. "All forty of those men are acting like they're in charge. Anyone who asked about their news from Will has been locked up, including Orton. No one is allowed to leave! I don't know *why* your father is doing this."

"Could you not call him that, please?" Joshua growled.

"I'm sorry," Ada replied. She pulled her hand off the tree next to her, glancing down at her palm with disgust. She grabbed one of the rags from the sack on the forest floor and soaked it in water. "Turn around. Your mother will kill me if you die from this."

Joshua complied, shivering in the cold predawn air when he pulled up half his shirt to expose his left shoulder blade. He bit his tongue when Ada worked the caked blood out of the cut, but he couldn't help swearing when she pressed the sticky mix Mistress Merheene had made into his skin.

"It's not deep," Ada muttered. She wrapped several dry cloths under his arm and around his chest, binding the cut. "But it's swollen. You should let that poultice do its job."

Joshua, however, had no intention of sitting still any longer. If Travok was taking over the camp for whatever reason, he had to go back and try to stop him.

"Thank you, both of you," Joshua said, looking between Mistress Merheene and Ada. "I know you hate this place, Ada."

Ada crossed her arms over her flat chest. "None of this would have escalated if you'd left him alone, and stopped cutting those marks into your skin like I told you to."

Mistress Merheene chuckled, a low, dry sound that engulfed the trees around them. "I can tell why you like her, little Rhethosian," she said, and Joshua felt his cheeks redden.

"I—" he started.

"And I know what you're going to do," she continued over him. "Since we can't stop you, I merely ask that you use caution . . . and this." When she extended her hand, Joshua spotted the blackened bundle of Sahma in her long, worn fingers.

"How did you know?" he began. He instantly remembered how the world lit up with bright clarity when he'd used the herb before. Perhaps, tonight, its connection to this realm and the Goddess' would help him.

"Umm, Josh?" Ada said skeptically, her eyes on the bundle of leaves. "What is that?"

"It's for meditating," he said, taking the Sahma. Now, with a set goal in mind, he wasn't as afraid of the herb's effects. "For getting close to the Goddess. It'll help me when I go back."

Mistress Merheene nodded, but Ada shook her head vehemently. Joshua gave her a hard look, hoping she got the message that she couldn't change his mind.

"You are being stupid, putting yourself in front of those men again," Ada snapped, turning to go. "I don't want anything to do with it."

"They won't see me, Ada!" Josh insisted. "I know the ropes system better than anyone. I'll stay hidden."

Ada raised her eyebrows. Maybe he didn't know the walkways better than *anyone*, especially the other young ones who'd practically been born there. But he was fast and quiet. "Do what you want," Ada snapped. "I'm sure you'll find Travok and his men over in the common hall."

Joshua didn't say anything as she left. Couldn't she see that something was wrong? If his father was locking people up and cutting off the camp from the rest of the kingdom, he had to find out why and do something about it.

"Goddess go with you, Josh," Mistress Merheene said. "Don't worry. I will be fine on my own for now." When Joshua glanced at her, he saw that she'd produced a candle from Ada's bag and somehow lit it. She held the flame up in his general direction.

Joshua lit the edge of the bundle, held the smoke under his chin, and took several deep breaths. His eyes closed, his heart rate slowed, and everything settled under a blanket of calm. The sweet, earthy scent of the smoke permeated his skin, ruffled his hair, and made all the aches from his bruises, cuts, and shoulder go away.

Putting out the crumbling leaves, Joshua pressed the bundle's remains into his pocket, opposite his compass. Maybe it was the effects of the Sahma, but when his hand brushed the compass, he felt an odd pang of pain. Traditionally, devices like it were passed from father to son, when a young man came of age in Rhethos.

He knew Gabriel had no children, and he treasured the unexpected gift, but Josh never expected such a thing from his own father he'd thought long gone. As the world shifted into vibrant hues around him, he thought of Travok with a sour expression his face when his palm met the brass casing.

Joshua exhaled deliberately and withdrew his hand. Having the Sahma leaves next to the device with Armellan runes on it made him feel more secure. There was no time to meditate as he'd done before, so Josh stepped forward with as much confidence as he could muster.

When he emerged from the woods and stood at the narrowest point trench surrounding the edge of The Forts, Joshua paused. An unfamiliar shadow sat up in the watchtower above. Beyond he could see dozens of armed, able-bodied men moving about the camp.

In the shadows, Joshua pulled out one of his daggers and let its weight balance for a moment on his palm. Then he cut a Protection Rune on the top of his left hand, wincing at each precise, little movement it took to break the skin in the dark.

The Sahma enhanced the feeling of giving blood to Cybarys, amplifying the desert warmth that originated from the rune. Joshua murmured a prayer, took three steps back, then ran to the trench, vaulting over it. Though his boots struck the ground loudly, no one turned in his direction as he made his way forward.

He headed for the common hall, seeing the most light inside its many-materialled walls. Ada was right; he could hear muffled voices inside, and he hoped one of them was his father's. Every movement of his, every sound he made, and every light and noise around him seemed to ebb and flow with confident, cool clarity.

Joshua licked his lips, sweat breaking out on his palms as he sidestepped a group of men he didn't recognize. He was barely in the building's shadow, but they didn't even glance his way. All five of his fingers were slick with the blood that Cybarys continued to pull from his body to keep him hidden.

Looking up, Joshua found the rope he wanted dangling just out of his reach. It was one of the first parts of the overhead system he'd learned how to use when he arrived. Pulling on it brought down the long plank on this side of the common hall to be used as a ramp to access the top level. But he only let the counterweight fall half-way; he didn't want to risk his luck with the noise the pulley system often made, especially while most were still asleep.

He jumped, grabbed the plank's edge, and hauled himself up onto the flat set of interlocking boards. His shoulder burned, the fresh binding around him limiting his movement. From up here, he could survey the main, open area of the camp, and he could make out the inside of the common hall through several gaps in the slat siding next to him.

But the price came at staying in a constant, low crouch; many of the weights and ropes met together on the building's side. They were mounted and knotted right above the platform, taking up almost all the free space above his head. There wasn't much room to bend, let alone stand from his uncomfortable position.

"Orton, Lackman, and the others are secured."

Joshua froze. As he gazed down into the building, he saw three men, one of them Travok, seated around a table made of used whiskey barrels. When Joshua squinted, the haze of Sahma sharpened what he saw with edges of green and gold light. Waves of color blossomed like airborne water when any of the men below moved. Despite the dull candlelight inside the common hall, Joshua saw all of them as if it were noon, and he was right next to them.

"No proper holding area in this shitty place, so that's not saying much," Travok snapped back. "Those storehouse walls won't hold a beast like Orton for long. We'll need to do this fast."

Joshua turned his gaze out over the camp's two-level system that was pressed against the curve of the mountainside. The storehouses were on the opposite end, but if he ran the planks, he could get there quickly and find a way to let Orton and the other rebel Masters out.

"We want to keep him and the others alive," Travok added, slamming the edge of the closest barrel for emphasis with his big, square fist. "They're worth more to the military that way."

Joshua ground his teeth, confused. *"The military"?* he thought. Fresh fury raced through Josh as it all became clear in his mind. *I knew it! He can't be a real rebel. He's got a connection to The Bradford's military. Probably has since he left Mum.*

That was all he wanted to hear. Now he had to move. Together with Orton they could fight back against these liars and get word to Will to stop this madness. Joshua planted his heels, ready to run, but then Travok spoke again.

"With Sarrett defeated, we can send news to the Rhethosian Captain himself. He used to be pretty interested in this part of the kingdom because of its connections to Armelle's Goddess."

Joshua felt the muscles in his thighs begin to shake, but he didn't dare adjust his stance. The Insane Captain had an interest in the Goddess? But why? When he glanced down, an iridescent shade of orange pulsed around his legs, as if reflecting the strain it took to crouch for so long.

One of the men across from Travok nodded, the motion overexaggerated by the colors of the Sahma. "Sarrett was a good bet, though, Travok," he said, and the others grunted agreement. "I know you were working closely with him for years. But control of this place will be worth more to the Captain."

"You think he'll make us Loyals?" another asked, his voice dripping with greed. "My family would take me back with open arms, then . . .kiss my feet, even."

"And that Goddess Touched boy," added the first. "Is that really your son? Wasn't there a rumor about the Captain needing pagan-blooded people? He could be another piece worth a lot to Caldrell."

There was silence, and Joshua put his hands down against the worn plank, shaking. The blood around his Protection Rune started to dry. His father was involved with the Rhethosian military, selling them rebel secrets, and, apparently, safe places where rebel families lived. And what did The Bradford's servants want with land associated with the Armellan Goddess?

Part of him wanted to hear Travok dismiss the idea of trading his own child for a reward or title. *Come on,* he thought, desperation itching the edges of his mind. *Give me something, anything to prove that you have a heart.*

"That would require finding Joshua first," Travok replied, "and then *keeping* him till we report to Captain Caldrell."

"We'll find him," returned one of the others. "We have men all around the edges of those trees. He won't get to Patten or Morely without us knowing."

Travok grunted like he wasn't impressed. "Orton was the one most concerned about him, and that young girl, she must be from Kaylyn too. Ask around the camp. Find out what'll break them, then maybe we can bring in Josh without killing him. Caldrell would appreciate it if our prize wasn't spilling his cursed blood unnecessarily."

Goddess, Joshua thought, conflicted. *What should I do?* Too many questions and options swam in his mind, and a wave of nausea induced by the Sahma smoke and his sudden headache made him clamp a hand over his mouth.

The edges of his vision began to glow in a dull shade of maroon. The color expanded in gusts before his eyes, like red, glowing wisps of sand in the air. Joshua stared, transfixed, until the red clouds filled the entire camp, the foothills of the mountains, and the dark clouds above. Then she spoke to him.

"Keep steady, little McKinlee. Stay hidden. You hold the key to a higher purpose than what currently stands in your way."

Joshua shook his head, frustrated. Did she just tell him to do *nothing*, after what he'd heard Travok say? Josh was beginning to understand why Will didn't want anything to do with Cybarys; their connection felt safe and reassuring, yet there were no clear answers when he needed them. Was he meant to blindly follow?

As he listened to his father and his men continue to talk, laugh, even, about what they'd done, Joshua didn't think he could remain silent. For sixteen years, he'd let his mother keep him blind. The last time he'd used the Sahma, the Goddess had told him he was "not meant to take lives, only protect them, and bring them to a free world."

I'm not here to lead anyone, he insisted in his head, and an immediate wave of heat flooded over him, as if protesting his refusal. *I have to stop Travok from hurting anyone else in this camp. That's what's most important.*

Suddenly, his compass flared with heat in his pocket. The smell of sea salt and rough sand met his nose, and Joshua hurriedly pulled the piece of brass out. It was almost too warm to touch. The Armellan symbols on the back glowed with a blood-red light. His throat went dry; it had never done anything like this before.

One marking in particular stood out, its outline sparking with a yellow-white color in such a powerful pinprick that Joshua couldn't make out the exact shape. He hovered his free hand over the compass, shielding it, trying to hide its light.

But there was no need; the Goddess seemed to have gotten her point across, and in the next instant, the compass ceased glowing and sat as a heavy, dull weight in his palm.

What was that? At the same instant Joshua thought the question, someone said it aloud inside the building.

"I don't know," another of Travok's men answered. "Who's on watch out there? I told them not to use torches."

"I'll head out and see."

"Here," Travok barked. "Take this with you and give it to a rider. We want to send word to Lorington that 'all is well' up here."

Joshua gathered himself, shoving the compass back in his pocket. He wasn't worried about the man emerging from the common hall; he didn't bother looking up. Instead, he started marching toward the corrals where the few remaining horses were kept. In the Sahma haze, Joshua made out the distinct outline of thick paper in his hand.

He moved silently forward, doing his best to stay in a low crouch even as the overhead pathway opened up. Bits of rope and canvas brushed over the top of his head as he kept pace with the man below. *Please, Goddess,* he thought, *let there be only a few people where he's going. I can't let them send out lies to Will.*

But as the corrals came into view, Joshua's hope disappeared: there were at least a dozen of Travok's men around the cleared, fenced area of dirt. Despite the early hour, with sunlight barely fighting its way over the looming mountaintops, they were taking no chances with the horses kept there.

He watched helplessly as the man handed off the message after talking with a few of the others. The messenger mounted a horse and Joshua balled his hands into fists as the rider headed southwest. There was nothing he could do to stop him unless he wanted to prove Ada right and throw his life away.

The storehouses, he thought, and grabbed the nearest rope. *I've got to try helping Orton instead.* His feet found the nearly frozen knots that ranged all the way down to the ground. From there, he wove his way through the early morning groups of rebels who were starting to emerge from their homes. He noticed they avoided speaking to Travok's men, shrinking back with fear. *This isn't right. This is where we're supposed to feel free and safe.*

Joshua spotted the storehouses, three large, thin structures that did indeed have the most sturdy walls. He knew his mother had made great strides here before she left with Lady Marselle, creating efficiency in the way the rebels gained, sorted, and distributed vital food and supplies. He hadn't cared less at the time, though; that was so similar to what she did in Kaylyn, and he wanted to do everything that had *nothing* to do with their old home.

Now, there were two men guarding the front and back entrances to only one of the buildings, where Joshua assumed that Orton and the others who had resisted Travok's sudden takeover were being kept. Travok's men, however, didn't seem to be too attentive. Was Orton even a threat anymore?

Joshua twisted his clotted Protection Rune, wincing as fresh blood issued forth. He made for the center of the long building, right in between several stacks of supply barrels. Even as he ducked in between them, magic remnants burst around him in a steady arc. *That must mean she really is protecting me,* he thought, and peered between the gaps in the storehouse's boards.

In between the towering shelves of supplies, darkened by shadows, Joshua made out slumped figures. From his position, he saw about a dozen of them, each bound and bleeding. Not far from him, chained against a shelf with blood coating his forehead was Orton. Joshua glanced around swiftly. What could he do to help the man who'd done nothing but help him since he arrived? His gaze fell to the ground and he got an idea.

Joshua ran his hands through the dirt, sifting the gem-like sparks of magic into his palm. After gathering a handful, Joshua aimed through the slats and threw the magic remnants at Orton. Any pieces that bounced off his skin dissolved. The man stirred, but only for a moment. When he shifted, Joshua saw thick globs of drying blood at the base of his skull, too. He'd put up quite a fight.

Joshua threw another handful of red sparks. Orton grunted, a deep, distrustful sound that Joshua associated with one of the old horses in the stables of The Hamond. To him, that meant stay back unless he wanted to be kicked. The chains around Orton's wrists strained, then slumped, as if he remembered his circumstances.

"That's not the smartest move, you know," Orton rasped. "How am I supposed to clean up this pagan mess around me when those men come in?"

"It doesn't matter," Joshua insisted. "I'll get you out. They aren't rebels, Orton. They're spies working with the Rhethosian military. He wants to sell you to the Insane Captain."

"Damn. And I thought your dad was a piece of shit deserter taking advantage of this place," Orton growled. "Don't think of coming in here, McKinlee. He's got forty men. We're twelve old men, and I'm not risking these families getting caught in a fight."

"Then what am I supposed to do?" Joshua insisted, desperation rising in his throat.

"Run." Orton coughed after saying the word. "You're useless here."

"I'm not—"

"What have I taught you, you ungrateful child? Your weapons are for stealth and defense. Balancing those daggers and avoiding your enemies are skills that don't translate to a forty-to-one brawl. And if you kill with your magic, you're done with that nonsense, too."

Joshua scoffed helplessly, knowing Orton was right. He was shocked to hear the man even mention using his Goddess' Touch.

"Be smart," Orton continued, "and you'll live through this."

A hand grabbed the back of Joshua's tunic, hauling him up and around. One of Travok's men held him up off the ground like a child, his muscles bulging as he glared at Joshua.

"You're the pagan boy," he snapped, and instantly clamped his second hand around the front of Joshua's throat. Everything began to darken, all noise dimming to a dangerous muffle. Joshua thought Travok told his men to keep him alive, that he was more valuable if he was still breathing. This man clearly hadn't gotten that message. In defiance, Joshua kicked, but there was hardly any strength left in his legs.

Orton said to be smart. He snapped his head back, then brought it forward, crashing it into the bridge of his enemy's nose. The man cried out and dropped Joshua, but as soon as he hit the earth, his head spun uncontrollably, aching from the impact. *Okay, that wasn't too smart.*

He immediately broke open the skin on the scabbed-over Strength Runes on his right hand. Dirt stung in the wounds as he shakily found his feet. Clutching at his bleeding face, the man growled at Joshua. There were other voices around the edges of the storehouse, and they would arrive in moments.

Thinking fast, Joshua drew his right hand dagger, found its balance, and flipped the hilt outward. He crouched low, wound his arm back, then swung forward with all of his might at the outside of the man's leg. He connected at the knee, and a wave of magic issued forth.

His enemy howled, dropping to the ground amongst the magic remnants. Shattered bone protruded from his knee joint, half of his leg turned at an unnatural angle. Joshua stared, dumbfounded by his actions.

Three men ran around the corner, but they stopped once they saw their cohort shrieking on the ground. One of them, Joshua noticed, had a set of keys. He needed those if he had any hope of getting the chains off of Orton.

That's when a fourth man came around the corner. Joshua stopped all other thought when he saw Ada, held roughly against the man's chest. She looked unharmed and Joshua saw fierce defiance in her eyes, but he knew this was bad: he couldn't fight all of these men. And he couldn't stop Travok's messengers by himself.

"Go, Josh," Ada snapped as his father's men cautiously advanced. "I can handle myself."

Joshua took a step back, inwardly cursing himself. The Goddess had told him to stay hidden and Orton had told him to run. All he'd gained was information, while his friends were still in danger. As he turned on his heel, kicking up dirt and heading back toward the tree line, Joshua thought of Cybarys' apparent indifference to all the little people in the way of her big plans she told him so little about.

"You hold the key to a higher purpose than what currently stands in your way."

Joshua, however, was more concerned about immediate threats than mysterious secrets. The question was, what would he do next?

CHAPTER EIGHTEEN

DENIED THE LORD'S FAVOR

At the age of eighteen, four years after Lily's death, Sarrett knew one thing clear as day: the Rhethosian military was loved and feared, a perfect representation of their Lord on every street corner. Sarrett felt it each time he stood watch, each time he patrolled outside the walls, and each time he apprehended someone who might disrupt The Bradford's peace. His newfound power gave him purpose and hope, two things he hadn't felt since he'd lost his grip on Lily's hand.

That strength trickled down from the Pure Palace to his captain and all the men he commanded. "Do whatever is necessary to uphold Rhethosian Justice," was repeated daily like a fervent prayer. And, over the last four years, that's exactly what Sarrett did, through every grueling exercise, backhanded putdown, and trial from his superiors.

The overly ambitious were both tested and rewarded. Out of all the new soldiers in Clancy, the Rhethosian Captain recognized Sarrett's face. He even spoke to him regularly, which, despite its assumed benefits, terrified Sarrett. His immediate superiors, clearly jealous of the attention, assigned Sarrett more arduous drills.

According to his family, who admired his newfound military determination, Caldrell was given more power than any previous captain by their latest Lord. Word was spreading that the impending threat of the foreign Goddess was more prevalent, and that required more force from the military, in every aspect of the commonfolk's lives. They needed to be kept safe.

Then, he finally did it: Sarrett earned an officer's jacket. It was nowhere near the splendor of a lieutenant's, and couldn't compare to his Captain's uniform, but it was the first step. He practically slept in the tailored piece of Rhethosian wool, feeling like part of his shattered heart mended itself.

"Do you know what the truth is, officer?"

At the end of a drill, supervising the newest soldiers, Sarrett blinked in the midday sun. Caldrell appeared at his side and prompted the odd question without preamble. This was how their conversations started, earning sharp looks from the other officers. Pleasant heat wafted down from the cloudless sky, bouncing off the grasses trampled outside the city walls by the constantly marching men.

Sarrett shook his head. He kept his eyes downcast, hands at the small of his back, pressed against his spotless Rhethosian Blue jacket. "Truth" was a dangerous word, and he was unwillingly speaking to a very dangerous man. He knew the right answer was The Bradford's truth.

Caldrell leaned in, bringing his tall, slim frame very close to Sarrett's shoulder. "The real truth," he whispered in a low, deep tone, "is we need our Lord desperately. He alone can keep us safe from Cybarys."

Sarrett thought for a moment, then shifted his polished boots. "Yes, Captain," he spoke up. "But. . ."

Caldrell snapped backward, as if Sarrett had slapped him. Sarrett met a pair of cold blue eyes. The right corner of Caldrell's mouth and his right eye twitched erratically. "But?" he repeated, in a tight tone.

"Shouldn't we fight back? Isn't there some way we can do more than defend ourselves from her and her pagan followers?"

He held his breath, not knowing what possessed him to ask both questions. It may have been a gnawing doubt that had been growing in his stomach that made him wonder why a pacifistic kingdom, so far away across the sea, was such a threat, and how it felt like more of a convenient excuse for evil Rhethosian men to freely do evil things.

Caldrell smiled at him. The expression made Sarrett want to wince, but over the years he'd trained himself to not let what should have been a show of warmth turn his stomach sour. Every time the Insane Captain smiled like that, on purpose or with an involuntary spasm of his muscles, Sarrett fully understood why some people dared to give him such a nickname.

"That, officer, is why you are worth a damn. You don't bathe in the free will your title gives you. You step beyond that and look to the future. It shows you are one to think of the long-term, not just the current personal benefits."

"My family has always been worthy of Loyal status," Sarrett dared to input. He shoved his doubts on the validity of the Blood Goddess' threat aside, focusing on what mattered most to him. "I think of hard-working Sarretts like my parents, deserving to be rewarded for their obedience to our Lord, and I think of my sons who will continue such honored service."

"That would require you to have children for your legacy," Caldrell snorted. His tongue ran slowly along his upper teeth, and Sarrett averted his gaze. How, in the Lord's name, was he supposed to find a woman and start a family if every second of his mental and physical strength was focused on advancing his place in the military?

There had to be some appeal, though, if he could find a free night. After all, who became an officer after four years? *That achievement alone was unheard of. He'd seen ambition draw women to other men in the ranks. Surely that could work for him, too.*

He hated the way his Captain seemed to know his every thought, every step in his plan to mean something in this world. It gave him the idea that, somehow, he was like the volatile, violent man beside him, and that truly frightened him more than everything else.

Now that is actually the truth, *he thought.*

Not two months later, when the weather started to cool into the serene, mild season that passed as winter in southern Rhethos, Sarrett dared to take a night off. With a group of his fellow officers, they drank for free at the nicest tavern, earning cheers from the staff, respectful nods from the tradesmen, and daring smiles from some of the women.

"Did you hear about the unit sent north last week?"

Sarrett could hardly hear the words of the man next to him. The hours had gone by, and the noise level, drinks, and dances had all escalated beyond count. His tolerance for the local wine was higher than the officers around him, but even Sarrett noticed his head starting to spin.

"What unit?" he asked, decidedly setting down his glass.

"Exactly!" exclaimed the officer in return, pointing his glass at Sarrett and spilling a bit on the table. "A hundred men and Master Fentrell marched out in the middle of the night. All I know is they headed north."

"He's not the only one," replied a man across the table from Sarrett. He

folded his arms over his chest, looking around as he spoke, as if, despite the roar of revelry, someone might hear him. "There have been special groups, hand-selected by the Captain for discreet missions. Heard the tasks come from The Bradford himself."

"To do what?" Sarrett prompted. He knew these men, but they had been officers much longer than him. They were all at least five years his senior, but, he assumed, now trusted him enough to invite him out this evening.

The first man shrugged, then buried his face in his drink again. The second, however, leaned both forearms on the table. It brought his officer's jacket close to one of the wine spills, and Sarrett grimaced. "They're looking for weapons," the man said. "To use against the Goddess and her people."

"Weapons? Against a Goddess?" repeated the first officer loudly, earning eye rolls from not just Sarrett. "How's that even possible?"

"Clearly you're not 'discreet' enough to lead a unit and find out," Sarrett snapped. The first man glared, while the others at the table laughed appreciatively.

"There's nothing discreet about you, either, Sarrett. Everyone knows you're Caldrell's personal lackey."

Sarrett tightened his jaw, holding back several retorts. He let a brief smile touch his lips; it was better, in situations like this, to let people think what they wanted.

He cleared his throat, studying the women who weren't currently dancing with anyone. There was one, with midnight-black hair, he'd spoken with earlier that he wanted to find again. Mayra was her name, he thought.

The other officers at the table continued to talk, the conversation drunkenly moving in other directions away from Master Fentrell's departure. Sarrett only partially listened, absently touching his wine glass stem as he scanned the room.

His interest was piqued by these "discreet assignments." Though he'd barely earned his officer's status, he was already wondering what it would take to keep moving up. He expected to spend at least another four years, working tirelessly, to even begin being considered for lieutenant. But something like this could cut at least a year off of his advancement if he could be trusted with whatever the task was.

Not a week later, he put in a request for a change. As the rumors suggested, he merely wrote "new opportunities" on the official slip of parchment.

Almost immediately, he received word back that his request was denied. When he dared mention it to Caldrell, Sarrett was only rewarded with maniacal, condescending laughter followed by harsh drills in the rain.

Despite the disappointment and embarrassment, Sarrett learned two things: there was, indeed, something secret going on in the ranks above him, and he had to work much harder to get there.

He believed his soul-sacrificing work would pay off. Instead, as soon as he asked for something, like the commonfolk never dared to do, he was tossed aside like a used scrap of paper. He did his best to perpetuate the "threat" of the Goddess and spread that fear to keep people in line despite his doubts. But now, he was slowly discovering that Cybarys was a propaganda tool for The Bradford.

The worst part was that he believed that a man like Caldrell could help make him famous and respectable, and fill the hole Lily's death left in his heart. Instead, his Captain used him as a toy to make him laugh and dismissed him the moment he dared rise higher.

So many lies he'd buried under grief and denial at the time, now placed together in order for the first time without Sahma wine to help keep them down. . .

Sarrett brought himself back to his cell in Lorington's dungeons. Over the last few days, he'd noticed new prisoners being added to the nearby cells, most of them men accused of assaulting local women. Sarrett grimaced as more and more Rhethosian folk were punished, screaming threats and indignations against the rebels who dared shut away those with Loyal family status.

At least the shaking in Sarrett's hands started to lessen as time went by. Every time he ate or drank, less of it ended up on his bloodstained tunic. Though several of the rebel soldiers had taken to taunting and mocking him from the shadows, Sarrett was getting better at ignoring them.

His mind felt like it was coming out into the sun for the first time. The mental image of daylight was one he constantly conjured, as if he could forget what real warmth could bring. It burned at times, but every memory he'd drowned in Sahma wine was unstoppable. It hurt more to hold them back in his new sober state, so he let them wash over him.

He shifted on the cold floor, then stood, forcing his muscles to move in circles. As an officer, he'd heard rumors about discreet missions to look for weapons that could be used against Armelle. Of course, the pacifistic kingdom had never tried to invade and probably never would. He saw that now, but if The Bradford was looking for ways to attack, and his notes mentioned "digging" up north, there could be something hidden in Lorington.

Now, he thought, *how can I get out of here and find it for Caldrell before Will and his men figure out what they're camped on top of?*

Surely that would win him back the respect he deserved. Delivering a mysterious weapon that could harm Armelle's Goddess? Mayra would run back to him with open arms, his lieutenant's status would be restored, and Lorington would sing his praises.

CHAPTER NINETEEN

THE PAIN OF DAYLIT TRUTH

Devaki didn't wait for her father's escort to Towne Centre. She was still frustrated with him, even though they'd had an open, honest conversation for the first time face to face. There was still so much to share, but as her heart was opening, he'd cut her off and blocked her out.

So, she sought out Sutton as soon as he finished his overnight duty at the gates leading into the barracks. Devaki saw a grin spread across his face underneath the surprise in his pale green eyes. All hints of tiredness from being awake all night disappeared in a blink.

"Miss Tarran!" he said, stepping into the shadows that graced the west side of the stone buildings that time of morning. Devaki looked at him from under the cover of her cloak's hood. "Where are you headed today?"

Vaguely, she explained the need to go to Lorington's castle and find the Towne Master's private libraries. Sprinkling in some pieces about orders from Will and the Fate's Strings of the Goddess, she had a feeling it would be enough to have someone she trusted keep her safe. It was.

Devaki's feet shuffled to a slower pace as they walked, steadily upward, toward the looming turrets. There was something different and yet also familiar about what she was feeling. The last time she'd been on these streets she had been running for her life. Was it possible that now, she felt something similar to her old home?

In Valsara, no matter how awfully she was treated, the air was always full of peace. Tension didn't string like tangible death traps between buildings and guardsmen didn't threaten passersby no matter what color they wore. She even saw some families hanging rebel violet cloths in their windows.

Was she really feeling such a shift toward those things now, in Lorington? Whatever her father was doing must be working if such a change was possible in Rhethos, where people were only supposed to be capable of violence, not creating spaces of safety. Inwardly, she marveled at the harmony she felt around her.

Sutton spoke with the rebels stationed at Towne Centre's entrance with Devaki not able to see much under the cover of her hood. She caught a glimpse of the rebels staring at the Blessing Rune cut into Sutton's armor, but then they muttered instructions to her young rebel friend, and they entered the castle without further issue.

"That seemed too easy," Devaki commented as they ascended one of the side staircases in the main hall. Drafts of the morning's wintery breeze blew through the stones against the folds of her cloak.

"I told them that I was on important business for Master Irvin," Sutton explained. He touched the curve of the staircase's wall and looked back at her as she opened her mouth. "I might be young, Miss Tarran, but I'm not stupid. I know that if you are bending a rule or two, like we did the other night at the dungeons, you use Irvin's name, not Will's."

Devaki thought on that as they continued to climb. From each level of the castle they passed, she briefly heard muffled laughter, accompanied by the warm smells of fresh bread and cut herbs and cinnamon. Despite the end-of-year chill, it made the granite walls feel pleasant.

She decidedly threw off her hood to let her hair spring free. Even though passing servants and rebel soldiers alike stared at her as they continued upward, Devaki refused to look down at her feet like she used to do in Valsara. One way or another, Will's people would learn about her, who she was, and what she stood for.

The libraries weren't hidden, she discovered, as they reached a wide set of double doors in a long hallway. She assumed that "private" only meant no one could enter except the Moores, and Lorington's people were under such fearful control that no one ever dared come here. The consequences, Devaki imagined, for defying the rules of one of The Bradford's servants, were severe.

But she was itching with excitement. Devaki loved books and was fascinated by what she could potentially find in a foreign place like this. Both Gardain Moore and his brother had mentioned that, for some reason, this Rhethosian city had old Armellan history books. Whatever was in them, she knew the Goddess was leading her to it so she could find out what Cybarys had to do with these people . . . in the past and the present.

Sutton worked one of the doors open for her, and she was greeted by a huge, circular room at the top of one of the castle's eastern turrets. The vaulted ceiling rose above her, coming to a point at its center, with innumerable rows of books ranging up twenty feet high. Everything, however, from the shelves to the surrounding furniture, was draped in thick white cloth.

Sutton whistled appreciatively beside her, then stepped inside and toward the large fireplace to their left. Devaki slowly walked in between the shelves and peeked underneath the coverings that appeared to be in place to ward off dust. It seemed like no one had cared to use this room in a long time.

With some effort, she pulled back one dusty sheet to unveil a large Rhethosian Blue chair. Now that it was visible, the fabric invited her to curl into its cushions so she could lose herself in the words of the past, if she could find them.

All of this knowledge, she thought, amazement and bewilderment running through her. *Just sitting here . . . what would the people of this towne do with what they could learn in these books, I wonder?*

The rough sound of wood being thrown in the fireplace caught her attention, and soon a warm glow echoed toward where she stood in between shelves. "Miss Tarran," Sutton called, and she found him dusting off his hands next to the growing heat. "Can you tell me what you're up to, or is it another of the Goddess' secrets?"

Devaki smiled and clasped her hands behind her back. "I'm going to read, of course," she told him confidently, not offering him more details.

He smirked back. "Right. Well, if it's all the same to you, I'd like to stay. This castle is still full of people who lived with and worked for Master Moore, and I don't trust many of them yet. Especially if they saw someone like you up here alone."

Devaki honestly hadn't thought about that. This was *her* lead that she'd heard Gardain Moore mention, and she wanted to seek out the books about Armelle's history here by herself, without Will's "help."

"You've been up all night, though," Devaki said. "Aren't you tired?"

Sutton shrugged, the movement camouflaged by the plate of his armor. "They put anyone my age on those duties on purpose. Say we can handle it. For you, I'll be fine."

Devaki blinked, not expecting that last part. "I'm going to gather some books, then," she said, and Sutton gave her a nod before positioning himself by the doors. She smiled again as the young man straightened his shoulders and put his hands behind his back, one of them close to the dagger on the side of his belt. She doubted the seriousness was needed, but she knew it made the rebel feel better.

As she worked her way to the back curve of the room, Devaki noticed that there were certain places the coverings were disturbed. Though the library had clearly been shut up for a while, there were cleaner spots on the dusted floor and drapes that had been pushed halfway back to reveal rows of books.

Devaki looked more closely, the crackle of the fire sparking distantly in her ears. Each time she examined a shelf that had been touched, she found gaps in the lines of books. Holes of black space stared back at her, clearly gathered by someone for the significance of whatever those pages held. Frustration mounted in her as she glanced through the surroundings books and found nothing intriguing.

Cutting a Guidance Rune on her wrist didn't help, either; the entire room glowed with red, magical heat, but it seemed that what the Goddess wanted her to find here were only empty spaces now. *Adlar said Gardain spent plenty of time here,* she thought, pacing back over to the warmth of the fireplace. *Would he really have hidden what could tell me more about that digsite?*

After a couple hours of searching high and low, Devaki was ready to give up. When she glanced over at Sutton, she saw that the young man had slumped down by the entrance with his eyes closed. She was glad he was resting. Why he felt the need to give up sleep for her was something she didn't understand.

Devaki sighed and settled, frustrated, on the east-facing window's ledge after grabbing a blanket warmed by the fireplace. *Where could those books be?* she thought. Worry filled her when she imagined that, somehow, Gardain's father had gotten a hold of them and burned them for the secrets they held.

Despair tried to take over next, but she refused to be brought down by the unknown. *Cybarys,* she prayed, *you brought me here. What am I supposed to do?* Mere heartbeats later, she was drawn to the unfamiliar weight in her pocket.

In the quiet space around her, Devaki came to a new conclusion: maybe the book she should read wasn't from this library.

With her search now at a dead end, she brought out Will's journal. The small bundle of pages was discolored and water-stained at the edges, smelling of leather and oil and years of use. Taking a deep breath, she cleared her head and said another small prayer as she opened the cover. In relatively new, deep black ink was a note addressed to her.

Valsara captured my heart. Its princess set it free. My brother cut it in two.

Devaki, this is a story of my truth, one so painful that it has never seen daylight before and never been spoken aloud. You are the first to have this heartache in its entirety, most of it written not long after such events took place. For that, I am sorry.

Please know that you deserve much more, and that I have dedicated my life to fighting for a better future for you. Do not let the past hurt you more than it must. Take it, learn from it, and grow from it. These pages contain the pieces of my heart. Do with them what you will.

Caulin

Devaki stared at that name for a moment, realizing that few people, if anyone, knew the *real* name of Rhethos' rebel leader. Then she slowly read about the life of a young Rhethosian second son. She saw neglect, abuse, and heartache that no one that age should have to suffer. And then, on top of it all, immeasurable, sudden loss.

Unbeknownst to her, burning tears rolled down her cheeks, unaware that she could hold such kinship with her father. Had they both been through so much while so young? Decidedly, she shut her eyes and skipped ahead. She already felt lost and alone herself in Lorington. Her thumb stopped on a random entry, and she shifted the blanket in her lap before continuing to absorb her father's older, faded handwriting.

Valsara Temple, age fifteen

Before the Night of Blasphemy, as they call it now, the royal family often came and went from the temple during the week. That was how Isaka and I were able to get to know each other and begin to love each other. We were drawn together out of loneliness, I suppose, her because all attention was on her older sibling, Railen, the queen, and me because of my Rhethosian skin.

Isaka would pray to Cybarys, each time taking a fresh roll of Sahma leaves I'd made from the basket at the temple doors. I'd watch her pray, kneeling on the black marble, calmly enough that no one around her noticed her slip a note into the bundle of leaves. She always wore her dark hair in tight, rope-like braids, woven with gold threads and silk ribbons. They fell in her face when she bowed before Cybarys' giant statue, obscuring her hands.

It became a routine for us, me picking up the Sahma bundle she left behind as I cleaned the smudges off the mirror-like floor, and her slipping into one of the alcoves off the main worship room. I wouldn't read her note right away; that was meant for the time when we couldn't see each other face to face. I always had a note wrapped in leaves for her to take back to the Silk Palace. We sat hidden, holding hands, talking about . . . anything and everything.

I don't think you've experienced anything like this yet, Devaki, but I hope one day you will. When you meet someone who connects to your soul, you find merely being together is enough. Everything comes easily; hours go by, full of meaningful conversation about one another and mindless rattling that in any other circumstance would be mundane. All of her concerns, all of my pain, were suspended in those hidden corners where we laughed and held each other and kissed.

In our naïve teenage minds, we were safe from all harm.

Remember, Brother Danvir and the other monks showed me the love found in the Goddess' words. Even though I was confined to the temple almost constantly because of my skin, I always felt the acceptance of everyone who lived in that beautiful building. With Isaka, I began to dream that I could heal from what had happened to my parents. What still hurt the most was my brother's rejection.

Mic hated the trusting complacency of the monks and hated even more how much the Valsarans adored the royal family. When he'd gone to his private lessons in Clancy years ago, they'd cemented that The Bradford was the only one worthy of our devotion, and where Mic and I were forced to live now was against everything in his being.

Somehow, he was able to escape from the temple, but I did not know where he went or with whom. All I knew was that when he came back from his secret expeditions was the only time I saw him smile. It wasn't lost on me that when he was happiest was when I wasn't around.

Because I never knew when to expect him, it was a shock to both Isaka and me when he showed up by our hiding spot one afternoon. What was even more of a shock was who he was with: Sehran Tarran. Before they spotted us, I saw the two young men arguing quietly. My brother and I had few interactions with the royal family, but I knew Mic hated them, even the many cousins like Sehran, who seemed kind enough.

Isaka froze when she heard their voices, her hands still in mine. She had been tracing Armellan runes on my skin to teach me more of the complicated symbols in her language, but in truth, I had just liked the way her fingertips felt on me. Her fear was well-justified because there was nowhere for us to escape from the dead-end alcove. We never really thought those things through.

"What are you doing with the Rhethosian boy?" Sehran had demanded as soon as he saw Isaka.

I remember her standing and facing her cousin, who was quite taller than her. "What are you doing with the other Rhethosian boy?" she returned.

Mic glared at the princess while Sehran brushed off a few excuses as to how it was no one's business what he did with his time, unlike her. She was of elite royal blood and couldn't be seen with someone as low as the temple monk's charity case.

But my brother's judgmental gaze focused on me as Sehran lectured your mother, and I felt his disappointment and distaste as much as I had ever felt from Father. There weren't any lies I could tell him that he would believe:

My brother was trained differently at a young age to see through any weakness, and that's what he saw me as (and our mother, when she lived): weak, stupid people who needed stronger, smarter men like him to keep us safe from our own mistakes.

"Oh, just go," Isaka was arguing with Sehran while my brother silently pulled all our secrets from my eyes. "I do not need your opinion on my safety, cousin. I'm fine where I am."

"Clearly you need an escort back to the Palace, where you'll find more suitable company." Sehran's words were polite, yet a fine political threat edged into his tone, very well-versed for someone only in his early twenties.

"For once we agree," Mic said, his voice a low rumble. His dark eyes were still on me, though he nodded in Sehran's direction. That alone nearly floored me. Though I didn't know it at the time, the two of them argued often and spent a lot of time together, making his chastisement of my meetings with Isaka entirely hypocritical.

"How long have you been doing this, Caulin?" Mic asked next.

I honestly didn't know how to answer, and when I glanced at Isaka, who stood very close with her shoulder pressed to mine, I didn't care. It must have only been weeks, maybe a couple of months, but it felt like the only time I'd really been alive. Counting those moments when we were alone was never a priority for either of us.

"Your father," Sehran urged next, "my uncle, would be furious if he saw where you are, let alone whatever you two have been doing." He barely glanced at me, like I was a dirty, stray mutt that didn't deserve his full attention. Then he straightened the collar of his silk tunic and gave the princess a sympathetic look. "But don't worry: I won't tell our Temple Leader a thing. . .if you come with me now."

He held out a hand, covered in the fine gold and jewels that all the royal family members wore, his brown palm out toward Isaka. "Walk back with me, with the rest of our cousins out in the worship room, and this will be forgotten. I promise."

As much as I objected to the idea, I knew he was right. And that she didn't have a choice. Mic was nodding, crossing his arms over his chest from where he stood opposite me. Sehran, from the little I'd seen him at that age, was a smart young man. He knew that Isaka was strong, defiant, and would not simply listen to his orders. Instead, he politely threatened her with going to her father, who would have no problem making sure I would never see her again.

"It's not fair," I spoke up. "You get to talk with him, but I can't talk to her?"

Mic unfolded one of his arms to backhand me. It was a simple, powerful move that our father had used on both of us countless times, more so with me. Second sons did not question or object to commands from their elders. Normally, I obeyed everything my big brother said, but when it came to her, I had a hard time staying silent.

It was complicated. My brother, who despised me and whom I still loved with desperation, was telling me to stay away from the one person who felt like vital air in my lungs. Couldn't he see we weren't doing anything wrong? At least not yet.

Isaka caught my eye. I touched my split lip, about to open my dumb mouth again to tell her to go; I cared about her, maybe was already hopelessly in love with her, but I couldn't see her shamed or hurt. She, however, was already on her own course, willingly following her Fate's String. She wouldn't let Sehran or anyone else tell her to go against her heart. I admired that about her so much.

Isaka sighed, then squeezed my hand. With her chin held high, she pushed past Mic and put her fingers on Sehran's arm instead, who guided her out into the main worship hall. The second they disappeared, my brother rounded on me.

"Have you lost your mind?" he questioned, mouth tight with disapproval. The scar across the left side of his forehead, the biggest wound he'd gained the night our parents died, bunched into ugly folds of skin when he was mad. He launched into another of his usual speeches: we were alone here, prisoners in a foreign land, and we had to stick together. They were the enemy that he was working to find a path away from, so we could go "home" to Rhethos.

"Promise me you'll never see that girl again."

"I'm sorry," I insisted, especially when he raised his fist at me this time. "I promise." I knew it was a lie, yet somehow Mic didn't catch that one as it was coated enough in my fear of him to be believable.

"What's the only thing that matters?" he demanded.

"Us. Our family."

He didn't seem entirely satisfied that day, however, nor any day after that until he died. If I had listened to him, Devaki, things would have been so different. I don't regret a moment of my time in Armelle, despite what happened. Your Goddess would call it our destiny. And, even though I hate the concept, your mother always embraced any challenge in life with dignity and a youthful brilliance that shone clearly.

She followed her heart, to a fault. I try to do the same every day, though often I fail, too. Please let these words be an example to you, so you may succeed instead.

Devaki sat back, numbly feeling her shoulder blades hit the stone window casing. She found her throat dry as she tried to swallow, a physical show of the mental digesting she was in the middle of conquering. Her entire life, her mother had only been mentioned in harsh whispers. She was a warning of promiscuous, blasphemous behavior that Devaki was the painful result of.

No one had ever told her what Isaka sounded like, what her body language was, or how she felt about life. It was like the statue of her Mother deity whom she loved, wrought in cold stone, had finally come to life and embraced her with real, warm arms. Her mother, the woman who gave birth to her, had dreams and fell in love and broke rules . . . all things that resonated with Devaki at a deep, guttural level.

She followed her heart, Will said, Devaki thought and found stinging tears forming in her eyes. *And she died for it. For me.*

On top of that, hearing about her Temple Leader, the man who'd unexpect-edly taken control of the kingdom after the murders of her aunt, uncle, and mother, was equally as jarring. Apparently, according to Will's recollections, Sehran had often been at odds with Will's older brother, but one thing they'd agreed on was the fact that Will and Isaka should never see each other again.

"Miss Tarran," Sutton said, and Devaki glanced up to see the young rebel was awake now. He stared at her with concern, and she realized her face was stained with tears. "What's wrong?"

He sat next to her on the window's edge, and Devaki decidedly shut her father's journal. There was a dizzying mix of emotions running through her, a combination of long-felt sorrow and growing tenacity. Confusion rose stron-gest when she felt Sutton take her hand in both of his. She felt the rough calluses of his soldier's skin, but his touch was soft and comforting.

"I'm fine," Devaki said, and pulled her fingers out of his grasp. "I didn't learn what I thought I would today, but I learned plenty."

CHAPTER TWENTY

CARRY YOUR TORCHES

ngelyn stared down at the beautiful dress that Marselle had delivered her an hour ago. The sun was down and there was a rebel escort waiting for her, but she felt . . . naked. As she carefully touched the fine fabric before her, she did her best to keep straight everything Will had announced that morning.

He and Irvin were hosting a celebration, publicly announcing Moore's "official cooperation" with the rebel cause. Though the Towne Master and his family all agreed to attend, no surrender had been given yet. Will hoped that, for Jeras Moore himself to see the progress made across all four districts of the city was a necessary push forward with the little time they had remaining.

After dropping off the dress, Marselle had informed her that her spies would be playing a large role that evening, plying the truth out of revelers about the digsite, while at the same time Will intended to make good on a promise he'd made to Gardain Moore about meeting the rebels' Goddess Touched "soldier." Apparently that young man held information about the towne's history that couldn't be found elsewhere.

It's a good plan, Angelyn thought, especially after the increasing amounts of progress she'd been receiving from Remora. But after Angelyn handed off a letter to Josh to a messenger headed up to The Forts (who mentioned all was well, according to the latest reports), she still had a hard time putting on the gown in front of her.

Her entire life, she'd worn practical, homemade dresses that were stained and patched. She did not want to stand out; plain and hidden meant staying alive. Though the dress she was wearing tonight wasn't by any means extravagant, to her, it was a luxurious gown.

Lightweight silver fabric flowed from a square neckline to a tight band at her waist. Drifts of different shades of gray wilted down to her feet in flattering waves, each one complementing her pale skin and blonde hair. She refused the jewelry Marselle tempted her with, but her friend had insisted that the white fur cloak she wore was clasped at her throat with a brilliant brooch made of tiny white gems.

Her hand went to Will's amethyst a bit lower on her neck, under the hollow of her throat. This evening was about unity and progress, not just distraction and politics. And, if all went well, Marselle's spies would learn the truth about Lorington's digsite.

Angelyn took a deep breath and left the barracks. Several rebels led her straight north into the heart of the city, and as they walked, bright lights, warm conversation, and sweet smells rolled toward her. It was odd to see the cold Rhethosian Blue awnings that lined the streets accompanied with such welcoming sensations.

When they rounded the next corner, her breath was suddenly taken away. "Just a moment," she murmured, and she put a hand against the nearest building. The escorts kept a respectable distance.

She had to take a second to marvel at the way the streets were lit around her. With Lorington's high walls, every bit of the stone-clad city was rarely warmed by the sun. But Will had outdone himself, both with the innumerable torches placed around the streets and the location he'd chosen.

The area was nearly the exact center of towne, containing a bit of each district. Despite the tight-knit walkways between buildings and the lack of any expansive, open courtyard that could be found elsewhere, this place was now the most logical location: each district had a reason to share in the joy of what the rebels had created since taking the city.

Spies of Marselle's, Remora's women, and armed rebel soldiers all spread the word that Master Moore had "agreed" to peacefully support the rebel cause tonight. Musicians played, children ran under every streetside awning, and couples dressed in bright colors danced down the cobbled roads. Angelyn spotted a few boys Joshua's age and her heart ached. She made a note to write to him next about how he could be free in this city now, too, if he chose.

Never in her life had Angelyn seen children run care-free through the streets, women laugh next to men in uniforms, and Loyals congregate in the same space with those who worked for them. She did notice that the latter were the least in attendance; those who enjoyed the benefits of The Bradford's heavy taxes and slave-like laws were either not present or stood disdainfully to the side. The rebel soldiers kept an eye on these particular folk.

Overall, though, it was a serene evening showcasing all she'd ever dreamed of as a child, the elegant dress she wore being the least of it all. Leaning against the building next to her, Angelyn sighed happily and then breathed in the moment again.

"Miss McKinlee, the last thing you should do is hide over here on your own."

Angelyn looked to her right and saw Will walking toward her. She opened her mouth to reply, but she stopped when she noticed his appearance. His hair was combed and tied back, and he wore an embroidered black tunic and open leather vest. The evening's chill didn't seem to bother him at all. None of his usual weapons were visibly present and the lack of any steel except the shine of his smile sent a chill down her spine.

"You look . . . different," she managed.

Will rolled his eyes, then sidestepped as a group of a dozen children skidded past him, squeaking with joy. In a quick flash, Angelyn remembered the night after she'd met him, when she'd seen him give up his only bodyguards to help two children orphaned by Sarrett's officers.

When he reached her, Will offered his arm. "Let me show you something," he said, and he pulled her forward to join the throng of grinning revelers. "Look, over there. Even Irvin is smiling. . .and I think, no, I'm sure, that's a real grin. Not long ago I would have agreed with his initial solutions to our challenges. But look at him now."

Will walked up to a woman who stood behind a cart, lighting candles tied with violet ribbons. She handed each of them one, and when Will led on, he lowered his voice. "It would've been much simpler to kill Moore and his leaders, and force the people into our cause. We might've had the offensive upper hand instead against Caldrell. But would you look at all this?"

Angelyn nodded, knowing what he meant. "Worth the effort?"

"Only because you showed me that this could be more than a dream." Will's tone became softer, and Angelyn glanced at him as they crossed another street. "You told me, in Kaylyn, that you didn't want your son around me because my cause was an excuse to be as violent as Sarrett. My means didn't justify the ends if all the people saw was bloodshed, and all they gained was more fear."

"Well, no one is afraid here tonight, except maybe Moore." According to what Marselle had said, the Towne Master and his family should arrive soon, free of their bonds and ready to join the celebration of their own accord.

Will smiled, and Angelyn loved how the genuine expression lit up his green eyes. "He'll fall in line. Adlar won't be far behind his father, and I have a feeling Gardain and his mother will be easy." He stopped on the next corner and took her candle from her hands. When a group moved around them, he gave them both candles with a nod.

"Thank you, Angelyn," he said, catching her eye, "for letting me see I could create something like this."

Angelyn shook her head, unable to take his direct praise. "I don't know how I ended up here. I. . .I admit, I never thought I could help this many people. It feels so—"

He grabbed both sides of her face and brought her lips to his. His kiss was firm, insistent, and Angelyn put her hands up to hold his wrists. The torches around them seemed to burn more brightly, making her fully aware of how many people could see them together. Still, she kissed him back, and her only thought was, *So this is what it feels like to be free.*

"When the last torch goes out tonight," Will whispered, his mouth brushing against hers as he spoke, "come with me. I—"

"Master Will."

Angelyn recognized Rowlann's voice. Will shut his eyes and grimaced, then turned, smoothly placing her hand back on his arm. The rebel Master had to be one of the few still bearing a serious face, in his full armor and weapons.

"Master Torald and some of the other tradesmen would like to speak with you," Rowlann said. "Miss McKinlee as well, I'm sure."

Angelyn glanced over to where she saw Lorington's Trade Master, standing under a lit awning and conversing quite animatedly with the men and women around him. Torald had, once his family's safety was secured, become a huge ally to the rebel cause. The star of that corner, however, was clearly Marselle, who, never to be outdone, had dressed herself more elegantly than the northern district's richest women.

"It seems, with the Lady Marselle entertaining the Trade Master, we aren't much needed," Angelyn commented, watching as Marselle laughed wholeheartedly at what Torald was saying. She'd chosen an iridescent gown of deep purple that bordered on black. Yet the artfully gathered layers of heavy fabric captured the light of every torch and candle, taming it into rainbows that hugged the curves of her corset as if she willed them to. Bright gems sparkled down her neckline into her cleavage, her red curls flowing with her laughter.

"For now, yes," Rowlann confirmed, not much emotion in his voice. He didn't seem to be anywhere near as enamored with the former southern Rhethosian lady as everyone else. "But Irvin is bringing Moore over soon."

Will nodded. "Thank you."

As they walked, Angelyn found that groups of people stopped them. Everyone, covered in violet and bearing appreciative smiles, wanted to speak with her and Will. Women from the northern district touched the sleeve of her silver dress and asked about where it was made.

Girls from Remora's area of towne begged to know how she gotten from The Hamond to the co-leader of the kingdom's rebellion. Angelyn noticed a few of them muttering about how she'd openly kissed Will moments ago, as if *that* was how she'd gotten to her current position. Before she could think of correcting them, a few of Remora's closest friends Angelyn had been working with set about putting those rumors to rest.

Rebel soldiers, both young and old, moved alongside them, inquiring how they could better assist those in towne who kept mentioning her name. Angelyn did her best to reply to everyone, though Will spoke whenever she became overwhelmed. They'd barely made it halfway to the corner where Torald and Marselle stood when she noticed Irvin reach the group, the Moores not far behind him.

Irvin did not need more than his usual bright display of rebel violet to gather attention; his personality demanded a space all on its own. He moved his long, thin limbs almost like a dancer, bathing in the spotlight as if the torches were the midday sun.

Angelyn watched as Irvin sidestepped toward Marselle, holding back the tip of his elegant Towne Master's sword. Even from a distance, with the crowds all around them, Angelyn swore she saw Irvin's hand brush across the small of Marselle's back. It was fast, hardly noticeable, but that touch was . . .intimate, possessive, almost.

"Brother!" Irvin exclaimed, gesturing widely toward Will and Angelyn. Several of Torald's trade masters had to step back out of his reach or risk being slapped. "We were talking about how so much incredible change has happened, in such a short time. All thanks to you."

"Yes," Torald agreed with a nod, and Marselle gave him a sweet smile. "Working with your northern Towne Masters has brought a whole line of trade back to us." His eyes drifted to Marselle, but then focused on Jeras Moore and his sons. Seeing the Towne Master out in public put a nervous expression on his face.

"Having Lorington fly violet banners will make all the difference," Will said. He knew the benefits Irvin had showcased so far to these men. Angelyn's grip tightened on his arm, and he looked over at the Moores.

"Impressive," Jeras muttered. His old gray eyes scanned the crowds, then the lights above, as if mulling over the plethora of violet flowers, ribbons, and gleeful gatherings from each corner of his city. Angelyn had no doubt that, on their walk over here with Irvin, Moore had heard many celebrating his "peaceful surrender" to the rebel cause.

Moore's wife, Angelyn saw, was beaming uncontrollably. She even thought she saw a sheen of tears in the older woman's eyes as she took in the display of unity amongst Lorington's people. Though her husband and eldest son stood coldly amongst the flickering lights, Angelyn clearly observed pride in Moore's wife's eyes. She, at least, was genuinely impressed.

"I'm going to make a speech before the night is over," Will said when Moore didn't elaborate on his one-word statement. "Your cooperation and announcement of your fighters joining the rebel's ranks would be well-received."

"I am sure," Jeras said shortly. His wife glanced at him, and Angelyn saw a silent pleading in her gaze. What was he holding out for? Angelyn knew this was the key that Will needed more than anything. When she looked over at Will, he bore an easy smile.

"The evening has just started, Master Moore. You can take your time deciding." Will's attention turned to Gardain, who stood with his arms clasped behind his back, straining his thin neck to look up at the torchlit buildings and walls. He couldn't seem to care less about the tension between his father and the rebels.

"I do have something to speak to your younger son about," Will added, and Gardain snapped his gaze to Will, eyes wide. Then bemusement touched his lips. Will nodded toward Rowlann, who stood to the side, waiting.

"Gardain, darling, you should stay with us," Moore's wife spoke up, reaching out toward her son.

"He'll be perfectly safe," Will assured her, and Angelyn echoed the sentiment even as Adlar Moore snorted.

Gardain straightened the sleeves of his pale green tunic and gave his mother a small nod. "Lead on, Master Will."

Angelyn caught a raised eyebrow from Marselle as she and Will stepped away from the group. Irvin smoothly picked up the conversation right where they'd left off, and Angelyn heard Marselle chime in as they strode down one of the side streets, Rowlann at their backs.

Gardain walked on Will's opposite side, an excited smile on his face. "I didn't think you were going to follow through, Master Will," he began. "We had just met, after all, and I assumed the only promise I could count on from you was a noose."

"Yet here we are," Will said simply. The further they walked, the fewer torches surrounded them, and Angelyn watched as shadows crept up the sides of Will's face. She knew he was worried about introducing this young man to Devaki. There was a stiffness in his arm that she hadn't felt until now. "But you must know that something has changed since the last time we spoke."

"You certainly have more of an upper hand, yes," Gardain said, as if this were obvious. He nodded, the curls of his hair moving with the evening breeze. "Let me guess? You aren't merely going to let me meet this Goddess Touched person, even if I wear rebel violet in front of everyone."

Angelyn halted when Will stopped their progress. He gave Gardain a smirk, then inclined his head. "Correct. I want to know everything about the ruins in that digsite. I will help and protect your people, but you won't see Devaki until I have your word that you'll share everything you know."

"It's a girl, then? Beautiful name," Gardain said, his round eyes lighting up. "I see. Yes, yes. Of course I'll share. In fact . . ." He paused and reached toward one of the satchels on his belt. Rowlann stepped forward, hand on his weapon, but Will shook his head.

"I'll do better because I am truly impressed with what you've done in Lorington in such a short time," Gardain said with a grin. He pulled out a tiny key, made of gold and inlaid with several miniscule rubies. "This matches a chest in my father's private library, one where I've put the oldest and most relevant history books. I'll hand it over once I meet this Devaki."

Angelyn caught Will's eye and saw from his expression he wasn't expecting this, either. Both of them knew Devaki had been in Moore's library for days, reading every book she could find, but she wasn't having much success discovering "forbidden" subjects. This was the piece they needed.

"Devaki," Will said over his shoulder. "I'd like you to meet someone."

The door of the building behind them opened, and the Armellan girl stepped out onto the street. Gardain looked genuinely stunned. His right hand worked nervously at the back of his neck, rumpling the ashy blond hair under his ears.

"You . . ." he began, then laughed unevenly. "You are beautiful!"

Angelyn smiled even as Will's fingers dug into her arm. Gardain seemed to catch the sudden tension in the air, then put up both of his hands innocently.

"Oh, I didn't mean t-to . . ." he stuttered, overwhelmed by both Will's and Rowlann's glares. "I just meant that . . . your skin . . . your hair, it's so . . . I sound quite stupid, don't I?"

Devaki, Angelyn was pleased to see, wasn't fazed by the young Rhethosian man gawking at her. She crossed her arms over her chest and gave him a genuine smile. "I wouldn't use the word 'stupid.' I'm Devaki. It's nice to meet you, Gardain Moore. From what I've been told, we can help each other." She held out a hand, her elbow stiff.

"No, no, no . . ." Gardain insisted and took a step back. "That won't do." He slowly worked his fingers together into a gesture that Angelyn assumed meant a formal greeting across the sea. Turning his palms outward, he placed his laced fingers against his forehead and bowed deeply. "The pleasure is all mine."

Devaki blinked, clearly taken aback. Angelyn thought she saw a touch of blush rise on the Armellan girl's cheeks when she returned the gesture.

"This is quite the honor," Gardain continued, "but I have to ask . . . can you show me your magic? I must see it. Something small, a little offering to Cybarys—"

"No," Will cut in firmly. "Everyone here will be terrified of a single spark of Bloodgems."

Devaki, however, was already turning the sharp ring on her hand toward a Guidance Rune on her forearm. Will moved to step toward her, but Angelyn held him back. If they wanted the information Gardain had and his support for their cause, he deserved to see what clearly meant the world to him.

"Dear Mother," Devaki murmured, her eyes closing, "guide us with your light and love. Bring us peace, on both sides of the sea."

When she broke her skin, dry heat engulfed the cobblestones. Sprinkles of red gems hit the earth, but as Devaki continued to murmur her prayer, the magic remnants around her began to vibrate. They gathered into a pile at her feet. Blood dripped down to her elbow, and when she gestured with her hands, the solidified red lights rose into the air.

Gardain's jaw fell slack as the magic remnants swirled toward him, traveled once in a circle around his body, then rained down into his outstretched hands. They tinkled against the gold key he still held, some falling back to the street. The ones that touched his skin faded away to dust.

"That's enough!" Will said quietly. "Please, Devaki."

"Sorry," she muttered, wiping at her oozing rune scar. "He wanted proof. I don't think anyone saw."

"That was brilliant," Gardain chuckled. "You are amazing!"

"Nice to see a positive reaction for once," Devaki smiled, looking pointedly at Will. Her mouth twisted into a frown when she got a warning look from Rowlann, too.

"How could a girl like you not get a positive reaction?" Gardain said. "Yes, I know that's a ridiculous question; I can't imagine what you've endured being here in our kingdom. But you must tell me, Devaki, what is it like to be connected to Her? How long have you bled, and what kind of power comes from being able to offer more—"

"The key," Will insisted. He extended his hand, palm up. "I'll take it now."

Gardain's excited expression dampened and he turned a cool eye toward

Will. Angelyn swallowed, her throat suddenly dry; there wasn't any nervousness or uncertainty in the young man's eyes now. "I'm sorry, but for all of your successes tonight, Master Will, you forgot to clarify one detail: I never said *who* I'd share anything with."

"You will give me that key," Will said, his tone dropping to a dangerous low. He brushed off Angelyn's hand and stepped forward.

"Devaki is actually the only one I'll give the key to," Gardain clarified. "And because I know your time is quite limited, I'll only speak to her about what I've put together from the fifty books she'll find in that chest."

Rowlann pulled a knife out of the back of his belt, stepping toward Gardain. "What part of him should I cut?" he growled, rolling back his shoulders. "He's gravely overestimating his worth."

"Rowlann!" Devaki exclaimed. "You're joking!"

"He may as well be," Gardain said. He gave Will an innocent smile, ignoring Rowlann. "Master Will here knows he can't harm me; not tonight, when the entire Moore family is 'making peace' with the rebels."

Angelyn heard Will swear under his breath, then sigh. The young man was right, and she didn't see the harm in him spending time with Devaki. In fact, she was impressed by Gardain. He was clearly fascinated by Devaki and willing to help the rebels solve the most dangerous mystery of this towne.

And Devaki seems quite interested in him.

"You don't need to be angry, Master Will," Gardain added. "I had to ensure that you wouldn't discard me after I stopped being useful. Many people have done that in the past. And Devaki . . . I just want to learn from you. Your Mother is in that digsite, and I want to help you find out why people are being hurt down there."

Will strode forward and stopped one pace from Gardain, standing to his full height, an entire head taller than the young man. Though he kept eye contact with Gardain, he said over his shoulder, "Put three of your men with them at all times, Rowlann. Escort Gardain to his father's private library tomorrow, in the light of day. Understood?"

Gardain nodded with approval, not the least bit intimidated. Rowlann only grunted. "I'm looking forward to it," Gardain said as he gave Devaki another bow. "Thank you. You don't know what it means to meet you tonight!"

CHAPTER TWENTY-ONE

YOU CHOOSE

The torches burned late into the night, as obstinate as the last of the celebrators who slowly filtered home. As far as Will was concerned, the evening was a success except for one frustrating piece: Moore refused to make a public admittance of joining the rebel cause, even though his wife and Gardain amicably spent time with the rebels.

Despite the disappointment Will felt, he knew it was only a matter of time till Jeras himself folded. And Marselle would have reports from her spies in the morning, who had carefully woven themselves throughout the very open and honest revelers. He planned to hear them out, then solve his last problem.

Will took Angelyn's hand and led her down the main road with several rebel guards a few paces behind them. All night, through the countless conversations and smiles, it was almost impossible for him to not stare at her. Now, however, there was nothing to keep him from admiring how beautiful she looked as the noise lulled to a serene blanket of quiet.

"We're not going up *there,* are we?" Angelyn asked, her eyes on Towne Center's turrets on the hill before them.

"Why not?" he said, eyebrows raised. "Haven't you had enough of those damned barracks?"

"I've just . . .never been in a place like that," she replied. "It doesn't feel right."

Will chuckled. "All the more reason to go now. Trust me." When they reached the castle Adlar Moore was so quick to brag about, Will led the way through the main foyer and up the staircases toward the eastern tower. Few lights were lit, but he knew the way by now.

"This is. . .?" Angelyn began when he stopped before a set of double doors guarded by one rebel soldier.

"The Towne Master's private library," Will finished, and waved away the man to open the doors himself. He bolted them shut once they were inside. "Devaki's been up here quite a bit. But right now I want to at least find that chest Gardain mentioned. Think you can help?"

She gave him a smile, then stepped into the high-ceilinged room after him. Its plentiful shelves and towering piles of tomes were overwhelming, and Will watched her gaze study the disturbed coverings draped over most of the furniture. Despite the shut quality of the room, at least the rebel stationed up here not long ago had kept the massive fireplace lit.

"This place is bigger than I thought it would be," Angelyn mused. She stared in awe at the books all around them. "It would take years to read everything; you were smart to let Gardain work with Devaki."

Will shrugged. "Let's not talk about that."

"Can I look around?" she asked. "I'm sure the chest is similar to that key he showed us."

"Please," he said, stepping over to a desk where he had attempted to organize stacks of documents the day before, after Devaki had left. Angelyn disappeared around the curve of the nearest bookshelf.

"Over here," she began a while later, and he found her standing near the back wall looking at a dozen large trunks, each with locks on them. She gestured at one inlaid with several rubies at the edges, its gilded lid covered in the same carvings at the key the Towne Master's son had shown them.

For some reason, seeing it was real made Will's heart settle. "We'll have to find out tomorrow what's in there," he sighed.

"You mean today," Angelyn corrected, indicating the nearest window.

The dawn's first light barely began to touch the windowsills on the east wall, and the soft firelight that filled the room lit Angelyn's face with a warm glow. Despite how long the night had been, Will couldn't see any sign of fatigue around the shapes of Angelyn's soft blue eyes, nor any tension in the smooth curve of her jaw.

He cleared his throat, then made his way back to the warmth of the fireplace, taking a seat on a long, overstuffed divan that was placed as close to the flames as possible. He moved several stacks of books over so Angelyn could sit next to him.

"It has been a long night," he said, running a hand back through his hair. She nodded. "We should get some rest."

Will reached over and put a hand over hers, covering her fingers with a light touch. Her muscles tensed, then relaxed. Turning his hand over, he drifted the back of his fingers up the length of her arm, till he could reach the locks of hair that drifted around her shoulders. He spun them around his palm, wishing he wasn't wearing his gloves that covered his rune scars.

"Will," Angelyn began, and when he glanced up, he saw that her eyes were closed. She rarely said his name, unless it was to point out the fact that it wasn't the one his mother gave him. He waited for her to say something else or to pull away, but her head tilted toward his touch, against his hand that lingered in the wisps of her hair.

Swallowing his last bit of self-restraint, Will pulled Angelyn close. He wanted to press his hands to either side of her face and kiss her, more passionately than he had earlier. He wanted to feel the heat of her body despite the roaring fire. He wanted to bury his hands in her hair and lose himself in the curve of her neck.

But Will wouldn't, no matter how badly he wanted to, because in her gaze, past the bit of surprise, was a lingering echo of fear. *That's what she felt when her husband pushed her around,* he thought. *That's what she's remembering, from the last time he forced her or hit her or put her down. She has to choose to move right now, not me.*

Unless she wants me, it doesn't matter how I feel.

"You choose," he whispered, surprised by the uneven tone of his voice. "I want you, Angelyn, but you have to choose."

Her eyebrows narrowed, and he watched thoughts play across her face. This woman was here, risking her life for his cause, away from her son for the first time, in his arms. And she wasn't pulling away.

Angelyn put her hands on his shoulders, then brought her mouth toward his. Her touch was tentative, unsure, and when her hands began to tremble, Will steadied her. Her hair brushed against his cheeks, sending an uncontrollable shiver down his spine. She kissed him lightly, as if she were testing him, daring him to do more.

Will couldn't stop his arms from tightening around her, then he leaned forward, pulling her underneath him. She inhaled sharply, but did not move her lips from his. It took a moment, but he pulled off his gloves, not wanting anything between his touch and her body.

Gently, he ran his hands up through her long locks, pressing his fingers up the length of her back till he reached the nape of her neck. Angelyn squirmed beneath his touch, and her lips parted against his in a small smile. A moan rose deep in his chest, full of a longing he hadn't felt for another soul in over twenty years.

His fingers danced over the laces at the back of her dress, beginning to loosen them. Will held his hands steady while she ran her own fingers along his chest, up his neck, and against the sides of his face. He pulled down one of the shoulders of her silver dress, running kisses down to her exposed chest. She shuddered, and he pulled back.

"Are you all right?" he murmured. "Do you feel safe?"

Her cheeks were flushed, though he couldn't tell if it was from the heat of the nearby fire, or if she was blushing. "Yes," she whispered. "I just . . . I haven't . . ."

"Neither have I," he said with a small laugh, then brushed long strands of hair out of her face. "Not for a long time."

He kissed her again, gathering up the layers of her dress' hem. Slowly, like the light of day attempting to enter the room, she melted into him. The amount of trust Angelyn gave was overwhelming, and he only hoped she could feel the same from him.

There wasn't anything else, in that time, that held a candle to the significance of the woman entangled in his arms. She encompassed everything that was broken in him, every mistake he'd made, every hurt he'd buried, and the rest of Rhethos fell away as night finally died, and morning came through.

Afterward, sleep was easy, and for the first time since arriving in Lorington, Will drifted off with nothing but peace in his mind.

CHAPTER TWENTY-TWO

BEFORE CYBARYS STRUCK THE EARTH

Joshua hated the safety of the trees. He couldn't meditate like Mistress Merheene did nearby. But every time he tried to train, either with the Blessing Rune scars he was developing on his skin or with his daggers, he shook too much with anger. Helplessness ranged through his muscles, making his grip on the blades weak and unbalanced. He recalled Orton's words before he'd had to run, breaking the leg of one of Travok's men with his magic: "Be smart, and you'll live through this."

But Joshua couldn't tell what "smart" was right now.

I can't go to the brother townes for help. Travok's men are guarding all the entrances as "rebel" fighters. I can't ride to Lorington to tell Will the truth because the horses are under lock and key. I can't kill those monsters in camp because they have Ada and Orton, not to mention I'll lose my Touch. What should I do?

"Deities are difficult, aren't they? She will never just give you the answers you want," Mistress Merheene said. Joshua glanced over to where she sat in the underbrush, wrapped in her warm cloak and tending a small fire over which she was heating their meager meal. "She will tell you what she feels you need to know now."

"That's not very helpful," Joshua muttered. He unsheathed a dagger, then let its weight balance on the edge of his index finger like Orton showed him. One tilt of his wrist forward and the tip was poised for an attack, but he had no enemy in his way.

Frustration boiled under his skin as he tried to find a solution. He'd wanted freedom his entire life, but this was too much. The last thing he wanted was to be back in Kaylyn, near his mother all the time, yet now the Mother whom he prayed to wasn't a good replacement.

"Let me tell you a story, young Rhethosian. To set your mind at ease until you know how to best follow Fate's String next."

Joshua ground his teeth, then sat on a rock between several towering trees. Still balancing the dagger, he looked at the old, blind Armellan woman with impatient indignation. She still fascinated him, and he wanted to know more about her kingdom, yet right now all he could think about was Orton being tortured to death, or whatever his father's men would do to Ada.

"I don't need to see your face to sense *that* expression," Mistress Merheene chuckled, the dry tone of her voice lit with humor. "I'll start with a question, then: where did your kingdom come from?"

"Umm," Joshua started uncertainly. He glanced above him, at the multitude of old, gnarled branches sparsely covered in stubborn orange leaves that hadn't yet fallen. It was an easy question, one his mother had taught him like every other child in Kaylyn. "The First Bradford set us free from The Blood—from Cybarys' chains. Two hundred years ago, he saved us so we could live under his protection."

"Yet right now you're fighting to be free of *him*. Interesting, isn't it? The truth of it all, little Rhethosian, is that none of us know *the truth*. 'Across the sea' is a common phrase used nowadays, but long ago, there was actually no sea to cross. Everyone was at peace, together on a single stretch of land. I'm sure your Towne Master's tomes did not teach you that."

Joshua raised his eyebrows. No Great Sea between Rhethos and Armelle? What could make or break the world itself? No sooner had he thought the question than the answer came: *the Goddess, of course.*

"Rhethos and Armelle were one kingdom that loved the Goddess," Mistress Merheene explained, pulling her brown hands out of her cloak to demonstrate with simple gestures. "Because of what your First Bradford did, however, Cybarys was so angered that she came to the earth itself and split the land in two with her rage."

"What?" Joshua demanded. "How?" And *why* was the last question he didn't say, too in awe of the seemingly impossible images in his mind.

"It isn't so hard to believe if you knew that she created each of us in the first place." Mistress Merheene paused, her breath echoing in silver clouds around her coils of white hair. "At the beginning of time, the Goddess came here, ready to give birth to her only children. She found the land already full of plant and animal life and decided it was a prosperous place for us to live.

"She walked across the earth and her bare feet began to bleed. From her blood soaking into the ground rose men and women, forming from the puddles that were left by her massive steps. It took nearly all of her magic blood for the miracle of life to take place, and when all of her children were born, Cybarys had to leave this world and watch us from afar. Because of how she sacrificed for us, we continue to give her what she asks in return: obedience and blood."

"That sounds . . .fair," Joshua mused unsurely. "If it was so peaceful, though, why did The First Bradford want to 'break free' of her?"

Mistress Merheene shook her head. "Some men are never satisfied; they always want more. More power. More wealth. More freedom. He wanted his own rules, with not even the Goddess herself above him, and he did the unthinkable to achieve that."

Joshua leaned forward, almost unaware that he was still balancing the blade that sat loosely in his grip. "What did he do, exactly? How could he hurt *her*?" He had felt Cybarys' strength, protection, and guidance through her magic. It was unimaginable that a human could cause any harm to the Mother deity.

"I wish I could tell you," Mistress Merheene sighed. "We don't know the truth of what existed before he angered Cybarys. After the breaking of the land and the creation of the Great Sea, we have been divided. Our rulers have written their versions of history, to sow distrust of the opposing kingdom. What I've told you is what Sehran Tarran and his monks preach in Valsara. Now Cybarys has shown me that Will is the one to lead us to true freedom, and that's why I'm here."

Joshua's head swam with these new concepts. He stood, and, without looking, turned the point of his dagger toward a Guidance Rune on his forearm. A firm resolution grew in him, calming his shaky rage and helplessness. "Well, right now Will needs our help. He has no idea the families of his fighters are in danger. It doesn't matter if Travok's my father; I need to find a way to stop him."

He broke open his skin, tracing the now-familiar shape as he winced. His mind was full of the story Mistress Merheene had shared, and the mystery behind what had happened between The First Bradford and Cybarys. He had so many questions to ask Will, but he wasn't here. His mother was living her new free life, and he didn't want to ask her anything, anyway. This was his Fate's String, as he'd been told, and he would solve this problem on his own, like he wanted.

But I would like to do this with your help, he thought to the Goddess as blood leaked around the circumference of his arm and onto the frosted forest floor. The heat that radiated around him felt more than comforting in the chaos of his life; it felt *right*, like he was doing something meaningful. *Show me what you want me to do, or I'll have to resort to my only other option, which will take away this magic. Please guide me, Mother.*

The heat around Joshua started to grow exponentially, until sweat broke out on his skin. Though his eyes were closed, it reminded him of what he'd felt the other night while listening to Travok and his men conspiring. That had been under the intense amplification of the Sahma haze, but what he felt now was very similar. Dry warmth ran down the length of his arm, from the Guidance Rune, to the pocket of his pants.

Once more, his compass pulsed like it had a heartbeat. Frustrated, Joshua pulled it out, flinging droplets of blood across its copper surface. Still, he couldn't read the language of the inscription, nor could he see that one symbol that glowed with a golden color instead of the usual red. What did this thing that Gabriel had given him for his birthday have to do with his current problems?

"This is the most important piece. You must keep it safe until the time comes to use its power. Stay true on this path, Joshua McKinlee."

He tensed when the Goddess said his name in his head, its echo like that of his mother's when he was little, layered with extreme power. He resisted. *The words on this compass and whatever they mean, they matter more than the lives of my friends? And the safety of the innocent people Travok will sell to the Rhethosian military?*

Despite his magic's heat, Joshua felt a sharp chill down his spine at the response he got: *"Yes. You are the keeper of what matters most."*

But what does it say? Josh demanded. *What is it for?*

"Destruction. . . or creation. It is a piece of spell that has been hidden from humanity for two hundred years. It was given to you because your String is the connection point: you, and the broken Armellan girl will be the keys to the world's downfall. . .or survival."

Joshua's head spun, with Cybarys' riddles and the blood loss from his Blessing Rune. He leaned forward, meaning to sit on the rock behind him, but ended up stumbling to his hands and knees at the weight of his connection to the Goddess. None of what she said made sense. He refused to accept that he had to abandon The Forts to his father's men to follow some unseen "destiny" about destroying or saving the world.

Help me save my friends, Joshua prayed fervently. *And then I'll do whatever you want with this damned compass.*

Immense pressure beat down on his shoulders, forcing him cheek first into the broken oak twigs. Mistress Merheene's white eyes snapped to the sound, surprise all over her features. Joshua coughed, tried to rise, but found he couldn't move a muscle.

"Destiny is not a negotiation, little Rhethosian. Follow the path of your Mother and become significant to this kingdom, more than you ever dreamed."

The magical energy that held Joshua pulled back, giving him more room to breathe and sit up shakily. Then an image was put into his mind, clearer than the real world around him: five lines of runes, each with a single symbol on every row that shone with yellow light. Somehow, Joshua was aware that there was incredible power in the foreign words before him.

She's showing me something . . . one of those lines is the same as the one on my compass. But where are the other four written down? And what do they mean?

Perhaps, Joshua thought, if the words from those symbols were spoken, their power that he felt could be released. Or, if they had to do with magic, maybe they had to be cut and bled to achieve something Cybarys clearly wanted.

No matter what, Joshua felt the otherworldly weight of them, and that amount of magical strength terrified him. What he saw could make or break anything: the rebellion, the kingdom of Rhethos . . . even the Goddess herself.

CHAPTER TWENTY-THREE

THE FINAL THREAD OF RESISTANCE

The knock that came at the door, many hours later, barely had the strength to wake Will. What could be more important than this? The sun had only woken him once before, and despite how late into the day he'd known it was getting, he'd reached down over Angelyn's sleeping form to grab the hem of her fur cloak. With the fire long gone, he'd draped the thick material over both of them, placed his cheek on top of her head, and shut his eyes once more.

The second knock was more insistent, just as sleep was ready to find him again. Angelyn startled awake, and Will steadied her before she could fall from the divan. She quickly blinked away sleep, and he gave her a smile.

"Messengers, I'm sure, at the door," he said, while clearing his throat.

"Good morning to you, too," she replied. She sat up slowly, holding her cloak against the front of her body.

"Afternoon is more like it," Will said, lying back on the cushions to look at her more clearly.

She shook her head, and tangles of her hair ran down her naked back. When she glanced over her shoulder at him, he saw her gaze linger on the band of scars around his waist. It took him a moment to recall that she'd seen them once before, in the cellar of The Hamond the night he'd been injured.

"Will," she began, meeting his eyes again, "I—"

The third knock was a solid pounding, followed by a shout from the other side of the double doors. Will swore under his breath, finally sitting up.

"One moment!" he snapped, loud enough for his voice to carry. Grabbing Angelyn's dress from the floor, he smoothed out the flowing silver fabric and handed it back to her. As soon as she struggled to find a way back into it on her own, however, he changed his mind.

"Don't," he insisted, putting a hand over hers. "I can do better than that. Just . . .stay here, like this."

Before she could say anything, he stood up, dressed quickly, then walked to the library's entrance. A man bearing a violet cloth around his upper arm handed Will a sealed piece of parchment the second he opened the door.

"Apologies, Master Will," he said right away. "Master Rowlann said you needed to receive this immediately."

"Who gave you this?" Will asked. There was Rhethosian Blue wax on the seam.

"One of Master Moore's guardsmen brought it to the barracks less than an hour ago," explained the man. "He said it was urgent and was only to be read by you."

Will couldn't help but smile; their celebration last night must have finally swayed the Towne Master. He thanked the messenger, then stopped the man as he turned to go. "Please, send up several clean dresses, and some food as well. If other messengers need to be seen, and I am not here, direct them to Miss McKinlee."

"Not Master Irvin?" the man clarified, and Will gave him a short nod before shutting the door.

He turned back toward the smoldering fireplace, where he found Angelyn wrapped in her cloak, taming her hair into a thick bun at the base of her neck.

"Are you all right?" he asked, then immediately regretted the question. Thankfully, she raised her eyebrows in a bemused expression. Was there a hint of embarrassment in her expression, or a tinge of regret? He wasn't sure.

"What does it say?" Angelyn asked, indicating the note in his hand.

Will thought for a moment as he sat next to her, then handed over the message without opening it. "You tell me, Miss McKinlee."

She smiled at that and broke the seal. Her eyes darted across the page, then widened. "Moore wants to see you," she breathed softly. "Right away."

Will took the note from her hand and read it twice, then a third time to be sure. "The benefits you've brought to Lorington are undeniable, but there is an issue that I fear cannot be solved without your assistance. As I'm sure you're aware, a curse lies on Old Towne, and I cannot publicly give into your cause until it is dealt with."

"What does he mean, 'Old Towne'?" Angelyn asked.

Will bent over, toward the stacks of books that he'd put on the floor last night. "Though I haven't had much time for reading. . ." he began, working his grip toward a few smaller tomes stuffed with loose papers, "I do know local history: the majority of Lorington was built on top of an ancient city that Armelle founded a thousand years ago, before their people were exiled across the sea."

Angelyn leaned against him as he opened one of the books, reading with her head on his shoulder. He kept his eyes on the papers, which made it easier to resist the urge to pull her close and kiss her all over again. Clearing his throat, Will continued, "That hole in the western district must lead down to what Moore calls Old Towne. There's something in those buried ruins that The Bradford wants."

Angelyn nodded against his arm. "But do you think Moore is sincere about wanting your help?"

"I don't know. But I definitely don't believe in 'curses,' just magic Rhethosians don't understand. And because people have been talking about the pagan magic that broke the city gates, I bet Moore thinks I used the Blessing Runes, not Devaki. He must believe that I can somehow solve this."

"Let him think that, then. He also might be trying to take advantage of how badly you want peace," Angelyn suggested, and Will caught her eye. "I don't trust him, so be careful."

"I will," he said, then put a hand up to the side of her face. He brushed his thumb along her skin, savoring the way it felt to touch her before he had to put his gloves back on. "Someone will be bringing you everything you need. I should go—"

"No one needs to bring me anything," she insisted.

"Believe me, I know that," he said. "But this once, humor me. After all, Devaki and Gardain will be up here soon enough. You don't have to stay, but I would be grateful if you were here with them. Speaking of not trusting someone . . ."

Angelyn smiled. "I planned on it. For your sake."

Will made his way down to the barracks where the Moores were being kept, the afternoon sun at his back. Three of his men walked with him, two on either side and one behind. Even as he thought of what to say to Jeras, his heart pulled back to the statement Angelyn hadn't had a chance to finish before the messenger arrived.

She said, "I . . ." Did she mean, "I think I just made a huge mistake"? Or "I think I'm in love with you"?

He shook his head. The time would come to finish that conversation, and now was not it. "You," he said to the man on his left. "Run ahead and tell Master Irvin to meet me where the Moores are kept. I'm sure he's not far."

The man nodded, jogging at a brisk pace around the nearest corner. It didn't take long to reach the barracks, then the building where the comfortable prison was arranged. When he arrived, his gaze immediately went down to the end of the hall that led to the underground cells. Jonathan Sarrett was still there, no doubt going through his own struggles. Will refused to deal with the man directly, preferring to wait till he could possibly be used when confronting the Rhethosian Captain.

"I'll be damned!" Will heard Irvin exclaim, and turned to see his friend approaching. "Moore reaching out the day after our 'celebration' is impressive."

Will smiled. Things were always better between him and Irvin when they were on the same page. "You know," he said quietly, "that I only want his version of this. Then we'll listen to what Marselle has learned last night and make sure he's telling the truth."

"I actually spoke to some of Marselle's lovely ladies this morning, since you weren't around," Irvin began. He waved a hand at the rebels around them, dismissing them so he and Will were alone. "Her spies confirmed the truth, about what Moore has said *and* what Torald said about Adlar."

"Good work," Will said and Irvin gave him a small bow. "We will use that secret if we have to. For now, it's time to hear what the old man has to say."

Irvin clapped him on the shoulder, then motioned for one of the rebel soldiers to step up and unlock the door. He bounced on his heels as if trying to contain his excitement. "After you."

The dark stone room was barely warmed by the small fire against one wall. Moore and his wife sat nearest the flames, while Adlar paced, only pausing to glare at Will and Irvin. Since approving the design of the prison, Will hadn't been back to see the family being kept here. He was glad to see that Gardain was gone, no doubt heading where Will had come from to see Devaki.

"I received your note," Will said in the chilly silence. He sat on one of the empty crates across from Jeras and his wife, though Irvin chose to remain standing over his shoulder. "And I'm glad you're ready to talk. Would you care to explain your problem further?"

"My problem?" Jeras Moore said, white eyebrows shooting up to his wrinkled hairline. "Since it seems you're set on not killing us, that digsite is an issue we both face, no matter what color our men wear."

"Agreed," Will said shortly.

"With your background, you must be aware of the pagan Goddess' curse down there. My ancestors never had any trouble with the Old Towne beneath our feet, till Captain Caldrell's men started digging."

"Well, Will here is *full* of Armellan magic," Irvin lied with confidence, leaning against the granite wall beside him. He pushed back almost instantly, brushing soot and grime off his violet tunic. "That Goddess loves him, so we'll take care of your little problem with pleasure. Just, of course, sign over the official leadership of this towne to the rebel cause. Its soldiers, too, since you know we'll be needing them soon."

Adlar rolled his eyes. "What makes you think any of our men would fight for you unless my father gives the command?"

"Some of them already share barracks with mine," Will replied, placing his hands in his lap. "And soldiers share stories, especially grievances. If you'd paid attention last night, you'd have seen that most of the women here would fight for the rebel cause as well. That's a force you won't want to underestimate, my friend."

Adlar full-out laughed, snorting and shaking his head.

"What kind of men does Lorington house who wouldn't act as bravely as their wives and sisters?" Irvin added over Adlar, in sync with Will's line of speech. Adlar quieted a bit, especially when his father glared at him.

Moore's wife smiled briefly at Irvin's words. "Will you tell them, then?" she asked her husband. "For all of our sake's?"

Jeras nodded stiffly. "The people in the western district have always had more sickness than the rest of the city before the Goddess' curse sprouted," he started. His words were rushed, like he was suddenly voicing a fact that had already been trailing through his head. "Lots of people crammed together, many of them not clean. But when bodies were brought out of the ruins fully drained of blood, things got worse."

Will looked up at Irvin, eyebrows raised. The man shrugged his thin shoulders, indicating this was something he hadn't heard yet either.

"Start from the beginning, please," Will said. "I'd hear the situation from your perspective, the day the Captain's men arrived."

Jeras rolled his tongue along his teeth with an irritated look, thinking for a moment. "Three months before your arrival, we received orders from Captain Caldrell, an unheard-of missive for us up north. He informed us that a garrison would be traveling to Lorington on The Bradford's private business. Our Lord desired something underneath the city, in the remains of the ancient Armellan village that used to stand here. We were to prepare an area of the western district, and he demanded that my soldiers could be used.

"They had an incredible sense of urgency as they began digging, demanding unpaid help from locals. Anyone who got in their way or worked too slowly was beaten and executed. It was easy to hand over those who disturbed The Bradford's peace to those soldiers, knowing they'd likely be worked to death."

He cleared his throat, then reached for a cup of water at his feet. "Now, think what you will about us Loyals, but this was a harsh invasion from our Lord's military. I did not know how to combat it. How could I?"

"Stand up for yourself?" Irvin suggested wryly. "Fight back?"

"We know our kingdom's history, Master Colwell," Adlar put in. "We are proud to stand on this land in the name of our true Lord. The First Bradford is memorialized in our courtyard because we serve the successor of the man who broke us free of the Blood Goddess' chains."

"Yet the commander of that man's army tore holes in your city and abused your people," Will said pointedly, and Adlar lowered his gaze.

Jeras stared coldly at his son, then shook his head as if reprimanding him was not worth the effort. Instead, he nodded in Will and Irvin's direction. "They dug for miles into the remains of something evil. My people have suffered when the sickness struck without mercy. Caldrell's soldiers easily killed anyone with symptoms."

"Huh," Irvin commented. "Sounds familiar."

Will nodded, also seeing the connection to Irvin's old home and the loss of his family. That prompted a new question that he directed at his friend: "And in Patten, when did the 'curses' stop?"

Irvin pursed his lips, as if it irritated him to speak further on the subject. "When The Bradford's men found what they were looking for. And there wasn't much left of my towne by that time."

"There have been few survivors from those who've gone in the digsite," Moore commented. "But all of them have spoken of things that cannot be true."

Will leaned forward, genuinely drawn into the old man's words, but also looking for any signs of lies in Jeras' face. From where he sat, he could not see Adlar's expression, but Moore's wife did not have trouble meeting his gaze. Fear darted across her eyes.

"The sickness must be in their minds," Jeras reasoned, "because they recount seeing the spirits of long-dead Armellans drawing every drop of blood out of the diggers to serve their Goddess. They look like ancient monks, wearing robes and chains, and they use outlawed magic like you, only it shines a different color."

Will felt his throat constrict with trepidation and confusion, and he saw that Irvin, too, was doing a poor job at keeping a straight face. He didn't know if his friend was about to laugh or protest at being insulted with lies. Blood-draining spirits? Odd-colored magic? Neither of those things existed.

Yet Will recalled something that Devaki had confessed to him, the night they spoke alone. When she had spied on the Moores, she'd heard Gardain mention "ancient spirits." Were the stories finally lining up, despite their unbelievability?

"Eventually, none of Caldrell's men were left, but the fallout continues to plague us. You spent time with those pagan bastards across the sea. Surely you must know some way to stop this. I am willing to die for this towne, for our Lord. But I will have *nothing* to do with the Blood Goddess."

Jeras Moore sat nearly face to face with Will. A graveness entered his eyes and seemed to encase the room around them in anticipation of his next words. "If the Insane Captain wants something to do with that kind of ancient evil, nothing good can come of it. If you survive, all the credit will be yours. As much as I hate the idea, you've given me no choice: the towne and Lorington's fighters will also be yours. I will see to any outstanding protests from my people whom you haven't already won over. Lorington's fighters will wear rebel violet. If you don't come back. . . I can't say I'll mourn the loss."

Will ground his teeth as he processed. He believed the man was telling the truth, and that he really had reached the end of his rope by asking for help. He needed the cooperation of Moore's army to have any hope of succeeding when Caldrell arrived.

One thing he had in common with Moore was that he wanted nothing to do with Cybarys, either. Yet she'd brought his daughter here and involved her magic in his fight. And she plagued this city from under the very ground where they sat. It didn't make sense to him; the Goddess did not summon spirits, drain the living of their blood, or curse innocents with illnesses. What was *really* in that hole?

Something The Bradford wants, he thought, answering his own question. *And if he wants it, so do I. Especially if it means resolving the illness in this towne, like what happened in Patten years ago.*

"Will," Irvin began, and tapped his shoulder in the growing silence. "Thank you for your candid storytelling, Master Moore. We will discuss our options and let you know what we decide."

"Take Gardain with you, if you go down there," Moore added suddenly. His eyes were on Will even though Irvin had spoken. "I'm sure he's happier helping you."

"What?" Moore's wife spoke up, standing at the same time as Will. "Please, don't. He's a smart boy, but not clever in practical things. Do you understand what I mean? He can't go."

Will did, now more than ever; Gardain was her only son, after all, and she didn't want to lose him even though to the public eye he was a mere safety net in case her "firstborn" was ever harmed. He wanted the opportunity to speak with Moore's wife alone, but he knew Jeras would never allow it.

"Gardain's a traitor, Mother," Adlar insisted. "Let him fight and die with anyone stupid enough to go into those ruins."

"He *can't* fight!" she said desperately, looking between Will and Irvin. "But he *will* die down there. I beg you, don't throw away my boy's life because his brother and father have no love for him. He's different, always has been—"

"That's *enough* of that," Jeras snapped, and he stood to push his wife forcibly back into her seat. She put a hand over her mouth, though Will wasn't sure if it was to stifle a helpless sob or fight back more protests. It only took a moment for her to regain her former composure that fit a "content" Towne Master's wife.

"I will let both of your sons make their own choices as they see fit," Will said, stepping toward the door. "As every free man should."

He couldn't add anything else, not wanting to upset Moore by promising his wife that he'd look after Gardain. No sooner had they shut and barred the door behind them did they hear Moore begin to berate his wife more emphatically. Irvin shook his head as Will did his best to walk away.

"Brother," Irvin began in a cautious tone, "I saw the look on your face. You're going into that pit, aren't you?"

"Aren't *you*?" Will shot back as they stepped into the afternoon sun. He stood still for a moment, letting his eyes adjust to the world of stark granite and high walls.

"Oh, no!" Irvin exclaimed. "Not for The Bradford's palace! I like my odds better up here, where I understand our impending military threat. Take Rowlann, even take Gardain Moore, if you want. Definitely take Devaki, if you're smart."

"That's not happening," Will growled, and Irvin held up both hands defensively. "She will not be a pawn to whatever the Goddess is doing underneath this city. I will solve this on my own."

"Today?"

"Today, brother," Will confirmed. He planned to hear out the full reports from Marselle's spies, put a group together, and move forward. Now that he had the information Moore was holding back and his promise of surrendering to the rebels, this was the final thread of resistance to his peaceful takeover.

"Do you think he'll make good on his promise?" Irvin mused. "To unite our armies if you pull this off?"

Will thought for a moment before responding. "I think he knows he won't have much of a choice but to concede. He saw what we've achieved in the city so far at the celebration, whether he liked it or not. Most of the people are won over. Towne Masters like him know when it's time to fold."

Irvin nodded, seemingly satisfied. "At least say goodbye to Miss McKinlee first, won't you?" he said with a joking grin. He elbowed Will, who gave him a silent, warning glance. "Oh! I didn't actually think that last night . . ." Irvin chuckled to himself. "You really put it all on the line, didn't you?"

"You're an ass," Will said shortly.

"A handsome one, at least," Irvin quipped back. "And I'm happy for you. I know you've been having Angelyn handle many things lately."

"And you'd like to thank me for the relief you feel?" Will insinuated. "There's a lot to manage and you deserve the help."

"I'll admit that's true, yes," Irvin said, "Just know I'll keep everything in order as best as I can without you."

Will glanced sideways at his friend. "Something tells me you'll be fine either way."

The sly grin faded from Irvin's face, and a rare, somber expression touched his high cheekbones and narrow jawline. "Be careful down there, Will. I mean it; we need you back up here. And don't forget to give that Armellan bitch a good smack for me."

CHAPTER TWENTY-FOUR

TO SWALLOW POISON

Sarrett waited for the rebel to return, slowly making two lists in his head: what he knew about the military because of his returning memories and what he would be willing to share about Caldrell for the right price, including the safety of at least his only son and heir. The darkness beat against the sides of his head as each day passed, as if it could sense his weakening defenses.

He wanted out. He wanted to be "free," even though the rebel tonality of the word stung like fresh salt in his healing wounds. But he was so jumbled between knowing what was right and what was wrong, and the maddening state of harsh sobriety in his square prison was making his nerves fray to their breaking point.

Leaning back and forth, he teetered between one option and the other. Some of his memories told him his captain was a liar, an evil man who had used Sarrett for his amusement. Other times, though, he'd shown Sarrett how to make a name for himself. Now, Sarrett imagined choosing his own future, free of the Rhethosian military for the first time in fifteen years. The idea, despite an undertone of excitement, made him sick to his stomach.

"Lieutenant," came a voice from the other end of the dungeon's narrow hall. Sarrett froze, his body reacting to the presence of another person nearby.

"You'll have to forgive me. More pressing matters are keeping me busy; you nearly slipped my mind. I bet you'd *love* to know what's going on up there. In fact, I would throw you these keys right now if you could make one correct guess."

Sarrett ignored that comment. Instead, he noticed that this time, the rebel wasn't alone. There was another person standing behind the torch that the rebel held in front of him, blocking Sarrett's vision of the other figure.

"Who's there?" he asked.

The rebel laughed, then licked his lips. "I have to admit I'm glad it came to this. Step forward, darling, where he can see you."

Mayra looked exactly the same as the last time he'd seen her, the day he left for Kaylyn with his new lieutenant's jacket. Though, as he looked a bit closer, he noticed some lines around her dark blue eyes. And instead of the usual, fine gowns she'd worn in colors that flattered her black hair, now she stood in a road-weary dress and dirty boots.

He imagined, from where she stood, that he looked even more of a mess. That final letter she'd sent him, before Lorington's attempted siege, only expressed her impatience and disappointment in him. Had any of that changed or was she merely being forced to stand in his presence?

"You're not hurt," Sarrett said. It should have been a pleading question, but the words instead came out as a weak statement.

Mayra shifted from one foot to the other next to the rebel. Her awkward stance helped Sarrett notice that her hands were tied behind her back. "I was, indeed, much better off than you. We thought you were dead," she replied, "when news reached us in the south, of your failure to follow our Lord's orders."

Sarrett grimaced. His brain was going through a dizzying loop in the dark, from the days he'd met this woman and the love and motivation she'd given him, to the pressure of giving their children a worthy, Loyal family name, to the harsh judgment of a lover who wanted more that he could give. He realized she'd been his drive, his desperation, his condemnation.

And he didn't want to talk about his failures now. The Lord knew he'd had plenty of time to dwell on those lately. Instead, he demanded, "Where are Keppler and Neera–?"

"Don't tell him about the children yet," the rebel cut in. He placed one hand firmly on Mayra's shoulder, making her jump. "Go ahead and let him know about your recent chat with his captain."

Sarrett's eyebrows narrowed as Mayra grimaced. A spark of redemption burst forth, then quickly died as her expression remained dour.

"He's finished with you, Jon," Mayra said flatly. "I sent him a letter before he left with the army to inquire after any possibility of your rescue. I was already beyond Clancy, trying to find a new, safe home for me and the children. I got his reply, not long before these rebels forced us to come to Lorington."

She glanced at the rebel, who gave her a nod before she handed a slip of paper through the bars. Sarrett ran a shaky hand over his face, recognizing the erratic penmanship of a man he wanted to please and wanted to hate all at once. In the lack of light, it was hard enough to read the message, but he found it was too painful to focus on its entirety. Instead, as he squinted, his brain could only jump from phrase to phrase.

". . .more important things than forgotten trash. . ."

". . .put him out of his misery. . ."

". . .for your suffering. . ."

"Are you letting that sink in, Lieutenant?" the rebel grinned. "Your captain gave Mayra poison to kill you. After laughing at the idea of rescuing you, that was his command, including a decent amount of gold for her trouble. But she's not going to follow that order now, are you, dear? Even if you want to."

Sarrett balled up the message and threw it out of his cell. His heart ached. Why did he feel nauseous? There was nothing in his stomach except empty bitterness. Too many questions rose with the wave of bile in his throat. Would Mayra do such a thing, to be rid of him for good? Had his entire life amounted to nothing, in both his captain's and his mistress' eyes? What good was he now?

When he caught Mayra's gaze, he found only angry tears.

"So, let's talk about the Insane Captain a bit more," the rebel spoke, filling the heavy silence. He trailed the back of his hand up Mayra's bound arms. She gritted her teeth when he grabbed the hair at the back of her head and forced her into the only chair across from Sarrett's cell.

"Clearly, Caldrell thought you important enough to have killed. So what you know is as important as I've suspected. With your mistress here, and whatever bit of hope you had in a rescue eliminated, I think I'm right in assuming your tongue will be more loose today."

"You're a son of a bitch, you know that?" Sarrett growled quietly.

"If you'd like to discuss facts, that's definitely one of them," the rebel snapped, "but I'd only concern yourself with this certainty: tell me all of the Rhethosian Captain's secrets, or I'll make sure Mayra drinks the poison intended for you."

Sarrett stepped up to the bars, gripping them tightly as the rebel pulled a vial from his pocket with his free hand. Mayra's frightened reaction was enough to tell Sarrett whatever was in that little glass was lethal.

"You have to admit it's poetic," the rebel chuckled. He put more effort into holding Mayra still by her hair as he spoke. "So let's move beyond whatever loyalty you may have to the man who tossed aside his favorite puppy as soon as it pissed indoors. I'll start with an easy question: why does Caldrell care about *you*?"

Sarrett frowned. He sank down next to the door of his cell, the movement heavy with defeat. His forehead nearly touched the lines of cool metal before him, his attention on the dirty hem of Mayra's dress.

"Around when I made officer," Sarrett began, "Caldrell was given an unusual amount of power. Military rule was harsher under his laws, taxes, and punishments. The other officers thrived under his. . .erratic behavior because it let them do whatever they pleased without consequence. We taught new recruits that they were entitled to abuse the commonfolk."

"But you?" the rebel prompted. He tilted the vial of poison back and forth in his free hand with impatience. "I remember when all of that began. Your Captain practically threw reasons at people to support the rebellion. Made our job easier than ever."

"I . . ." Sarrett faltered, then cleared his throat. There was no point in holding back. Not anymore. "I was always afraid of him," he confessed. "He liked me, though I never knew why. But all I wanted was the ranking. The Loyal status. The immortality that serving men like Caldrell could bring me and my family."

The rebel chuckled, and Sarrett felt hot rage fill his uneasy stomach. What did this man know about him? About working tirelessly, shamelessly, to achieve something noteworthy in this lifetime? "I'm sorry," the stranger laughed. "You and I just have some things in common. The difference is, I was *born* with everything you want. And I've chosen the winning side, unlike you."

"What's your next question?" Sarrett demanded.

"Well, the sentiments about Caldrell are interesting, but what I want are tactics. Military secrets. Weaknesses only you would know about him because he 'liked you' at one time. *Those* details help me, Lieutenant, and therefore will help you and help your mistress here. And I really don't want to do anything more than feed and house your little bastards."

"But you will do your worst, I'm sure," Sarrett growled. "At least let her tell me they're alive. I'll believe *her*. I want proof you haven't already killed them."

Mayra opened her mouth, but the rebel dug his fingers deep into her hair till she screamed.

"I'm not inclined to reveal that yet," the rebel said. "After all, your 'family' wasn't easy to find. But it just so happens that I have an excellent connection, quite the beautiful one, who found all three of them. I promise the children are safe for now."

Sarrett heard Lily whimper out of the corner of his vision. She appeared less often, and her form was weak compared to when the Sahma wine flowed through his veins, but it was apparently impossible to make her disappear. He didn't want to admit it, but his clear, sober mind knew that she was more than a hallucination; she was a manifestation of his conscience, something he thought he'd sacrificed to the god they called The Bradford years ago.

"They are all tools to you, aren't they, Jon?"

Water garbled Lily's words, bits of filth from the river drifting over the floor toward Sarrett's crossed legs. He knew better than to shy away from it or think it would actually soak his tattered pants.

"But now is your time to stand for them, as if love and fatherhood are more than rungs in life's ladder to step over for better things. Fight for them, big brother."

"Sarrett," began the rebel, and the former lieutenant looked up at the odd tone of sympathy in the man's voice when he said his name. "This is your only option. Talk."

Sarrett shut his eyes, then let out a breath. Lily was right, and so was the heartless man on the other side of the bars. He had made his choice. "Leave my family be. I will tell you everything I know about Caldrell."

CHAPTER TWENTY-FIVE

REMNANTS OF THE PAST

"Tell me one more time. Please."

Devaki laughed. She kept her eyes on the book in her hands, feeling how hot her cheeks were. It seemed trivial, but she repeated herself anyway.

"Once a month on prayer day, the royal family goes down to the temple to give offerings to Cybarys with the community. Goddess Touched are stationed on each street corner, casting Blessing Runes. The magic remnants are gathered after one of the Tarrans has walked over them, then cased in metal cages or glass to be fashioned in jewelry. People think they're 'blessed' and bring good fortune."

Gardain beamed at her, somehow even wider than the last time she spoke. It was so commonplace to her, a tradition as simple as lacing one's boots or putting out the candles before bed.

Yet the young Rhethosian man hung on her every word, standing across from her in his father's private library, asking her question after question about her home. Gardain knew a lot of facts of his own, easily talking about his thoughts on how Goddess Touched were utilized in service to Armellans in need, or how the language in certain prayers said by the monks had changed slightly with each passing decade.

"You must think it mundane, to repeat such things to me for entertainment," Gardain commented, as if reading her mind. "I'll do my best to focus on the task at hand." He stepped over to her, where she stood next to the opened chest of books. The key still stuck out of its lid, forgotten now that it had revealed the contents Devaki knew were more valuable than some magic remnants on a string.

Within were at least two dozen books, each too large for her to hold with one hand. Gardain had read them all, collected them all, and hidden them all, although Devaki doubted the last part was necessary as no one but him seemed to care about them.

His memory was incredible; every time she skimmed a book, knowing she couldn't possibly read every one with the limited time frame her father presented, Gardain could comment and then reference his words nearly to the paragraph in moments.

Devaki held very still as he touched the book in her hands, noticing how delicate the weight of his hand was. "This one is quite old," he commented. "It's spent at least a century sitting here on a back shelf. It's a beautiful thing, isn't it?"

She knew he was remarking on the inlay of the cover, but for some reason Devaki couldn't stop thinking about how he'd used that word to describe her last night. No one had ever said she was pretty, let alone beautiful. To be fascinated with her culture was one thing, but to find *her* so interesting? She didn't know how to react to that.

After all, it wasn't as lovely as it sounded when she shared the daily life and teachings of her youth in Valsara. Yes, the royal family was adored, especially their Temple Leader Sehran, but those parades through the city on prayer days had been torture for her.

Devaki could go, but she was forced to walk behind the procession, singled out, caught in the dust cloud of her "betters" before her. To be seen, but not to be honored. To be known, but not to be spoken to.

The one time she had tried to cut a Blessing Rune and contribute to the magic remnants in the sandy streets, Sehran had beaten her later in private. His blows were precise, below the collar, and carried heavy threats that he could do much worse. . .and had, in the past.

"Devaki?" Gardain prompted. "What do you think?"

She shook her head, forcing the Towne Master's son to step back as her wild curls moved about her face. "Sorry, what?"

Across the library, in a chair near the fireplace sat Angelyn. She glanced over at them, concern on her face when she seemed to notice the change in Devaki's demeanor. Since Gardain had arrived and opened the chest of books,

Angelyn had kept her distance, though Devaki had no doubt that the woman was here to keep an eye on both her and Gardain.

"Everything all right?" she asked as she set down her own book in her lap.

"I'm fine," Devaki insisted. On the other side of the closed library doors were three of Rowlann's men, the ones who Will had commanded be watching Gardain at all times, but Angelyn had dismissed them. She said she trusted Gardain, and she always kept them in eyesight.

Devaki wasn't worried either; it seemed that the only enemy in here was the one in her head. She was ready to move forward and not dwell on painful pieces of the past.

"What were you saying?" she asked Gardain. She met his gaze, still surprised at how odd it was to see someone completely opposite of her: gray eyes, ashy curls, and pale skin.

He had stared at her since arriving, so she didn't feel bad about looking at him longer than necessary now. Angelyn had mentioned he was about five years older than her, though his youthful manner made him feel like a teenager in her eyes.

Gardain broke their eye contact to glance down at the book once more. "That page you're touching, it talks about rituals similar to what you've described on prayer days in your home," he repeated. "I was merely commenting on how certain elements of habit withstand the passage of time, albeit details may shift."

"Yes," Devaki agreed. The script under her fingertips was faded, though still in runes she could understand. "I'm sorry, I don't have a lot of good memories on those days. I wasn't allowed to cut runes with the rest of the Goddess Touched."

"Why not?" Gardain asked.

Devaki grimaced. "I don't think that's important," she insisted, then shut the book in her hands, as if that should indicate she was done talking about that subject. Gardain, however, seemed clueless to the hint, opening his mouth no doubt to ask yet another question. Angelyn cleared her throat loudly from her seat, and that, thankfully, seemed to get through to the young man.

"Well, why don't you pick next?" Gardain began. "We've been here for hours and I just realized I've been handing you book after book and interviewing you constantly. Rather rude, right? I'm sorry." He stepped back, till his slim shoulders touched the nearest stack of shelves, displacing more dust onto his sage green tunic. There was now plenty of room between Devaki and the ruby-crusted chest.

Devaki shook off the last of her memories, staring down into the neatly organized piles before her.

"You could. . ." Gardain added in the silence, clearly unable to help himself, ". . .you could cut a Guidance Rune now to see what book the Goddess leads you to."

That got Devaki to smile again. After all, the other day when she'd prayed in this library, it had led her to nothing in particular till she opened her father's journal. Now, with all the answers before her (and someone who had a positive reaction to her magic), she thought that was a great idea.

Devaki sat in front of the trunk, its massive, studded lid now taller than even the top waves of her hair. She shut her eyes and took a slow, deep breath, full of the welcoming scent of innumerable sheets of paper and dusty daylight. Feeling Gardain settle beside her, she turned the intentionally sharp edge of her ring against the raised scar tissue of a Guidance Rune on the inside of her left forearm.

"Dear Mother," she murmured as she broke open her skin, "we are looking for the truth. Help lead us to the answers we need to help your children."

A warm energy swirled at the back of her ribcage, as if a bright, hot torch was being held behind her at her back. When she reached forward, eyes still closed, she heard both the splash of blood and the tinkle of magic remnants hit the floor in front of her bent knees. Her fingers danced along the edge of the trunk, inching forward, following where the heat of her magic was pushing her.

Devaki grasped a book, then moved it aside. She did the same thing two more times before she blindly touched the binding of one tome that burned like a roaring fire. The sensation eased after she grasped the leather tighter and pulled it out to rest in her lap. Only then did she open her eyes.

Gardain stared, openmouthed. He pulled out a handkerchief from his sleeve to gather the magic remnants from the floor, shaking them into a pouch on his belt. "You. . ." he began, then cleared his throat. "I really don't think you know how special you are, do you?"

Devaki's eyebrows narrowed. "Special?" she said, her voice quiet. For some reason, she felt tears sting her eyes. It was difficult, going from being referred to as a cursed bastard to a beautiful, special person.

Leaning forward, Gardain placed his kerchief on her bleeding arm. He squeezed gently till the blood flow from her Guidance Rune began to clot. After wiping the red trails on her brown skin and the floor between them, he met her eyes. She wasn't sure what to say, and, for once, it seemed he didn't either.

Devaki nearly jumped when Angelyn threw a fresh piece of wood into the fireplace. Then another. . .very deliberately. Glancing at the woman, Devaki caught a knowing smile and a wink from Angelyn before she sat down with her book again.

"I didn't have to keep my eyes closed," Devaki said with a casual laugh. "I was just showing off."

Gardain tilted his head, confusion furrowing his brow.

"That was a joke," Devaki added.

"Oh." Gardain's laugh didn't have much emotion behind it. "So. . .this book, it's interesting you were led to it. We were, a few minutes ago, talking about prayer days and rituals. This is actually the oldest book in my collection. I can't even read the language it's in because it's long since died, though over time I've been able to translate a few characters."

"What have you learned?" Devaki asked. She sat back on her heels, gently opening the yellowed pages herself.

"From what I understand, it details some of daily life in ancient times. Seasonal ceremonies that took place for survival, those sort of things. You know this kind of information was purposefully lost two hundred years ago, after The First Bradford . . . did what he did."

Devaki frowned. The symbols before her were hard to make out. There were even pages missing and ink stains that blotted out entire blocks of texts. What she could see didn't mean anything to her and neither did what Gardain said.

"Ceremonies to help my people survive? I don't know anything about those," she replied, "and trust me, I had plenty of time to read over the years in Valsara. You must have your translations wrong."

Gardain scoffed. "I assure you, what I've managed to read here is accurate," he insisted. "The rituals described here were performed at the start of each season.

I'm not clear on the logistics, but I can tell that without them Cybarys would be angered. Mind you, the bloodletting back then, centuries ago, was much more intense than what your people do today. Quite sinister, from what I–"

"Our Mother never asks for more of us than we can willingly give," Devaki returned. It was an old adage, one she thought would resonate with this young man, but he seemed determined to tell her more.

"Yes, but look," Gardain said. He leaned closer, turning a few pages of the book she held, to where a fresh sheet of paper sat. "These are my notes. This language has extremely complex runes, some shapes containing an entire phrase in one character. I've done my best to work through translations to modern Armellan, though it takes nearly all day for a seemingly simple piece. Like here."

He tapped one long, slim finger to a shape full of intricate slashes. "That loosely means, or at least captures the concept, of 'magic.' Related to this rune here on its right, regarding 'change' or 'season,' as I mentioned before, you can see how I came to the conclusion that magic had to be conducted regularly in certain ceremonies."

A chill had run down her spine when he spoke. "Why does any of that sound sinister?" Devaki dared to ask. She stared at the faded content of the book and Gardain's detailed notes before her, hardly understanding any of it.

"Well here," he added, passion filling his voice, "is another shape that has characteristics of your language that apply to several different words: this arc looks like 'to survive' and this piece combines modern runes that mean 'servitude' or even 'giving life'. . . similar to 'death,' as you can see on this page."

Devaki clutched the book a little tighter as Gardain spoke. What he was hinting at was not a subject that could be found in books in Valsara anymore. She knew her cousin, since rising to power, had changed the narrative of history to suit the current hatred and fear her people had of violent Rhethosians.

As a child, older nurses and palace staff told stories about ancient times with darker connotations now forced to be forgotten.

"It is fascinating Cybarys led you to this book," Gardain was saying. "You must have heard of Dead Runes in Armelle."

Devaki felt that shiver run through her again. "Those are a myth," she dismissed. "Frightening children's stories that are not supposed to be talked about anymore."

The Towne Master's son leaned back a little, studying her face intently. "You can't believe that. You're too smart to believe that."

She scoffed. "I said Dead Magic and its Dead Runes *aren't real*," she told him definitively. Her hand went to her chest, where that unreadable rune was scarred into her skin. Fear of the unknown gripped her ribcage.

When Devaki dropped her gaze to the book again, she stared harder at the translation process on the new paper, hoping that somehow she could understand it, find a hole in Gardain's logic, and prove him wrong about a time when people may have been forced to "give life" to the Goddess, but all of it merely gave her a headache. Frustration filled her as she prayed silently for further guidance.

Why lead me to this if we can't even read what's in here?

Devaki got no answer. In a huff, she set the book aside. "This doesn't help us if we can't read it properly. How about you show me something we can both understand, in modern Armellan, that's more relevant?"

Gardain blinked. "Of course. I didn't mean to offend you, Devaki. That's truly the last intent I have here today. I'm, uh. . . not great with social cues, if I have indeed done something wrong." He rubbed nervously at the back of his head before standing next to her. "Maybe *you* should have opened your eyes when using that rune. . .for accuracy."

Angelyn chuckled from the other side of the library, and it took Devaki a moment to notice that Gardain had, in fact, tried to make his own joke.

"Maybe you're right," Devaki replied. "Show me something else."

Gardain smiled and reached into the chest, pulling out three different books that each had precise locations marked with extra pieces of paper covered in his handwriting. He opened his mouth to speak when the library doors opened.

Devaki glanced around the shelves just as Angelyn stood from her chair. Her throat went dry when she saw her father. Will stepped over to Angelyn and spoke quietly in her ear for almost a full minute. Devaki frowned, watching the Rhethosian woman's eyes go wide. After a while, Angelyn nodded, gripped Will's hand for a moment, then stepped out into the hall.

"You two," Will said suddenly. "Come here."

Devaki stood and followed Gardain over to the fireplace. Will only glanced at her briefly, his eyes on the Towne Master's son.

"Your father has told me everything he knows about the digsite," Will began. "And he's agreed to publicly support my cause if we go down there and resolve what Caldrell disturbed."

Gardain blinked several times, then grinned. "And he volunteered me to go with you, didn't he?" he asked.

Will nodded wordlessly.

"Well, *I'm* going," Devaki spoke up before Gardain could even open his mouth. Excitement rushed through her body, pushing back any fear or confusion she'd felt during the last hour. It was finally time.

"No, you're not," Will said emphatically.

"But we've been waiting for weeks to–"

"I said no," Will cut in.

Gardain stepped back a few paces, wincing.

"Please–" Devaki tried again.

"I said *no*."

CHAPTER TWENTY-SIX

INTO THE CITY'S WOUND

Will didn't think it was possible to disappoint his daughter further and yet, here he was. She stared defiantly up at him, her dark brown eyes full of frustration. He noticed that Gardain stepped even further back to avoid any conflict. The silence held, more painful with each passing second.

"Rowlann is here," Angelyn announced from the doorway. "I've told him everything."

Will sighed as Rowlann entered the library, breaking eye contact with Devaki. This man, at least, would not ask questions or debate his orders. Sometimes it was good to have an elite fighter at his side.

Will watched, however, when his daughter marched up to said elite fighter. She had a serious look on her face, one of a person addressing a friend who needed to hear unwanted news.

How did they become so close? Will thought, realizing this was the first time since the night of the siege that he'd seen Devaki and the man he'd sent across the sea to meet her together. It was odd, like looking at a child and a dangerous weapon, entirely juxtaposed to one another.

"Rowlann," Devaki began. Will watched the man's expression set itself into a hard grimace, as if he was preparing himself for her words. "You have to see reason, out of everyone here," she continued, desperation in her voice. "This place you're going into has to do with *my* Goddess. You'll need my magic, I know it."

Rowlann worked his jaw, then opened it slowly. "If Master Will hasn't asked you to come, it's not a possibility."

"I, uh, personally would suggest taking her along," Gardain spoke up, then flinched when Will and Rowlann both glared. "Of course," he added, "I will happily report any findings to you, Devaki, supporting or disproving any of my theories we've been discussing."

"About Dead Magic?" Devaki scoffed, rolling her eyes.

Will looked between the two of them. That was not a phrase he thought he'd ever hear again. "You mean the ancient myths? That's what's in your books up here?"

"I can only guess, for my translation skills are rudimentary at best," Gardain confessed.

"Guesses will not help us, with time being of the essence," Will dismissed, "especially if you're talking about lost stories."

"They are more than mere stories, Master Will," Gardain insisted. His eyes darted to the trunk and the piles of old books stacked around it. "I've found accounts confirming the existence of a different form of magic, one that existed before The First Bradford's time. Even if my translations aren't entirely accurate, we shouldn't dismiss this based on mere language alone."

"Gardain, please," Devaki snapped, clearly not in the mood. "He doesn't care. I'm sure he heard the old tales in Valsara, like I did. But that's all they are: purposefully lost fiction."

Will agreed, though the comment about him not caring did sting. "We leave now," he declared, "to face what's actually in our way."

Rowlann nodded in approval, though Will couldn't take his eyes away from his unhappy child. Letting out a breath, he knelt in front of her so he had to look up at her stubborn face and fiery eyes. He understood her points, but he refused to accept that the one person he'd wanted to keep safe for sixteen years had to put herself in danger for his cause. "You are just like—"

"If you say something about my mother," Devaki snapped, "I will cut open this Strength Rune and punch you in the face."

Gardain stifled a laugh, and even Rowlann's lips twitched.

"What I meant to say," Will started again slowly, "is that you are right. Cybarys is calling you to that digsite, but I have a feeling, a *strong* feeling, it is not for what you think. When I see what's in those ruins for myself, I promise to go back with you when it's safe. You will find your answers. But do not pay for them with your life."

"Princess. . ." Rowlann began, and Will looked up at him, surprised at the sentiment in his voice. Apparently, that single word, a bittersweet title that held more pain than Will could begin to understand, got across a message his words could not.

Devaki sighed, then nodded. Will almost reached out a hand to comfort her when she turned sharply and went back over to the books from Gardain's locked chest. Will watched her grab and flip the ruby-studded key Gardain had given her in her hands, almost as if it was a token of trust, one she seemed to value more than the journal he'd given her.

"I decided I will join you," Gardain spoke up, as if just making the choice. "I've been wanting someone to lead a proper expedition into that hole for months."

Rowlann gave the young man a skeptical look. "Wouldn't you be more useful here? Can you even carry a sword?" he demanded.

"Carry?" Gardain repeated, rubbing a hand over the back of his neck. A reluctant smile lit his youthful face. "Yes, of course. As long as it's not as big as yours. How are you planning on wielding that in narrow, underground passages, anyway?"

Will stood and stepped away from the two as Rowlann launched into a speech about different forms of weaponry he was extremely proficient in. He glanced briefly at Devaki, but he could not think of anything else to say to her.

Instead, Will motioned for Angelyn to join him in the quieter hallway. He dismissed the rebel outside, then turned to face her. She wore a plain brown dress now, and somehow she looked more rested even though she'd slept the same as him.

"I had a feeling you'd rush off, if your talk went well," she said. She reached out a hand to him, and he pulled her close. With all of the weapons he'd put on after speaking with Moore, it wasn't as pleasant a feeling as it was the previous night. "Are you sure about this?" she asked. "Did Moore really say that spirits are draining people of blood down there? I don't understand."

"That's why I'm going. For answers, to solve this so we will have his public surrender. This morning," he pressed on before she could reply, "you were going to say something, when it was just the two of us."

Angelyn frowned, playing with the collar of his tunic as she thought. "Oh. I was going to say . . . that I was happy. I've never woken up feeling just . . . happy before."

He let out a breath, blowing back wisps of her hair.

"Has that been haunting you all afternoon?" she asked with a smile.

Will pulled her tighter against him, then buried his face in the side of her neck. "You have no idea," he murmured, covering her skin in kisses. "Please keep Devaki out of trouble."

Angelyn leaned back and gave him a serious look. "She's your daughter."

He laughed briefly. "I'm doing the right thing, aren't I? By making her stay?"

For a moment, Angelyn seemed to consider his words. He knew that, when he'd asked for her advice before regarding parenting, she'd been willing to share. But she never flaunted her sixteen years of experience in his face and seemed to respect the boundary of what he chose to do or not do about his daughter's willful spirit.

"Yes," Angelyn shared. "She shouldn't go anywhere near that place until you've been down there first. Just . . .come back, for her sake. And mine."

Will nodded, then did his best to let her go. There were other things he wanted to say, things he'd never told another person, and most of them surprised him when they pressed to the forefront of his mind. But time was ever-shorter, and he had to move.

It took an hour to travel down to the western district from Towne Center, but Will agreed with Rowlann that they should go slowly on foot. His men needed time to clear the streets of the slums. Those who were sick still wanted to attack anyone who came near, and Will didn't want anyone getting hurt because of his choice to enter the digsite, innocent or otherwise.

The closer they got to the precisely cut hole in the ground, the more Will's head began to ache. The presence of the Goddess was as strong as before, pressing against him like an oncoming tide. This time, however, there were no voices that assaulted his mind or overwhelming pain to incapacitate his body.

Does that mean she wants us to come now? Will thought, telling himself that either way he didn't like it.

He shuddered, then stopped at the mouth of the hole before them. Looking back, he took the time to make eye contact with Rowlann, Gardain, and the four guardsmen who had volunteered to accompany them. Two were of Rowlann's company and two were some of Moore's men, whom he knew were familiar with what had happened when the captain's men ventured underground.

"Can any of you tell me how far down the excavators managed to go?" he asked.

"My brother was forced to work with the Captain's men down here," spoke up one of Moore's guardsmen. "They tried to map out the remains of Old Towne as they dug, but very few made it back. He was one of the last and mentioned finding piles of countless bones at the end of a tunnel."

"So the spirits of dead men are waiting to curse us?" repeated one of Rowlann's men, his deep tone skeptical. "I don't believe it. We're more likely to get crushed by some unstable rocks down there than drained of blood by a vicious spirit."

"I lost my brother to this cursed place!" the other man snapped back. "Let's go down there, and we'll see who makes it back out."

"Quiet," Rowlann said, and the men obeyed. "The Armellan faith doesn't even believe in souls lingering after death."

"I, uh, actually," Gardain put in, "I could debate you on that."

"Or we can all see for ourselves," Will said. He paused, a chill creeping up his own spine when he looked into the black pit. Before continuing, he pointedly caught Gardain's eye. "Unlike The Bradford and his Captain, I won't force anyone into this place. None of you would be shamed for turning around now."

None of the guardsmen spoke up or turned away. Gardain swallowed, a bit of fear touching his gray eyes. "Thank you, but I'll come along. There are worse ways to die than if something goes wrong down there."

"Also debatable," Rowlann muttered.

"Well," Will said, "if you're looking for knowledge, revenge, or whatever else made you agree to be here, it's time to go."

He forced himself to step down into the range of walkways that lined the edge of the digsite. Dry dust and sharp metal stung his nose, combined in the stagnant air. Silence encompassed them as they observed abandoned digging tools, towering mounds of dirt, and tents full of what appeared to be the personal gear of many military men.

"The tunnels down there are narrow and dark," Gardain spoke up, his soft voice bouncing off the edges of the hole they slowly descended into. "But there is only one entrance to them that they were able to stabilize."

It was clear, from the way the pathways of molded earth and rising scaffolding moved downward, that it focused on one particular spot. Will had seen what he thought was an entrance the night of the siege with Devaki. Even now with the day's light barely reaching into the hole, he could have found it in the dark.

Cybarys pulled him to it and pressed him back at the same time. It was dizzying. He was glad when they finally reached a reinforced doorway that led down into the earth. Gardain stepped up to it immediately, while Rowlann and the guardsmen hung back.

"It *is* sandstone," Will muttered, investigating the material of the entrance before them. Gardain nodded beside him. He fiddled with the short sword Rowlann had given him, clearly displeased with where it hung on his belt over his green tunic. Will wondered if the young man could feel the conflicting energies around them as strongly as he did, but if Gardain did, he gave no sign.

Will curled the edges of his fingers around the sandstone archway and stared down to find crumbling steps that led into the darkness before him. Even the smell of the stone brought back memories, which he firmly pushed away.

Sandstone forms in the desert, he thought, pressing his fingertips against the curve of the cool, porous structure. *And this style of stone-laying is only present in the oldest parts of Valsara.*

Behind him, he heard Rowlann striking and lighting several torches as Will took the lead and stepped into the shadows with his hands free.

When Will inhaled, an odd odor drifted like strands of silk along the air, making him flinch. The air in here wasn't stale, nor was it rank; the only label that seemed to fit was "old. . ." very, very old.

He breathed in deeply once more, and as he descended, one hand on the sandstone, the black air around him seemed to settle like an encompassing weight across his body. That smell pulled at him in nostalgic drafts.

Nostalgic. Why would he use that word in an ancient place like this? His boots sunk into the palpable layer of dust along the steps as he pressed downward, aware of Rowlann and the torchlight behind him.

"Oh," Will said suddenly.

"What's wrong?" Rowlann demanded, his deep voice echoing off the narrow passageway.

"It's Sahma," Will murmured, realizing what the smell was that permeated through his clothes and into his memories. "Sahma and dust."

That "old" smell was a combination of two things that he had never experienced together; the Sahma smoke must have burned almost constantly in this ancient place and its scent had bled into the surface of the stone. That created a new aroma all together: the earthy musk of the Sahma and the gritty dust of times long past.

Every time he breathed, that scent lit up his past like the torchlights that danced to either side of his vision. He adjusted his pace to step over the uneven ground that chipped in bits as he walked. Silence surrounded them, though he could feel more than hear Gardain constantly looking around, muttering to himself.

After some time, Will felt something touch the corners of his mind, itching like the Blood Fortune rune scar on his hand that Isaka had cut for him when he was fifteen. Suddenly, he had to put his hand against the tunnel's cold wall to steady himself. Painful memories were forced to the forefront of his mind, hitting him with a sharp impact equal to a blow to the side of his head.

Crying when Mic left for a year's training . . .

His father's harsh smack when he dropped the rigging . . .

His brother setting temple prayer books on fire . . .

Hearing Devaki cry and not being able to hold her . . .

"Will—" Rowlann began, and he heard a strain in the man's voice.

"There's something," said one of the guardsmen, the light of his torch quivering uncontrollably. "In my head—"

Two of the others cried out and bent over. Will grimaced, then found that, when he stopped trying to advance down the tunnel, the voices and memories halted, too.

"How do they know these things?"

"It's the Blood Goddess, trying to break us–"

"This was a mistake to—"

"*Stand strong!*" Rowlann's command broke through the sudden chaos of voices, both in and outside of his head. But one of Moore's guardsmen kept screaming. He tore at the skin on either side of his face, as if the agony inside of him was too much to bear.

Blood leaked from his self-inflicted wounds, dripping onto the dusted, cracked floor. Almost instantly, Will felt a presence in the tunnel, emerging from nowhere. He touched a knife on the inside of his arm, searching in between the gaps of torchlight for whoever had appeared.

A burst of hot air rushed in between them, and Rowlann put out an arm to press Will back against the tunnel's wall out of reach. Over the armored man's shoulder, Will thought he saw the outline of a man hover over the injured guardsman. Blood rose unnaturally from the floor, then from his scratch marks, flowing at a rapid, terrifying pace. The liquid pulsed with an ethereal golden light.

The guardsman fell silent and slumped forward with a harsh, dead thud. The space around them was covered in silence once more, everyone unable to speak.

"Will—" Gardain began, whispered awe in his voice.

"We should go back—" said another.

"I was about to say," Gardain pressed on, "that I'm not sure which way is back."

Will looked behind him, then ahead. Every time he was able to focus on the lit spaces, the pathways shifted. What had been one passage now split into three, and behind them ranged six different narrow openings. When he dared step forward, pain filled his head again, along with an onslaught of the worst memories he could imagine.

"Blood," echoed a demanding voice in his mind. *"Give her more blood."*

CHAPTER TWENTY-SEVEN

BENEATH REBELLION'S SMILING FACE

T he night fell, but no one slept. Angelyn stayed in the libraries, watching Devaki read while messengers from throughout the city came to her. She told the men in charge of the army's supplies how to properly organize dried goods and fresh ones that had arrived from northern townes, as the storehouses were beginning to fill once more.

Then she looked over a list of the latest digsite widows who were taking over their former husband's or family's businesses, as well as the women from Loyal families now distributing clothing and offering their homes to Remora's pregnant girls. Many of the messengers merely brought regular reports from each district, and she couldn't help but smile at the positive results despite how worried she was about the rebel leader himself.

Sometime in the middle of the night, while Angelyn was rebuilding the fire in the large hearth with her cloak clasped at her neck, Devaki suddenly screamed. Angelyn spun, her heart in her throat. She held a cup of warm wine in one hand that was helping calm her nerves, but she nearly spilled it across her dress sleeve.

"What?" she demanded.

The Armellan girl was just visible above the half circle of books piling up around her, her chunks of curled hair standing up. "I cannot believe this!" she cried, and her auburn eyes filled with tears. "This says that children in Rhethos, every twenty-five years, are killed if born under the Goddess' Moon!"

Angelyn grimaced and tossed the last piece of wood in her arms into the growing flames. Hours ago, Devaki had been reading as much of the books from Gardain's chest as she could, mentioning how she wanted to find something to prove one of the young man's theories wrong. She must have not had much success if she'd moved onto reading pages of Rhethosian history.

"It's called the Blood Moon here," Angelyn said with a nod. Memories of Joshua's birth surfaced. "Most folk avoid creating a family during that month. The consequences are truly horrific, but we are told removing those children from the kingdom will keep us safe from the curse of the Goddess' Touch."

Devaki angrily wiped her eyes, then stood. "Everything here is so different, but this is awful beyond words."

"My son is the same age as you," Angelyn began, sitting in one of the chairs by the fire. She gripped her cup a bit tighter, bringing it close to her nose to inhale the comforting smell of berries and cinnamon. Talking about Josh was a good way to keep her mind off of worrying about Will. "He is only alive today because a friend of mine used his outlawed magic to keep my boy's magic hidden. He loved your Goddess very much."

Shock blossomed over Devaki's features, highlighted by the fresh shadows made by the renewed fire. "Really?" she exclaimed. "I would love to meet—"

The library doors swung open. They both turned, Angelyn expecting to see yet another messenger, but this time it was a young woman. She recognized her as one of the kitchen staff who regularly brought and cleaned up food throughout this wing of the castle. Now, well past midnight, the girl's wispy brown hair flew wildly around her worried eyes.

"Miss McKinlee," she began, completely out of breath, "I'm so glad I found you. There's trouble in the northern district streets. Several Loyal families are arming themselves, and we think they intend to harm some of the women you've worked with. Somehow they've heard word of Master Will's departure this afternoon. We need to do something—"

One of the doors swung open again, cutting off the girl and letting in Marselle, who was nowhere near as distraught. "Just in time," she began, flattening the rumpled edges of her skirts.

"I was telling Miss—" the servant began.

"No need to trouble her," Marselle cut in smoothly. "I have that rabble handled on my own."

The girl looked between Angelyn and Marselle, touching the violet scarf she wore around her neck that was drenched in sweat. "It's only that we saw the fires through the kitchen yard," she continued. "We're all worried about our friends."

"Darling," Marselle insisted, and Angelyn knew that placating yet firm tone of hers very well. She put a hand on the girl's shoulder, steering her gently toward the door. "Master Colwell himself oversees this district and is helping me handle those rich bastards just fine. Get back to your duties."

Angelyn stood, her eyebrows narrowing. Something didn't seem right in the overly sweet tone of Marselle's voice. As the young woman left, Angelyn decided to choose her words carefully. "That sounded serious. Are you sure there isn't anything I can do to help?"

Marselle shut both doors, then came to collapse elegantly in a seat farther back from the flames. Even at this time of night, she sparkled with jewels and smelled of cloves and citrus. Brushing back a long curl from her cheek, Marselle flashed Angelyn an appreciative smile. "The people here in the northern district are a delicate part of this situation. Rest assured, I will take care of whoever thought it was a good idea to share the fact that our leader is risking his life underneath this city . . . after I've given my feet a moment."

She lifted her skirts to slowly remove her tall boots. "Your people," she added, glancing at Devaki, "are very smart not to wear these."

Devaki smiled politely but didn't say anything.

Angelyn wasn't distracted by Marselle's latest words. In fact, she felt more suspicious than usual; Marselle had mentioned Irvin's name, which meant he was well-aware of the unexpected conflict before anyone else.

Did that mean he was the first to know everything, including any tasks she'd recently begun to handle? She and Irvin certainly didn't get along, and it wouldn't surprise her if he felt slighted by her newfound leadership role.

"So what, exactly, is being done to help those women and put out those fires?" Angelyn asked, trying again for more details. Seeing Marselle show up at the exact same time as the worried castle staff made her feel like Marselle was hiding something . . . something Will certainly wouldn't approve of.

Marselle didn't meet her eyes. "Irvin has men handling those who'd dare put a hand on any girl recently inclined to own her voice," she said smoothly.

"Yes, but *how* are you two handling it?" Angelyn demanded, taking a step forward. She knew how aggressive Irvin could be and had seen Marselle coldly slit enough throats to be wary of violence that Will strictly forbade.

They had fought so hard for amenable peace and she couldn't stand by and watch that crumble because Will wasn't here to stop it himself.

Marselle snapped her attention to Angelyn. "I'm handling it probably as well as you *handled* our leader last night."

Angelyn felt her jaw drop as her throat constricted. She put her hands on the luxurious pattern of upholstery on the back of the chair opposite Marselle. Her friend had never said such a crass, hurtful thing to her before. Angelyn felt her grip tighten on the soft blue and rust-orange fabric.

"Go ahead," Marselle added. "If we're sharing details, I'd like to hear yours first. How good was he?"

Angelyn's eyes quickly flashed to Devaki, who merely sat in stunned silence. When a blush rose on her cheeks, Angelyn also felt a simultaneous flash of anger. Jealousy, she decided, did not suit Marselle well.

Doing her best to swallow past her embarrassment, Angelyn searched for how she could possibly respond. Maybe going to find Remora would be her best bet–

This time, Devaki jumped when the library doors burst open. Three women, dressed in black, entered, and Angelyn knew they were some of Marselle's long-time spies. They didn't even spare Angelyn or Devaki a glance, looking only at their leader.

Marselle raised her eyebrows expectantly at them as she put one of her boots back on. "Let's hear the basics only," she ordered.

"None of the girls who were targeted were harmed," spoke one of them. Angelyn let out a sigh of relief.

"Those who started the fires, somehow, found themselves trapped in them," shared another, and the other two smiled as if this pleased them.

"Good," Marselle said shortly. "Head back to the evening's gathering point. You can give me a full report in an hour."

Angelyn felt a sour feeling rise in her stomach as the spies left. Marselle, however, was putting on her other boot without concern. "You aren't encouraging any violence against Lorington's people." She said it as a statement toward Marselle, letting the words hang in the tense air between them.

"Leave it be, McKinlee," Marselle hissed. She sat up and straightened her sapphire necklace.

But Angelyn refused to let it go. If Irvin was circumventing any of her new responsibilities, she wanted to know. If Marselle was going too far and keeping secrets, she wanted to know that, too. It wasn't right, and with Will risking his life that very evening, under their very feet, her patience was short.

"Marselle," she began as calmly as possible, "you know the rebel cause is all about honest, open change. Our new freedoms are supposed to be justly, peacefully gained for any who've suffered violence in the past."

"Of course," Marselle replied. "You have mastered the rhetoric, McKinlee. Excellent pillow talk, I'm sure."

Angelyn almost blushed again. Part of her was wondering how Marselle knew about what had happened between her and Will last night, but another part of her figured it out. Will had meant well when he asked for new clothes to be brought up to the library for her, but anyone who saw (and then spread the news), would have been able to put it all together.

"How much does Will know?" she snapped. "About what you and Irvin do, in his name? You stood with me in The Butterfly's Breath that night, and you felt how tender and powerful the promise of nonviolence was. I love how proud you are of *who* you are, triumphs and mistakes, Marselle. What is it you're hiding from me?"

Her mind unwillingly went back to the first nights she'd encountered Will in Kaylyn, when he unashamedly shared how anyone who dared betray him to the lieutenant would find their throats cut in the streets. He preached freedom but condoned murder if it was in the name of his definition of the "greater good."

She'd seen him change, yes, and had fallen for the new man he'd become since they met, but this exchange between her and Marselle . . . this dark energy of Rhethosian Justice between them felt like what the rebel leader emitted in her old home.

When Marselle said nothing in the silence, Angelyn drove on. "I'll make it easy for you, my friend. I'll list all of the horrible things that I've seen happen in my life. They got results, but they are, at their core, evil. If I say anything you haven't done since we arrived here, stop me."

Marselle stood and crossed her arms over her corseted chest. A chilled, challenging gaze sparked in her green eyes as she waited.

"You've spread lies for our benefit," Angelyn began. The words tasted like soured milk on her tongue.

Marselle remained silent. That was true.

"Blackmailing to keep someone in line."

Nothing. Also true.

"Cheating . . . stealing." The wine in Angelyn's stomach suddenly felt like a bubbling storm.

Marselle sighed, but kept her mouth closed.

"False imprisonment. Hurting men, women, and children. Torture. Murder."

"Now hold on, dear," Marselle finally spoke up. "I have never stooped low enough to do anything to a child. Irvin, on the other hand . . ."

Angelyn felt nauseated numbness creeping over her. Out of the corner of her eye, she saw Devaki shift, no doubt uncomfortable. "But *murder*?" Angelyn demanded. "In the name of the rebel cause? Behind Will's back? That's not too much for you?"

Marselle's expression became pained for a moment, as if she might suddenly cry, but then her lips tightened into a cold sense of practicality. "You fell for Will's words like everyone else. That's the way it's supposed to be. Did you think all those northern townes joined our fight 'peacefully' like he proudly tells people? We want Rhethos to think that, and I think even Will likes to think it sometimes. But people like me. . .broken people. Dirty people. We do what needs to be done so a leader like Will can be 'different' and make real change we all need."

"Marselle. . ." Angelyn found that words were now failing her; each one felt painful in her mouth, like poison. She knew Will wasn't perfect. However, the idea that people beneath him did horrible things like the Insane Captain and his master while Will preached about a better way to the kingdom's face?

She knew Irvin could be an awful man, but her new friend who she looked up to admitting casually to such crimes? It made her furious and sick at the same time. This cause she believed in was supposed to be *different*. Was she really so lost in her dream of a peaceful rebellion at Will's side that she forgot what arguably had to happen to reach their goal?

"Like I said, let me handle the northern district. You and our young Armellan hero can conquer the imaginary 'monsters' in our way," Marselle said mockingly. "I'll take care of the human ones."

After the rebel guards closed the double doors yet again behind Marselle, Devaki faced Angelyn. "Well, this . . . is all a mess."

Angelyn thought Devaki's voice sounded much too weary for someone her age, but she found she couldn't disagree.

CHAPTER TWENTY-EIGHT

FAITH OVER FEAR

"**D**on't move!" Will shouted. "Keep your feet still!"

The sobs from the men around him began to subside as everyone stopped scrambling around in the tunnel. "Make it stop," whimpered the last of Moore's guardsmen as he stumbled on the uneven bits of sandstone beneath their feet.

"Keep still and it does stop," Will insisted. "They don't want us moving forward."

Several feet away from him, one of Rowlann's men was on the floor, his torch sputtering next to him. He held his hands against his ears, his nails dragging against the sides of his face, close to drawing blood.

Will glanced at Rowlann, who shook his head. But Will couldn't let another man die down here already, especially one of Rowlann's elite force. Every man, despite his fighting prowess, had demons. Whatever was in these tunnels was using their past's pain against them . . . literally.

Pressing past Rowlann's protective arm, Will stepped over to the soldier. As soon as he moved, his head lowered under immense pressure. He cried out and fell to his knees when an image of a bundle of Sahma leaves pressed forward from his memory, one he'd woven together and dried with his own fifteen-year-old hands.

At the center of the bundle was a rolled piece of parchment, its tail end just visible. Somehow, he remembered the love poem he'd written on it word for word, as well as the chaotic events that took place after it was read. The voices in his head raked across his brain, as if digging insatiably for more.

"You loved her, and she died.

You betrayed your brother, and he died.

You broke the rules, and all of Armelle suffered."

"Enough!" Will screamed, but he stumbled on the loose rocks. Sharp sandstone cut into his palm and he felt wet blood leak between his fingers. For a moment, his heart stopped with terror . . . but nothing happened. No unseen enemy drew the liquid from his cut out of his body.

Will pulled Rowlann's soldier's hands back from his face. "Don't do that," he said, his voice much weaker now.

The man nodded shakily. "I'm sorry, Master Rowlann, Master Will," he stammered. "I can't take what Cybarys is putting in my mind. She wants us to suffer down here! But we can't go back either."

"It's hard to even tell which way *is* back," Gardain mused once more, twisting back and forth with his torch, keeping his feet smartly rooted in place. "That's clearly not where we came from."

Will stood, fighting a wave of nausea that attacked the pit of his stomach when he glanced around him. Each flicker of the torchlight illuminated a new path on either side, some heading sharply to the left or right, other branching off in weaving patterns. When Will spun backward, he saw not one but three more pathways behind them, even though they'd come down one single route.

"They keep changing," Rowlann scoffed with disbelief. "How is that possible?"

"Well, magic," Gardain said quickly. Caution and awe tinged his voice when he continued. "But I agree that it should be impossible. Blood powers the Goddess Touched Blessing Runes, but only one of those three things are present. No one has cut a Blessing Rune, and no one here is Goddess Touched . . . one who can use their magic, anyway."

"Not to mention magic doesn't create illusions or mental torture," Will snapped, his irritation growing. How could they find the source of all this trouble if they didn't know whether they were making progress?

And every time we move forward, these souls try to split our heads open and use our memories against us, if we don't give them blood.

All three of the remaining men raised their torches higher, their arms shaking with fear from where they stood behind Gardain. The vibrating light split unnaturally and redirected itself across the dirt walls, shifting as it spilled into different pathways each time one of the men looked to either side.

"Just hold still for one moment!" Rowlann snapped. "And give me that."

He took one of the torches and Will turned in place to look at him. Even though he knew the consequences, Rowlann still stepped toward Will. Pain distorted his face, and he gripped the edge of the narrow pathway to steady himself. Seeing the large, armored man walk toward him in the confined space made Will dizzy.

As the lights flickered, new pathways blossomed into view on either side of Rowlann like spontaneously growing tendons. That made something click in Will's mind: the light. Every time the torch shone onward, the light split into misleading mazes. *So it's magic that comes from light?* he thought. *That's not possible.*

"Maybe just . . . stay there," Will suggested. "I might be sick."

Rowlann halted. "What are you thinking?" he asked quietly.

"At this moment? This place is old, and whatever is awake down here should never have been touched," Will mused.

Rowlann grunted in agreement, though he didn't seem pleased with the response.

Will glanced over at Gardain, guessing the young man's fascination might be fading about now. However, he found that the Towne Master's son caught his eye with a rather determined look.

"Master Will," Gardain began. "You must see that this relates to my research I tried to share earlier. I don't understand how it specifically works yet, but this *is* Dead Magic, from the old world."

Will grimaced. *My brother,* he thought uneasily. *It was the only part, the forbidden part, of Armelle's history that he was interested in. I didn't believe him then, and even though I've seen things in these tunnels that I can't explain . . . is that really what this is?*

He tried to steady his breath and collect his thoughts. Instead, he chose to focus on what he knew, including his determining drive: find what The Bradford wanted down here to stop the disease plaguing the city above him.

"You," Will started, glaring at Gardain. "Stop talking. The rest of you, put out your torches." When only the rebel soldiers obeyed, he repeated the command with more force.

"Care to tell me why I should do that?" replied Moore's guardsman.

"Whatever this magic is, I think it's fed by the light," Will explained. "The false pathways are appearing when we shine light on the walls, and every time we look back the way we were heading, the light confuses us with even more misleading tunnels."

"But without the light, we won't be able to see where we're headed," the man snapped back, panic twitching around his eyes.

Will shook his head. "Without the light, we'll only be left with the right path. We have to not see it to travel it."

"'Have faith over fear of the unknown,'" Gardain quoted the Armellan scripture with approval in his voice. He lay his torch on the ground and smothered the flame with the bottom of his boot. "Smart."

Will stared pointedly at Moore's guardsmen at the rear of the group. They gave each other skeptical looks, but, having no other solution, they waved the brands violently till the flames went out.

The tunnel plunged into a black cloud, one that seemed to thicken with intensity the more Will tried to see. When he shut his eyes, there was no difference in the level of darkness, and a smile touched his lips.

Of course, it comes down to faith, he thought. *And I have it, but not in you, Goddess, or your ancient tricks. I have faith in myself, and my ability to outsmart whatever may be down here. I'm done with your games.*

"Master Will," began one of the rebels. "I don't like this."

"Put a hand to the wall and keep silent," Will insisted, pulling his voice down to a calmer level. "We are *not* going back. I need a moment to think about how we can survive traveling further into this hole."

Without the light, the crackle of the torches, and the audible worries of their group, the tunnel took on another setting completely. Will's other senses heightened: the smells of mold and dust and Sahma remnants all flowed through the air, moving on the breaths of his companions like a stale breeze.

A phrase Angelyn once said to him sparked in his mind, one of many instances where she'd murmured something profound in a passing manner, like it was common knowledge: "Control what you can control, and you'll make it to another sunrise."

The ancient Armellan spirits that had been seen down here, or lost souls, he guessed, said they wanted blood. Every time they'd been denied what they thirsted for to serve their Mother, the souls tore at their minds, rifling through memories and ripping through pieces of their past with maddening speed.

Will shivered, not wanting to experience that again. If they wanted blood, why didn't they take his from the cut along his palm? Did it have to do with him being Touched by the Goddess? He recalled what Devaki had told him about her journey to the digsite alone; when she'd cut her Blessing Runes, the attacks on her had ceased.

Reaching down, Will pulled several inches of his sword out of its sheath and ran the top of his forearm over its edge. He winced as he made a fist, increasing the blood flow, catching the liquid in his opposite hand. Placing his sticky fingers against the wall to his right, Will took a deep breath and stepped forward.

Every muscle in his body tensed, anticipating the mind-wrenching torture, but his head remained clear. With more confidence, Will took another two steps and pressed his bloody hand to the stone.

So there is something about Goddess Touched blood that they don't like, he thought. *Even if my "gift" doesn't work, it's still in my blood.*

When his hand slipped in the dark, however, to a dry spot on the wall, his head began to ache again. Adjusting his fingers, Will found that the pain ceased once he stepped forward with his touch on the bloodied stone. *This will be interesting,* he thought.

"Walk forward, with your right hand on the wall," Will instructed. "Touching the stones with my blood on them should keep the souls at bay while we press on."

"Fascinating," he heard Gardain murmur in the dark behind him.

Will heard the group start to walk, the soft whisper of their skin against the stone wall echoing in his ears. It was slow going, with the others feeling blindly for the right places along the wall that he'd touched. Every time Will felt the pathway bend, he kept close to it and stayed on their current course.

It was a shot in the dark (literally), but he refused to go back, glad that he could feel a steady decline in their steps, leading them further into the earth. He only hoped they'd stumble upon an opening or another clue soon before he bled himself dry.

CHAPTER TWENTY-NINE

PEACE, PROSPERITY, SERVITUDE

Silence and darkness descended on the digsite tunnel in a heavy blanket. Will could still feel the ancient souls trying to break into his head, trying to throw their group off course, but each time he gave them what they wanted, they screamed in frustration at his blood. It felt as though two giant hands were pressing against either side of his head, trying to overcome his new defenses and crumble his skull into pieces. His feet tested the blind steps he was taking, and his hand remained slick against the tunnel's walls.

What was The Bradford digging for? Will thought. *What did he want badly enough to sacrifice some of his best soldiers and upset one of his most loyal townes?*

Will paused for a moment, feeling the cut on his forearm starting to congeal. He twisted it as Rowlann bumped into him.

"Sorry," Rowlann muttered. "Everything all right?"

"Yes," Will lied, his body shaking.

"How much longer can you bleed like that?" Rowlann asked quietly, even though everyone in the passageway could undoubtedly hear him.

Will knew Rowlann had experienced how Devaki's magic only stayed active when she kept bleeding. This wasn't something he could do forever. "It's not the blood I'm worried about," Will grimaced. He could hear the spirits on the edges of his thoughts, begging for light, whining for blood, longing for freedom. He clutched at the stone with his wet fingers, flaking away bits of ancient dirt.

"Will?" Rowlann began.

"Keep moving," Will insisted. The pain in his head made it feel like the opposite side of the pathway he wasn't touching would crash into his shoulder any moment. He resisted the urge to duck, sure the ceiling was going to press into his body and finally crack him open so nothing could stop the ancient Armellan souls bent on breaking him to pieces.

"Can you hear that?" Gardain spoke up.

Will strained his ears, but he found that the effort made him want to scream; he could barely hear his own thoughts over the persistent whispers on the edges of his conscience.

"It sounds like water," commented one of the others. "An underground river, maybe?"

"No one digging here said anything about a body of water," Rowlann said, his voice very close over Will's shoulder.

"Then we might be further than any of the previous expeditions," Will suggested, unable to keep the edge out of his voice.

The next step Will took, his foot met air. He tumbled forward, weightless for a single heartbeat, then landed hard on a cool, flat surface. He barely managed to roll sideways before Rowlann and the rest crashed down next to him.

"Is everyone all right?" Will asked, then realized that he could see his hands and his arms. In fact, the more he blinked, the more aware he was of the light change in this space they'd fallen into. He noticed that the ground underneath his hands was no longer rough sandstone but black and smooth, like marble.

Ten years old, he had scrubbed the temple floor clean after hundreds of Cybarys' worshippers knelt against its smooth surface.

His hands stood out against the dark surface, white against black, different from all of the monks who gave him and his brother a home.

Will pressed back the nostalgia that tried to touch his heart, barely letting it past the surface of his skin. When he found his feet, he saw he was in a huge chamber, one supported by giant sandstone pillars and full of unearthly pale light. Its dome-like shape and dark floor reminded him of the Valsara Temple but in a dark sort of way that made him extremely uneasy.

Instead of prayer candles lining the edges of the room in welcoming arcs like they did across the sea, here there were deep grooves cut into the stone. The divots ran like small tributaries toward the far wall, where he saw a likeness of Cybarys, human-sized and cut from the stone around her. At her feet was a deep catch basin, now empty.

His throat dry, Will looked upward, along the curved walls of the chamber to see half a dozen sets of shackles, fashioned to hold a person above the grooves in the floor, as if to catch falling blood.

The sound of water was much more prominent here, and when Will glanced to the left wall of the chamber, which curved inward on itself, he saw the smooth flow of a river, its waters dark except for bits of white froth at the edges. Even in the pale lighting, he could see the moist smoothness of spotless rocks.

"Are those chains?" asked one guardsman, staring upward. "As in, Cybarys' *literal* chains?"

"I don't know," Will replied, though in his mind it was an ancient form of a temple, the term for which he remembered his brother mentioning many years ago. "This used to be called a Harvest Room." As he said it, his attention was pulled to the statue. Though her features were shadowed, he could make out the tips of the Goddess' outstretched fingers, calling to him.

"Why does that sound much more sinister than it should?" Rowlann demanded.

"I read about those!" Gardain exclaimed. He had gained his feet on the black marble floor, turning steadily in circles, his gray eyes wide. "Ancient Armellans would gather here at the change of each season, and the community would give blood as their Temple Leader conducted rituals . . . a *lot* of blood. I *knew* I'd gotten it right! I can't say what those shackles are for, but I can definitely guess."

Will muttered to himself. He hated guessing, but he couldn't deny the heavy energy in this room. When he looked at the rest of their group, everyone had frightened expressions on their faces.

"Why were they forced to endure such sinister acts?" Gardain was musing, stepping forward. He couldn't seem to stop himself from sharing his theories aloud. "Everyone talks about the Blood Goddess' chains, as if she used to force people to bleed for her to the point of death, harvesting blood from her children to ensure their loyalty? Or their survival in a more dangerous world—?"

"Gardain," Will growled, rounding on the young man. Will could tell the Towne Master's son was making everyone else progressively more nervous, on the edge of panic.

"Sorry, sorry," Gardain said, though he continued to murmur under his breath. "It's just an odd riddle to me. Cybarys herself bled to give birth to the first humans; we literally came from her blood. To give back to her through her magic we now know makes sense, but this here . . . it feels wrong. Evil."

Will did not respond to that, not necessarily believing the creation myth that was preached in Armelle. Gardain just wanted the truth, and he was risking his life being down here looking for it. Old times and ancient events were purposefully lost, both by The Bradford and the Temple Leaders in Armelle. He also knew history had been twisted by both kingdoms since then, and he was hesitant to believe anything till he experienced it firsthand.

His brother, however, had been bent on showing Will that the foreign kingdom Will loved was not what it seemed, often trying to find forbidden pieces of their world's long-lost magic. As a child, Will could never understand why; the appeal of Cybarys, a loving, compassionate Mother was what he needed after losing the woman who'd cared for him.

Despite how drawn he was to the modern teachings of Armelle's monks, he still faced more tragedy in his youth. After Devaki's mother died, Will had cultivated a harshness toward Cybarys that was well-justified, but this . . . this feeling in the Harvest Room was different. Despite his hatred, he always felt the Goddess' love in return. Here, his anger was met and overcome tenfold.

An icy wave of fear bit at his spine. When Will stepped toward the middle of the room, the black surface cracked underneath his left boot. Dust plumed around his knees, thick with sand and forgotten times. It had been centuries since people had knelt in this place, supplicating the Goddess for her love and safety.

Squinting, Will looked up and knew the silver light was being created by some unseen magic. He noticed that chunks of the floor were broken in haphazard shapes, jutting out of the ground. Pieces of the domed ceiling had fallen, splitting the ancient marble. No one, not The Bradford's nor Moore's men, had been here in countless years.

"I don't see another pathway out of this room," Will said. "What we're looking for must be down here. Search every corner. We will *not* return empty handed."

Each of them spread out, though what they were hoping to find Will still couldn't guess. An artifact? An old book? Some secret of Cybarys' that somehow served The Bradford now? He ground his teeth at the lack of answers.

Moore's remaining guardsman had moved close to the Goddess' statue. When he neared the basin at her bare feet, the man started to grunt. Then he screamed, falling to his knees. As he clutched his head, Will knew the same magic they'd experienced in the tunnels was attacking the man here.

Will reached down to break open the cut on his forearm, knelt on the cold marble, and smeared his blood against the dusty stone. A murmur of laughter rippled through his mind, and a fast glance at Rowlann showed that he heard it, too. The guardsman shrieked, his sudden agony amplified around the circular Harvest Room.

Whatever fear the souls had of his blood in the tunnels, it wasn't a factor now in the Harvest Room. Will felt terror root in his chest and spread through his limbs rapidly. This energy was stronger and wasn't afraid of his Touch.

Blood streamed down the guardsman's face as he tore at his eyes, bubbling over his cheeks and into his palms.

"No!" Rowlann shouted, but it was too late.

Will barely took a step when the pale light of the chamber shimmered around the bleeding guardsman. When it cleared, three figures stood around the man, or rather, the outlines of them became clear. Will tore his sword from its scabbard, but Rowlann put a hand on his arm. The figures, shining in the same color of the room's light, stooped toward the guardsman, their ethereal fingers dipping into the tears on the man's cheeks.

"We bleed for peace, as one."

Three voices echoed forth, and though Will assumed the sounds came from the ghost-like figures, his attention was drawn back to the statue of Cybarys on the far wall. The light around her form began to solidify as well, back to the dull gray the room used to be when they entered.

"We bleed for prosperity, as one."

A new cry of pain ripped from the guardsman's body, and when Will looked at him, he saw that the transparent forms around the man were gaining more shape. He could make out the brown color of their skin where they touched the guardsman's blood, and intricate chains of linked metals that ran up and down their arms.

"We have to help him!" one Rowlann's men demanded, yet he stood rooted to the spot several yards away.

"We bleed in servitude, as one."

One of the figures took hold of the bleeding guardsman's chin. Will could make out his dark robes, gathered in leather braces at his wrists, elbows, and waist. He reached inside the left sleeve of his garment and pulled out a small knife.

Will ran forward, closing the distance between himself and the guardsman with his sword raised. The ancient Armellan soul did not look at him but brought his blade down across the guardsman's back, weaving it in a practiced motion. Somehow, it cut through armor and cloth and flesh like water. His slashes came together in the shape of a rune, one that shone with blinding gold light to the point that Will couldn't see its full shape.

Shock and confusion rattled through Will. That was *not* a Blessing Rune. In that single moment, he couldn't stop the realization from screaming clearly in his mind. *It's real, then. That's a Dead Rune, a piece of Dead Magic.*

When Will thrust his sword through the soul, who was quickly solidifying, his blade passed harmlessly through the man. The other two figures knelt next to the guardsman, placing their hands over the rune their leader had cut. The blood from the wound coursed up into the air instead of down the man's back, against the tips of the ancient Armellans' fingers.

"Get him!" Will snapped at Rowlann. He grabbed the guardsman's wrist and tried to pull him away from his attackers. Rowlann took hold of the man's opposite wrist, and Will marveled at how difficult it was to pull the guardsman backward. It was as if an unseen bond was holding him in his place as the old souls pulled wave after wave of blood from the guardsman's body.

Finally, they yanked him free, and Will and Rowlann skidded backward on the marble floor. His muscles ached as though he'd lifted an enormous weight, and when he looked at the guardsman's wrist he held, his stomach turned. The man's arm had been reduced to dry skin, which flattened to an unnatural thinness against his bones.

"There's nothing left," Rowlann said, and he tossed aside the drained man's arm.

Will shook his head angrily, finding his feet. The three ancient Armellan men had vanished, leaving behind not a single drop of blood. He turned toward Cybarys' statue, fury filling his veins. Renewing his grip on his sword,

Will marched toward the statue, ignoring the light distortions dancing across his vision. He wanted his answers. Now.

"What are you doing?" Rowlann demanded.

Will split open the cut along his forearm and rubbed his palm with fresh blood. "I'm going to have a talk with the damned Goddess."

CHAPTER THIRTY

FORCING HER HAND

Will heard Rowlann protest, and Gardain began to mutter, but Will was no longer listening. He set his sword down at the feet of Cybarys' statue, then held his arms out to either side, almost mirroring her image.

Breathing deeply, he set his mind back to when he was nine or ten, learning how to meditate, to connect with the Goddess, to hear her wisdom. His fingers twisted into a prayer knot, which he pressed against his forehead. He could envision the statue in the center of Valsara's main temple chamber, a hundred times the size of the small one before him.

All right, you passive bitch, he thought, still calm and reverent despite the vile intention behind his words. *It's been too long since I've given in. Let's hear what you want, so we can make a deal. It's time to end this, here and now.*

Silence met his ears, defiant and strong. Will kept his breath even, taking time to fill his entire chest with air. In the space between his inhale and slow, controlled exhale, he kept his head and his heart open, waiting for any response. When the silence persisted, he let his fingers fall out of their knot. He twisted his forearm, let out fresh blood, and heard the droplets hit the statue's stone basin with wet clarity.

This passage is a dead end, he tried next. *What were The Bradford's men looking for in here? What are these old souls protecting? And why do you keep calling out to my daughter?*

"Will," Gardain began, and from his meditative state, the man's voice seemed miles away. "They're back. . . well, one of the spirits is, and he looks rather important."

Will opened his eyes to see that one of the ethereal men had reappeared. He stood on the raised section of stone next to Cybarys' statue. In his hand was the dagger he'd used to cut into the guardsman's back, a small collection of drying blood on its tip.

"She will not answer your demands," the Armellan soul spoke. His words echoed in the air around them, but his mouth did not move.

"What else is new?" Will sighed. "You want blood, don't you? Take mine." When he held out his dripping forearm, the man's wavering form shimmered as he stepped backward. "That's what I thought," Will smirked. "If Cybarys won't answer my questions, you better say something. Religious patience was never my strong suit."

"No one forces the hand of our Mother," the old soul began, dismissively straightening his voluminous robes and glancing around the chamber's high ceiling. "What the remains of Kaladir hold is as dead as I am, and it will stay that way. Your Lord's men disturbed our peace and awoke us to ensure her secrets are kept."

"You don't understand," Will insisted. "I only want what you're protecting to keep it from those who would do much worse. I am not like the men who tried to come here before me."

The Armellan soul's face split into a nasty grin, and when he raised his hand that held his dagger, the pressure he'd felt on his head in the dark passageways returned, and he clenched his jaw against the fresh wave of pain.

"You will change nothing." He laughed, motioned with his dagger at the guardsman on the floor that he'd cut open, and the other two Armellan spirits reappeared. They turned toward Gardain, who didn't even seem to think of drawing his weapon. One of Rowlann's men stepped forward, protecting the Towne Master's son.

In mere heartbeats, the spirit's weapons connected with the man in front of Gardain, drawing a wave of fresh blood. No matter what Rowlann or the others did to try and stop them, the spirits latched onto the man's open wounds and began pulling the rest of his blood from his trembling body.

"Let him be!" Will insisted, helplessness filling his chest.

"We will not," declared the dead Temple Leader. "Why can't you quietly follow your Fate's String and obey your Mother, Caulin?"

Will couldn't stop his jaw from dropping. "What did you call me?"

"Master Will, he's dying!" Gardain shouted, and when Will glanced back at Rowlann's fighter, there was hardly anything left of him. His skin draped over his face like a wrinkled sheet of paper, and his mouth hung open in a silent cry of agony. When he tried to breathe, his body convulsed, then he lay still.

The ethereal men had nearly solidified now, and when they rose from their victim, their weapons looked real enough when they faced Rowlann. He glared back at their leader and spat defiantly at Cybarys' statue.

"I envy your free will," the Armellan soul murmured. He held his hand up and his men waited for his order to attack once more. "But we are slaves to her whim. We always have been, and even in death, to protect her lost magic, we can do no more than what she commands."

Will growled, his frustration mounting. He was here to fight for Rhethos' freedom. He wanted nothing to do with Armelle, or its ancient curses, yet the damned Goddess had once more forced herself into his fight. *Why? What does this place's mysteries have to do with my enemy?*

Silently, Will knelt and retrieved his sword. "Enough, then," he said. "Enough names from my past, enough insults, and enough mysteries. You look real enough now. Let's see if *you* still bleed."

"Oh," the ancient form shook his head, even as he menacingly twirled his dagger. "The Goddess will not let us harm you, Caulin. But we can take all of your men's blood for our Mother."

Will stepped back from the statue's pedestal to face the two Armellan spirits that advanced toward Rowlann, Gardain, and the remaining rebel soldier.

The Armellan soul drew a second dagger from within his robe's sleeve. He used its tip to cut a rune scar Will didn't recognize on top of his opposite hand, and a brilliant yellow flash filled the room. Will noticed that his two men faded slightly as their leader prepared his magic, as if he drew from the blood source they had provided for him.

Light is the residue of this old magic, Will noticed. *Not heat, like the Blessing Runes. Bright yellow light, not a warm red glow. And instead of giving his own blood, he has to pull it from the body of another. . . or is that only because he's dead and has no blood of his own to give? Does he need every drop in a man's body for the full effect of the magic?*

There were too many questions, too many secrets. Complications did not help his cause, nor did they keep his rebels or Lorington's people safe.

"There is only one way you will get all of your answers, Caulin."

Will heard Rowlann and the others cry out as they clashed with the undead, but the scrapes of metal and the shuffling of feet did not turn his attention from the ancient form in front of him. Golden light poured from the symbol on his hand, leaking like blood onto the dusted stone floor. The Armellan soul raised both of his arms above his head and held suddenly still.

"Bring your daughter down here," he said with a cruel smile. "Cybarys *will* speak to her."

Will took a firm step back with his left foot, then swung hard and low at the ancient man's gut. In the same moment, the man brought down both daggers, and when they met the edge of Will's sword, a wave of visible force ran through the Harvest Room.

Before he could react, Will was thrown through the air as if pushed by an insurmountable tide. He slammed into the back wall, right below the ledge where they'd entered the chamber. Will gasped, fighting back the urge to scream. A small groan escaped his lips as the pain from the impact ran its course through his body.

All of that power came from him? he thought, shakily trying to find his feet. He motioned for Rowlann and the others to get behind him, blocking the reach of the Armellan souls' weapons.

"Will," Rowlann began, "you can't take another hit like that."

"I know," Will snapped. "You should go."

"What?" Gardain questioned. "You can't be—"

But Rowlann motioned for his man to grab Gardain's arm and pull him up the wall to reach the raised ledge.

"I want whatever The Bradford came here for," Will insisted. His eyes were on the brightly lit rune cut into the Armellan soul's hand. "And you," he added, taking a step toward the spirit, "you're going to give it to me, or you'll have to kill me. How does the Goddess feel about that?"

The ancient forms paused, unable to raise their weapons against Will. It gave Rowlann enough time to climb to safety, forcing Gardain farther back. The light pouring from the rune on the man's hand melted to a darker, more dangerous shade of deep gold.

"You're as stubborn as she said you'd be," sneered the Armellan soul. "You give her your blood out of defiance and we give it to her as unwilling slaves. No matter what, in the end Cybarys wins."

The wave of energy that met Will's chest blew him back into the wall. This time, in every direction around the chamber, he heard a series of cracks issue forth. Stone split and crumbled in web-like patterns, spewing dusty rubble onto the floor. Will's vision wavered as he collapsed, dropping his sword. He coughed, and a bit of blood spattered the floor.

Inhumanely strong hands gripped the front of his jerkin, hauled him upward, and held him suspended in the air. Will met the eyes of the ancient form before him, staring into their dark orbs with as much strength as he could muster. He held his hands out from his sides as he had when he'd meditated by Cybarys' statue, leaving himself open for whatever came next.

Frustration peppered the spirit's face, and he shook more magic out of his right hand in a flurry of bright flashes. The next burst of incredible force threw Will to the left, and his shoulder smashed into one of the chamber's enormous pillars. Will screamed, feeling his arm punch out of its socket. He clutched his left limb to his side, his jaw quivering with overwhelming pain.

"Let it go, Caulin," the Armellan spirit ordered, and Will shivered when he heard the tone of the man's voice shift. Perhaps he had hit his head, too, but now there was a dark, powerful undertone to the man's words that reeked of the Goddess herself. The sound was heavy and menacing, weighing over him like a physical knife at his throat.

"Show me what you're hiding," Will rasped, "and then we'll see how I feel." He tried to stand and failed; his body was beaten down, lacking too much blood, and the edges of his vision stayed black no matter how much he tried to blink the unconsciousness away.

Two of the Armellan souls appeared on either side of him and took hold of him with rough hands. He noticed their limbs were transparent, as if the blood of two men didn't sustain their corporeal forms for long. When they yanked on his dislocated shoulder, Will passed out for a moment, unable to take the anguish that spread through him like fire.

"We bleed for peace, as one." The voices that spoke the chant seemed to echo directly into his head as the world faded away. "We bleed for prosperity, as one. We bleed in servitude, as one."

CHAPTER THIRTY-ONE

RHETHOSIAN JUSTICE

The streets of Kaylyn ran with blood in Joshua's nightmare. The field outside his old home was covered in bodies, and a man with blinding yellow light radiating from his chest screamed with laughter. It was chaos, carnage, and complete ruin that he didn't understand.

Through it, he heard the Goddess' voice, pounding like a guttural beat. *"You can stop all of this, little McKinlee. Together, we can bring peace. At the center of the woods, you will find the key to your freedom."*

"Joshua!"

He struggled to wake, but something held him pinned in the dream. The same images rushed by like the jumbled pages of a book caught in a frenzied storm.

"Josh, wake up!"

He brought awareness to his limbs and how they ached from sleeping on the forest floor night after night.

"Josh, you have to get up! He's dead."

Finally, his body disentangled itself from the grip of his subconscious mind and came back to the cold, dark world. The last of the trees' leaves littered his blanket, frost forming at the cloth's edges. He sat up, nearly crashing into Ada's forehead. The icy clouds of her breath burst in his face as he blinked away the last of sleep.

"Ada," he began. "How are you here? Didn't those men. . .?"

His throat constricted when he really looked at the girl who used to serve drinks for his mother in The Hamond: a gray and indigo bruise ran across the left side of her face, from her temple to the edge of her neck. Her normally smooth brunette locks were strewn in knotted clumps down her shoulders.

"Those aren't men," she snapped. "They're monsters. I got away. But you can't hide out here anymore."

Joshua glanced over at Mistress Merheene, who slept curled against the trunk of a large oak underneath the majority of their blankets. The small fire they'd had earlier to eat and keep warm by had burned down to maroon embers. "You said, 'he's dead,' didn't you?" Joshua asked slowly. "Who did you mean?"

Ada's brown eyes filled with tears, rimming the edges of her bloodshot gaze. "Josh, I'm sorry . . ."

"No." Joshua shook his head. His hands tightened in fists at his sides, crunching the frozen underbrush beneath him. He refused to believe what she was implying, and the denial came out in a rush. "They said that they needed everyone alive! The Rhethosian Captain wants us alive! We're worth more that way! That's what he said!"

"They couldn't keep Orton quiet once he heard that they were sending messages to the Insane Captain," Ada explained bitterly. "So they gathered the rest of the men . . ." She leaned forward, taking hold of Joshua's hands.

When he looked down, Joshua noticed blood under her fingernails. He knew that the dozen or so men left in the camp had to be twice Orton's age, but still, they were the only decent fighters left.

"Are you saying they're all dead?" Joshua breathed. His heart ached for the rebel Master who had taught him so much in a short time, as well as the others left behind who couldn't fight with Will. "There's only women and children?" he asked aloud.

Ada nodded bitterly, a few tears running down her cheeks. "Your father's men are telling the Rhethosian military exactly where we are and what they want for turning us over to be used against Will. They . . ." She paused, and her grip tightened on his hands to a point of sharp pain. "Tonight they cut all of their throats, right in the middle of camp where everyone could see. It . . .wasn't pretty."

Joshua fought down fresh outrage. His father had lied to and hurt his mother for years, working as a spy for the Rhethosian military. He came to the rebel camp when they were vulnerable, attacked Joshua, threatened innocent lives, and murdered men Joshua looked up to.

"How can we stop them?" Joshua thought aloud hopelessly.

"I saw what you did to that man's leg by the storehouses," Ada replied. "You're smarter than your father's men, smarter than *her* people." She jerked her head in Mistress Merheene's direction, barely lowering her voice. "Even though I don't like it, you can use that magic to bring them down. *I'll* kill them. The other women will join us if we're brave enough to make a stand."

Joshua hesitated, despite how much it hurt to realize he'd never see Orton again. He looked into Ada's eyes and saw all the mental and physical pain she'd endured in such a short period of time.

"What matters more to you, Josh?" Ada leaned in, so their faces were inches apart. "The pagan Goddess out here or your people in there?"

But something held him back; Cybarys had shown him incredible power in his last vision, with the five lines of magic she said were lost to the world. If he could stay on this path and bring that back, somehow, he could either save or destroy *everything*. In his heart, he wanted that so badly, to be significant and independent of his mother's old cage.

Ada let out a huff as she stood. "Fine," she growled, her lower lip trembling. "I'll do it myself. Stay out here with your *destiny.*" She spat the word as she turned to head back through the trees toward camp.

Joshua glanced again at Mistress Merheene, still asleep in a cocoon of her cloak and blankets. He stood abruptly and added his blanket on top of the Armellan woman. "Wait!" he called after Ada. Picking his legs up high to weave through the brush on all sides of him, Joshua stumbled after her.

I told Cybarys I wanted to help my friends. She told me to wait, that Her riddles were more important. Now Orton is dead. I've had enough of sitting here.

"We should go to the corrals first," Ada told him. "To stop the messages. Whatever lies they're telling Will stop now. And we don't want them informing the Captain, either."

"Good plan," Joshua agreed.

"Give me one of your daggers," Ada demanded.

"Are you sure?"

She gave him a cold glance, more visible now that they neared the edge of the forest and were greeted by the moon's light. "I already killed one last night with my bare hands." Her voice was tinged with a numbness that frightened Joshua. "It would be easier now if you gave me whichever dagger you're weakest with."

Swallowing, Joshua handed over the blade on his left hip. It was the one Orton had given him when he chose this fighting style over a typical sword, the right dagger being the one Will had given him the night his home burned.

"We've got to go all the way through camp, back where the horses are kept," he said, whispering now that he could see the outlines of men in the watchtower and dirt paths beyond. She nodded.

Joshua gripped tightly to a Protection Rune on his left shoulder, ready to twist it open. Then he thought of Ada; how could his magic keep her safe, too? For all her defiance, he could tell Ada was drained and injured, and he needed to make sure she wouldn't lose her life trying to get revenge for Orton and the others.

"Wait a second," Joshua said, breaking open the rune scar on his shoulder till he felt beads of blood form on his palm. He turned to Ada, noticing that bits of snow were beginning to fall around them, turning into fat, frozen flakes. He had an idea.

"What?" she insisted impatiently.

"Just trust me." He grabbed the end of her long leather belt she wore looped around her waist and brought the tip of his dagger against the supple material. Tracing the blade in the shape of a Protection Rune, Joshua cut enough to break halfway through the leather. He smeared his blood on the mark, then made sure the cut on his shoulder was still open. *Maybe this will help her,* he thought. *Goddess, please keep her safe.*

"We have to be smart and quiet," he added. "There are a lot of them in there."

Ada looked warily at the mark he'd etched into her belt but didn't complain. Joshua stepped in front of her, out of the trees and toward the plank that ran over the camp's eastern trench. Just as they emerged, the two shadows on guard above in the tower turned away, looking south instead. Their voices echoed down, like the falling snow, and Joshua felt fresh heat bloom on his arm.

They kept to the sides of the roads, darting in between the torches that burned away the winter chill and ice attempting to encase the camp. Ahead of them was a group of seven men, wrapped in fur cloaks and carrying several torches. They stood next to the doorways on the ground level buildings, underneath the raised platforms above, blocking their path.

Ada glanced sideways at him, and Joshua sheathed his dagger. His gaze darted around above them until he found the rope he was looking for. Pulling it released a counterweight down the line of planks, lowering an opening above their heads. He helped Ada put her feet on the large knots in the rope meant for climbing, keeping his eyes on Travok's men not far away.

When it was his turn to haul himself up onto the second level, his stomach dropped; he'd forgotten to whisper to Ada to keep tension on the rope. When she let go of it, the counterweight slammed back into place with a loud thud. The noise echoed throughout the quiet camp, and Ada swore under her breath.

"What in the Lord's name was that?" said one of the men below. Joshua saw his torchlight whirl as he looked left and right.

"Something up there," said another. "Better go look. Travok said no one's allowed out of these little shitholes after dark."

"How do you get up there? I don't know how this damned rope system works."

"Go," Joshua hissed. Back the way they came, another counterweight slammed down and lowered one of the main planks to the ground below.

Staying crouched down, they rushed forward as fast as they could, skidding occasionally on the snow-slick planks and ducking underneath bunches of ropes and chains. When the open area of corrals emerged out of the gloom, Joshua's heart fell when he saw more than twenty men ranged around the fences. They were dispersed throughout, routinely checking the gates.

"Okay," Ada began quietly, extending her arm over his shoulder to point at a group of men. "They're the ones Travok gave messages to. Some will ride to Lorington, others will head straight south to Clancy."

Joshua squinted and saw four men covered in thick riding gear, each with satchels on their belts and horses waiting nearby. They stood close together at the front of the enclosed area, talking quietly.

"Back there," Ada continued, "is where I'm headed." Her finger hovered over the stables at the very back of the corral, pressed against the looming mountainside. "I'm going to set those horses loose and create a distraction. The watchmen should come back to the stables, so you can handle those four messengers in the commotion. When I give the signal, the rebel families will come out to help us take these men down."

Joshua thought fast, frowning. "You sure you want that job, with twenty men coming toward you? I could—"

"I know what I'm doing," Ada insisted. She gripped his dagger tighter in her hand. "After the horses are out, I'll lure as many of the men into the stables as I can . . . then cut these." She smacked her palm against the frosty post next to them on the upper level of The Forts, the remains of a massive oak that held up this end of the rebel camp's narrow buildings.

Joshua nodded in approval. The support beams here were built the same as the ones on those stables, and if Ada timed it right, she could collapse the wooden structures on Travok's men.

Ada let out a slow, deliberate breath, then turned toward the ladder at the end of the plank system. "Be careful, little Josh," she whispered. "For Rhethos." She descended to the frozen ground.

Joshua slid down the icy ladder after her. Ada's form disappeared into the dark night air, obscured by the snow that fell more heavily now. He waited, counting the seconds, then counting the minutes as ice formed on his eyebrows. Then, there was the sudden groaning of wood. A loud crash echoed out, and a plume of dust rose from the far end of the open area. Horses and men screamed in unison, but Joshua had his eyes on the riders set to go out.

The watchmen currently making the rounds ran back toward the stables, leaving the messengers alone at the entrance. Two of the messengers got on their horses, while the other two held the mounts' bridles and stepped toward the sudden chaos across the corrals. All four murmured in confusion to each other, their eyes on the horses set free within the enclosure.

Joshua darted forward, dagger in hand. With all of their backs turned, it was simple for him to run up behind the two mounted riders and slash at their belts to remove their pouches packed with papers. The two messengers on the ground chuckled to one another, pointing at the rest of Travok's men scrambling about to collect and calm the horses.

The Protection Rune on his shoulder was starting to clot, the blood down his arm drying in the freezing air. He was creeping toward the backs of the dismounted riders when Joshua heard Ada shriek in the distance. Through the latest sheet of snowfall, he barely spotted her grappling with a man who was unarmed. Her opponent lunged at her, but she sidestepped, swung her arm back, and drove her dagger into his gut.

"What in the Lord's name. . .?" growled one of the messengers.

"We should ride out, in case there's more rebels with her," said another.

Joshua grabbed desperately at the man's belt as he turned, hoping to get one more bundle of papers, but he wasn't fast enough. His hand slipped and the edge of his dagger missed the leather wrapped around the man's waist. He cursed as all four men snapped their attention to him.

"Grab him!" barked one of the messengers on horseback. "He's got my bag!"

Joshua dropped both satchels he'd cut free onto the snow-littered earth. With his free hand, he broke open the Strength Runes he'd cut onto his knuckles. Balancing Will's blade at its center point, he dropped low and waited for one of them to make a move.

Both messengers on the ground let go of their horses' reins and stepped toward him. One darted forward as if to grab Josh's tunic, and the other took the time to pull out his sword. Joshua pivoted on the ball of his right foot and tilted his wrist at the same time. Ducking underneath the first man's reach, he flipped his dagger backward so his punch landed into his enemy's gut. The dagger's pommel connected underneath the middle of the man's rib cage, as Orton taught him to do. That messenger collapsed, unable to move. Red magic remnants sprinkled into the white snow.

The second man had his sword out and drove the point toward Joshua as he came out of his low position. Joshua skidded to the side, his foot sliding on the wet earth. His blade met his enemy's next attack and the sound echoed around the empty land. He ducked inside the man's swings, narrowly avoiding several slices close to his arms. Twisting his dagger downward this time, letting the weight drop the tip toward the ground, Joshua cut at the man's shoulders. Two precise hits sliced into the joints of the man's leather jerkin. Blood flew, and he dropped his sword.

Ada screamed again, but through the dozens of horses running wildly around the corrals, the falling snow, and the night's blackness, Joshua couldn't see her anymore.

Why wasn't his magic keeping her safe? What good was it if he could only protect himself? Glancing at his Protection Rune, he noticed it wasn't bleeding anymore. His attention was drawn to the two remaining messengers on horseback, both of whom had drawn weapons and were glaring at Josh.

He flinched backward; Orton had only taught him so many tricks, and how to survive a frontal assault from mounted riders wasn't one of them. Dropping his stance low again, Joshua focused on what was important: getting those letters away from Will and the Rhethosian Captain.

"*Boy!*"

Joshua spun. Fear dropped low into the soft spot of his gut. He recognized his father's voice. The bulking man strode toward him from the main camp, a torch in each hand. Josh watched Travok's gaze snap to the collapsed stables in the distance, underneath which now lay many of his men.

"Caused me enough trouble!" Travok roared, and he spun one of the torches like a mace. "Caldrell be damned. I'll give 'em yours and Orton's heads in bags, and he'll pay for the rest of these rebel shits in gold!"

The messengers backed off, their horses frightened of the towering, bellowing man wielding brands of fire. Only two bags of notes lay at Joshua's feet. The other two were in the riders' possession, both of whom looked ready to flee. He couldn't stop them, not with his father barreling toward him with outrage in his eyes.

"*Be smart, and you'll live through this.*" Joshua remembered Orton's words (his last words to him) yet again. He turned his back on Travok and darted behind one of the messenger's horses. The frightened animal was prancing in place, terrified of Travok's torches so close to its face. Despite his best efforts, the messenger couldn't get the scared horse to budge.

"Get out of my way!" ordered Travok, brandishing the fire in the messenger's direction. The horse only reared this time, neighing in distress, rooted in place between father and son.

What is wrong with him? Joshua thought, bewildered. *Can't he see he's terrifying those beasts with that fire?* Then he looked closer, around the horse's legs, and saw how uneven his father's gait was. He noticed ale stains down the front of his tunic, like the ones he'd seen on men who spent every night at his mother's bar.

Joshua jumped, grabbed the back of the distracted messenger's belt as he tried in vain to control his horse. When Josh pulled, the satchel ripped loose as the horse's hooves slammed back into the ground. With a cry, the horse finally darted forward and ran into the night, bucking off the messenger as it went. The man landed with a shout and clutched at one of his ankles.

"You are ruining everything!" Travok spat at Joshua. "Should have stayed long enough to force your mother to smother you at birth, with the rest of the cursed children."

"Strong words, for a spy and a traitor!" Joshua replied. He sidestepped away from the remaining messenger and his horse as they lunged toward them. The man took a swipe at Joshua with his sword, but with his mount darting away from Travok's fire, his attack missed completely. Joshua scurried back and forth with the horse's movement, trying to keep it between him and his father.

Travok snarled in frustration and threw one of the torches to the ground. He stumbled around the horse, waving his remaining brand at Joshua in wide, blinding arcs. Joshua ducked low, keeping his dagger parallel to the ground in a defensive stance. It was getting nearly impossible to avoid Travok, and Joshua didn't think he could fight him off . . . not without potentially dealing out lethal damage.

His father's next swing connected with the leg of the messenger in his way. The man cried out as fire spread up his trousers. Both horse and rider shrieked and rode past Joshua in a growing burst of deadly heat. The sight and sound of the burning man made Joshua sick, but he felt fresh rage wash over him when Travok, the man he had to call his father, *laughed.*

When Joshua heard that sound, the entirety of his predicament rushed over him in an overwhelming wave.

His mother's shaking hands whenever she was around conflict or heard the angry shouts of men.

His dream to be free and make his own path in the world shattered because this man showed up as a violent traitor.

His goals to learn about his magic, train with Orton, fight for Will, and make his kingdom proud were all destroyed because this man had murdered his friend, turned his new home into a prison, and hurt Ada.

Travok drunkenly lunged at Joshua with his torch once more, and this time Joshua let out a cry that encompassed every injustice and swung back. He barely felt the impact of the length of his blade sliding across his father's throat. The motion was quick, smooth, and almost effortless. Then the flaming brand dropped to the ground and a warm spray of liquid splashed across Joshua's face.

Illuminated by the torch sputtering on the snowy earth, Travok clutched his thick, square fingers against his neck. Unable to breathe himself, Joshua numbly wiped at his face, not feeling his hand as it smeared blood from his eyes. Travok staggered as he choked, lashing out viciously with one arm in Joshua's direction.

No, Joshua thought, but he found he couldn't take his eyes from the pulsing wave of black blood pouring from the long, precise cut on his father's throat. He didn't mean to . . .or did he?

His mind suddenly flashed back to the night The Hamond burned, when Will had cut the throat of the Rhethosian officer who had captured him. Then, Joshua had been too afraid to look at the bleeding wound. He was terrified to find that, now, in this moment, he *did* want to watch this happen in the satisfyingly sinister glow of the torchlight. "Rhethosian Justice" was what everyone in Kaylyn called such an action, and it made him sick to realize how good it felt.

Vomit filled the back of his throat as Travok pitched forward and twitched on top of the torch, smothering the flames. Plunged into the night's shadows once more, Joshua gagged as fresh snow hit his cheeks. He doubled over and spewed hot liquid on his boots as his body shook.

"Joshua!" Ada ran up to him, but he couldn't stand straight and see more than the hem of her dress. "Are you hurt?"

He couldn't respond as another wave of vomit coursed out of him. Vaguely, he felt Ada's hand on his back, small but strong. When he dared glance up at her, she only caught his eye for a moment before whistling shrilly. She repeated the sound, this time turning in the direction of The Forts.

"Here they come!" Ada shouted triumphantly.

Joshua could barely stand straight. It was hard to take his eyes away from his father's body. Then he saw them: the rebel families started emerging from their homes on both levels of the structures.

They came out of the shadows armed, cutting down the remains of Travok's men. Some of the women shouted for the rest of the "true violet bearers" to come out and stand for their cause against their traitor captors.

"Yes!" Ada cried triumphantly at his side, observing what they'd set in motion. "Look at them fight back, Josh! Just look!"

Joshua spat a mouthful of bile on the ground, near his father's motionless form. His lips trembled, and, even though he knew he should feel like he did the right thing, something was wrong. Empty. Like a bit of his soul had bled out onto the ground with Travok's lifeblood even though he bore no wound.

"Goddess," he said softly, and he dropped his dagger into the snow. He touched the rune scars on his hands, ran his fingers along the Protection Rune on his shoulder that had barely scabbed over, and pressed his palm against his compass in his pocket.

Nothing.

Pulse quickening with dread, Joshua squeezed his shoulder till the shape bled fresh, but no sparks of magic flew. His body remained chilled instead of pleasantly heated with desert air. *Cybarys,* he thought, *please. I didn't mean it . . . I had to do it . . . I . . .*

Even though Ada wrapped her arms around him, even though it was a pleasant feeling he wanted to enjoy, Joshua felt tears burn in his eyes. He'd broken the Goddess' most paramount rule of not taking another's life. Blood could only be shed in devotion to her, through his Blessing Runes. And now, his Touch was gone.

CHAPTER THIRTY-TWO

TRULY LOST IN SALVATION

"**I** have one more question for you."

Sarrett swallowed a groan, both his head and his throat weary from talking. The rebel had been questioning him for what felt like days. He couldn't remember how many secrets he'd shared, about Caldrell's favorite battle tactics, how often he grouped men in certain formations, what the sizes and weapon choices of his elite forces were.

"I can tell you've nearly had enough," the rebel said with a smile from where he sat comfortably against the wall outside Sarrett's cell, next to the chair where Mayra remained in silence. He leaned back and took a long drink from a cup that had to be filled with Rhethosian whiskey; Sarrett could smell the awful stuff from his prison. "But you have to understand that's exactly where I want you."

Mayra shifted, one of the few movements she'd made since Sarrett started talking. At some point, the rebel had looped her bonds around the back of the chair, even though she'd never tried to stand. Sarrett couldn't tell if she was relieved by his confessions or disgusted by his surrender, even if it meant saving her life.

"What else can I tell you that hasn't damned me already?" Sarrett snapped. The skin on his hands was dry almost to the point of bleeding from how often he'd been wringing his fingers against one another.

"Oh, you're on the way to redeeming yourself!" the rebel grinned. He brushed a hand back through his thin blond hair with ease. "There's just something I'd love to hear from your side, Lieutenant, since you were there *and* you were a big part of it. The events that led up to Caldrell's wife and daughter being executed for associating with the rebellion . . . it was your Mayra here who tipped off the Captain, wasn't it?"

Sarrett slowly met Mayra's gaze. Every question so far had been about Caldrell, not himself or his family. "Why does that matter?" he asked tentatively.

The rebel shook his head, then bit his lower lip. "You realize you asking questions instead of answering them will lead down a nasty path for both of us?" He broke the seal on the poison vial in his hands, tilting it toward the whiskey cup he held. "Mayra looks awfully thirsty, doesn't she?"

"Please . . ." Sarrett began. "Wait." What harm could there be in telling this man a story about a day that lived in infamy in southern Rhethos?

He decided to stand, stretching his sore legs. Putting one hand on the chilled bars next to him, he was surprised to find his grip steady. "Not long ago, rumors of the rebellion reached Clancy. I know now that you already had hold of several northern townes, but they didn't tell us that, not even in the military. The Captain was choosing when to release the fear of the rebel monsters into the public's ears. We were cracking down on anyone breaking a single law, with Caldrell making grand displays of as many public executions as possible, even for petty theft. Have you ever seen him when he hangs a man? It's one of the only things that makes him truly . . ."

"Happy. I know," finished the rebel. There was a grim undertone to his voice. "I've seen him do worse than that. Inflicting violence on others is what satisfies him."

Sarrett nodded, suppressing a shudder. All of a sudden, in this environment, talking about the man he once idolized made him nauseous. "I was doing my part," he continued, "bringing Caldrell anyone who breathed a word about rebel violet." Pausing, he looked at Mayra, who merely gave him a nod. That sparked a bit of hope in his chest; maybe she did approve of his confessions after all.

"Mayra heard whispers one evening of a group of women who were trying to reach Master Will. They were all unhappy with their lots in southern Rhethos, it seemed. When she told me about it, she mentioned someone called the Lady Marselle as the main instigator. I knew she was high up in Clancy society and was a good catch that would earn serious respect for me."

He sighed, recalling that moment when he'd crushed Mayra against him with an overwhelming feeling he assumed most called love. At the time, it was only gratitude for what he knew would come his way because of her information.

"Such a scandal," the rebel agreed. "And what about the others?"

Sarrett grimaced. "When I went to my Captain, I had no idea how high up the insurrection went. The day of the public execution, I was as shocked as everyone else when Selise and Miri Caldrell were brought to the noose."

"The man you idolized killed his own family when they were implicated in the Lady Marselle's rebel plans?" the rebel confirmed.

Looking at Mayra again, Sarrett grimaced. "I had no idea his wife and daughter were involved. For a man to watch them swing and smile, it . . ." He faded off, remembering the afternoon when the Insane Captain officially earned that title in Sarrett's mind.

He ground his teeth, then took a deep breath, barely noticing the stench of his own skin and hair. "I don't know if Miri Caldrell was guilty of anything. She was only twelve, after all. I don't even know if her mother Selise acted on anything she'd heard at Lady Marselle's meetings. I just know that the Captain made such a public display of the rebels that no hint of rebellion has been spoken in Clancy since. He reveled in the fact that he got to kill what he was supposed to treasure most in the name of the kingdom that cowered before him. Some of those rebel women got away, but I didn't care. Caldrell was so pleased that I reported the bitches that I got this."

He touched the filthy remains of his lieutenant's jacket reverently, recalling the first moment he'd put it on and gained his new title. So many years of suffering, manipulation, and the harsh torture of his soul led to that promotion. Everything he'd wanted since Lily's death was being placed in his hands, and, at the time, it had felt glorious; it had all felt worth it, even.

"Brilliant," said the rebel dryly. "And then you got your first real assignment in that ugly jacket in Kaylyn Towne. What a mess you made of *that,* and here we are today."

Sarrett's grip tightened around the bars, and he let his other hand fall off his jacket to make a fist around where the lock sat on the door. "Are you done torturing me, then?" he snapped, his patience at an end. "I've told you everything I know about Caldrell. I've said more than enough for that man to draw and quarter me as slowly as he can manage. You're throwing every bit of my life on the ground and spitting on it. What more do you—?"

"More?" cut in the rebel, and Mayra shrunk back in her chair. He stood from his seat and walked up to the cell. The torchlight danced in his pale blue eyes. "What I want more than anything is to see your Captain begging at my feet. He ruined my life, and Marselle's life, too. You don't know how lucky you are to have the *chance* to spill secrets to me."

Sarrett's eyes narrowed. So this was personal. Whoever this man was, he had a deep, vicious hatred of Mercer Caldrell and seemed to care for the Lady Marselle, too. With this rebel as his only lifeline, Sarrett made sure to lower his voice as he swallowed nervously. "I've told you everything—"

"No, you haven't!" the rebel roared. He reached through the bars, grabbed Sarrett's collar, and yanked him forward. Before he had a chance to blink, Sarrett felt a sharp blade against his neck. "I know military pricks like you. Caldrell trained you better than to break all the way. You've told me how to handle the Captain in battle, and some of that will help me greatly. But you're *still holding back.*" The man pressed the tip of his knife into Sarrett's skin and blood leaked in a line down his chest.

Sarrett closed his eyes, trying not to tremble on his exhale. This wasn't the first time this rebel had done this to someone. He could tell there was something else Sarrett hadn't confessed, and . . .he was right. But it wasn't anything about Caldrell. He'd truthfully spent hours sharing everything he knew, personally and professionally, about the Insane Captain. The only thing that remained was bigger. Even Mayra had no idea what was left.

If I tell him, I'll truly be lost. There will be no way that the kingdom I've dedicated my life to could forgive me. Have I really come to the point where I have to cross this line?

"Master Sutton!" snapped the rebel, looking over his shoulder, his patience clearly gone. "Bring the children in here."

Sarrett could barely turn his head with the rebel's weapon cutting into his skin, but out of the corner of his eye, he spotted movement. Down the steep, narrow stairs came a young rebel soldier, one who looked terrified to be in the depths of the dungeons. He held a torch that illuminated the uncertainty in his youthful features.

"I don't think I should. . ." Sutton began slowly.

"Leave them alone," Mayra began. "They don't deserve–"

"*Now!*" ordered the rebel, and Sarrett cried out when a fresh line was sliced through the skin under his overgrown beard. The rebel shoved him back from the bars and Sarrett wiped the wetness from his neck as Sutton turned and left once more. A moment later, he returned, and Sarrett immediately forgot the stinging pain in his fresh wounds.

Though it had been years since he'd seen his children, Sarrett found that they looked nearly the same as he remembered. Keppler was much taller than his little sister now, who cowered behind her brother's form. They looked clean, unharmed, and well-fed, but a hollow expression lit both of their eyes. They looked to their mother, whose dark blue eyes were filled with tears.

Deep in Sarrett's beaten, weary heart, something began to ache.

"Both of you should step up closer," the rebel suggested. His tone shifted from cold and commanding to sweet and welcoming when he looked at the six-year-old and four-year-old children at the dungeon's entrance. "Take your time and observe what a deadly combination the poisons of greed and The Bradford create."

Sarrett didn't dare move, didn't dare speak as Keppler put an arm around Nira and led her forward. Neither of them met his eyes. The rebel cleared his throat and beckoned for Nira to come toward him, which she did slowly. Her brother stepped forward as if to stop her, but Sutton put a hand on his shoulder and kept him still.

"You needn't be frightened," the rebel said kindly. "You know me. I'm the one who's been taking care of you. But *that* man," he added with a drop in his voice, gesturing at Sarrett, "he should be the one you're afraid of. You see, he's supposed to be your father, but instead he chooses to put all else before you and your brother. Your mother, even." He reached out and picked up Nira to set her on his lap. "So if any harm befalls you, it's his fault."

"You don't understand," Sarrett began. For some reason, seeing his son and daughter in this setting actually hurt more than he imagined it could. His pulse quickened as his nerves tightened like a noose around his entire body. "I *can't* say anymore. I shouldn't even know it!"

His heart constricted to a wracking knot of pain as the rebel pushed a few strands of auburn hair out of Nira's face. The rebel soldier who held Keppler looked like he might be sick, but he kept his grip steady on the boy. Mayra fought against the bindings on her arms but seemed too frightened to do much more.

"Father," Keppler started, his voice strained. "Tell this man what he wants to know. He said he will let us leave with Mother if you will."

"I don't like this place," Nira muttered, toying at the sleeves of her cream-colored dress.

Sarrett turned and paced his cell, refusing to look at any of them. He hated the man torturing him. The rebel knew that his family was a necessary piece in Sarrett's life, but he also knew that, deep inside, Sarrett cared about them. Even though it seemed he just discovered this fact himself, it was nonetheless true. It was such a fine line to walk, with destruction of his very being teetering on either side.

But they were only children, after all; they had no idea what he'd sacrificed to get this far, what he'd endured at Caldrell's hands in the name of notoriety and Rhethosian Justice. He needed them, yes, to advance his career, to further his family's name. Even though he'd lost everything in this cell, if he gave up what he knew, it would be real, undeniable treason . . . defeat.

"He doesn't seem like he wants to share, does he?" the rebel said in Nira's ear. "He's making it hard for all of us. Sutton, take the boy and his mother back for a while. They don't need to see what happens to the little girl."

"Master Co—"

"Good *Lord*, you're a soft one, aren't you?" snapped the rebel, his eyes flashing dangerously in the torchlight. "Where did Will find you?"

"I just don't think this is right. I'm not comfortable with—"

"I told you, Sarrett is the monster here!" the rebel insisted, pointing harshly at the cell. "What do you say, *Lieutenant?* I know you're not telling me something. Will you let it out or do I need to start removing her little fingers?"

Nira squirmed, but the rebel soothed her with whispered words Sarrett couldn't hear. Instead, he listened to Mayra say, "Please, Jon," over and over.

Sarrett clung stubbornly to his last bit of restraint, but in his mind, he already was reliving that night several years ago when he had been invited to drink with the Rhethosian Captain himself. The military leader's barracks in Clancy were almost as decadent as the Pure Palace itself, and Caldrell's room had been arrayed with golden chalices, countless wine barrels, and gorgeous women.

The other men were more seasoned officers and seemed used to the atmosphere involved in such an exclusive, private event, but Sarrett had *not* been expecting the wine. It was incredible in itself, imported from Armelle, yet after only two sips everything in the room lit up with brilliant color. Movements were amplified, tastes were more intense, and every touch was a shimmer of shivering delicacy.

That was the first night he had Sahma wine.

Everyone else faded away as the hours went by, and Sarrett found his tolerance for the oil-infused liquid higher than many others. It bolstered his courage and enhanced his senses to a brilliant degree. Before he knew it, he found himself face-to-face with his captain, and from the look in Mercer Caldrell's eyes, he was more far-gone than anyone.

As the rest kept drinking, Sarrett cut himself off. He teetered on the brink of complete euphoria, but even as his body begged for more of the drug, he merely pretended to drink from his cup, determined to remember any secrets spilled that night. Overindulgence, back then, could still be controlled.

In the Sahma haze, Sarrett doubted anyone could understand one another, and now that most of the other officers had left with different women, it was startling to find that he could still hear every single word his captain slurred.

But how could he tell this rebel bastard what Caldrell had unknowingly shared that night? Besides the Captain of the Rhethosian Army, Sarrett was the only living person who knew that their current Lord was the only Bradford who hadn't completed training at The Academy. Sarrett himself had wanted so badly to enroll after Lily died, so to hear that their revered leader came from such unconventional circumstances was just wrong.

"I can't," Sarrett murmured, and sank to the floor of his cell. "I can't do this anymore. It's too much."

The rebel merely waited in silence.

"Caldrell told me that The Bradford didn't complete traditional training like everyone else who's held the title before him," Sarrett said, his tone dry and empty. "He said he was a brutal monster worthy of the position, yes, but the man himself was a disgrace to centuries of Rhethosian tradition . . .an orphan, even. Caldrell went as far to say he knew that foreign hands had a role in placing our Bradford into power."

The rebel leaned forward, his mouth open slightly. He set Nira on the ground and patted her arm reassuringly before sending her back over to her brother. With a wave of the rebel's hand, Sutton quickly gathered up the children and left. Mayra gazed after them, almost toppling over her chair.

"You are certain that's all true?" the rebel whispered.

Sarrett held out his arms to either side in his prison, his once-splendid jacket hanging off his thin form. A brittle laugh crackled past his lips. "On my life, for what it's worth anymore, I swear it." He could only hope his expression showed how sincere he was. After all, he didn't feel like he was worth a damn thing. There was nothing left to give. Now, he was an empty man.

But, like Lily said, perhaps he could do something right before this was over. He needed to believe that the choices he'd made were going to help save him and his family, not condemn them all.

CHAPTER THIRTY-THREE

THROUGH ANCIENT EYES

The image of a desert forced itself into Will's mind. He didn't generate the thought himself; it was as though an unseen entity took hold of his head and shoved a memory into it, making him feel violated.

He strained against the mental bonds holding him, not knowing if he was alive or dead. When Will tried to move or think on his own, his body and his brain did not respond. All he could experience was what was put in front of him.

"In this space between life and death, observe what transpired, back when the world fully served me."

Will saw a distant part of the Armellan desert that ranged before him, full of rolling hills spotted with harsh shrubs and rust-colored rocks. Mud huts lined the shady sides of the hills, forming a sprawling town with wheel-rutted paths connecting each dwelling. The heat bore down on everything like a physical weight, putting pressure on each grain of sand that reflected stinging brightness into the air.

People rushed in the open land between the huts, hurriedly keeping out of the sun. Beyond, there was nothing but unforgiving hills of death-like sand in every direction. Everyone, however, seemed to be gathering somewhere ahead, with desperation on their brown faces.

Will watched as the ancient Armellans came together in a large, sprawling area covered in flat brown stones. All around the space were towering trees, bare of leaves except at the very top where deep orange canopies stretched out like countless burning fingers. In the center of the stones was an elongated pool of water, glistening in the precious bit of shade.

Never in his youth in Valsara and the many books he'd consumed there, had Will heard of a place outside the kingdom's capitol that had so much water. The spring before him was pale periwinkle at the edges, but deep blue at its center, indicating immense depths.

Will marveled at the little tributaries flowing like sparkling veins of life into the main pool. Seeing such isolated abundance outside what history mentioned made him feel small compared to this place forgotten by time. An instinct in him, however, told him to pay closer attention to the brown stones paved across the sand; they appeared to be stained with rust-colored splatters that couldn't be scrubbed clean.

Monks clad in rich robes painted with golden prayer scriptures guided what looked like the entire community to the stone-patterned area at the water's edge. Along the deeply tanned skin of their arms ranged tiny rings of copper, their circlets in different shapes and sizes. The chains were bound at the wrists, elbows, and shoulders with leather straps painted the color of blood.

The man front and center was clean-shaven and had his chest exposed to the gathered crowd. A rune the size of his entire torso had been cut there many times, thick scar tissue puckering his otherwise smooth skin. Though Will tried to focus on the symbol and memorize it, it blurred and shifted in his vision, making it impossible to see clearly.

The crowd formed a circle and looked to their Temple Leader with longing and devotion, falling to their knees as if their lives depended on what he did next.

"Do you see the power he holds, this ancient acolyte of mine? Those entrusted with my magic wielded my power and my will over the subservient masses."

The feminine voice permeated through Will as if someone was speaking directly beneath his skull. The feeling was akin to sticky spider webs trailing down the length of his spine.

"You are a leader, are you not, Caulin? Do you not wish for the world to bow to the fulfillment of your dreams? All peace, all prosperity, all unity, all reassurance of continued life came from the Temple Leaders who bore my magic. Any who dared disobey were sacrificed entirely."

Will squirmed when a flash of another image raced through his head: a human body hung upside down, cut open like an animal, bleeding every drop of its blood into the earth in repentance to its Goddess.

Anxiety gripped him as his vision was unwillingly turned to observe the gathered people in the desert. Nearly no one wore jewels nor metal except for the rune rings on their left hands. The blood red stones on them glowed dully compared to the finery Will saw on their leader.

"Today, we hold our new year devotion," the Temple Leader began, and everyone quieted. "Our Mother watches us and protects us as we serve and obey her. She gave her blood for us to be born, and we give ours so we may live on."

"From sacrifice comes safety," chanted those around the circle, children and elderly alike. "We give to our Mother, to keep her favor and stay her wrath."

Each member of the community turned the sharp edges of their rune rings toward their palms and cut open their skin. One by one, they stepped forward and bled into a large basin in the center of the circle. The Temple Leader spoke in a language Will couldn't understand, then brought out a knife and pointed its edge toward the sprawling scar on his chest.

Instinct made Will want to move forward, to put a stop to the bloodletting, but no part of him could move. He watched men, women, children, and elderly bleed collectively until the basin filled to the brim. Then bright yellow light filled his vision.

The Temple Leader had cut the large scar on his chest open, and both blood and the gold light leaked from the wound. It reminded Will of the magic he'd seen the dead man use in the ruins beneath Lorington, but on a much larger scale. The earth began to pulse beneath his feet, as if the magic from the rune was connected to the sand itself.

"You can wield this power in your time. Bring the world back into my chains and you will want for nothing."

Though Will felt suddenly sick, he couldn't deny the power that now surrounded them. Unlike the Blessing Runes, this ancient, darker form of bloodletting created immersive, encompassing energy. Every piece of his body, the ground, the trees, and the water in this desert oasis thrummed with incredible, magical strength.

Hopelessness and helplessness were suffocating weights. This was a space between life and death. That phrase made him fight harder against his bonds, desperate for his survival. The spirits beneath Kaladir said he could not be killed, but their existence proved there were fates worse than death within Cybarys' bonds.

"Find the only remaining written piece of this rune, claim its power, and build a new home for those you love . . . for your daughter."

Was it supposed to be that simple? Will couldn't accept that all of his problems could be solved if he merely submitted, right now. Despite how tempting the precipice was, he refused to give in. Instead, on the edge of his brain, itched a shadow of an image:

He remembered Angelyn and how she'd felt in his arms last night. She deserved to have someone fight for her and her son.

Will pressed back against the enormous force holding him captive in this unconscious state. He would not be the Goddess' puppet no matter how tempting the power behind this magic felt.

Next, he thought of Irvin and how he'd given up everything, including his luxurious title, to support the rebel cause. He deserved to know what they were up against in their war.

Will reached with more effort, even as the power controlling his mind fought to keep him down. She would not break him.

Then he thought of Devaki and how she truly had faith in her Mother. She deserved to have the real truth about their kingdoms' histories, even if it broke her heart.

The edges of his consciousness seemed to take shape again, like he was coming back into control of himself. A flicker of pain, real, physical pain, brushed over him. He was barely able to form his own thought for the first time since blackness overtook him: *I have to get out of that Harvest Room or I'll be nothing but the Goddess' slave.*

His next thought he directed at the Goddess, knowing that with each passing second that he fought back toward consciousness, her grip on him was loosening. He would not leave without fighting back with all the spite he'd held for this deity since he was sixteen.

If I find and use this magic, what do you want me to do with it? What do you actually want?

The voice that had full control of his mind previously was now just a whisper that Will could barely hear. It tried to retreat from him, but he would not let it flee. Instead, he used all his mental strength to steal something new from the entity around him.

Five men, each of them with a respective rune cut on their chests, stood in a circle. Five corpses lay at each of their feet, drained of blood. Yellow light bloomed in a star-patterned glow as they spoke in unison.

"Stand and break the Goddess' chains
Hold her in this trap of judgment
Dissolve all fear of her bloody constraints
So freedom may rise triumphant."

Their spell in its ancient language overwhelmed all sound, all thought. Though he could tell the Goddess didn't want to share all these details with him, Will demanded every detail be laid before him. Each line of the spell and each man present represented a different, single Dead Rune, a rhyme of power to create a massive amount of energy. *But why,* Will thought, *are there five men, five pieces of Dead Magic, but only four lines of the spell?*

The magic felt like what Will had experienced in the Temple Leader's ritual in the desert, but the golden light looked infected, twisted with a sickening green tinge that came from one man.

Staring at him more closely, Will felt shock and recognition hit him; that man's face was carved into countless statues throughout Rhethos to remind the world of the day he broke the world free of the Blood Goddess' chains. He was looking at The First Bradford. No one in Rhethos knew what, exactly, he'd done so long ago, and here Will was witnessing it.

An unearthly shriek filled Will's head. The sound was like nothing he'd ever heard, full of shock and agony and fear. He realized it was the Goddess herself who was screaming, due to the effects of the spell the five men had cast with their Dead Runes.

Then one member of the group broke away, interrupting the flow of power and breaking the connection. He covered his open wound with his robe and fled into the shadows.

Will felt the Goddess try to renew her strength, but she was now broken somehow . . . weaker . . . split. She sealed the wounds of the four remaining men, no scar of the Dead Rune shape remaining. Searing red light touched each of their heads. The same light rattled across the earth in a rush of inhuman magical power.

It erased all forms of the Dead Runes, leaving behind ruby-colored remnants. Conflicting voices rang out, one a dark golden boil and the other a warm maroon wave. They were so strong, too much for any human to stand against.

"Break the cycle of centuries of uprisings in the name of 'freedom.' Use

this magic in its full capacity to recreate this world in your image, Caulin. Claim the power of a God at my side."

When he could feel his eyelids again, Will tried to force them open even as his mind reeled with what he'd seen. He swore, underneath that final, stubborn level of unnatural unconsciousness, he could see golden light . . . or was it actually white daylight? Then something or someone put pressure on his injured shoulder and he fell, unwillingly, back into death-like black.

CHAPTER THIRTY-FOUR

BREATHE TO SURVIVE

Angelyn kept holding her breath. She didn't realize she was doing it until her chest started to ache. Taking shaky inhales, she tried to calm her restless heart, but nothing helped. Marselle was nowhere to be found, though that wasn't surprising. When coral colored dawn lit the battlements, Angelyn stood resolutely in Moore's private library.

She had to do something or she'd go insane, and an idea suddenly hit her: Sarrett.

The former Rhethosian lieutenant had hardly crossed her mind since she'd been swept up in Lorington's challenges, but now she became well-aware of how the man who'd murdered her best friend and burned her home was so close and entirely helpless. She knew Will was purposefully ignoring him, but her intuition said she shouldn't waste the opportunity to resolve the final thread of her old life.

"Miss McKinlee?" Devaki began, stirring from where she sat by the window. The girl had been half-asleep moments ago. "What's wrong?"

"There's something I have to do," Angelyn began. "Down at the barracks."

Devaki followed her as she stepped toward the library's doors. "I'd like to come with you," she said. "I don't like the idea of being alone right now."

"To the barracks, that is fine, yes," Angelyn replied. She nodded at the two rebel soldiers who followed them, ready and waiting to escort them through the city. "To my final destination, however, no. Can you stay in your room down there and wait for news?"

Devaki nodded, not asking any further questions. Angelyn wasn't sure if the girl's mind was as frantic as her own, worrying about her father and Gardain and Rowlann, all men she clearly cared for. Since Marselle had stormed off, Devaki had been incredibly silent and Angelyn guessed her inner turmoil was ultimately related to her faith.

A sharp winter chill met Angelyn full blast when she stepped out onto the street. Her stride was quick and determined in the shadows of Towne Centre's spires that seemed to follow her as she strode away from it.

Normally, seeing more and more violet banners flying from the homes of Lorington's people would have brought a proud smile to her face. Now, all she saw were fearful shades of gray. She had gotten so used to having a purpose, fighting for something she believed in, that being uncertain about everything since Will's departure and Marselle's harsh words made her extremely nervous.

She gasped again. She had to stop forgetting to breathe like that.

"Could you slow down?" Devaki asked behind her. "I can't keep up."

Angelyn tried to regulate her steps, but it only made her body shake further. When they arrived in the southern district, she saw Devaki safely to her room before making her way to the prison itself.

Though she'd spent plenty of time in the barracks, she'd never gone into the large building that led down into the dungeons. The rebel soldiers on guard gave her odd looks when she asked for a torch and to be led to Sarrett's cell. It took more courage than she thought to walk through the floor-to-ceiling iron gate and down the dark, sharp stairwell.

The light she held illuminated damp stones and cobwebbed corners. When she reached the landing, Angelyn strained her eyes further. The space was isolated from other prisons, dark and silent. On her right was a small square cell, encased in rusted iron. The man sitting in it looked calm at first, but he started backward at the sight of her.

"Please . . ." The word was barely spoken loud enough to reach Angelyn's ears. "No more. Leave me be."

She paused, holding the torch a little higher. Had the rebel soldiers really sent her to the right place? That certainly didn't sound like the man who'd ordered a Kaylyn guardsman to cut Gabriel's throat on her cellar floor. She squared her shoulders and took a few steps forward.

"You should know," Angelyn began, "that I haven't thought about you very much. But I wanted to ask you something today."

The man leaned toward the bars, his hands in his lap. Angelyn started to recognize him, though it was hard with a tangled beard and soiled, plain clothes. He was younger than her by at least five years from what she could tell in Kaylyn, but he looked like he'd aged a decade after spending almost a month in this place.

"McKinlee?" Sarrett began slowly, as if he were asking a complicated question in another language. His eyes focused, and a glint of recognition sparked in their Rhethosian Blue shade. "Good Lord," he chuckled dryly. "Bleeding rebel violet now, are we? You're even weaker than I thought."

Angelyn bristled, not expecting harsh words from someone who looked so helpless. The fire she'd built inside of her since joining Will's fight and falling in love with him made hot anger rise in her stomach.

She looked over the ruined military jacket in the corner of Sarrett's cell, and the grime that caked his face and neck. The curled ends of his brown hair were lank with sweat and oil, matted against his forehead in clumps. Pity mixed with her rage, making her wonder if his words were old weapons, ones that once held power but now left no mark.

Angelyn gathered the edges of her dress, stepped toward the cell, and knelt very slowly. She kept her eyes on Sarrett as she set her torch on the ground beside her, remembering everything that had happened the night Gabriel died.

Sarrett came into my business, my home, and searched it like it was a common whorehouse. He insulted my family name, threatened my son, and put his hands on me like I was a disobedient servant. He questioned my honor, and when I spoke back, he killed Gabe and forced me to thank him for keeping me safe from conspiring rebels.

Her jaw quivered with fresh fury, and, surprisingly, Sarrett looked away. "It's only one question," she said. "Do you feel sorry for any of it?"

He glanced back at her, the dirty creases on his face creating wrinkles around his tired eyes. "Sorry?" he repeated. Angelyn watched his expression, expecting more resistance, more of his initial sharpness. But now she could see that this place had indeed done damage to the man before her. Sarrett slumped forward, his shoulders weak with defeat.

What has happened to him down here? she wondered, not liking the questions that immediately followed: *What's been done to him down here, likely without Will's knowledge? And, better yet, who has done it?*

"I am living with many choices, in this Goddess damned place," Sarrett murmured. "Shifting through years of pain, layers of shame and stupidity and your home? That little inn? To be honest, it hasn't even crossed my mind."

Angelyn grimaced. She was hoping, somewhere in this man's eyes, she'd find remorse, so she could offer forgiveness and receive peace for herself, maybe.

"In fact," Sarrett continued, his gaze now far away, as if confessing was routine, "not long after the night your sad establishment burned, I told him where to find you and your boy. You know, to see the irony in it all."

She blinked at that, confused. "Who?" she asked.

Sarrett shifted on the floor on the other side of the bars, then caught her eye. "Your husband, of course," he iterated. "Did you not find him in the rebel ranks when you fled north, right where I put him?"

Angelyn felt her legs go numb against the stone space in front of the cell. What could this man possibly know about her husband? "How do you. . .?" she started, then her voice caught. "How do you know my. . .?" For some reason, her words suddenly came out constricted and tough, like a dried piece of meat sat in her mouth instead of her tongue.

Sitting up a little straighter, Sarrett leaned close to the bars, a small grin rising on his face in the torchlight. There was, apparently, a sliver of the Rhethosian lieutenant still intact, and she'd just, regrettably, found it.

"Travok i-is dead," Angelyn stuttered. "He abandoned my son and me a long time ago."

"Dead?" Sarrett cackled, then coughed briefly. "He left you because your little seaside dump bored a man like him. He worked for the military for *years* before beginning to spy within the rebel ranks. I thought when you ran off with Master Will, there would be some poetic justice in you finding your husband at a rebel-filled towne, where he'd put you quickly back in your place as a 'rebel wife' while he kept feeding secrets to me."

Pins and needles scraped over Angelyn's body, making her wish she was still numb. Her mind reeled with the overload of unexpected information: not only was her husband alive, but posing as a spy in Will's ranks. Where was he now? Will's reports said the northern rebel townes and The Forts themselves were safe, but how could she be sure? Joshua hadn't replied to any of her letters.

"I . . . don't believe you," she whispered weakly.

Sarrett shrugged, as if this didn't matter to him. "Before I left Kaylyn, I met with him. He gave me the information I needed to burn the rebel supply line. And I told him about a rebel camp supposedly hidden in the cursed woods, that it would be a good place to look for you. He's a big man, dark brown eyes like Joshua's, fighter's scars on his knuckles? Should I describe him further?"

Angelyn felt nausea flicker throughout her throat. Suddenly coming down here to find some sort of closure seemed rather naive. *This is all wrong,* she thought, standing shakily. *It can't be true.*

She nearly screamed when a hand clamped down on her shoulder from behind. Spinning, she came face to face with Irvin.

"I was quite displeased when one of my men told me what Miss McKinlee was currently up to," Irvin hissed. Usually he was curt with her, rude, even, but now she made out sheer anger in his pale blue eyes.

Angelyn stepped back, then realized how close she was putting herself to Sarrett's cell. But when she looked over her shoulder and down at the man, she found that he'd already shrunk to the very back of the filthy square space, as far away from Irvin as possible.

That initial countenance she'd seen when she came down here returned to the former lieutenant's face. *"No more," he'd said. "Leave me be . . ."*

Irvin looked between Angelyn and Sarrett, a smirk rising on his face. "Here I was, thinking I'd drained everything noteworthy out of this pitiful man, yet you've discovered something new."

Angelyn felt her throat go dry as Irvin bent and picked up Angelyn's torch, holding it at a practiced height so they could clearly see each other, as if he spent plenty of time down here and was used to the poor lighting.

"So you're lawfully married to a violent, lying traitor?"

She watched several more vicious accusations dance across Irvin's expression, though he didn't voice them aloud. He didn't need to. "Please," Angelyn began, "you have to do something. We need to send men north, to The Forts, to stop Travok. My son is–"

"I don't have time for that," Irvin sighed.

"You must–"

"I do *not* take orders from you!" When Irvin shouted, his words cracked sharply off the dungeon's walls. Out of the corner of her eye, Angelyn saw Sarrett shrink back further.

Then she heard a child cry.

It was soft at first, an echo of a whimper, but then she heard another sound, slightly higher and full of fear. She stared open-mouthed at Irvin, who winced.

"Irvin. . ." Angelyn began slowly. Her eyes darted around the cell and the dark area beyond as the sobs of two children grew louder. In the flickers of light, she spotted tiny, shuffled footprints in the dirt.

"Leave them alone," Sarrett said, suddenly gaining his feet. "Haven't you done enough to my family?"

His family. . .? Angelyn couldn't breathe.

Irvin plunged the torch in his hand into a bucket of water at his side, enveloping them in sudden darkness. He took hold of Angelyn's elbow and yanked her back up the stairs. Blind, she didn't have a choice but to trip alongside him, fear rising to the back of her throat.

When they reached the landing, Angelyn had to fight hard to break away from Irvin's grip in the large, empty holding area of the prison. She gathered her courage, despite how intensely her heart was beating. "You have his children imprisoned?" she breathed.

Irvin glared at her silently for a moment, then folded his arms over his violet tunic. "I don't need your opinion on the things I do for your lover so this cause can survive."

Tears filled her eyes and her stomach roiled. When a bitter breeze pressed into the dark space, she shrank back a step. After what she'd learned about Marselle's actions and her hints at Irvin's, she knew it was bad . . . but this? She couldn't get the whimpers she'd heard in the dungeons out of her mind.

"You've gone too far," she managed.

"Says the wife of a spy," Irvin shot back.

"I'm also a mother, Irvin, and my boy is in danger," she admitted, not realizing how frightening the possibility was until she voiced it aloud. She took a step toward the thin man before her. If there was a chance Josh was at risk, that he might even have to face his father alone. She had to risk Irvin's wrath for that.

Desperation clawing up her throat, she dared to push further. "I know you don't like the role Will has given me lately. But because of it, I've learned some things about you. There's a balance, between you and Will in this fight. I know how good and bad can clash, and how they can work together. As much as I don't like it, he needs you. And *you* need him, to get what you want out of this rebellion."

"What are you getting at?" Irvin cut in. He shifted with impatience.

Angelyn took a breath. "I will tell Will every nasty, evil thing you *and* Marselle have done. He may look the other way about torturing Sarrett himself, but *children*? If you don't want to incur whatever wrath Will would have against you . . . you'll take those orders of mine to heart."

The glint in Irvin's eye darkened dangerously. He reached out and grabbed her upper arm, tighter than before, as if he had half a mind to drag her down to a cell buried even deeper than Sarrett's. "You do not want to make an enemy of me like this, Angelyn."

"I'm on your side," she insisted. "We can't be enemies, Irvin." His grip on her arm increased, and a cry of pain escaped her lips. "Please, l-let go."

Irvin's jaw worked back and forth, then he finally set her free. "I will send a messenger, one I trust, to the camp immediately. A messenger *only*. We cannot afford, with the Rhethosian Captain so close, to have any of our fighters gone."

He paused and her heart raced further. Angelyn knew sacrifices had to be made, especially when an entire towne like Lorington was at risk. A messenger would have to do.

"The only way this works," Irvin continued quietly, "is if you keep silent about what you heard in that dungeon, and I won't mention every dirty detail about your husband to Will."

Angelyn nodded wordlessly, her mind still reeling with the emotional shock of knowing Travok was alive. With the snow up north, she knew that it would take time for anyone to reach The Forts. But it would have to be enough until she could find a way to reach Josh herself.

A moment later, a sharp horn blew through the dawn air. Outside the entrance to the prison, Angelyn saw several men rushing past. Everyone had been awaiting news of Will, and at this early hour, Angelyn doubted it could be anything else.

One of the guardsmen at the door spoke quickly with a man rushing past, then glanced into the holding area where Angelyn and Irvin stood. "You should head to the main barrack, Master Colwell. They're back."

Angelyn met Irvin's eyes briefly, then she followed him out into the freezing cold air. It didn't take long to reach the main building, where she'd met with Will and Torald previously. She almost jumped when she felt Devaki skid to a halt beside her, coming from the opposite direction. To their right, she heard more racing, approaching footsteps.

Three men were rushing toward them from the district's main road. Devaki let out a cry beside her and rushed forward before Angelyn could stop her. That's when she recognized Rowlann's armored form, with Gardain at his side. Between them, mostly supported by the elite fighter, was Will.

Irvin swore, then snapped orders to the rebels stationed at the barrack's entrance, demanding the healers be woken.

"What happened?" asked Devaki, her gaze darting between Rowlann and Gardain. "Is he. . .?"

Gardain stepped back once Irvin offered to take his place holding up Will. As far as Angelyn could tell, the Towne Master's son wasn't visibly harmed. Angelyn reached out a shaky hand toward Will, then pulled it back. The rebel leader's face was deathly pale, fresh cuts along his face and palm and forearm. It reminded her of the night he'd been brought unconscious into her home, but this felt worse, with even higher stakes.

She took a breath, focusing on what Rowlann was saying in a rushed tone to Devaki. Why was she so terrified to touch Will? Angelyn took a step forward and put her hands on either side of Will's face. His head was a heavy weight in her palms, and it took some effort to lift his chin from where it rested on his chest.

"He told us to leave, but I disobeyed that order," Rowlann was saying. "I would not abandon him down there."

"The Goddess and her servants let us take him back," Gardain added.

"What? How?" Devaki demanded.

"He's so cold—" Angelyn started. Her throat constricted before she could utter another word. Under the tips of her fingers, beneath the curve of his jaw, she felt a faint, uneven pulse.

Rowlann shifted Will's weight between himself and Irvin, clearly not sure how to answer Devaki's questions.

"I want him in the healer's barracks, down that road," Irvin ordered. "Now, before the streets are filled with people. Explanations can come after."

Gruffly, he shifted past Angelyn, forcing her out of the street. As they strode away, Angelyn's jaw trembled. When she glanced down, she saw her hands were shaking, like they used to all the time before she met the man whose skin had felt like ice under her fingers.

If he's gone . . .

Devaki clasped Angelyn's hands in hers. "Come on," the girl said with soft urgency. "It'll be okay." She pulled Angelyn forward, after the retreating group, and this time Angelyn had to make herself keep up with Devaki.

They managed to bring Will into the healer's quarters without too much trouble, though many of the rebels awakened by the horn craned their necks when they spotted who Rowlann and Irvin were carrying. Within one of the squat, stone buildings was a room with a bed set next to a roaring fire, where several healers hurriedly began doing their jobs.

Several chairs were pressed back against the walls, making room for countless shelves of healing supplies that ranged from floor to ceiling. The conflicting scents of harsh alcohol and fresh herbs swirled around them. Between the ever-moving arms, bottles of tinctures, and weaving of bandages, Angelyn couldn't take her eyes off Will's sallow face.

Vaguely, she still knew Devaki held one of her hands. "You could try praying," the Armellan girl whispered, "to help you feel better."

Angelyn found it touching that she offered, but she had no idea what to say, and frankly didn't think it would make a difference. She noticed that the girl's attention had already gone back to Gardain, who stood out of the way in the corner by the door. Angelyn glanced at him briefly, knowing the young man must be bursting at the seams with his educated assessment of what happened underneath the city.

Devaki no doubt wanted to hear it, but everyone waited to see if their leader would awaken. Outside the closed door, Angelyn could barely make out the tones of Rowlann's and Irvin's voices snapping back and forth at one another.

When the healers were done, hours had passed. One of them pressed a warm, clay mug into Angelyn's hands. She would have thanked the woman, but her voice was still gone, and it took all her effort not to let her trembling fingers spill the liquid onto the stone floor.

"Well?" Irvin demanded as soon as the healers opened the door. He blocked the exit with his slim shoulders.

"Keep him warm," they replied. "Keep his arm still. And wait."

Angelyn took another deliberate breath. With the three healers gone, there was room for Irvin and Rowlann to come back into the small room. When the door shut once more, Angelyn looked between them, then at Devaki next to her, then at Gardain in the corner. Now she would bet she wasn't the only one holding her breath.

"Enjoying your time supporting our cause yet?" Irvin muttered in Gardain's direction.

Gardain stared, as if unsure how to respond to the comment. "After what we saw down there," he began, "I am here to solve this, no matter the cost. If it'd help for me to officially wear violet, I suppose I can do that."

"My bleeding rebel heart is aching," Irvin drawled dramatically.

Finally, Will groaned. Angelyn nearly screamed as she stood, toppling over her chair. His eyes opened, full of immediate pain. With Rowlann's help, Angelyn was able to help Will drink some water.

"Will," Angelyn began, finally finding her voice when his gaze met hers. "I'm here."

The corners of his mouth faintly lifted into a smile. When she gripped his hand, there wasn't much strength behind his touch. "How did I. . .?" he began slowly. For some reason, Angelyn thought his mind was still far away, deep beneath the ground under their feet.

"Rowlann disobeyed your command to abandon you," Gardain explained simply. When the elite fighter glared at him, Gardain only stared back, as if he wasn't sure what offense he'd caused. "We . . . well, *he* mostly carried you after you fell. Blood from your cuts kept us safe through the passages. Though, I'm sure at this point you're feeling extensively drained. Not completely, of course, since they made it clear you were not to be fatally harmed. Pretty battered nonetheless, I'd say–"

"What in the damned Goddess' name happened down there?" Irvin demanded. "I mean– sorry, I am glad you made it out. Small blessings, and all that. But please tell me you found whatever is cursing this place so we can move on."

Will grimaced, shook his head, and motioned for more water.

"He almost died, Irvin," Angelyn snapped. "Look at him."

"And we're almost in deep shit," Irvin insisted. He stepped forward, to the foot of Will's bed, and pulled several messages out of his cloak. Tossing them onto the blankets, he added, "forgive me for receiving correspondence without consulting you first, Miss McKinlee, but these are the latest scout reports. Caldrell will reach Kaylyn in less than a week. Five days at best."

Angelyn ignored the personal stab, instead taking the papers with broken seals. She felt that heavy weight, always present in the background of her mind, force its way forward as she read the words, holding them so Will could see, too. "He can barely sit up," she said to Irvin. "Let him regain some strength before you jump down his throat–"

"It's fine," Will cut in. With one arm bound tightly to his chest, he used his free elbow to prop himself up fully. "You," he added, looking at Gardain, who blinked rapidly, "go get those books of yours from the library. We need every tool at our disposal now to figure this out."

"As you wish," Gardain replied immediately. "Glad you're, you know, alive."

To make sure Will was eating something, Angelyn reached for some food that the healers had left after Gardain was gone. They had mentioned several specific items that were good for the body after large amounts of blood loss. He still looked so pale, like he could fall back to his death-like state any moment. After a few minutes of silence, Irvin cleared his throat.

"You should begin telling us what happened before that odd young man returns," Irvin suggested. "But can I first say that I knew it would be a disaster?"

Will sighed. Angelyn watched as his attention shifted toward Devaki, who sat very silently in a seat next to her. "Devaki," Will began, "this will not be easy to hear."

She leaned back without much expression on her face. "Let's hear it anyway."

CHAPTER THIRTY-FIVE

SPLITTING LIES AND TRUTHS

Will took a deep breath. As he gathered his thoughts, he noticed that Angelyn's hand was trembling in his, something that hadn't happened since they'd fled Kaylyn Towne. He gave Irvin a firm look when he opened his mouth once more. It would take several minutes for Will to fully encompass what he needed to share; it wasn't just what they had experienced together but also what he'd seen since his brush with death.

"Kaladir is the name of the ancient towne beneath Lorington," he began when he was ready. "The spirits in those tunnels were woken up when the captain's men began digging. Cybarys forced them to remain there in case anyone ever tried to find what she intentionally buried."

Devaki bristled at that. "Kaladir is an old name," she spoke quietly. "One of the Goddess' first settlements, a place that stood before the Great Sea existed."

"And what did she bury, exactly?" Irvin asked. He leaned casually against the edge of the hearth. "And why does The Bradford want it?"

Will nodded. "As much as I'd like to deny it," he replied, looking toward Irvin, "what is hidden down there is exactly what Gardain suggested. An old magic, one that requires a large amount of blood, to create an even larger amount of power." He shivered and put his free hand to his head. There were still tendrils of the Goddess' hold on his mind, clinging to his subconscious, calling him back to her.

He nearly jumped when the door opened again. There stood Gardain with a rebel soldier, both of them holding large crates filled with books. "Sorry," he muttered. "I had a cart bring the trunk down to expedite the process. Hope I didn't miss anything."

Everyone stared at him as he went back to the corner of the room, rummaging for fresh paper and ink amongst the healers' supplies. Irvin tapped his foot through the process, though Gardain hardly seemed to notice as he arranged the crates of books and settled into his spot.

"So, you saw this magic?" Devaki asked. "With your own eyes?"

Will swallowed dryly, then took a drink after Angelyn refilled his water. "Yes. It emits gold light, not red gems. It feels bright and strong, not warm and comforting. We ended up in a Harvest Room, Devaki. Did you ever hear stories about what those were used for?"

She shook her head, though he wasn't sure if she was telling the truth. It made him uneasy, to see the teenage girl who was usually so passionate and assertive remaining so short-spoken, coiled back, as if each of his words could act as a devastating blow.

"In that room were places to chain humans," Will continued, "to bleed them dry like animals–"

"That can't be true," Devaki snapped. "How hard did you hit your head down there?"

Angelyn put a hand on the girl's shoulder, but Devaki shrugged it off immediately, pulling their chairs farther apart.

"I'm sorry," Will insisted. "You wanted the truth. An ancient Temple Leader showed himself to us, and had a shape carved into his chest. I couldn't see the exact character no matter how hard I tried."

His daughter looked away, her hand covering the space above her heart and rubbing it softly. Gardain shut one book and quickly opened another, scrawling notes with precise speed. Will craned his neck far enough to see the young man tracing runes in a language he didn't recognize, then writing out pieces of modern Armellan underneath.

Devaki leaned forward in the silence, placing her forearms on the tops of her legs. Will met her brown eyes again, which were full of an emotional weight that he wanted to carry but still shied away from. "And this spirit," she began, "he needed all of the blood in one of your soldiers to cast this spell?"

Will nodded again, though Gardain held up a finger.

"That is a fair conclusion, though I wasn't sure of it till now." He held up one ancient book gingerly, accompanied by his notes. "This shares several personal accounts of seasonal ceremonies. A basin was filled collectively, equal to that of a single life."

Will winced, remembering that detail of his vision he hadn't shared yet, and the deep basin at the base of the Goddess' statue in the Harvest Room.

"But," Gardain continued, "we couldn't tell if this Dead Magic required the caster to sacrifice his own blood, similar to Blessing Runes. After all, the man was dead and had no choice but to pull his source of energy from our unfortunate companions."

"When they started draining the blood from my men, his monks were able to attack us," Rowlann input from where he'd stationed himself at the door.

"And when a life's blood was taken in total, *then* he could throw you around like a doll!" Gardain concluded, flinching a little when Will gave him a frown. "The full effect of the rune must equal what it translates to, no? This old magic and your Blessing Runes, Devaki, no doubt have that in common. Something meaning 'push'? 'Pull'? 'Break'? It's definitely related to the motion he used to hurt you, Master Will, and to damage the chamber . . ."

Devaki stood as Gardain trailed off, then walked over to where the Towne Master's son sat. He didn't seem to notice her coming closer, too busy grabbing yet another book to support his current theories.

She glanced down at his latest notes, then back at Will, who wished more than anything that he could tell what she was thinking. Pain tinged with denial cut across her young features.

"If there are more differences than similarities in what you encountered, this cannot come from Cybarys. Whatever you faced down there must be something else."

Gardain tilted his head back and forth, still muttering under his breath. His quill began scuttling across his paper again.

Will could see how Devaki made that assumption. But there was more, and his brain ached at the idea of recounting what he saw before waking in this room. The Goddess' final message to him was something that still circled like a dark omen around the inside of his head:

"Claim the power of a God at my side."

He shook himself, then grunted at the pain in his shoulder. Obeying such a command was something he wouldn't dream of doing, yet . . .

"Will," Angelyn began. "What happened when you were unconscious? There's something else you haven't told us."

He shivered, no longer feeling the warmth of the fire so close to him. Was it that obvious that there was more to say just from the expression she could see on his face? Shutting his eyes, he let himself go back to that place, where he was powerless in every terrifying way.

"I had a vision," he said, aware of how silent the room had become, with everyone's gaze on him. "Or, rather, the Goddess revealed things to me. She said because she'd beaten me down to a space between life and death, she could reach me directly."

"Good Lord!" Gardain and Irvin said at the same time. Will heard awe in the former's voice and disbelief in the latter's.

"In ancient Armelle, before The First Bradford's time, the offering equal to one human being's life ensured their survival. If anyone questioned the power of the Temple Leaders, who wielded the only written copies of this Dead Magic, they were sacrificed to Cybarys until no blood was left, further ensuring the village's safety and keeping back the Goddess' wrath. She showed me these things taking place, Gardain, so your guesses are correct."

Devaki inhaled sharply. When Will opened his eyes, he saw her cross her arms over her chest. "That is not something our Mother would do," she insisted.

"She gave you this knowledge, in your mind, communicating with you through images of the past?" Gardain breathed. "That's fascinating."

"It's *wrong*," Devaki said.

"Do Goddesses lie, though?" Irvin questioned. "Can they?"

Will had his own answers to those questions, but he knew they'd upset Devaki even further. She took a step toward him, desperation tight in the muscles around her mouth and eyes.

"I've stood at the edge of that pit twice. Both times, I felt Cybarys' love." She turned slowly as she spoke, looking at everyone in the small room. "It was there, alongside that other, darker energy . . . the thing you're describing, the thing that put these lies in your head. They conflicted with one another, pushing and pulling me simultaneously. These have to be two different entities."

"Remember, Devaki," Gardain murmured, "we haven't found anything to support that theory of yours."

Will, however, frowned as he contemplated the elements of her resistance. He had felt exactly what his daughter described. Yet, in the Harvest Room, the only things present were hate and vengeance and a thirst for control. There was no undertone of motherly compassion or protection related to what he'd felt from Cybarys his entire life, even when he broke her rules.

He knew the Mother whom Devaki loved would never tempt him with the ability to find and use her Dead Runes, the only price being his free will to gain god-like strength.

No. The Cybarys he knew would welcome him back into her loving arms if he repented and regained his use of his Goddess' Touch to peacefully serve her children. This thing, which took slave-like control of his mind and showed him what would be possible if her Dead Magic was found; it wasn't her *exactly*.

"Will. . .?" Angelyn touched his leg and offered him more water.

But he shut his eyes and put up a finger, silently asking her to wait. Slowly, each piece fell into line, from what he knew of the Goddess today . . . to what he'd learned of this ancient magic . . . to what he'd seen the Dead Runes do when put together by The First Bradford.

They are separate, as Devaki says, he thought, *but that doesn't mean they both aren't the Goddess.*

After The First Bradford's spell failed and Cybarys was not destroyed, what remained of her in this world was a small part, a weaker aspect of the entity. The Mother whom Devaki loved. What only dwelled around the space where her Dead Magic was hidden was the rest of the Goddess. And it was much, much stronger.

Will felt the truth of the realization like a heavy weight in his stomach. He could not tell Devaki this, knowing how badly it would break her faith and her heart.

He had to keep the rest of his vision, the lines of the spell he heard, its potential effects, its previous failure, and its damage to the Goddess to himself or his only child would be ruined.

"Okay," Irvin said suddenly. He stood up straight, dusting off his violet tunic with a definitive flourish. "Because all of you are too caught up in the mystical theology of this mess, let me break down what I'm getting here."

He sighed and steepled his long fingers, resting them on the tip of his chin. "The magic in that hole is something The Bradford wants. He dug around my home, too, remember? And eventually the captain's men left Patten when they achieved their goal. We chatted about this with Moore when he shared his story, remember, Will? Now, with what you've just told us, I think we really understand how deep this shit runs."

Will's eyebrows narrowed and Angelyn's grip on his leg tightened significantly. "You're saying he already has a piece of this Dead Magic?"

"The insane military leader who's almost at our doorstep?" Irvin clarified, his voice jumping an uneasy octave. "His master does, yes. So, no matter what Will's bleeding heart feels, Miss Tarran here has to go back into that digsite to help us reach that old magic with her new magic. So you, Will, can possess whatever the bitch of a deity tempted you with. You know why?"

Even though he felt protests being prepared by everyone else in the room, Will still stated the obvious: "Because if we are enough of a threat to Caldrell, The Bradford will use what's in his possession."

"Damned right he will!" Irvin returned. "You said this stuff is extremely powerful? We need an even battlefield, brother."

Gardain set down his quill and pursed his lips as he looked up at Irvin. "You realize in order to use a Dead Rune to the full extent of its power you have to essentially sacrifice someone?" he pointed out.

Irvin let his hands fall to his sides. "Yes. And our enemy will not hesitate to bleed his soldiers dry, so–"

"That kind of evil violence goes against everything this cause stands for," Angelyn interrupted. "How can you be all right with that?"

Will watched as Angelyn and Irvin glared at one another, perhaps more vehemently than usual. There appeared to be, the more he looked, a significant amount of tension between those two.

"I will sleep just fine because I always have our ultimate goal in mind," Irvin dismissed. "Whatever needs to be done. Will must at least agree that we need to find it, even if we don't end up using it."

"I've said as much," Will grimaced. "But Devaki, you *cannot* go down there. Please, if you believe nothing else I've ever told you, trust me now."

His daughter stared at him, just as defiantly as he had stared at the Armellan monks when he was her age. "Gardain said your blood kept the spirits back," Devaki replied. "If I help this time, you will succeed. My faith in my Mother will keep me safe. And you have no other option."

Will exhaled. The logic was sound. His only winning argument lodged stubbornly in his heart, knowing he couldn't tell Devaki the truth about her broken Goddess and what truly awaited her in the digsite. Even Angelyn, when he met her eyes, silently told him that he needed to let Devaki go to that Harvest Room.

"Bring your daughter down here," the dead Temple Leader had told him. "Cybarys will speak to her."

With less effort this time, Will managed to sit up completely. He looked back at Devaki, who pushed some of her curls off her forehead, forcing them to spring in bunches along the sides of her face.

Finally, he gave in. "Can you give me three days?"

She blinked for a moment, and he saw dozens of thoughts fly through her eyes before she nodded. Will remembered something Angelyn had told him, after they'd spoken to Torald, when he'd asked for her advice regarding Devaki:

"Don't lie to her, don't keep things from her, and don't make her feel small."

When Devaki smiled at him, it hurt more than Will could have ever imagined.

CHAPTER THIRTY-SIX

FORMS OF BRAVERY

Will hardly slept each passing night. It wasn't just because of the constant tension in the air or preparing for the threat of the Rhethosian army or the pain that ebbed too slowly in his injuries or the way Devaki kept looking at him like she finally approved of his choices.

The worst part was the nightmares. No matter how exhausted he felt at the end of every high-strung day, he was haunted by his vision of that group of five men and their sacrifices. Cybarys nipped at his mind every time he dared fall asleep for too long, as if in the confines of rest that ancient, powerful form of the Goddess could still tempt him.

On the third night, before he'd agreed to go back into the digsite with Devaki this time, Angelyn was the one restless beside him. Her hands balled into fists against his chest. Suddenly, she bolted upright, eyes wide with terror.

He put out a hand to steady her, but she shoved him away, breathing rapidly. "Angelyn," Will tried, sitting up and pressing back the warm layers of blankets and furs around them in their bed. "You're safe. It's okay."

She wrapped her arms around herself, tangles of her hair falling around her naked body as she shook. Slowly, she looked around, as if recognizing the room in one of Towne Centre's towers where they'd met after sunset each night.

"I'm sorry," she murmured. "That was awful. Did I wake you?"

He shook his head. "Nightmare?" he dared to ask.

She gathered a blanket against the front of her body, then pressed her hair around to one side of her head.

Reaching out a hand toward her, Will offered, "You can tell me about it."

"No," she whispered. When he tried to catch her eye, she stared far into the dark corners of the room. "I need to deal with this on my own. I have to."

Will frowned. He respected her independence, now more than ever, but he couldn't lie there while she silently suffered. "At least say who it was about," he prompted. "They can't hurt you now, when you're here with me."

Before he'd gone into the digsite, Will had felt the urge to tell her countless memories and secrets he'd never uttered to another person, and also hear anything she would want to express to him, but now that desire was even stronger. When he met her eyes, a deep shade of blue now that the hearth at the end of the room had long since turned to ash, he could tell she felt the same way, even though it was hard.

The truth was, if he did make it out of the digsite a second time, they had even larger enemies to face. Time had truly run out and, after tonight, he had no idea if he would ever be with her like this again.

Angelyn nodded and turned so she could face him, though she didn't take his hand. "I was dreaming," she began softly, "of the night Joshua was conceived."

Will watched her as she spoke, realizing now why she didn't want him touching her.

"You already know what they teach children growing up in Rhethos," she continued. "But as a girl, life had an additional challenge. We didn't just submit to the law of our loving Lord; we also had to blindly obey the man we married, serving him day and night."

Will grimaced, not liking the tightness that grabbed low in his stomach when Angelyn mentioned Travok. He resisted the urge to reach out and gather her in his arms, doing his best to respect her wishes.

"Travok was not a kind man, to say the least," Angelyn continued, "but I knew no different. What was normal for many women in towne wasn't cruel or unjust. It just . . . was."

"You've always had the courage to stand up to people like him," Will commented when she paused. "That's not something I suddenly gave you."

"Permission, to a Rhethosian woman, is a precious, forbidden gift," Angelyn corrected. "I did have the capability to stand, but I firmly believed it was right to stay kneeling in the dirt. There were times when I dared to rise, but when my brutal father passed and my husband ruled over me, things got worse."

She shifted, swinging her legs to face the foot of the bed, away from him. Now, Will could only make out the profile of her face and body, the curve of her bare back a pale shadow in the evening's light that shone through the single window of the room.

"It was one of the nights nine months before the Blood Moon, the cursed month where every woman feared getting pregnant. The consequences of public shame and a dead baby were enough to deter many couples, but Travok never listened to anyone. He had been around less lately, taking more work I didn't know about to help keep the inn open. At least, that's what he said when he occasionally brought in mysterious gold with no explanation. That night, no was not an answer, as if it ever was. But I said it anyway, and that was the first real time I fought back."

Her left arm wrapped around her torso, till the tips of her fingers landed on her right side of her ribcage, under the curve of her breast. "His fist actually slammed into my head," she whispered, "but the force knocked me across the room into the doorway, breaking four of my ribs. They never healed well." Angelyn cleared her throat again, and before Will could think of anything to say, she began again.

"What he did to me after that was more brutal than usual, as if he was trying to prove a point. I won't go into any more detail than that." Her shoulders shook on her next inhale. "The result is my Goddess Touched son. That is the good that came from one of the worst nights of my life. Travok never stopped, not when I was pregnant, not when I had a newborn, not until he decided to leave one day."

"Angelyn," Will began. Yet he couldn't find the words that, in many other circumstances, came to him so easily. Anger pulsed through him when he watched her grip her ribcage.

"I haven't dreamt about how badly all of that hurt in a long time . . ." she whispered, tears in her voice. "I wish I could just face him myself. I'm *not* that girl anymore."

Unable to sit still any longer, Will slid forward until his chest was pressed against Angelyn's back. He let his hand rest delicately on hers and softly pressed her fingers away from her ribs. He could feel the uneven bumps in the damaged bones, and her breath quickened under his touch.

Will let his hand fall, gripping the blankets in tight bunches. "You are much braver than me," was all he could manage to say.

She still felt tense, as if there was something else bothering her.

"Is there more?" he prompted quietly. "More about him?"

"I. . ." Angelyn broke off. He could tell she was struggling with something in her mind and waited patiently. "No, there's nothing else. All of that is in the past," she insisted, and, to his relief, she leaned back against him. "There isn't even a scar on me. Unlike you."

She turned around again, so they sat face to face, in the middle of the bed, their foreheads nearly touching. Will didn't break their eye contact when one of her hands drifted down to the thick layer of scar tissue that ran diagonally around his torso.

"Tell me," she said, "how old you were when this happened."

Will sighed. He wanted to tell her everything, details that went beyond scars, of childhood and adult hurts in the little, precious time they had left. But all the secrets caught in frightened, frustrated knots at the back of his throat.

In the silence, he hugged Angelyn close. She squeezed back, not strongly but with a firm level of compassion. When she wrapped her arms around him, everything seemed possible, and when they were together like this, everything felt whole . . . for the first time. He didn't want to lose that, but he also didn't want to let what might be a final chance go by in silence.

He collected his courage, pressing away the concerns of the Insane Captain's arrival and the threats of Dead Magic to recall a piece of his buried childhood. "I was eight," he began. "That's when I lost everything. My life ended, and I was forced to begin a new one. These scars . . ." He faded off, much sooner than intended. His gaze fell to the raw amethyst that hung around her neck and he held it lightly between his thumb and forefinger.

"I'm sorry, lovely," Will tried again. "I have a hard time finding the words."

"It may be now or never," Angelyn pointed out kindly. Her eyes glossed over with fresh tears for a moment, and Will wondered if it was because of the term of endearment he'd hardly realized using for the first time. "If it helps," Angelyn added, "I have wanted to know since the first week I met you."

He gave her a tight smile. His resistance began to fade, and when the memories of that night came up again, he let them form into solid images and emotions. "Let me tell you, then, Miss McKinlee, about one of the worst nights of my life."

Will sat back against several pillows, offering her a space under his good arm. She sat close to him, but he barely felt her warmth. For the first time in thirty-two years, Will felt his big brother tie that thick length of rigging around his waist to keep them together. He felt the merciless, stormy sea whip his body until the rope shredded his skin to the bone.

CHAPTER THIRTY-SEVEN

THE ADRIADNE

"Have you ever been on a Rhethosian trading galley?" Will asked.

Angelyn shook her head.

Will let the images of his family's ship play across his mind as he spoke. "Well, they're cramped. And musty. And the cargo hold was where my big brother and I were supposed to sleep. Even in calm waters, I couldn't get comfortable down there." He shivered, then let out a slow breath. "I couldn't grasp the concept of floating on so much violent water without panicking and jumping to the nearest piece of land. But it was how we made a living, sailing regularly across the Great Sea. And there was no room for weakness on my father's ship.

"The hull was always full of crates and boxes. That night, the ones with Armellan runes on the sides were empty, ready to be filled with wine when we reached Valsara. Everything smelled like dried fruits and salted meats and stale air and burned lamp oil. And the planks above my head would scream at me like they were alive with each passing wave. I only told my parents about how frightened I was of the open sea once. My father beat me pretty hard that day. He preferred my brother's brutal sense of practicality, while I took after my mother."

It wasn't hard to conjure a perfect picture of her from that particular voyage. Will shut his eyes before continuing. "Her name was Adriadne, and my father named our ship after her. A romantic notion, yes, but only for appearances. He was not a sentimental man, though he did acknowledge that my mother had seafaring skills, and she became a trusted member of his crew. Being so little, I didn't really care about how she could navigate treacherous waters or tie knots that made my head spin. She was just . . . strong."

He opened his eyes when he paused to see Angelyn nodding. Her expression was calm and contemplative in the moonlight. "You were lucky, to have one loving parent, at least," she input quietly. "Take comfort in that."

"I try," Will murmured. He glanced down once more at the necklace Angelyn wore. "She gave that to me," he said, motioning forward with his chin, "to try and calm my nerves that night. When I went above deck I found her at the railing, standing like all the sailors did, confidently moving with the rocking of the ship. I never figured that part out and got sick all the time. We could see masses of flat, black land on the horizon, the desert in the distance that we couldn't reach soon enough.

"That's when she told me something I've told countless people in the last decade: 'fear is the enemy of freedom.' She added, 'When we choose to not let fear of the unknown hold us back, little things like waves won't scare you anymore.'"

"And did that help?" Angelyn asked.

"No," he laughed. "Neither did the necklace, honestly. She didn't wear any other jewelry, so I should have understood how important it was for her to share something with me that obviously gave her great comfort. She called it a stone of hope but never got a chance to explain why a tiny amethyst meant that in particular to her." His voice wavered. "I had no idea at the time . . ."

"You were just a child," Angelyn said. "I'm sure she thought you were brave, coming up on deck on your own."

He sat up further and pressed back his hair. "What made me brave were her stories. She taught me everything, more than most of the young Rhethosian men on our crew because I was so willing to learn, especially when Mic started going away for private lessons in Clancy. If he'd been back in Rhethos that night instead of below deck, sound asleep, things would have been very different.

"But I was the only one who ever listened to my mother paint a vivid picture on a regular basis, dreams that I knew, if any military officer or Loyal family member heard, would instantly damn her. She had a vision about what the world could be . . . what it could be like if fear didn't rule us all."

The next sentence caught in his throat and he had to pause. For some reason, he couldn't stop thinking of how fear came from The Bradford now, though it used to come from the Goddess in ancient times. Cybarys used to demand blind devotion with fear of an awful execution as consequence of disobeying her rules.

A sour taste rose in his throat when he realized it made sense for The First Bradford to want to break free of her. Yet, many generations later, his descendants were the haughty leaders Will himself now fought against, in the name of his own definition of freedom.

Was it all really a meaningless cycle of what certain men defined as worth living or dying for?

"She planted those seeds, didn't she?" Angelyn asked in the silence. She turned slightly, tucking her knees up to her chest, leaning forward, no doubt to try and catch his eye.

"I . . . yes." He found his voice unsteady, tension gripping the pit of his stomach. His throat ached, and, for some reason, it hurt to swallow.

Angelyn leaned over the side of the bed, finding her shift that lay on the floor. After slipping it over her head, she stepped over to a pitcher of water that stood near the fireplace. "Keep talking," she said over her shoulder, giving him a small smile.

Will cleared his throat as best as he could. "Storms on the Great Sea hit fast, out of nowhere, really. One moment we were at the railing, my mother reassuring me, putting that silver chain around my neck, then a large swell passed. That moment of suspension before the bow hit the surface again was always harsh. The next tall wave was worse. Freezing winds picked up, and I remember the deck taking on some foam and sea water at that point. Land was still far away on the horizon."

Angelyn brought two cups of water over, sitting next to him and handing one over. He drank slowly, hoping it would help, but his throat still felt clogged. "My mother knelt next to me and put her hands on my shoulders. I tried to look brave. Then the lightning flashed through the sky, coupled with thunder, and we heard my father start to give orders from the helm. Even though the wind had escalated to a nasty gale, I still heard the last thing she said to me: 'Don't be afraid, darling Caulin.'

"When the ship pitched violently, it knocked me off my feet and rolled me away from her. The warning bell echoed from the wheelhouse, ringing on a pulley system down below deck to bring up the members of the crew who were sleeping. With the people instantly all around me, I couldn't find my mother anymore. Then Mic was there, hauling me to my feet."

He flinched a little, caught enough in the memory that he swore he felt Mic's hands grasping his forearms. Angelyn reached out and touched his shoulder, giving him a soft, patient smile.

"When he helped me up," Will continued a moment later, "I remember holding tightly to his soaked shirt. It was mere seconds, with not even a chance for me to open my mouth before we saw lightning strike the top of the mast. There were flames and black smoke and the sound of splitting wood. When it fell and hit the deck, fiery rope and canvas rained down everywhere."

He gripped his cup tightly for a moment, then handed it to Angelyn. "While the deck disintegrated, my brother wrapped a rope around my torso." He indicated the band of scars with his free hand. "A big knot sat under my right arm as he tied the other end similarly to himself. Mother always told him to look after me when he was home, so I suppose he was listening to her command.

"Mic told me to hold onto him when the rest of *The Adriadne* gave way under our feet into the sea. I spotted my mother, pinned under some rigging, sinking fast. When I reached for her, the rope between Mic and me held me back. I think I screamed over and over for her, right to the point of my head going beneath the waves."

Silence fell and his gaze drifted to the stone ceiling, clad in shadow. His heart pounded audibly and he decided to shift his attention to the dark window, where he could make out the horizon, not water, not suffocation, not clouded vision reaching toward death. Will made sure he could see land, filled with air and life, before he could speak again.

"The world became brutal water. That rope hurt as I got pulled in every direction, with the wreckage sinking around me. Then I saw Mother's dress, her fingers stretched in my direction through the water. But that damned line yanked me away from her. I tried instead to find my brother on the other end, but his weight made it impossible to get to her; up was down and it started to get very dark."

Angelyn touched his hand. "You know he didn't keep you from her on purpose, right?" she asked quietly. "If he was fighting for air, too, he wouldn't have wanted you swimming toward her; he'd want you heading up, to stay alive."

Will shrugged one shoulder. Even with the sympathy he saw in her eyes, it still felt like he was back beneath the stormy sea, losing air, floating unwillingly toward the end. He quickly put his attention back on the window.

"Till then," he managed next, just above a whisper, "my mother had always been there, to hold me steady, to keep me warm, to tell me the answer to any endless question, to wipe my tears when Mic left me behind. I knew I couldn't fail her yet. Everything she taught me couldn't be swallowed by the violent sea.

"I knew I was drowning, but I also knew that I wasn't ready to die. It took two seconds of stillness to figure out which way was up, and I swam as hard as I could, with death inches behind my feet. I hit air for a moment, then got slapped with one wave, another breath, another wave. There was nothing but black sky pouring rain into black water."

"And . . ." Angelyn began slowly, "your brother?"

"That's part of what was weighing me down," he replied. "When I tugged on the fraying line leading back down into the water between my legs, no one tugged back. So I hauled on it, hoisting inch by inch, bringing myself back under with each effort. It would have been easier . . ." He faded off, pressing back his hair again. "So much easier to wriggle out of that knot and just keep myself breathing. But I couldn't let him go."

Will laid his head back against the pillows behind him for a moment, then turned to meet Angelyn's eyes. "Now I know I would have been better off. Innocent lives could have been saved. Devaki's mother would still be alive if I'd only stopped hauling on that rope."

She blinked, her mouth falling open slightly. "You're saying," she began, "that your brother was the one who murdered all those members of the Armellan royal family? The Night of Blasphemy? He. . .?"

Swallowing with more difficulty, Will grimaced. "Not only did he commit those crimes, but he made sure I was blamed. But please, you can't ask me to tell you all about that night along with this, lovely. I'd rather you throw me back into that digsite alone."

He was surprised to find that Angelyn was wiping tears off her cheeks. She leaned against him, resting her head on his chest. "You pulled him up, then?" she murmured.

"Yes," he replied. "It took all my strength to punch at his stomach, to get him to breathe, while I choked down plenty of water myself. When he came to, he fought me at first, then when the rope pulled taut, he seemed to come to his senses. I'm still in awe of how quickly he regained his composure, swimming confidently to crest each wave and see farther than I could have hoped.

"Just like our mother, he tried to command the respect of the ocean; a born leader, I suppose. He pulled me with him to the remains of some crates. We barely fit on the debris, but those tiny islands of life kept us afloat. In the lightning strikes, Mic's face was calm, except for a massive injury on his forehead. A large flap of skin hung off of his skull, coating half of his face in dark blood. He didn't seem concerned, and later it turned into a nasty scar."

Will shook his head. "You know, for all of his determined calmness, I couldn't stop shaking or crying or asking for our mother. He held my hand till I passed out. Waking the next morning on a beach outside of Valsara was awful, like realizing your worst nightmare has come true. When I took that rope off my waist, my chest was rubbed raw, shredding me to the bone from my armpits to the bottom of my ribcage. Most men would be proud of such scars, I suppose, but I'm ashamed of mine."

"Why is that?" Angelyn asked. She touched the middle of his torso, so lightly that he could barely feel it. "You are alive now, with me, in spite of what you faced that night. They're proof that you were right: you were not supposed to let your mother's dream die. That's not something to be ashamed of."

He smiled briefly. Reaching down, he put a finger under her chin, tilting her head back so she could look up at him. "I love you," he said.

Shock raced across Angelyn's features. She opened her mouth, but he leaned down and kissed her deeply. Her arms tightened around his waist and, remarkably, the weight in his throat and on his heart started to lift. He realized that this was what life used to feel like, before that night *The Adriadne* sunk. Some of his burden, however self-righteous it felt to bear, could be shared with someone without damning them, too.

Angelyn pulled away. "Tell me what happened next."

"Danvir found us," Will said after a moment. Suddenly, he felt quite tired . . . satisfied, even. "The monk was a man my brother hated and I adored. Mic just wanted to find a way home, but after we learned no one else survived the shipwreck, we had nothing to go back to. I started to really resent Mic for tying us together and keeping me from swimming to my mother that night. And when I fell in love with the temple teachings and the love of Cybarys and, eventually, Devaki's mother, we grew even farther apart.

"Mic was terrified of all the Rhethosian biases against Armelle that my father had ingrained in him. He insisted on proving to me that Cybarys was a lie, a monster that our Lord kept us safe from; little did I know how right he was."

Angelyn's gaze narrowed. "Don't worry about whatever's in that Goddess-damned pit tonight," she told him. "I can tell you need to rest."

He pulled her close and nodded, his cheek brushing against the top of her head. His brother was gone and their real enemy would be unstoppable, unless he accomplished what needed to be done beneath this city, with his daughter, soon.

CHAPTER THIRTY-EIGHT

WHERE A STRING LEADS

"Joshua, you're doing it again."

He frowned down at Ada from where he sat on one of the raised planks of the rebel camp. She gave him a worried look and nodded at his gloves sitting next to him in the fresh sprinkling of snow.

Though his fingers were turning bright red from the cold, Joshua still had his hands out so he could trace the rune scars on his knuckles. For three days, while everyone worked hard to rebuild the corrals, find the last of Travok's men, and reach out to Patten and Morely for help, Joshua mainly sat, alone, running his fingers over the foreign shapes on his skin.

They no longer echoed any magic heat back at him, nor did they glow red or scatter magic remnants on the frozen ground if he dared cut one open. And the Goddess wasn't answering his prayers or speaking to him, either in the camp or in the woods, with or without his dwindling supply of Sahma.

"Can you come down here?" Ada prompted. She was wrapped in several layers of furs over a heavy woolen cloak that covered her long, brunette locks. "I could actually use help, you know."

Several groups of women marched past Ada on the snow-covered pathway between the shacks of the camp, moving around the tall, slim girl to reach the shelter of the overhanging plank system. There were no men left, and it made Joshua feel even more out of place.

"You're fine without me," Joshua muttered, though he slipped his gloves back on and shoved his hands in his armpits, trying to feel the tips of his fingers again. "I'll stay out of your way. I'm no use to anyone anymore."

Ada rolled her eyes, then handed off the armful of firewood she'd been carrying to one of the passing groups. Those women glanced up at Joshua, his legs dangling over the frozen plank above them, and they smiled. He knew they were grateful for what he'd done, but he felt sick and empty.

It took Ada a moment to work down the icy counterweight that lowered the nearest section of the walkways, but before long she scrambled up to where Joshua sat. After kicking off several inches of fresh snow, she curled up beside him. Her warmth was comforting, especially when she unfurled one of the long furs around her shoulders and draped it over his damp cloak.

"You don't have to sit here and pity me," Joshua muttered softly, watching the bustle of older women, girls, and even children below them.

Ada sighed and locked her elbow with his. "You're right. Pity doesn't do anyone any good. Getting up and helping with the work, that might start warming you up, you know."

Joshua's jaw tightened. Just a few days ago, he had an unimaginably powerful deity speaking in his mind. He had the potential to experience everything he'd ever wanted as a child.

And he'd ruined it by straying from his Fate's String and breaking his connection with her Touch. Now, he couldn't accept that this was what he had left for himself: distributing firewood, tending to horses, and sorting the meager supplies that Patten and its brother towne could share with them on the other side of the trees.

With the harsh, unrelenting descent of winter in northern Rhethos, it would take twice as long for the messengers from Patten to reach Lorington's walls. And they still had no idea what had been going on down there for the last month. Even though he still didn't want to see her, Josh wondered if his mother was all right.

It's all a big mess, he thought miserably. *And I don't know how to fix it, or if I even can.*

He leaned against Ada, and her head rested on his shoulder despite how she was a few inches taller than him.

"It'll be better, I promise," Ada insisted. "Once we're able to get through the snow and reach Will, you can explain everything. We're grateful for what you did."

"You are?" Joshua asked. "You're grateful I killed my father? I've felt horrible ever since that night."

Ada sat up, shifting under the cover of their shared length of fur. Fresh snow still landed on her eyelashes and cheekbones. She put a gloved hand on his jaw and made him look at her. "But it felt good in the moment, didn't it?" she whispered. "It felt *right* to stop the people hurting us? To help us be free again?"

Joshua blinked. Her face was so close to his, and there was a spark in her eyes that for some reason made him want to look down at her mouth, just inches away. But a sour feeling grew in his stomach when she spoke so easily about violence. She seemed to enjoy the idea of Rhethosian Justice too much.

"I think I should go," Joshua said.

"Go?" Ada repeated with a small laugh. "Where?"

"I . . ." He was about to say, "I don't know," but somehow, deep inside of him, he knew that wasn't true; even though his magic was gone, there was still a pull that he felt, softer than his heartbeat, that told him he wasn't done. That he was meant for *more*.

"Josh?" Ada questioned. She gripped his arm tighter. "Whatever it is, don't. It's better this way. *You're* better this way."

He stared at her plainly. "Broken? I don't think so." He pulled away from her touch. "I'm sure I'll see you again." For the briefest moment, he thought of leaning in and kissing her. But it didn't seem right. Instead, he stood up and put the puff of fur back around her shoulders.

The cold ate at his aching muscles that had sat too long in one place the last few days. But he forced them to move down the slippery raised walkways and underneath frozen chunks of extra ropes hanging above. When he reached the place where Mistress Merheene was staying once more, he knocked gently.

Joshua knew the blind Armellan woman had been grateful to go back to her old home, at the back of the camp. She wasn't meant to live in the middle of the woods, especially with winter now rolling in at full strength. People mistrusted her as well, but she played their ignorance to her strength; they didn't know anything about her, whether she was Goddess Touched or an old witch or a foreigner to be feared. Therefore, they let her be.

"I've got my fire going, little McKinlee," came a voice from the other side of the rickety door. "Don't make me get up to let you in."

Joshua smiled and pressed open the thin piece of wood that didn't have a handle or latch. The space was small and had meager furniture. The Armellan woman sat on the floor, next to a pit full of flames. The smoke rose to a soot-covered opening in the ceiling above them, any falling snow melting before it had a chance to dampen the fire.

When he shut the door behind him to keep out some of the chill, Joshua breathed in the smells of bread and stale Sahma. One reminded him of his old home, the other reminded him of the Goddess, and both made him inexplicably depressed.

"Aren't you going to ask how I knew it was you?" Mistress Merheene questioned. She patted the planks of the floor beside her with one wrinkled hand, the rest of her wrapped in the same dark blue cloak she'd worn when they were hiding in the Goddess' Woods. As he walked over, she used the same hand to brush back the long, white dreadlocks of her hair down her back.

"Because I'm the only one who comes to see you," Joshua replied. He sat next to the fire and let its heat sink into his freezing bones. He'd spent too much time outside in the snow recently, too stubborn to be completely alone indoors and too ashamed to move about helping others.

The Armellan woman grinned with her remaining teeth, an expression that lit up the blank whites of her eyes. "Good to see there's still some humor left in you. I'm glad that you came today. I feel things shifting, and you are part of them."

Joshua grunted, staring at the swirls of dancing yellow and orange before him. Even though he didn't know what she meant and he knew she couldn't see his nod, some part of him was aware that he wasn't done. The Goddess had only been in his life briefly, but they had been the most terrifying, exciting days of his life so far.

"I have this feeling," he began unsurely, "that I'm not supposed to be here anymore. It doesn't seem right; none of it does. But I can't pray. I can't find answers—"

"Of course you can pray," the old woman cut in. A smirk wrinkled one side of her mouth. "Anyone can, especially when there is no one else to talk to. But you're just like the rest of us, McKinlee. She can't speak back to you. All you have now is . . . blind faith." A small, dry chuckle escaped her lips at her choice of words.

Joshua sighed, the self-pity he'd been drowning in lately rising up to his chin once more. This time, he didn't know if it was worth fighting to stay afloat. "Isn't there something I can do?" he murmured. "Anything that can fix this?"

Mistress Merheene grunted, then shrugged one of her shoulders. "I don't know. If we were in Armelle, you could go to the temple and pray."

Joshua blinked. "A temple?" he asked. "The Goddess' Woods, they have temple ruins in the middle of them. I could go there!"

The Armellan woman's mouth twisted into a deep frown. "Without your Touch, Joshua, you cannot safely navigate the depths of those trees."

He glanced down at the rune scars on his knuckles, feeling a spark of hope in his chest for the first time since he'd watched his father fall to the ground at his feet. "But she said I was special," he insisted quietly. "I don't care if it's dangerous."

Mistress Merheene let out a small sigh, reaching toward the fire between them. "You should keep in mind that those who ask for forgiveness from Cybarys across the sea are simple people like myself. The Goddess Touched do not break their Mother's rules. I do not know that, if you even reach those temple ruins, she will give you your gift back."

Joshua stood up, not really hearing the last of her words. "I have to try," he said determinedly. His mind was racing forward, thinking of what he wanted to gather before setting out. One thing was certain: he couldn't stand another day of sitting here.

Somehow, it felt right. In fact, he remembered something Cybarys had told him before he'd gone back into the camp with Ada. *"Together, we can bring peace. At the center of the woods, you will find the key to your freedom."* She'd wanted him to go there all along.

"I understand. It is a place of power, old power. And, no matter what, you need to remember she still loves you, Joshua," Mistress Merheene said softly. "What do you need before you go?"

Joshua reached out and touched her hand in thanks. "I'd like to send a letter to my mother before I go."

CHAPTER THIRTY-NINE

ACCORDING TO PLAN

"Don't you have that book memorized by now?" Devaki asked Gardain. She paced across the moonlit alcove on the opposite side of the library, anxious, knowing they would be summoned to leave for the digsite any time now. The Towne Master's son lounged comfortably, surrounded by books near the crackling fireplace, as if he wasn't about to risk his very life's blood again so soon.

His gray eyes gleamed when they met hers. "After what Master Will shared, I don't feel like I know anything anymore. Lately, it's like I'm seeing the world through an entirely new lens," he replied.

She gave him a curious look, not sure what he meant. No matter how hard she tried, she'd given up learning the complex translations of the dead language Gardain had discovered. She'd even given up trying to find a book, even a page, that proved him and her father wrong that what they were going to face under the city was something unrelated to Cybarys. There was nothing to be found, yet her stubbornness held.

"I, um, let me clarify," Gardain said, no doubt seeing the confused expression on her face. "The last weeks with you have changed everything. You've created many questions and going into that digsite brought up even more. As I'm sure you can tell, finding answers gives me purpose, potential meaning in a place where I've been essentially nonessential."

Devaki raised her eyebrows. She went over to the hearth as Gardain spoke, sitting beside him. "That's how I've felt since coming here," she said, leaning toward him. "About my purpose. Despite other painful things happening, too."

Gardain's mouth twisted up into a half-smile. "I didn't say those new lenses were painless," he pointed out. "But they are new, nonetheless. I've been reading about the Goddess my entire life, to everyone's frustration and shame, but here you are, a solution to it all."

"That's a bit much," Devaki laughed unevenly. She felt a heat rise in her cheeks at the way Gardain was beaming at her, and he suddenly seemed to realize how his words made her feel.

He cleared his throat and brought his attention back to the books in his lap. When Gardain brushed some of his ash-blond curls out of his face, Devaki saw he was still smiling a bit.

She wasn't sure what to think of Gardain. He'd volunteered to go back into the ruins with her, even after lives had been lost. *Is he doing this to gain more knowledge about his "hobby" or is he doing it for me? Because I "fascinate" him or. . .?*

She glanced down at the old runes and scriptures notated on the pages of the book he read. "You know," she began, "you don't have to come."

Gardain laughed. "Of course I do," he replied calmly. "You're going now. I'll be there."

Devaki knew he might be better off than those who could merely wield swords, but she marveled at how unafraid he was of the threat before them all. She thought that this young man was perhaps braver than her, and though she was worried about him, she found herself glad she could count him as a friend going into danger at her side.

A knock came at the door, and Devaki turned while Gardain didn't seem to notice. With her eyes adjusted to the firelight, it took a moment for Devaki to recognize Sutton's face at the library's entrance. "Miss Tarran," he said, "they're ready down at the digsite. Are you prepared to leave?"

Devaki bit her lip, then stood. "Yes. I don't think I need an escort," she said. "But it's nice of you to offer."

Sutton's eyebrows narrowed. "I'm one of the volunteers going with you," he explained. "I'd like to see this through to the end. For Rhethos."

"For ourselves first, I'd say," Gardain corrected, definitively shutting his book. "Let's not waste time." He made his way past Sutton, not even looking at the young rebel.

Devaki followed, silently bolstering her courage as they went. When they arrived at the digsite, she noticed Will and Rowlann waiting. Descending the scaffolded walkways felt like marching willingly to her destiny; finally, she would prove her faith in her Mother to everyone who doubted.

Will had mentioned that when he'd come down without her, there were no mental assaults out here under the open sky. The same was true now; instead, all was eerily silent, the stale air shrouded in mites of dust and sand. All she heard was the shuffling of Gardain's feet beside her and Sutton at her back.

Near the entrance, she saw her father and Rowlann waiting. "It's the five of us then?" she asked Will when she reached him, and he nodded.

"There were other volunteers," Will explained, "but I've sent them back, in case the Rhethosian Captain arrives while we're gone."

Devaki understood that. She also knew that she was supposed to keep all of these men safe. That responsibility, resting on her Blessing Runes and faith in Cybarys, suddenly weighed more than her desire to find out if Dead Runes were indeed real.

She glanced at Will, who still favored his injured left shoulder. Under his black garments and leather armor she knew he had plenty of bruises from his last encounter, but when she caught her father's eye, she saw resolve and trust.

He was finally ready to work with her to solve this mystery, earn Moore's cooperation that was key to their survival, and keep his rebellion alive under his peaceful terms. A warmth grew in the center of her chest at the idea of him treating her like an equal.

"Remember what we've discussed," Will said. He put a hand on her shoulder, his tone low. "Stay at my side."

"Don't bleed unless I have to," Devaki added, knowing what he'd told her earlier. She had every piece of their plan memorized. "I'm ready."

"It'd be best if she led, I think," Gardain spoke up. Despite the trepidation in his voice, Devaki saw him bouncing on his heels a little, as if excited anticipation was keeping him from standing still.

Will gave a stiff nod. As she walked toward the entrance, her gaze was fixed on the archway, one of the only intact pieces of the ancient city of Kaladir that was visible aboveground.

Broken heaps of steps descended at a sharp angle into blank, musty space. A tight pull at the back of her heart beckoned her forward with increasing strength, whispering to her of centuries past and the secrets they held.

That pull came with a question: could she handle what she could potentially find here? What would she do if Will's and Gardain's theories about a darker, brutal form of her loving Mother were real?

Devaki cleared her throat, facing the four men with her. "Before we go. . ." She turned the edge of her rune ring against the chest plate of Rowlann's armor. She carved a small Strength Rune next to the Protection Rune already in place, then split the tip of her finger and smeared her blood across both. He was someone, she already knew, whom she was willing to bleed for, and she knew he'd do the same for her.

A memory rose of the night they'd crossed the Great Sea, when she'd nearly died bleeding to stop the storm. Rowlann had offered his own blood to the Goddess at her side. The unreadable rune on her chest itched under her tunic, but she ignored it.

She couldn't say a word now because her father had made it clear that he only allowed honest communication between them on his terms. He only shared what mattered most in a pre-scripted journal. He didn't care if she was terrified at what had been magically put into her skin. So she kept her mouth shut, just like he wanted.

This venture . . . it was what would prove her worthy of his love.

Following suit, Devaki stepped up to Sutton, who kept a very serious face even though his eyes were drawn to the entrance of the underground passage. His armor already had a Protection Rune cut into it, but she placed several drops of fresh blood on the symbol.

When she glanced at Gardain, he waved a dismissive hand in her direction. "I know how you feel about using those in a nontraditional manner. I don't want to contribute to that."

Rowlann scoffed, and Will gave the young man an uncertain look. Devaki, however, did not want to take any chances. Despite his protestations, Devaki cut a Protection Rune on the end of Gardain's belt, then pressed a drop of her blood onto the symbol.

It must have had something to do with the bravery she possessed in that moment, but Devaki reached down and briefly grabbed Gardain's hand in hers. Out of the corner of her eye, she noticed Sutton frowning.

Without another word, she turned her attention to where her feet were being urged forward and gave in. A cloud of dusty air hit her face as she stepped underground. She flicked her hand at her side, spraying droplets of blood onto the steps as she made her way downward. Magic remnants trickled around her.

It did not bother her to actively bleed in a place like this. After all, her Mother, the very Goddess herself, had bled to bring humans into this world. The least Devaki could do in return was have faith and step forward.

Lead on, Mother, she thought resolutely. *I'm not afraid.*

She tuned out all sound, ignoring the wisps of torchlight blossoming from behind her. No one spoke as they went into the earth. She felt the weight of every chunk of dirt above them, every interlocking stone of the passageway, as if they all rested on her shoulders. But Devaki sloughed off her fear like an unwanted cloak in the heat of the desert.

She didn't need it. And it didn't serve her.

"Devaki," she heard Will murmur later, his tone calm. "About now should be when—"

But she cried out in the middle of his sentence and slumped forward. Intense pain struck her head and tore at her skull. *I thought I had more time before this part happened.* Will put an arm around her, propping her up. With his free hand, she was vaguely aware of him pulling out a knife as more shouts burst out behind them. Viciously sharp memories slapped across her vision:

Sehran banning her from royal family meetings and celebrations . . .

Being bullied when she dared visit her mother's shrine . . .

Slurs and threats whispered by women when she went out in public . . .

The night she never spoke of when her cousin came to her room . . .

"Enough!" Devaki cried. That was too much. The rest she could handle, but that last memory of Sehran's deliberate abuse was something she would *not* tolerate being used against her.

She shook off Will's support, then cut the Protection Rune on her arm. Heat encompassed the space around them and the memories in her head dissolved like melting clay. She heard something shriek and shivered when she realized the sound came from a real, unseen thing in the dark space around her. Cries of protest echoed around her, and Devaki saw the glow of her runes on her companions' forms wink in the darkness, attempting to also keep them safe.

The ancient spirits down here were *not* happy with her magic.

Devaki cut open a Guidance Rune, too, and deeper red energy filled the underground passage as she prayed aloud, "Dear Mother, keep us safe in your merciful embrace. Lead us forward with your love and light in these dark places. Keep back our enemies."

The air around them calmed, and when she took a tentative step, there was no pain and no harsh echoes of the past in her head. She could feel the Goddess pulling the blood from her body, taking what she needed to protect those she'd placed magic markings on. Even the bad taste in her mouth at that last memory of Sehran went away eventually, and she clamped a hand over both cuts, staunching the wounds. She needed to conserve her strength.

"Move forward," Will said beside her, encouragement in his tone. "Soon, we will have to put out the lights to find the right path."

"I know," Devaki agreed. They went over what had happened to him previously, and how she would combat those obstacles. His blood would suffice to keep them safe during that particular hurdle. She knew what to expect. She could do this.

"Oh, child. How little you know."

A dark, twisted voice hit her like a physical blow to the center of her rib-cage. It crawled over her skin like ice, permeating an ancient power and fresh fear into her veins. Devaki opened her mouth, but no words came. Reaching out, she touched Will's arm, wondering if he heard what she had. In the dull flicker of torchlight, she could hardly see him.

Her body was so heavy. In fact, *everything* felt heavy, like the world had the Goddess' hand on top of it, pressing down with infinite strength. The walls began to shed away dusty layers, and the compacted dirt above them quaked dangerously. Every "safe" place where she'd shed her Goddess Touched blood so far was now covered in Sahma-scented clouds.

What is this? Will said nothing about this!

She heard Gardain and Sutton scrambling behind her, and she turned to see them raising their arms over their heads to shield themselves from falling debris. Will tightened his grip on her shoulders, and she thought she heard Gardain shouting but couldn't make out his words.

How can either of them manage to do anything with this weight? she thought. It felt as though her heart was being forced down into her stomach, being pressed into mush along with the rest of her organs.

Then the floor of the passageway under Rowlann's, Gardain's, and Sutton's feet gave way. They fell into the dark, followed by countless rocks. There was enough time for Will to wrap his arm around her before the pathway underneath them disintegrated and she free-fell for a terrifying amount of time. Her head hit solid rock. The air slammed out of her lungs and blackness took over.

CHAPTER FORTY

IMMEASURABLE STRENGTH

Devaki felt the cold rubble of broken stone on top of her, but she couldn't find the strength to pull herself up. Something else was still holding her down, as if she belonged on her hands and knees before the unseen entity that held such strength.

She groaned and fought back. Whatever collapsed the passageway and spoke in such a condescending tone in her mind wasn't her Mother. Cybarys was loving. Cybarys cared for everyone, for her.

"We bleed for peace, as one."

The words echoed in her aching mind as she tried to sit up in pitch-black space. It sounded as though they were being spoken by countless people, plastering the phrases to the inside of her eyelids.

"We bleed for prosperity, as one."

"We bleed in servitude, as one."

"Devaki, get up."

She felt Will shake her, and the ritualistic words in her head jumbled like a bundle of rocks against the inside of her skull. They tangled with Will's voice, creating nonsense.

Her father grabbed her shoulders and hauled her off of whatever she'd landed on, pulling her instead onto smooth stone. The motion made her vomit between her shaking hands. Blood dripped down the back of her neck from a throbbing spot on her head.

"Where are we?" she rasped. She blinked, trying to focus her vision. Everything was dark and blurry and full of dank clouds.

"Another chamber, I think," Will replied, helping her sit. She noticed he held tight to his injured shoulder with white knuckles. "We fell pretty far."

Devaki tried swallowing, then fought back another wave of nausea. The floor beneath them was cracked and smeared in fine dust. When she looked up, she could barely make out a sloped ceiling fifteen feet above them, and dark walls that encased a small, squat chamber. *How far underground are we?* she wondered.

To her right, she heard more stirring, then recognized Rowlann's voice, ordering Sutton to try and light the remains of a torch. Sparks flew, then died, then flew again, making Devaki dizzy. When fire sprang to life, she winced.

As her vision sharpened, Devaki saw bodies piled where they'd fallen. They ranged in varying states of decay, several dozen in broken heaps, all of them in either Rhethosian Blue military uniforms or worker's garments. She felt sick once more.

It took a moment for her to realize that her group must have free-fallen onto the remains of the digsite's original excavators, landing on them had ensured their survival.

Will stood beside her, touching a blade at his belt as he studied Rowlann and Sutton. "Are you injured?" Will demanded, stepping in front of Devaki. "Are you bleeding at all?"

As the other men checked themselves in the flickering light, Devaki saw Gardain for the first time. He scrambled back from the pile of old bodies, running his hands along his dirtied tunic, no doubt looking for fresh blood of his own.

She saw Will protectively pull out his weapon.

"Surprisingly, I believe we're intact," Gardain announced. He stared up at the large hole in the ceiling, then shook dust from his hair.

Rowlann nodded at Will on his and Sutton's behalf before Will sheathed his dagger. The elite fighter held the splintered piece of a single torch high, though the dark walls seemed to absorb the light with vehemence. Devaki finally managed to stand, keeping her gaze away from the shadowed corpses.

That could have easily been us, she thought with a shudder, *if we hadn't fallen where we did.*

Will put a hand on her shoulder, then stood to walk around the perimeter of the empty chamber, examining the clouded space. She didn't miss the fact that he was limping slightly on his right side. When Devaki tried to follow, everything spun and blackened.

A hand grabbed her elbow, and she saw that Sutton was at her side to catch her balance. His face was covered in grime and one of his eyes was partially swollen shut, but she could still make out concern in his expression.

"Are you all right, Miss Tarran?" he asked, holding her up.

Devaki took a slow breath, then shook off his touch. "Fine. I don't understand what happened. Will said he was able to get farther in before—"

"The Goddess doesn't like us anticipating her moves," Gardain cut in.

"It's *not* her," Devaki snapped at him, though the sudden passion behind her words made her head scream with pain.

"It feels like her, doesn't it?" Gardain replied. He glanced over at Rowlann, who was circumventing the room, lighting the stubs of old torches that hung on the curved walls. "I truly believe, Devaki, that this *is* your Mother, in some way, some ancient form of her–"

"Please," Devaki began, though her argument didn't seem to want to come out of her mouth.

"Clearly you're upsetting her," Sutton said in Gardain's direction. "Maybe less theorizing and more inspection of this new space."

"Agreed," Will spoke from the far side of the chamber. "It's time to find a way out of here." He ran his hands along the dark stone of the walls. As far as Devaki could see, the only opening was the one high above them. With the fifty feet of cold, black room now dimly lit, Rowlann and Sutton spread out as well.

"She's put us here for a reason, I'm sure," Gardain began, still standing at Devaki's side, his youthful features contorted with deep thought. "I don't see any way to get out of this room."

"I don't believe that for a second," Will snapped. He continued to circle the room that had no other passageways leading into it or doors leading out of it, feeling each rounded section of the wall. Devaki noticed he'd taken his gloves off.

"Over here, Master Will," Sutton called. His hands rested on a section of the wall high above his head, his fingertips barely brushing one particular spot of stone.

Devaki walked over, gingerly touching the back of her head as if that would help stay the dizziness. Being the shortest person in their party, she couldn't see exactly what Sutton was touching. As she squinted, Gardain stepped in front of her and blocked her view. Much taller, he pushed Sutton's hand aside and traced the area with his long fingers.

"Good Goddess!" he exclaimed. "There's a carving up here . . . runes, but they're in that ancient language."

"What do they say?" Will asked. His attention was on the empty space around them, as if he expected something to appear while their backs were turned. It gave Devaki chills that she couldn't ignore.

"Well, I only memorized certain symbols in the old texts of my collection. Certainly not the entire alphabet which could very well contain hundreds of shapes," Gardain explained. He took a step to the right, moving his hands along slowly.

"Those old words were even more complicated than Modern Armellan," Devaki reminded him.

"And there's something wrong about this," Gardain added, although he nodded at her words. "Or, rather, something odd: these sentences are carved upside down. It's like the person who carved them was-"

"Hung by their ankles from the ceiling?" Rowlann finished. A coldness touched his voice, one that she didn't like. A sour feeling bubbled in her stomach.

"Devaki," Will started. He reached out to her.

A ripple of laughter fell into the room, leaking down the chamber's curved walls like thick sludge. It made Devaki shiver as Will, Rowlann, and Sutton pulled out their weapons. Gardain's face turned pale, almost the same shade as his ashen curls. Devaki reached for the Guidance Rune on her arm, refusing to be frightened by any more mental games.

I know you're here, Mother, she insisted, splitting open the skin of her left forearm. *Show me the way. Prove to everyone who you really are.*

She felt a familiar comfort surround her. Ruby magic remnants sprinkled at her feet on the black stone. A soft touch landed on her shoulders, pulling her in the direction of where the lines of runes were carved high on the wall. *That* Guidance from her Goddess was something she knew well.

Even though she reveled in the magical connection that still held strong between her and Cybarys, she didn't understand what she was supposed to do. How could they find a way out of this sealed room with a message left by a dying man in a lost language?

The dark, feminine laughter rang out stronger, as if reveling in her confusion.

"Lift me up so I can see those carvings!" Devaki insisted, spinning toward her father. The Guidance Rune on her arm glowed deep red as if in agreement that this was their only clue. "Will—"

He swept her up by her waist, dropping his sword at his feet in the same movement. Balancing as best as she could, Devaki leaned toward the wall. The runes were uneven and faded, but she could still make them out now that she was higher and closer. She touched the blood flowing from her Guidance Rune and began to write out what she saw on the inside of her forearm, right side up.

Halfway through copying the line of ancient script, she heard Sutton scream. Will kept hold of her as Devaki turned to see her friend and his commander drop to their knees. They gripped the sides of their heads and reeled. A fresh wave of laughter rained down, and Devaki cried out herself as she saw beads of blood form on Sutton's forehead.

"*Don't!*" she shouted and tried to squirm out of Will's grasp. Gardain started to grunt with pain next to the rebel leader, putting a hand heavily against the stone wall.

Will held her still. "Finish it!" he snapped, but Devaki couldn't take her eyes from her friend's blood. Over Sutton's shoulders, near the center of the room, two figures formed in the dusty darkness. Transparent almost to the point of invisibility, they reached toward the red droplets that ran down both rebels' faces from where they'd torn at their own skin.

Will yanked her back, forcing her to look again at the runes on the wall. With a shaking finger, Devaki traced the last two intricate symbols as best as she could onto her skin. She rammed her elbow back into Will's chest until he dropped her. Still, he was faster and blocked her from running into the center of the chamber toward Sutton and Rowlann.

"Keep her away!" Will ordered at Gardain, who was standing hunched over, mouth twisted with pain. "And translate those runes!"

Will stepped forward and cut open a straight line of a scar that ran along the top of his arm. After making a fist, he smeared his blood along the length of his sword and ran toward the spirits that reached for his men. It seemed, this time around, her father had some new ideas of his own.

Devaki stared at the solidifying forms of ancient men shrunk back. Disgusted or terrified of Will's blood (despite his lack of magic), they shrieked when his blade passed through them. Still, his weapon didn't seem to actually harm them.

Will offered a hand to Rowlann, but Gardain took her by the shoulders and guided her attention away before she could see what happened next. Frustrated tears filled her eyes as she met Gardain's gaze instead, who purposefully blocked her view.

"You don't need to see that," he stated with some effort. The same agony she saw on Rowlann's and Sutton's faces was clear on Gardain's, but he wasn't tearing at his skin.

"Doesn't it hurt?" she asked.

"Yes," he replied, his voice strained. "But I can still focus. Bad memories are harsh in living color, yes, but they will not kill me. May I?" he asked, indicating her forearm that was drying with the tracings of runes from a dead language.

Devaki nodded, and Gardain rotated her arm toward him. He pulled it close, till her limb rested against his chest. Will shouted again and she heard his sword scrape stone. Devaki tried to look around Gardain's shoulders, but he held her still with surprising strength.

"That one," he murmured, and his grip tightened as he touched one bloody symbol. "And that . . . don't you recognize that one?"

Devaki tried to focus, but she couldn't remember anything beyond what she was seeing and realizing in that moment. There were *spirits* in here, ones that were cursed to harm anyone who tried to get too close to a secret thought to be legend. Could it really be a Dead Rune, capable of more sinister destruction than any magic she possessed?

Across the sea in Valsara, no one would believe a single piece of this. Cybarys was a loving Mother who blessed her children. She kept them safe from evils like The Bradford. Her magic was given to those who could help the world, bless Her people, and spread the peace of their faith.

Furthermore, for Devaki herself, her Goddess' religion was comfort in a place where she only felt pain. It was meaning in a world that took everything from her before she could walk. It was the backbone of what made Devaki *Devaki.*

There had to be another explanation, one that somehow made more sense than what Will and Gardain had told her and what she was starting to see with her own eyes. However, deep inside, she felt something at her core begin to crack.

Gardain murmured in recognition, piecing together the puzzle scrawled in blood on her skin, but she wasn't listening. She couldn't help him. Will swore, his weapon clashed with something, and Devaki craned her neck to see Sutton starting to turn a deadly shade of white.

The two Armellan spirits were more defined now, their brown skin covered in heavy robes held on with brass chains and circlets. One wielded a sword, the other a long knife, and Will was doing his best to keep both of their weapons at bay with Rowlann's help. Each time he swung, his hits glanced off their blades and did no harm.

"Blood," echoed a heavy voice. It filled the chamber instantly like vicious, powerful poison. *"Bleed for your Mother!"*

Devaki shuddered. "We have to help them!" she demanded, trying to pull her arm away from Gardain so she could cut another scar open on her skin. She'd marked Sutton's armor with a Protection Rune, so if she bled more and prayed harder, she could stop those spirits from draining him dry . . . couldn't she?

But for the first time in her life, her faith was wavering, and Gardain would not let her go.

"Please hold still," he insisted. "I've almost got it; I just have to think . . ."

"You're hurting me!" Devaki snarled, but he merely tightened his fingers till she whimpered.

One of the Armellan monks, the man who held the dagger, turned away from Will and looked in their direction. His dead eyes flashed a shade of magical gold in the darkness as he took a few steps toward them.

Sutton, on his hands and knees, crawled forward and dove for the spirit's ankles. His fingers passed through the transparent form, causing the monk to glance back at the rebel on the floor.

"No!" Devaki shouted as the spirit raised its weapon toward her friend. She tore her arm from Gardain's grasp, his nails running fresh scrapes through her skin. Devaki broke open the Protection Rune on her arm, said a desperate prayer in her head, and saw the rune she'd carved in Sutton's chest plate spark a shade of maroon. She reached out to grab the spirit's wrist as he plunged his dagger toward Sutton.

Her palm met hard, cold skin. A shock wave of deep red light blasted through the chamber and magic remnants sparked over the ground. Shock stunned her breath. Devaki had just *touched* a ghost. With a cry, she pushed back against the spirit until he stumbled, then fell to the ground several steps away from her. An unearthly shriek echoed from the man's dark lips, along with a whine of pain.

She offered Sutton a hand. "Get up," Devaki said, and she helped him to his feet.

His face was stained with tears and blood. But Devaki saw gratitude blossom over his features as he gathered both of her hands in his. "Thank the Goddess," he murmured. "And thank you, Devaki. I'm—"

Blood burst into Devaki's eyes, blinding her. She blinked, terror rising in her. Sutton gripped his throat, dark liquid running between his fingers. She screamed, then saw the spirit close behind her friend, his dagger stained red.

Sutton fell to his knees, but his blood stopped flowing downward. Instead, it rose in the air, hanging in a suspended river till it began to float toward the Armellan monk's outstretched hands. It disappeared and the spirit grew visibly stronger.

"He is nothing." The same feminine voice beat down and Devaki felt anger rise in her chest when it held an echo of her Mother's tone. *"Do you want the truth, girl? All of you are here to serve me. Every drop of your blood will be paid for your trespassing in this ancient place."*

"Devaki, get back!" Will shouted. He stood on the opposite side of the chamber with Rowlann, still fighting back the other undead monster that now almost looked like a real, living Armellan. Will ducked under his enemy's next attack, dropped his bleeding arm from his weapon, and came up to punch the spirit hard in the jaw. The magic in his blood caused the spirit to squeal in anger and bought Will a few breaths of reprieve.

"I think I've got it!" Gardain cried. He had backed up against the wall, standing underneath the carvings. His fingers were pressed to his temples, eyes scrunched shut with intense concentration. But now he let his grip fall so his arms hung loosely at his sides. "Devaki, I know what it says!"

He rushed over to her, trying to catch her eye. "'The belly of the Goddess'," Gardain translated, touching one looped symbol on her forearm. "That must be the chamber we're in. 'The belly of the Goddess is a prison for the worthless. But immeasurable strength will break its weakness.'"

Part of Devaki was shocked and impressed that Gardain had somehow translated what some poor soul had carved into these walls countless years ago as they bled to death upside down. But she couldn't bring herself to even look at Gardain. Instead, white noise began to take over her senses. A terrifying numbness washed over her from head to toe.

"Immeasurable strength," she whispered. Right now, she felt anything but strong.

She dropped Sutton's lifeless hand. Falling to her knees beside him, her back to Gardain, she stared at the spirit that stood before her, its bloody weapon pointed at the ground. It was as if it was waiting for its Mother's cue to attack, after seeing Devaki break into pieces.

Why didn't my magic protect Sutton? I believe in Cybarys with all my heart; no one's Blessing Runes could be stronger than mine right now. So why didn't my Mother save him?

The pressure of it all beat against her skull, but she didn't feel any pain. Everything pressed in against her heart, as strongly as the heavy, earth-crumbling weight of the Goddess' magic that had collapsed their passage above.

But was that the Goddess? Did my Mother do that to me? Is Gardain right, and this is an older piece of Cybarys, an element of her that's been lost to time down here?

Is it her real voice taunting and punishing me now? Where is that peaceful, loving presence I've known my whole life? I can still feel her, and yet, there's something else, too.

The truth of it hit her, harder than the blow she'd taken to her head falling into this horrible place.

They're two pieces. Two sides of the same Goddess.

And the ancient, evil one is stronger.

Devaki screamed. Everything else in the chamber fell away as her entire body wretched with sadness and rage. This was not what she thought would happen down in Kaladir's ruins. Somehow, she imagined she'd prove Will's visions and Gardain's research wrong. Instead, the reality she now faced compacted in her chest and she had to let it out. Her screams, however, weren't enough.

She raised both of her arms above her head, tightened her hands into fists, and slammed them down against the stone floor. Overwhelming magic energy radiated and the open Blessing Runes on her body burned with red light.

Plumes of suffocating dust engulfed everything. The floor shuddered, and finally, mercifully, the Ancient Form of the Goddess stopped laughing.

The entire chamber shook with incredible force, and on the wall across from her, a massive crack formed. It split five, then ten feet up from the floor until an unnatural gray light melted in from the other side. Vaguely, Devaki remembered Gardain's translation, though it had been far from her intention moments ago: *"The belly of the Goddess is a prison for the worthless. But immeasurable strength will break its weakness."*

When the chaotic dust began to settle, Devaki coughed and looked at her fists and forearms. They had sunken several inches into the solid rock floor on impact, but none of her bones were broken. In fact, she still felt nothing at all. When Will rushed to her side and tried to help her stand, she barely noticed that the two ancient spirits were gone.

"Master Will," Gardain said from somewhere behind her. "Does that look familiar?"

Will, however, had his attention on Devaki. After she gained her feet, he knelt in front of her so his back was to the cracked opening in the chamber wall. His hands gently rubbed her upper arms, as if that was supposed to console her. She'd bled a lot, and she saw her body shaking from the exertion. Yet it was like she was covered in ice; she couldn't feel his touch.

Frowning, Will glanced behind him where the strange, magical light was seeping in. "That's the Harvest Room," he said briefly in response to Gardain.

The young man nodded, then asked, "How did you do that, Devaki? What magic did you just use?"

She couldn't respond, though there was no real answer even if she could. How was it that everything hurt and was painless at the same time?

"Are you ready?" Will's voice lowered when he asked her the question.

Swallowing, Devaki told the biggest lie of her life so far: "Yes."

CHAPTER FORTY-ONE

IF I EVER LOSE MY FAITH IN YOU

Devaki stepped into the Harvest Room with numb feet. Will walked beside her to her right, Rowlann to her left, and Gardain was just behind her. Her skin crawled when she saw the similarities between this place and the great prayer room of the temple in Valsara.

The ancient black floor was made for kneeling, broken votives ranging along the walls where blood candles could be burned and Sahma could be lit. She shivered when she saw the divots in the stone made to receive large amounts of blood.

Above them, a spot in the ceiling was torn open, designed to spill light into the perfect spot, where the Goddess' statue stood. But this old place was underground now, and the only light here was the unnatural gray sheen that Will had mentioned before.

She glanced at Rowlann, who did not meet her eye; instead, he was focusing on their surroundings, highly strung and ready for another attack. Gardain looked calm enough. He took in every detail of the room again as if he'd been too stunned by this place to really absorb it the first time.

His pale green tunic was stained with dirt and blood, but it had to be someone else's. It might have been Sutton's, for all Devaki knew, and that idea brought fresh tears to her eyes.

I wasn't strong enough to save him. If I couldn't do that, how can I find this Dead Magic and put this place to rest?

Slowly, she took a step toward the dark form that stood at the end of the chamber, shrouded in sinister shadow. She would confront this piece of her Goddess, no matter how hard.

Will kept in step with her, while Rowlann stayed close to the Towne Master's son. "She's been speaking to you," Will said, his tone a low murmur as they walked slowly toward the Goddess' statue. "Tell me what she's been showing you in your mind."

Devaki tightened her jaw, grinding her teeth. "I can't."

"Don't shut me out, Devaki," Will insisted. "Not now."

She halted abruptly, spinning on the dusty black floor to face him. "So *now* it's okay to let you in?" she cried. "You shut *me* out since the moment I came here, risking my life for you, saving your soldiers, but all I get is one brief conversation and an old book? After sixteen years?"

Will's attention darted to Rowlann and Gardain briefly. "I am sorry–"

"Don't be sorry!" Devaki yelled. Tears rolled down her cheeks. For some reason, it felt like she was still in the other room they'd just escaped, banging her arms against solid rock, except the rock was now her father. "Don't be a hypocrite, either! I'm supposed to tell you about how my heart is broken after you've–"

She cut herself off, her last word echoing eerily in the ancient space around them. Eyes growing wide, she felt her throat tighten. Somehow, she saw in Will's gaze that he could tell what she would say next.

"It's because you feel guilty," Devaki breathed hoarsely. "You knew. You'd already figured it out and you still let me come down here and . . ."

"I couldn't stop you," Will replied. She saw his jaw shift with frustration, and there was clear, cold practicality in his eyes. "And I needed you, as you said. But I also couldn't tell you what I'd been shown. She's damaged. Your Mother is a fragment of what Cybarys truly used to be."

"Wait, sorry," Gardain spoke, holding up a hand. "But are you saying you've left out some details from our last expedition? You withheld information that could have made this easier for her?"

Even Rowlann, whom Devaki knew wanted nothing more than marching orders, frowned at that.

"Nothing could have made this easier," Will snapped.

Devaki could feel compassion from all three of the men around her, but the one she wanted honesty and love and respect from the most didn't seem capable or willing.

She'd had enough and wanted all of this to be over.

"I'm facing her, now," Devaki managed to croak through the emotion in her voice. She balled her hands into fists, her bloodshot eyes on the statue of the Goddess once more.

"Not alone," Will insisted.

"I can't stop *you,* can I?" Devaki retorted. She wasn't sure if she was angry at her father specifically; she just felt upset at the entire world, almost wishing for the numbness she'd experienced not long ago to wash back over her.

When she stopped in front of Cybarys' form, the cool shadow of the far curve of the chamber touched her trembling skin. She expected, when she got to this point, that she'd have more to give. When she looked into the narrowed eyes of the ancient carving before her, she thought she'd have more of a fight in her. But what had happened in the sealed antechamber next to this room, the prison called The Belly of the Goddess, left her with no remaining resolve.

She felt Will's hand on her shoulder. She noticed that he'd cut open a Strength Rune on his skin, and even though she was bitter, the act still touched her. Devaki couldn't look up into his eyes, not wanting to see any more pity there. Instead, she broke the clotted form of a Guidance Rune on her right hand, grudgingly grabbed her father's fingers tightly, and faced Cybarys' statue.

Mother, show us the way. Break through the lies and expose what we need to lead your children to true freedom.

No sooner had she said the prayer than the light in the chamber shifted. The sickly gray color that seemed to come from nowhere distorted in her vision like a curtain of slow-falling rain. It made her eyes itch and burn nastily, but she kept her focus on the stone depiction before her. A warm red glow pulsed from her skin and Will squeezed her hand.

"Devaki," Gardain began uncertainly behind them. "I hate to be a distraction, but . . ."

The meditative state she was trying to slip into to reach her Mother was broken when she glanced over her shoulder. Devaki felt her throat go dry when she saw his round gray eyes swimming with blood. Rowlann's pale blue gaze was similarly clouded with red.

She winced when she split open a Protection Rune, but nothing happened. Why wasn't her magic keeping them safe? Was her faith destroyed so quickly that Gardain and Rowlann were now in danger, too?

"I don't know what else to do!" she exclaimed, helplessness leaking into her tone.

"Think of what we've learned," Gardain insisted. "This place was used for sinister purposes, a dark trade of an entire body's blood to ensure Cybarys' protection in ancient times. But *you* have new magic different from those Dead Runes. Your Blessing Runes have power here that those spirits don't know how to handle."

"You can do this, Princess," Rowlann added.

Devaki tried to take their words to heart, but they hadn't been spoken to by two different voices that both sounded like her Mother. They hadn't felt the evil force that cackled in her head and demanded slave-like obedience while also encompassing the power she'd grown up loving without limits.

How could she have faith after that?

"With haste, preferably," Gardain said. Pain distorted his features and his jaw trembled. He winced, touched the side of his head, and fell to his knees. Rowlann cried out next to him but kept his feet.

When Gardain looked up at her again through his ashen curls, Devaki saw bloody tears fall onto his cheeks. Behind him appeared the faint outline of an ancient spirit. From the looks of him, Devaki knew he had to be the Temple Leader Will had spoken of before.

"Will," Devaki began, "help them, please!"

When Will tried to pull his hand from hers, Devaki found she couldn't release her grip. An echo of dark laughter came from the Goddess' statue, and with it that pressure she'd felt in the descending passageways above. It bore down on her hand where she gripped Will's, then she felt it at the back of her knees. Both of them were forced to the stone floor.

"You will find nothing. Bow, and bleed for your insolence!"

The voice tore through Devaki's head, and when she heard Will scream next to her, she knew he'd heard it too. Any bit of warmth she felt from her Blessing Runes was crushed down with that weight, pummeled to dust along with all of her hopes. Will tried to pry their hands apart, tried to stand, but he couldn't move any more than she could.

Her shoulders slumped forward. Even when she heard Gardain shout in pain behind her, Devaki couldn't turn to see him, let alone help him. The force was too strong. Though she could feel her magic and her Mother underneath it all, there was no way she could gather what she needed to try and make a difference.

Everyone in Rhethos who had spoken about her faith was right. Cybarys was an ancient monster who was full of lies, vengeance, and bloodlust. Everything she'd believed in was a farce, a laughable dream of a child who thought that, without a real mother, her deity could possibly care enough for her to take her place.

"Fight, Devaki," Will muttered. His words were strained as his forearms slapped down against the stone steps before Cybarys' statue. "You don't need to believe in her. I believe in you . . . and you can believe in yourself."

Devaki's breath caught in her throat. Everything always rested on the Goddess' love; never had anyone told her that *she* was capable of great things, all on her own. Will had held back so much, shutting her out since she'd met him, but those two sentences were enough to make her think it was worth it to gather the last of her strength.

Devaki balled her hands into fists and forced fresh blood from her Blessing Runes. Heat engulfed her, and a dry breeze cast back the sweaty chunks of her hair. She didn't pray, didn't think, but instead focused on standing. Slowly, she gained her feet. It took immense effort, but she turned toward Gardain and Rowlann.

I will not let them die.

The Towne Master's son was bleeding from his eyes, clutching his cheeks with shaking hands. The ancient Temple Leader gained more clarity with each passing moment, drawing on the young man's blood while trying to avoid Rowlann's advances. No matter what, the elite fighter kept himself between his enemy and Devaki.

Beneath the opening of the spirit's robes, Devaki could make out the steady yellow glow of a rune scar on his chest, covering his entire abdomen. The more blood he gained, the brighter the shape shone, indistinguishable but full of a terrifying power.

"Leave them alone!" Devaki screamed, and ran at the spirit, her arm with a Strength Rune on it coursing fresh rivulets of red.

The Temple Leader sneered, sharp lines creasing his brown face and dark eyes. He grabbed a handful of Gardain's hair to keep him still, then struck

Rowlann with amazing strength, sending the elite fighter sprawling across the floor.

He turned his other hand and its dagger in Devaki's direction. She caught his attack in the palm of her hand, the sharp side of his blade slamming into her grip. Despite the fact that it should have cut through her fingers completely, it barely broke her skin. Shock widened in the dead man's eyes as Devaki pressed back.

She brought up her right foot and kicked hard at the spirit, sending him flying away from her with the power behind her Strength Rune. Gardain was blinking furiously, as if trying to clear his vision from where he knelt on the floor. He reached for her, grabbing at her bloodied clothes.

On the opposite end of the room, Rowlann was trying to stand, though Devaki saw how pale he was. It frightened her deeply to see the man who never showed any weakness in such a vulnerable state.

The Temple Leader charged back toward Gardain this time, weapon ready, but the young man flung something at the spirit that made it shriek and retreat. Devaki stared, noticing that Gardain had gathered a handful of the magic remnants he always kept in a pouch on his belt. The crystalline red pieces scattered over the black floor and the undead monster stepped cautiously away from them.

"I was hoping that would work," Gardain said, a shaky smile on his lips as he adjusted the glove he'd put on his left hand. Red tears still leaked down his cheeks. "Devaki, he needs *all* of my blood to make that Dead Rune fully work. Get rid of him now, while you have the chance. He may be the final barrier between us and that rune."

She looked toward the ancient spirit, who was gathering his strength once more. Gardain threw a handful of the magic remnants toward Rowlann, who caught them in his own gloved grip, ready to use them to ward off their enemy.

There was malice in the Temple Leader's eyes, but Devaki didn't look away. She'd mustered enough hate today to throw back at him, and it rose to a point that she felt it might consume her. But that emotion actually weakened her resolve; hate was not something she wanted in her heart. She was taught that it tainted her magic, that it saddened her Goddess.

And what did she *hate*, exactly?

"You are so lost, sister." The Temple Leader sighed the words, shaking his head and straightening the chains that held his transparent robes to his shoulders. "I am glad you are here so you can learn the truth and follow your Fate's String as your Mother commands."

"That *thing*," Devaki snapped, gesturing back toward the statue, "it's not my Mother."

"She is the core aspect of Cybarys," the spirit said plainly. "Much greater than your shred of a 'Mother.' You cannot deny her what she demands. Her power lasts even after death." He held out his hands, as if his existence proved the fact.

Devaki glanced back at Will, who was still held motionless on his hands and knees before the Goddess' statue. Rowlann seemed incapable of doing much more besides gaining his feet.

When she looked down at her own hands, Devaki found them paler than usual and shaking uncontrollably. Gardain stood beside her and put one hand under her elbow to steady her quaking legs. She'd bled too much in this cursed place and she didn't have another drop to spare.

Instead, she decided to offer a final prayer, one that had all she cared for in its words. If that didn't achieve anything, she knew she would pass out and die from blood loss in the remains of a city long forgotten.

Goddess . . . Mother. Hear me. Show me what is right. I am lost, and I need your guidance to stand strong. I want to fight for this kingdom, for your people, but I only ask for the truth. All of it. Please, I believe in you. I . . . I love you.

Familiar hands touched her shoulders, an unseen yet deeply felt touch that she knew was the deity she loved. Devaki let out a sob of relief and fell to her knees before the Temple Leader, who had lowered his weapon. Tears filled her eyes and a weakness close to unconsciousness coursed through her body.

"There is no reason for you to be afraid, Devaki Tarran."

Devaki flinched; that voice sounded so familiar, like the loving tone of her Mother she'd heard deep in Sahma trances. But it was layered with the voice of that ancient, dark side of her Goddess that hurt to listen to. They echoed each other simultaneously, making her brain ache.

"We have shown you the truth today. You are the one to rediscover these Dead Runes and cast their magic properly. Find the four pieces of magic and their final, fifth companion to complete The First Bradford's spell at its full power.

"Doing so will bring the world back into your Mother's arms. War will cease. Prosperity will spread. Love will rule. Cast the spell with the blood of one human per rune and fulfill your destiny.

"Fate's Strings all converge at this single purpose, and you are at the nexus. Prove your faith. Reap the reward of being your Goddess' chosen child."

Devaki whimpered. A spell cast by The First Bradford? She hadn't shared anything about that, but Will had just admitted that he'd kept knowledge from her.

It was all too much. None of this should be real: this ancient magic, this heartless deity, this idea that with a dead magic and her father's war, she could bring peace to the world. Besides, war meant the death of countless innocents; how could her Goddess be condoning that?

"Sacrifice is necessary for rebirth. But you always have a choice, my sweet girl."

That was her Mother, breaking through in a kind yet practical tone, telling Devaki she was approving such murderous acts. Devaki sobbed further.

"Find the Dead Runes to use them—" snapped the Core Aspect of Cybarys.

"Or find the Dead Runes to destroy them—" insisted the Mother Aspect.

"Do as your Mother commands of you, girl."

"You are capable of so much, dear child."

Suddenly Will's arms wrapped around her, picking her up off the floor. He gripped the bleeding Blessing Runes on her arms, staunching her slowed blood flow. The connection between the two sides of Cybarys and Devaki broke, and an unearthly shriek filled the room.

Devaki curled into a ball as her vision darkened. Vaguely, she was aware of Will setting her down near the Goddess' statue and snapping at Gardain to bind her wounds while he went over to Rowlann.

In her wavering world, she saw the young man with streaks of dried blood smeared across his cheeks kneel next to her, tear his tunic, and wrap the fabric around her arms.

"Caulin . . ."

The two feminine tones rose yet again, addressing Will now, and Devaki moaned. She couldn't take anymore; it hurt to breathe, let alone suffer under the strength of her Goddess' words for a second longer.

"You were meant to lose your family, to lose your love, in order to find your path to your true purpose."

"Enough, you twisted bitch!" Will roared. He supported Rowlann's weight, trying to get the elite fighter to respond, but Rowlann seemed hardly capable of opening his eyes. "You've tortured us plenty. Show us where the Dead Rune is!"

"Though you deny your Mother, she loves you dearly," crooned the voices together. It was impossible to tell, unlike before when they spoke to Devaki, which was which. *"Your war was meant to merge with our purpose. Find the pieces of this ancient puzzle before your enemy does, or he will be truly unstoppable. The power from the Dead Runes' spell is strong enough to give The Bradford the true godhood he's always desired. Those who aid him are just as dangerous. Help your daughter and save your kingdom."*

"Master Will, you've got to stop it or it'll kill her," Gardain warned.

Devaki felt her skin getting cold, and his words echoed like they were being spoken from far away. She looked toward the Towne Master's younger son, trying to focus on his face above her. Was he worried about *her*, or the potential loss of knowledge if she died right now?

As if in slow motion, she saw Gardain's eyes widen as if he'd realized something while looking at her. He reached down and tossed a broken piece of stone over to Will.

"Break that statue," Gardain ordered. There was a demanding tone in his voice as he tightened another binding around Devaki's left forearm. She'd never heard him speak like that before. "Break her connection to us."

Though she was numb, Devaki wondered how Gardain came up with this idea as he dragged her backward, away from Cybarys' stone feet. Will set Rowlann down against the floor, where the man held his head weakly in his hands. Devaki rested back against Gardain's chest, unable to open her mouth. The chamber around them was so cold now.

Will smashed the stone in his hand against the Goddess' face, sending a spray of dark shrapnel everywhere. Gardain put up an arm to protect Devaki, and she felt her eyelids flutter dangerously. After two more strikes, Will paused. There was utter silence in the Harvest Room now. No laughter echoed, no distorted rain clouded their vision, and no voices wreaked havoc in their minds.

That's when Devaki saw it: a faint golden glow echoed from the fractured chest of the statue, where Cybarys' heart should be, and Devaki felt Gardain start behind her. Will slammed the stone against the Goddess' form one more time, shattering her entire torso in large pieces that cracked again on the floor. He knelt with his back to Devaki so she couldn't make out what he reached for. In her heart, though, she knew.

He'd just picked up a chunk of stone that had an ancient carving on it, hidden on the smooth inner surface of a statue that had stood for many years. When Will straightened, he held a fist-size piece of black rock to his chest, muffling the yellow glow of its ancient magic.

"Is that ?" Gardain began. There was fascination and fear in those two words.

Will nodded. His face was set in a hard expression, one Devaki had seen him use only in extreme circumstances where his authority might be questioned.

"L-let me see . . ." Devaki murmured, and found that her words were barely above a whisper.

Silently, Will shook his head.

". . .y-you heard her," Devaki rasped, her jaw heavy with the weight of death. "It's too dangerous. Destroy that n-now."

Her eyes were closing on their own, her body shutting down despite how desperately she wanted to stay awake. Why wasn't he smashing the only written carving of the Dead Rune to dust? The Bradford wanted it to use it against Cybarys, so he could truly enslave the whole world.

And it wasn't like they could use it anyway; her father wouldn't be willing to sacrifice an entire human's blood to cast an incredibly powerful piece of magic. . .

Or would he?

Devaki tried to move, to shout at Will like she'd shouted at her Goddess. Will said he loved Devaki. He said he was making this new world *for them*, so they could finally be a family. That world didn't have Dead Magic in it.

Gardain suddenly picked her up, and Devaki saw Will slip the Dead Rune into his coat. With that last action, the final piece of her heart broke. Then she let go.

CHAPTER FORTY-TWO

LIFTED WEIGHT FROM NUMB SHOULDERS

Angelyn had never prayed before. She had wished desperately for many things, begging for safety and stability for her and Joshua back in Kaylyn, but she'd never centered herself like she'd seen Will and Devaki do. She'd never focused on something greater than herself and asked for help.

But when Will had failed beneath Lorington on his own and come back, still holding hands with death, Devaki had told her she could pray to find some relief. Without faith in the Goddess, especially with what Will had told her about the deity, Angelyn was cautious about the idea.

That night, many hours after Will had gone back into that pit with his daughter this time, she wrapped a thick cloak around herself and went down to the western district, alone. The slums around her were guarded by rebel soldiers, keeping watch over those who lived here who were still suffering from the illness spreading out of this cursed hole into their homes.

She stood on the edge of the digsite, the toes of her boots pointed over the precise cut in the land. Taking a deep breath, trying to open her mind, she felt a pain grow in her head. It was an ache that expanded the longer she stood still, warning her that she didn't belong.

But Cybarys was supposedly a mother, the Mother. That was something Angelyn valued about herself more than anything. She hoped, when she had so little hope left, that that connection might be enough to make a difference.

"Please," Angelyn began, just above a whisper, "I am not here for you. I've never wanted you in my life, yet your magic is in my son's blood. I don't have any love or hate for you. But I do care about the people under this earth. Give them back to me. Set them free."

That pressure on her brain increased, though it now pulsed along with her heart, in a steady, warm rhythm. Angelyn knelt, balancing on the digsite's edge. Her fingers brushed the edge of a sharp rock and she gathered it in her grip. Putting the tip against her palm, Angelyn pressed hard until it punctured her skin.

Red liquid pooled in her cupped hand slowly. With a shaking breath, she extended her arm over the open air of the massive hole before her. Several drops of blood overflowed past the base of her little finger and between her thumb and forefinger.

Please, she repeated in her mind. She had no idea how to pray or if her blood meant a damned thing to the powerful pieces of a Goddess that dwelled in this land. *I'm a mother, too. Don't let my husband hurt my child. Don't let Will lose his child tonight. Please . . .*

She heard motion, a faint echo of sound very far below her. Beyond the walkways edging the sandy digsite bathed in shadow, Angelyn saw a plume of dust. She put one hand over her mouth as she wiped the other, bloodied one on the skirt of her dress. Squinting, she drew in a shaky breath when she saw four figures emerge from a dark opening: Will, with Rowlann's arm up over his shoulders, and Gardain, carrying Devaki in his arms.

When the rebel leader stepped out into the open air, Angelyn felt something shift in the space around her. The headache plaguing her melted away, and somehow, her shoulders felt lighter. She rose quickly, looking back at the nearest rebel soldiers.

"I need some help!" she cried, waving them over. When the men rushed down into the digsite to help their leader and his companions, Angelyn glanced up at the ramshackle homes around the edge of cut earth. Faces appeared at open windows, many of them rubbing their heads, staring at the dark sky as if seeing it clearly and pain-free for the first time.

Did he do it? Angelyn dared to think.

Will barely made it up the last walkway before she collided with his chest. She held him close, pressing his sweaty face into the side of her neck, taking the full weight of him against her heart. He stumbled to his knees at the lip of the digsite, and she fell next to him with her tears falling onto the top of his head.

"Are you hurt?" she asked. Running her hands over him, she couldn't find any new injuries, but only one of his arms held her weakly, his breathing shallow.

She didn't care if he held her back; he was here, under the night sky, in her arms. When he'd come back before, she'd been terrified to touch him, but now she promised herself she'd never let him go again.

Angelyn glanced up at Rowlann, who was now held up by two rebel soldiers. The man's skin was a severe shade of white, starkly contrasted with his black hair and beard in the pale moonlight. Dried blood arced across his chest plate and gauntlets. "The princess," he began, his voice strained.

"Oh, no. . ." Angelyn looked toward Gardain, who insisted on holding Devaki without any assistance.

Will stirred against her shoulder, shifting to look at his daughter. "She needs to see the healers, now."

When one of the rebel soldiers offered a hand in Gardain's direction, he shook his head. "She is quite light, I assure you; there is hardly any blood left in her."

Angelyn felt Will try to stand and put her arms underneath him till they both gained their feet. Shuffling over to Gardain, they looked down at the Armellan girl, who was muttering quietly and trying to open her eyes.

Will tentatively reached out to touch Devaki's cheek, his own hand shaking. Her eyes fluttered open for a moment, but when her dark brown gaze settled on Will, tears filled her vision.

"Get away from me," she whispered, then she shrunk back against Gardain's chest.

Angelyn shot a worried glance at Will. "Here," Angelyn began, and she let go of Will long enough to take off her cloak to gather it around Devaki's still form as Gardain supported her weight. She shivered as the cold night air hit her, running straight through the fitted fabric of her pale green dress.

Before covering her up, Angelyn noticed that every Blessing Rune scar on Devaki's arms was split open, shoulder to fingertip, her skin like ice. She hoped the bit of warmth would help keep life in her still form.

When Angelyn helped Will stand once more, sticky blood met her touch when she grabbed his forearm. She noticed small, clotting cuts along his skin, too. The palm of her hand burned as she held him close.

"One of you," Rowlann ordered at the rebel soldiers. "Get a horse for her, now."

One man took a few steps forward, away from the digsite, but then he froze. So did everyone else. Angelyn saw that, on the outskirts of the buildings, in doorways and alleyways, stood dozens of people. Their cloth was poor and their faces were gaunt, but none of them had old expressions of hatred that they'd borne toward the rebel soldiers and the Armellan girl in the past.

A wariness still filled Angelyn, remembering when she'd first met Devaki several weeks ago when the girl had been running away from the people who lived here. Now, they took tentative steps in their direction, awe and respect in their eyes.

One older man looked at Angelyn. He held a little girl in a night dress on his frail hip. "My granddaughter," he began, "her fever has broken. She's been ill for months after this place took both her parents."

"Have you lifted the Blood Goddess' curse?" asked another from the crowd. "Are we free?"

Murmurs of thanks rose in volume, though when Angelyn glanced sideways at Will, she didn't see any touch of emotion on his face. "The evil woken here by The Bradford's men will not hurt you anymore," he said. The usual volume in his voice wasn't present, but his message was still clear. "Spread the word of how the final plague of your Lord's oppression has been removed from your city because of our cause."

"Because of Devaki," Gardain muttered, and Angelyn stumbled as the young man pushed past her and Will. Out of the corner of her eye, she saw that the rebel soldiers had come back with a horse.

"The barracks are closer than Towne Centre," Gardain said as one of the soldiers helped him and Devaki into the saddle. "I'll make sure she's taken care of by the right people down there."

"Thank you," Will said. Angelyn frowned, wondering why he sounded so forlorn and Devaki had briefly looked at her father with such . . .betrayal.

She knew, now that Devaki would be taken care of by the nearest healers, something had to be done about Will and Rowlann, both of whom couldn't stand on their own.

"We need to go up to Towne Centre, to coordinate next steps," Will said.

"But you can't even–" Angelyn began.

"Now, Angelyn. Please."

"If you need to get to Towne Centre, we can help," one of the women from the western district spoke up. "It might not be the fanciest form of transportation, but . . ."

She indicated the edge of a wagon around the nearest street corner, drawn by a large, old horse. Angelyn's throat went dry when she saw that in the bed were several bodies of those who'd recently succumbed to the fever racing through the district.

"Thank you," Angelyn murmured as the bodies were moved by some men nearby.

"You've already done a lot for many girls from our district, Miss McKinlee," the woman added. "Thank *you*."

Angelyn did not expect that as she helped Will into the narrow wagon's bed, lined with old straw that was stained a deep shade of copper. It took more time to get Rowlann on board as well, so Angelyn took a moment to embrace the woman. She discovered her body wasn't fevered, either.

The wagon moved much faster once they were out of the narrow streets of the slums, back onto the main road leading north. Several times she asked Will what had happened, desperate for details, but he remained silent, his hand over one of the pockets of his vest.

He still leaned against her, but there was something in his eyes, deep in their green spheres, that held a broken darkness. Even when she'd first met him and he'd been a colder man, she hadn't seen that glint in his gaze.

When they arrived at the castle's entrance, Angelyn still kept a firm hold on Will's arm as rebel soldiers and servants from the castle all gathered around the wagon. Not far behind them, in the distance, she spotted many from the western district, following them, spreading news of their recovery.

In front of this important place, surrounded by those who looked to Will as their leader, he seemed prepared to give formal orders, burying whatever else was troubling him.

"Bring Master Moore to the digsite at dawn. We will show him proof that his people are now safe. Prepare the audience chamber in the east tower, with a scribe, ready to have Moore sign an agreement with us to join our forces. I want men ready at the barracks where Lorington's fighters are, ready to set them free as soon as their Master bids them to wear rebel violet. We don't have time to spare."

The soldiers around them nodded, determination on their faces.

"Rowlann," Will added, lowering his voice as he turned to the elite fighter, "if, for whatever reason, Moore goes back on his word, I want you to make sure Adlar and his mother are also present. We will use his illegitimacy against his father if needed, today."

"And Devaki?" Rowlann asked. He had to keep a hand on the wagon's edge to keep from swaying.

"Please check on her, then *rest*," Will instructed firmly.

Several rebels stayed with Rowlann, helping him stand but also listening to him give orders to his own men. Something told Angelyn that he would have to sit at some point or risk passing out entirely.

Angelyn led Will inside, into an alcove within the castle's main foyer. The open space was eerily silent in the dead of night, empty and cool, save for a few remaining torches.

"This is good news, yes?" she asked softly. "You've fixed every problem in this city. Devaki will be all right, I'm sure."

Will grimaced. He leaned back against the cold stone and Angelyn put her hands on his shoulders as he avoided her gaze. "She will recover physically, yes," he replied, "but the truth about Cybarys cut much deeper. I knew better, but I kept silent and I still let her go."

Angelyn's breath caught in her throat. His words about keeping silent bit at her conscience, reminding her how she couldn't tell this man about Irvin's dark deeds in the dungeons, to have someone go make sure her son was safe.

"Did you at least feel it, at the digsite?" she said after a moment. "When you walked out of there, something changed." She didn't mention her prayer or her drops of blood. They were likely a meaningless coincidence with his return. She just wanted something from him, an emotion other than weariness and sorrow, to show that it was, indeed, worth it.

"I don't feel anything, Angelyn." The statement seemed to awaken something in him as she saw the muscles around his mouth contort briefly. "I put Rhethos before my child and I don't think she'll ever forgive me." He still held a tight grip over that spot on his shirt. She looked down at his white knuckles.

"That's it, isn't it?" she whispered.

He nodded. When she put a hand over his, she felt his fingers tense. A hard lump of rock rested there, and it emitted a power that frightened her greatly, as if the strength of the sun itself was encased between Will's fingers, but touching it would cause excruciating burns. She didn't want anything to do with it, and she had a feeling it was hurting him.

Slowly, she pulled his hand away from what rested in his pocket. Instead, Angelyn placed his palms on her cheeks. "You can feel me," she said. She pressed his fingers against her skin, then up into her hairline. "Can you feel this?" She leaned in closer till their lips met. He did kiss her back, but only for a moment.

His knees buckled and he slid down the stone wall, till he sat in the shadowed space with his head in his hands. Angelyn crouched down in front of him, not sure what to do. When Will started to cry, she leaned forward so his head could rest on her chest.

His broad shoulders shuddered, his fingers clenched tightly in his long, dark hair. She just knelt there, a barrier between his unspoken sorrow and the silent, empty castle beyond. He shook for a long time, long enough for her own legs to start to ache, but she didn't dare move.

This man moved many people with his voice, inspired even more with his actions, and now stood at the brink of a large victory in this city despite incoming threats. But whatever had happened in Kaladir with his daughter was devastating.

"Will," Angelyn began sometime later. She tilted his head up enough to wipe the tears from his cheeks. "Come with me. Rest, if only for a moment. It'll be dawn soon."

He cleared his throat and gave her a small nod. With some effort, Will stood and created a bit of space between them. "Thank you, lovely," he murmured, taking hold of her hands. "I will be fine." Rotating her palms upward, she watched his attention go to the puncture wound in her skin. "What happened here?" he asked.

"Well, I . . ." Angelyn started, then faded off when she saw torchlight out the window opposite her. "A small accident." She led him out of the foyer, into a bedchamber, where he collapsed almost immediately. Sitting beside him, Angelyn waited for first light. It came much too soon.

CHAPTER FORTY-THREE

HER LAST HOPE

"*Wake up, Devaki. Wake up and listen.*"

WBut Devaki didn't want to do either of those things. She'd never felt so cold, so weak in her life. And what was the point of waking up? Everything she'd built her identity on was a dark, dirty lie. Sutton had died in Kaladir's ruins because of her, and Will had kept the Dead Rune instead of destroying it.

"*Wake up, dear child. Listen.*"

Still, Devaki refused.

The Mother Aspect, however, pushed against her consciousness, refusing to be ignored. Amidst the darkness that surrounded her, Devaki saw an image begin to form that unwillingly tugged at her broken heartstrings. She saw the Goddess' Woods, as she had on her last day in Valsara in the city's temple.

The trees that her people worshiped but never got to see, far away in northern Rhethos, were up in flames. At their center were the remains of Cybarys' first temple, still revered but long ruined. Just as before, Devaki watched as sinister smoke devoured the serene oaks. But this time, as quickly as the image formed, it began to reverse itself.

Devaki saw the flames suck downward, encasing the tops of the innumerable trees instead of rising above them. Leaves turned from burnt black to lush emerald, blossoming from ashes to vibrant life. The smoke faded backward to soft white, then clear blue. Before, all she'd seen was destruction, but now she was presented with a vision of possibility: the possibility of rebirth.

"*Your Fate's String leads you here, daughter. Find the tainted Rhethosian boy and the key he holds. Together, you are the ones who can bring either death or salvation to this world.*"

Devaki tried to shut her eyes, to tune out the words from the Mother whom she now knew was a broken piece of an ancient monster who had no problem sacrificing thousands in her name. None of her orders mattered when she was the weak piece of a more evil whole.

It hurt so much to even think about. Then Devaki felt that anger inside of her that had risen in the Harvest Room when the Mother she loved told her it was acceptable to spill blood on both sides of Will's fight to achieve Her ends.

"Wake up. Listen."

Devaki refused to do either.

"Devaki, wake up."

Those words, however, came from a human being, even more so, someone she cared about. She heard Gardain speak and dared to stir. At first, the movement was only in her mind, becoming aware of the space around her as the vision of the Goddess' Woods started to fade. Then she actually felt her body and became starkly aware of how tired she was.

So this is what it feels like to almost bleed to death.

Devaki forced her eyes open, then tentatively, she sat up in an unfamiliar bed. She saw the Towne Master's son at her side, and he reached out a hand to steady her. That human contact brought everything back: this young man carrying her from the ruins, her father keeping the Dead Rune for himself, the carvings on the wall written upside down by a dying soul, the way an undead monster's knife sliced through Sutton's throat. . .

"Glad you're back with us," Gardain said with a small smile.

"Should I be?" Devaki asked, shaking the memories away and clearing the hoarseness from her voice.

"Be what?" Gardain clarified, handing her a cup of water. "Glad?"

Devaki nodded silently, taking a drink.

"I think so," Gardain said, sitting back against the wooden rails of his seat. "Though I understand why you wouldn't be. I've seen that look before, the one on your face."

Devaki swallowed, then let the cup rest in her lap. Her fingers trembled on its smooth surface. She noticed that her arms were bound from shoulder to wrist in fresh bandages, and she could feel the sticky salve underneath them lining each of her healing rune scars. When she glanced over at Gardain, she saw pity in his pale gray eyes and didn't like it.

"What look?" she dared to ask.

He sighed and leaned forward, resting his forearms on the tops of his legs. "The one that says you aren't sure if you actually did want to wake up. The one that says nothing is what you wish it was. I've seen it in the mirror quite a bit myself."

Devaki felt tears touch her eyes but deliberately forced them back. She wouldn't cry for Cybarys. She even thought that, if she tore off a bandage and used her rune ring to cut a shape on her healing skin, nothing would happen. For the first time in her life, she had faith in . . . nothing.

But she did open her eyes, so that had to mean something, just like Gardain's words had hit her straight in the heart. She wasn't going to give up yet.

Before Will had taken the Dead Rune for himself, he had told her something that wouldn't leave her mind. *You don't need to believe in her. I believe in you . . . and you can believe in yourself.*

That reminded her of the times she'd merely touched Blessing Rune scars on her body and felt magical energy hit her system. It was such a practiced motion of comfort to her, with no one around her entire life to watch or care, that she was puzzled when it had astounded Will several times in the last month.

She didn't bleed for Cybarys in those moments. And, when she'd broken open The Belly of the Goddess last night, she had bled, but she hadn't prayed for a specific magic effect. She also hadn't cut a Dead Rune of any sort. Gardain had even asked her what magic she'd used, and she didn't know how to answer.

"Gardain," Devaki began, sitting up straight. "I'm leaving."

His eyes widened. Turning in his seat, Gardain brushed several ashy blond curls back from his face. "What? Now?"

"As soon as I can ride a horse," she replied firmly. "It may take a few days, but I can't stay here longer than I have to. And I'm telling you this because I trust you, and I hope you won't try to stop me."

"Could I?" Gardain said with a small, practical laugh. "I know you're not well, but I've seen the magic you're capable of."

Devaki winced, then decided it was best to let him think she was still able to use her Blessing Runes. She needed to go back to the beginning, to the First

Temple, somewhere where she could start new. She didn't want any magic or any connection to either side of Cybarys anymore. Even if her Mother wanted her to head there, Devaki would keep her blocked out in pure defiance.

"The temple ruins in the middle of the Goddess' Woods," she began. "That's where I need to go, to decide what to do next in this fight. I'm not going to be the same after what happened last night, and I have a feeling I can find answers there."

"But you're not telling Will?" Gardain clarified.

Devaki shook her head. She didn't want to see her father, hear his excuses or rationalizations, or even face Angelyn or Marselle. She'd had enough of Lorington. She hoped that Gardain could see how, right now, she wished she didn't have a father at all.

"I suppose your father is quite busy right now, anyway," Gardain conceded. "And my father will no doubt follow through on his agreement to officially add Lorington's army to the rebels, just like Will wanted. So they should soon be united and planning to take on our approaching enemy right away. Of course, none of that really concerns me. They couldn't care less where I am, as usual. You think this would be different, considering the historically unprecedented circumstances, but . . . I am rambling quite a bit, aren't I?"

Devaki smiled. She knew Gardain did that when he was nervous, or had something else on his mind that he really wanted to say more than the endless words tumbling from his mouth. "Do you want to come with me?" she asked. For some reason, heat rushed to her cheeks when she said the words.

Gardain blinked with surprise. "I. . .yes," he replied. "Yes, of course I would. I don't know what use I'll be if you're going to this ancient place for personal reasons." He stood from his seat, faced her, and then took her hands. "But you fascinate me, Devaki Tarran. I am so glad you asked."

Despite the cracks of pain and sorrow that ranged through her heart, Devaki felt something warm stir in her chest. Part of her was still confused about whether this young man was just intrigued by her race, her faith, and her magic, or if he truly cared for her as a person, but she didn't have the strength to question any of it right now.

"Then we better go, as soon as possible," Devaki said. She pulled her hands away from Gardain's, slowly flexing her elbows to see what her healing skin would soon be capable of. "If they are all as busy as you say, hopefully it won't be too difficult. Will's men will stop us, I'm sure, if they see us leaving the city."

"Don't worry," Gardain grinned. "I'll get everything we need, so we're ready when you're able to travel. I know some creative ways out of here."

CHAPTER FORTY-FOUR

RHETHOS' UNITED FRONT

Winter rose in a crisp, bright curtain of frost on the city's walls. Normally dull gray, when they were touched with icy periwinkle light and careening shafts of pink, the whole of Lorington slowly began to sparkle. When Angelyn inhaled, taking in the brisk, fresh sight, she felt alive.

Even with four small hours of sleep, she embraced the immense shift that seemed extremely close, barely at their fingertips.

The audience chamber Will had specified was the top room in the tallest building she'd ever seen. Its high ceiling arched into a dark point, enclosed in innumerable, tiny pieces of carved granite. Unlike most of the city built from the stone so common in this area, the talented masons of central Rhethos had saved the best cuts for this hall. Their polished edges shone in the early dawn's light that poured in through wide, rectangular windows.

Moore was currently being led around the digsite and the surrounding western district, along with Remora and Torald and a few others who were eager to take in the sudden change in the energy and the people. They would make their way to this room soon, she knew, when the Towne Master was satisfied and would officially unite his army with the occupying rebels.

Turning from the window, Angelyn saw Will, standing at a table, speaking quietly with a man about the paper between them. He still favored his healing arm, but his calm confidence had returned. There was no sign of the man who'd broken down beside her mere hours ago before the sun's light rejoined the world.

They had received news from the healers down at the barracks that Devaki was alive and eating the specific foods that the healers recommended, supposedly helpful for those who had suffered great blood loss or injuries. Gardain was keeping a close eye on her.

Angelyn had seen relief in Will's eyes when they got the news, though it didn't seem to lessen any of the heavy loss he clearly felt under the surface of his calm demeanor.

When a rebel guard entered the circular room and told them Moore would be arriving momentarily, Will actually gave Angelyn a smile. He reached for one of the seats that were arranged around the outer curve of the wall, where the Towne Master undoubtedly had his closest confidants sit for important meetings.

Will brought that seat over to the far wall, where a raised dais held a single chair above all others. The idea of being up there, next to him, in a space of power, made Angelyn very uncomfortable. *If this will make him happy, it has to be done,* she thought. *Whatever will mend the hole in his heart.*

Angelyn cleared her throat and took the offered seat next to the rebel leader. Two feelings hit her heart.

The first was that, even though she knew the position was one he'd taken for ceremony alone, he looked like he fit the part perfectly. The second was that he reminded her of someone, situated like a ruler above all others, and though she couldn't pinpoint why, it sent shivers down her spine.

Jeras Moore entered the receiving hall, and something about his stance made Angelyn think he'd never come into this room from the main doors. For many years, he'd sat in the chair next to hers, analyzing every person who had to walk step by step up to his raised position. From that place of power, he could look down on whoever approached.

Now, he shuffled across the expanse of the room with his oldest son at his heels, and Irvin and Torald on either side. Angelyn saw Marselle and Remora not far behind, speaking with several women and rebel soldiers who were holding the doors open to let in representatives from all of Lorington's districts. The open chamber quickly filled.

A spark of hope rose inside of Angelyn; the previous tension she'd felt in the air between this towne's ruling family and the rebels was gone, dissipated almost like the fever that had left the homes around the digsite. In the room, Angelyn noticed divided classes, once permanently kept apart by old ideals and their oppressive Lord, now gathering together as one, each touched by rebel violet in some way.

"I trust you're as pleased as I am that your city is now safe?" Will asked when Moore reached the edge of the dais. The Towne Master and his group had taken nearly two hours of the morning to explore the area and speak with many of the locals. She felt her hands tighten into fists, hoping that it would be enough and Moore would make good on his promise.

Will indicated an empty chair nearby, but Moore remained standing. The old man held his arms out, expanding the burnt orange and deep blue fabrics of his robes away from his thin form.

"Yes," he replied, only a little grudgingly. "It is a miracle, what I've seen down there. Those poor people are actually in their right minds, free of their disease. Your magic has banished what the Rhethosian Captain dug up. After what they've suffered and what I couldn't stop, I am grateful."

Murmurs of awe and agreement rose around the chamber.

"It was not an easy task," Will said, his face somber, "but I hope you can truly see that I'll do whatever I must to free more than just Lorington; we intend to bring our cause all the way to The Bradford's city. Your army should be at our side."

"I understand the truth of that, yes, but I only have one more question, Master Will," Moore insisted. "What did you find? None of your men will tell me, but I know there was something evil down there."

"Unfortunately, I chose violence over questioning when it came to undead monsters," Will replied, sitting back in his seat. There was cold practicality in his voice. Instead of explaining further, he indicated the table at the foot of the dais and rose to meet Moore at its surface.

Moore nodded, resignation settling into the deep lines of his face. He leaned back and forth, reading the paper slowly. Then, he bowed at the waist in front of the rebel leader. "Master Will," Moore announced as he rose, "I'm a man of my word. Lorington is yours. Its people, its defenses, and its fighters will bear rebel violet this morning."

With the scrawling of his name complete, Angelyn watched a genuine grin of triumph touch Will's face. Irvin was beaming, though she couldn't fathom why the man also looked rather smug. Light fully broke in through the vertical windows on the eastern wall, bringing with it warmth and comfort.

"Shall we go down to the barracks?" Will asked Moore. "Your soldiers will be glad to see you, and they undoubtedly need to hear of our new alliance from your lips. They have been treated well this whole time, I assure you."

Moore nodded. "That I don't doubt," he replied. "You've just killed the monster under our city; I no longer think you're one yourself."

It took some time for the two of them to make it to the door, as many present in the chamber wanted to speak words of encouragement, both from Lorington's people and the rebel Masters. Angelyn noticed how Torald held back, and Adlar kept a consistent, silent pout on his face.

Several men stopped Moore and Will, wanting to know when they could begin discussions about filling in the digsite. Now that the area was safe and the people were cured, it felt important for people to move forward, and from the look in Will's eyes, Angelyn knew he felt the same way.

The southern district was bathed in light by the time they arrived, not long after midday. The usual activity of the rebel fighters stationed there filled the freezing air. Will sent several men on horses ahead of their main group, to alert the rebels guarding the barracks where Moore's ranks were being held that they would be released soon.

She also caught Will whispering something to Marselle before mounting his own horse beside Moore outside of Towne Centre. Marselle gave him a nod, then set off with Remora and several other women, in an entirely different direction. Angelyn held back, letting many of the others, both on horseback and on foot, follow Will and Moore down the main road.

Through the entire morning going by, word was spreading quickly as the rebel leader and Lorington's Towne Master were finally seen side by side. *That's exactly what he intends,* she thought with a smile. *And it's a beautiful thing that he should drink in every second of right now.*

When they crossed underneath the wrought iron gate that led into the city's barracks, Angelyn couldn't help feeling fresh anticipation rise in her chest. It floated above the worry she felt for Devaki, the concern she felt for Will, and the revelations that had come with their trips underground.

She'd never been a part of something so significant, so . . . liberating. Soon, the rebel cause would truly own this city, without any violence done against his people, just as he wanted. Part of it, however, felt tinged with an uncomfortable shade of darkness. Will was keeping secrets about what had happened in the digsite with Devaki, she knew Irvin and Marselle were committing crimes beneath the surface of the rebellion, and Angelyn herself . . . A lump formed in her throat when she thought of her husband's existence and traitorous ties.

"Miss McKinlee," began a woman to her right. "Do you need a hand?"

Angelyn cleared her mind and dismounted, taking the woman's fingers to help steady herself. She shifted her attention, like everyone else, to the stretch of land between the barrack's entryway and the grids of buildings.

When she craned her neck, she noticed that rebel soldiers had gathered as far back as she could see, but the main focus was on the area where Lorington's troops were being housed. Afternoon cook fires burned, gracing the air with fresh smoke, but food itself had been forgotten.

Under the awnings, along the walkways between the structures, everyone waited, their eyes trained on the rebel leader and the Towne Master, still on their horses for all to see. When the doors that had been bolted for an entire month were opened, Angelyn watched in silence along with the rest as those they'd had to imprison the night the gates were broken were finally set free.

Those in front, with prominent rows of gemstones on their uniform jackets, stepped immediately over to Moore. The old man leaned down over his horse's neck and murmured several orders before sitting up to address the rest who were quickly filling the empty spot of land.

"This man," Jeras began, projecting his voice as much as possible, "has done more for this city than we've ever received from The Bradford. That is a fact I cannot deny." He let his horse turn slowly in the crowd, looking over all of the gathered Rhethosian officers and guardsmen around him.

Pausing also gave time for his words to be repeated back, Angelyn noticed, beyond the first few hundred who could hear the man speak.

"Thanks to the rebel cause, we are free of the Blood Goddess' curse, but we have to stand together to be free of yet another evil." Moore waited for another moment, his gaze shifting to Will, who gave him a small nod. "We are united with the whole of northern Rhethos, to ensure that abuse from military leaders and neglect from their masters will not harm Lorington again."

That statement rippled along the air like an arc of unseen magic. Through the bursts of clouds that issued from thousands of lips in the cold, Angelyn could see the message spreading, past the open entryway, back along the stone pathways, in between the many square structures.

The waves of emotion reminded Angelyn of the first night she'd heard Will speak, unwillingly, in the parlor of her inn. Though she hadn't yet supported his cause, the undeniable sparks of hope and determination to stand and fight were encouraging things to see in the eyes of his supporters.

Another memory struck her as she breathed in the wintery air. When she'd made the decision to go after the supply barrels in the flooded caves, risking her life for the first time because *she* chose to. That initial flame of hope had been given permission to grow into an actual fire.

Looking around her, pulling her heavy cloak tight, she noticed the same emotions flowing through each person around her.

First the spark, then the action.

A few cheers resounded over her shoulder, breaking the silent ambiance like the thin sheen of ice cracking on the roofs under the morning sun. Fresh echoes reached her ears from even further back, and those around her started smiling. As the sounds of unity and celebration grew, Angelyn locked her gaze on Will.

Even from where she stood surrounded by the crowd, Angelyn saw how his eyes lit up. Moore muttered something to Will, and Will laughed. A sweet heat grew in her chest at that sound.

This means everything to him, she thought, feeling her own smile grow. *I don't think I've ever seen him this happy before.*

Over by the iron gate, she heard a new commotion. Many of Moore's men were running forward, though she couldn't see why. Stepping up in between those around her, weaving her shoulders through the crowd, it took a moment for Angelyn to see that the men were slowly being joined by women and children.

Angelyn put a hand over her heart when she realized what was happening: the families and friends of the Rhethosian soldiers were finding and reconnecting with their loved ones. She saw wives pull their husbands close and fathers gather up their little ones with joyful tears in their eyes.

To her left, she saw Will thanking Marselle, and Angelyn realized the assignment that he had given Marselle a couple of hours ago.

Then Angelyn heard what the families were saying to each other: women from the northern district were proudly telling their husbands how they were now housing young girls fallen from grace in the western district, something unheard of a month ago. Men who'd been disconnected from Lorington's society listened as those who, for many reasons, couldn't speak before could finally share what they'd suffered, and how much had changed in such a short time.

Women from across the eastern district shared even more news with the soldiers: the business owners who'd abused the young girls they employed or those who followed suit with Caldrell's soldiers' actions were finally imprisoned, thanks to the rebel leader who cared enough to listen to their stories and take action on their behalf.

When Will's name spread through the waves of people, Angelyn heard stories of how he'd risked his own life to break the Blood Goddess' curse and heal all of those who were sick in the city. All of it confirmed Moore's words from his speech, solidifying the new bonds being formed across societal ties.

"Miss McKinlee!" someone shouted, and several girls pushed through the throng to wrap their arms around her. "Come meet my brother! I told you about him, at The Butterfly's Breath."

Angelyn listened amongst the noise that flowed around her, taking in one story after another, being introduced to many men with wide eyes and grateful expressions. A lump formed in her throat as she shook their hands, proving there were more than monsters in this city.

She didn't know how much time passed, but at one point Marselle was at her side and beaming humbly at the many women and men wanting to speak with her. She gave Angelyn a mere sideways glance. It wasn't long enough for Angelyn to tell what genuine emotion dwelt underneath it.

When she felt a gloved hand on hers, with bare fingertips touching her skin, she squeezed back before turning to face Will. He wasn't grinning anymore, but a warm, soft smile still touched his lips. Out of the thousands of men and women filling the entire stretch of the southern district, he still found her and made it to her side.

Angelyn threw her arms around his neck and, without thinking, whispered, "I love you" in his ear.

Will pulled back, staring at her. She surprised even herself; she hadn't expected those words to leave her mouth. They somehow did, as naturally as the breath that came before and after them. He pulled her close again, and she savored how it felt to be held safely in his arms.

"I love you, Miss McKinlee," he murmured before kissing her. Fresh shouts and whistles rose around them.

A new sound rushed through the chilled air, low at first, then louder as it grew closer. The blast of a horn, insistent and strong, cut across the combined ranks of soldiers. With it came three men on horses, all wearing dirty travel cloaks as they shot through the crowd.

Shouts of joy died quickly when everyone saw the hard, cold faces of the messengers looking for their leader. Those around Will stepped back and took the reins of the three horses when they stopped in front of them. Sweat and steam, along with drops of brown snow, trickled off the animals' chests and legs.

"Master Will," began one of the men, "we've ridden directly from outside Kaylyn. The Rhethosian army has arrived and has started garrisoning the locals' homes and businesses. Hundreds are already building fortifications, with thousands more close behind."

"And the Captain?" Will asked, his voice low even as mutters of concern grew around them. Angelyn felt his grip on her fingers tighten.

The messengers all looked at one another before one replied, "He is there as well."

CHAPTER FORTY-FIVE

CHALLENGING INSANITY

A heavy weight hit Will's shoulders. For just a moment, what he'd consistently felt for the last ten years had been lifted when he saw Moore's signature and saw their people united and heard Angelyn say she loved him, too. The tension he willingly let rest on his back was removed for a seemingly insignificant amount of time.

The messengers' news was not something he was expecting . . . not yet. His last updates from scouts along the coast that he'd received before heading to the digsite said they had a couple more days. He had hoped for at least forty-eight hours of solidifying bonds with Moore and his army before the Rhethosian army would officially block their advancement toward The Bradford in Clancy.

"We came straight here once we met on the crossroads," the lead messenger told Will. His tone was more even now that he'd caught his breath after arriving so quickly. "Each of our reports confirm that half the army is in Kaylyn, with the rest still marching slowly up the coast."

Will felt the crowd start to shift around him as he took in the news. "You," he said to the first messenger, "request that Master Moore, his best officers, and his sons meet me in the central barracks. Make sure that Master Colwell and Master Rowlann have the same orders."

He looked to Angelyn next to him, her eyes swimming with worry. "Can you find Marselle and meet me there? Her spies have done wonders in this city, but they will soon be needed elsewhere."

"I . . ." Angelyn stuttered. Will wasn't sure why she hesitated; as far as he knew, she and Marselle were still on good terms. "I can do that," she finished before heading off into the crowd.

Will took only a few steps forward before Irvin was at his side. He put a hand on Will's shoulder and let out a sigh. "Always short-lived, these little triumphs, aren't they?"

"It will be the last time, I promise," Will replied, getting a small laugh out of his friend. "This is what you've been waiting for, to have the Rhethosian Captain in our sights."

Irvin's grip tightened for a second. "Then let's walk a bit faster, yes?"

They quickened their stride till they reached the larger building in the central area of barracks, where Will had spent plenty of time over the last month. There wasn't much temperature change from the late afternoon air to the inside of the drafty stone room. Silently, Irvin worked on the fireplace while Will spread out the dozen chairs to allow room for everyone who'd no doubt arrive soon.

"Tell me your initial strategy," Irvin asked over his shoulder as he sent sparks into the soot-stained hearth. "Before anyone else gets here."

"We hit him hard," Will began, "before he can fortify too much of Kaylyn. Caldrell may be there, but as the man said, the majority of his ranks are still slowly getting up the coast. We use our new numbers to–"

"I know that," Irvin cut in. He straightened his back when the fire welcomingly grew, trying to compete with the bright ball of red light that was the sun coming into the western window. "I mean, what's your plan about the Dead Magic? The unreadable rune that The Bradford has? I'm assuming, with what little you've told me, that you've now got one, too?"

Will heard voices approaching outside and slowly met Irvin's gaze, his hand resting on the wooden back of the nearest chair. He gave Irvin a silent nod. Whenever the damned rock he kept close to his heart was mentioned, all he could see was Devaki screaming and bleeding and staring at him like he was a monster.

"You don't have to spill your guts over every detail that happened down there this time. I just want to know, are you going to use it?" Irvin pressed.

"We can determine that later," Will returned, "if we must."

"Of course we must," Irvin said quickly. "And you know it. Honestly, it didn't used to be so much of a chore to speak privately with you. Since Miss McKinlee's arrival in this city it's been nearly impossible."

Will wasn't sure how to respond to that. He held his tongue as a knock came at the door. It was a perfunctory action only, since the entrance opened immediately afterward, letting in those Will had requested.

He offered Moore the seat he'd purposefully placed closest to the fireplace. The Towne Master sat, with four officers taking seats on either side of him. Will noticed that the men, who ranged across decades of age, had already taken off their Rhethosian Blue jackets and placed violet sashes around their arms. That was a good sign.

Marselle came next, pushing in front of Rowlann, who gave her a scowl. Will waited for her, as well as Angelyn, who entered last, to take their own seats. Rowlann stayed standing by the door, leaning more heavily on the wall than usual though his hand still rested near his weapon.

"Shall we wait for your sons before beginning?" Will asked Moore.

The old man shook his head. "Adlar doesn't have the patience for military matters, so I've given him different tasks to keep busy. And I couldn't tell you where Gardain is."

Will knew the answer to that, though he doubted it would do more than further degrade Gardain in his father's eyes. The young man had refused to leave Devaki's side since they'd left Kaladir, and he was sure Gardain was still with her now as she rested. He wanted to check on her himself, but that look she'd given him, barely conscious on the edge of the digsite the previous evening. . . his heart ached and he chose to focus on everything, anything, else.

With the room getting much warmer by the minute, it was a shock when the door opened once again to let in fresh, cold air and one of the messengers who had arrived earlier. Dark circles leaked down under his eyes, but he stood with his back straight nearby Rowlann.

"I've sent my companions to rest," he explained, "but I would like to be here to provide any further information."

"Start with numbers," Will invited. Standing with his back to the wall opposite the fireplace, there was enough room in the rectangular space so all ten people present could clearly see him.

"Of Caldrell's fifty thousand troops," the messenger said, "we've guessed only half of them are actually in or around Kaylyn, which has housed merely five hundred soldiers since Sarrett left. They're staying away from the

Goddess' Woods, of course, and there's no hope with the winter seas of him bringing in men faster by boat."

Will let out a slow breath as he thought for a moment. With the more or less ten thousand rebel soldiers he had brought to Lorington's gates, combined with Moore's army of twenty-five thousand, they could have a chance of initially outnumbering the captain, if they acted fast.

When Will caught Irvin's eye, then Rowlann's, he knew both men had reached the same conclusion. "We have a unique advantage, my friends," Will said. "The people of Lorington no longer fear Cybarys because we've just lifted her curse from its streets. But the people of Kaylyn live in constant fear of the trees on their doorstep."

"And Caldrell, whether he believes in the wrath of the Blood Goddess or not, cannot stray from his Lord's warnings against her," Irvin added.

"So he and his army will not go near the trees, which would be a smart place to hide troops," confirmed the messenger.

Rowlann muttered with approval from the door. "I would like to move several forces to the tree line immediately, then, especially knowing that our fire-loving opponent cannot burn the woods to the ground in this winter weather."

"We would like to add several thousand men as well," added one of Moore's officers, "if you can, in fact, guarantee our safety."

"I can," Will promised, though the officers still looked to Moore, who gave them a silent nod of trust. "Though we must do more than that. Our unexpected loss of our supply line when arriving outside Lorington has been something I've thought of often. Without the vital food and weapons that traveled with our army, we were set back in a nearly devastating way."

"Thanks for bringing it all back," Irvin muttered as he crossed his arms over his chest, shifting his boots closer to the fire.

"I say this," Will continued in a patient tone, "to relate to our current situation: the huge threats behind Caldrell are his sheer numbers and the cult-like loyalty of his brutal men."

Moore cleared his throat, and when he spoke his voice was low enough that Will leaned forward, off the cool stone wall, to hear him. "Mercer Caldrell may be insane, but he's quite the tactician. Even with our forces combined, we will have a hard time meeting him in Kaylyn."

"That is why we must delay the other half of his army as long as we can," Will continued. "Lady Marselle, I have a proposal for you, if you're willing to take on the task of crippling and obstructing a very volatile enemy."

"I do like where this is going," Marselle smirked, though her playful nature only lasted for a moment. "My girls are used to dangerous supply runs and dealing with small encounters with Rhethosian bastards– no offense," she added, glancing at Moore and his officers. "But they don't have much experience sabotaging a force like the Insane Captain's."

Will nodded. "I do not expect you to openly burn supply wagons or cut the throats of sleeping men. Those aren't our tactics. So I suggest a more subtle approach. Ways of delaying his approaching army and their supply line that don't seem deliberate. Meanwhile, the rebel troops arriving at Kaylyn Field will seem miniscule, with many hidden in the Goddess' Woods."

Marselle's mouth twisted, her lips pursing as she smoothed the sleeves of her dress. "Master Moore," she began, "do you have spies who can help strategize details with my supply runners to make this happen? Men who would work beside my girls so we can all survive this?"

Before Moore could respond, one of the officers, the youngest of the four, opened his mouth. "I have several men who would readily volunteer. Their wives have been speaking about what you and Miss McKinlee have done for our towne. So they'd have no issue joining the effort beside any female fighters."

"I know a few more guardsmen who would feel the same," added another officer with a small nod. "I'll summon them when we're through here, so you can meet."

"Well, I'll be damned," Marselle chuckled. "I never thought I'd see the day when I'd ask such a question of men like you, let alone get that reply."

"Yet here we are," Will said, earning a smile from both Marselle and Angelyn. It was an initial strategy, the best that he could set in place on such short notice. When he looked around the room, everyone was in agreement, though he did see some concern in Irvin's eyes.

Will knew exactly what his friend was thinking. *Moore and his men know nothing about the Dead Runes or the terrifying power that The Bradford possesses beyond his military captain. They are going into a fight that, if escalated . . . if we dare win, could ignite the anger of a man who holds Dead Magic capable of unimaginable destruction.*

And that same question remained: when the time came, would Will be willing to sacrifice another person's life to counteract one Dead Rune with another one?

He shivered, then shifted his attention to the messenger and Rowlann standing on either side of the door. "I need all of our messengers accounted for immediately, so we can implement these orders across our ranks before another hour goes by."

"That I can do," Rowlann said. "If you asked me to march out to Kaylyn right now, I might have to decline." His pallor, even in the warm glow of the fire that bathed the barrack's walls, was indicative of how much blood loss he'd actually endured facing the spirits beneath the city.

"You also have the use of all my messengers in Lorington right now," Irvin offered, and Rowlann gave him a thankful nod.

Will glanced at Angelyn when he saw her stir. She'd been silent the entire time, which didn't surprise him since he knew she had no knowledge of military matters. He had been ready to offer her a choice, to help Marselle with the task he'd assigned or ask her to take on the responsibility of feeding the rebel army or even staying in Lorington and continuing her work with Remora.

All of it, of course, was her choice.

But Angelyn was staring hard at Irvin, lines of suspicion sharpening the pale skin around her eyes. He watched her hands ball into fists on top of the arms of her chair. "All of your messengers are here except for one, correct?" she asked Irvin pointedly.

Irvin opened his mouth, then closed it . . . then grimaced, as if he'd made a mistake that Will didn't understand. There was usually tension between his friend and Angelyn, Will knew, but right now the space was more taut than ever before.

"Irvin?" Angelyn insisted. "Tell me you actually sent that man north."

The fire crackled and a couple of Moore's officers shifted uncomfortably in their chairs.

"North?" Marselle questioned, and Will saw confusion in her green eyes, too. "Why send any of our men north?"

Will studied Irvin for a moment, then glanced back at Angelyn. Was there something going on here that she hadn't told him about? He delegated important tasks to those he trusted most, but everyone always reported back to him. He wasn't left in the dark.

But he realized that with both of his ventures into the digsite so quickly and close together, he'd been gone for long periods of time, leaving these people before him to either work together. . .or clash.

"Of course I sent him, Miss McKinlee," Irvin said. He rubbed an errant hand against his thin, blond hair in a dismissive manner.

Angelyn stood from her chair. Everyone else in the room stared at her and several blinked rapidly when she snapped, "You are a liar."

"I've been called worse, darling," Irvin returned smoothly.

Will took a step toward Angelyn when he saw her start to shake. For some reason, passion was clear in her stance and she didn't even notice him.

"I kept quiet for you," Angelyn hissed at Irvin, "even though I didn't want to because–"

"You had best keep your silence now," Irvin snarled. He didn't move from his seat, but the glint of a threat in his voice made Angelyn step back.

Will cleared his throat and paced to the middle of the room, putting himself evenly between Angelyn and Irvin. "It seems as though we have some additional matters to discuss. Master Moore, would you be kind enough to work with Master Rowlann to organize which fighters are best suited to be hidden in the trees, versus those who would prefer to encamp in the open fields? We don't have time to lose placing each man where he will best stand for our cause."

Though he looked briefly between Angelyn and Irvin, Moore stood and motioned for the officers to follow. The rebel messenger at the door left with them, as well as Rowlann, ushering in a cold bout of air to match the barrack's cold energy.

CHAPTER FORTY-SIX

THE COST OF FREEDOM

Angelyn had never felt such an overwhelming combination of ferocity and terror. Irvin's disregard for their agreement hit her sharply, igniting rage in her belly at being lied to and fear when she realized there would be no updates on Joshua's safety any time soon.

To speak up in a group, especially one as important to the kingdom as those in the room, was hard enough. When she imagined Josh encountering his father or the rebel camp being at risk because of her violent husband or what Will would think when he learned that she was still lawfully bound to such an awful person . . .

It sent blinding white heat in front of her, burning away any decorum or formality or manners that might have held her back. And now that Moore and his associates had left, she was ready to unleash every bit of anger in her bones at Patten's former Towne Master.

"You don't care about anyone except yourself, do you?" she spat at Irvin.

Will put a hand on the sleeve of her pale green dress, still placing himself between her and Irvin. "What in the Goddess' name is the matter with you two?"

"He lied," she continued hotly, "about sending a messenger north to make sure Joshua is all right."

"Why wouldn't he be?" Will started.

"The only way he would agree to send someone to The Forts," Angelyn barreled on, "was if I didn't tell you about what he's done to Sarrett and his children."

Marselle sat up in her chair, wincing. Angelyn noticed her attention go to Will for a moment, then to Irvin, where she shook her head minutely. But Angelyn couldn't be stopped; it was as if the emotion rolling through her held so much weight that its forward momentum from her mouth was completely unstoppable.

"Sarrett?" Will began. "What does any of this have to do with him?"

"He's been torturing that man, in the dungeons, for weeks," Angelyn declared. "When I went down there, I heard those poor children crying. I couldn't stand how frightened and alone they sounded."

Will held up a hand in her direction, even as she watched multiple questions rush across his eyes. Crossing his arms over his chest, he kept his attention focused on Irvin. "We agreed that you'd leave the lieutenant be, until things aligned with his masters."

Irvin shut his eyes, pinching the bridge of his nose as if a great pain sat there. . .or merely an inconvenience. He opened his mouth once, then shut it slowly.

"These were details we were going to bring to your attention shortly," Marselle began in the silence. "I was–"

"Don't do that, darling," Irvin cut in. He opened his pale blue eyes to give Marselle a thin smile. "You are not responsible for any of this." He stood to his full height, demonstrating an effortless confidence that told Angelyn to brace herself. "I had to take advantage of you sparing that man's life, Will. Caldrell favored the ambitious little prick over the last few years. He told him secrets during their Sahma wine gatherings that no one else knows. He's even got something on The Bradford himself."

Will frowned more deeply at that, and Angelyn stood as well. She didn't know that Irvin had carved so much out of Sarrett, though, by the looks of him, whatever he confessed had to be true. It shocked her that a man like Sarrett who had burned innocents in their homes had broken because his own little ones were being threatened.

"Miss McKinlee here took the liberty of confronting the man who ruined her home," Irvin pressed on. "And, because I did what needed to be done, he confessed an interesting fact to her."

"Don't," Angelyn began. "Please."

She knew that Irvin would openly tell Will all about Travok's existence if she dared mention what the former Towne Master was doing in Lorington's dungeons. Part of her hoped that Irvin would stop, until she could tell Will about that unexpected layer of complication when she was ready.

She almost heaved a sigh of relief when Will shook his head at Irvin. "Leave that be, for a moment," Will said. "You have my trust, Irvin, more than almost anyone else in Rhethos." He swallowed, as if physically trying to make peace with the fact that, in order to learn what Irvin had learned, the man had to do things that Will himself would never do. "But we promised each other," Will continued, "at the start of this cause, that we wouldn't commit the same crimes as our enemies. Caldrell and his military torture men, rape women, and harm children. They oppress and attack and lie."

He stepped up to Irvin, turning his back to Angelyn. "Don't tell me," Will said in a tight murmur, "that you've harmed innocent children while wearing that rebel violet."

Irvin paused, then held his hands out away from his body. "Not so much *physically*, but—"

Will grabbed Irvin's tunic in both of his fists, practically picking the slim man off the ground. "You've gone too far," he hissed.

When Marselle jumped to her feet, Will turned his temper toward her. "And you are defending him because you're involved as well. Did you use your connections to find Sarrett's family? Did you willingly bring his children into a dungeon?"

Marselle cleared her throat. "I did not harm either of them–"

"And *you* . . ." Will interrupted. He set Irvin down and shoved him back several steps. Angelyn met Will's gaze from the other side of the room when he turned back toward her. "How long did you know what he was up to?"

"I. . ." Angelyn began unsurely. She felt herself shrinking, her hands starting to shake where they were clasped against her arms. Will hadn't spoken to her like that in a long time, definitely not since the night of Lorington's celebration.

For some reason, her mind flashed back to the night in Kaylyn when she and Josh had watched Will risk his own life to protect the newly orphaned Luwenn girls. He valued the safety of children above all, but so did she. How could she make him see that Irvin gave her no choice but to keep silent?

"I went down to question Sarrett myself when you went into the digsite for the first time, three days ago," she said in a low voice. When the logs in the fire cracked and shifted, she jumped nervously. "And I didn't say anything to you because Irvin made me promise to keep my mouth shut, or he wouldn't protect Josh."

Escalated anger and betrayal flashed in Will's eyes. He stalked across the room toward her, eliminating the space between them. Angelyn put up an arm to shield herself and shut her eyes. Heart pounding, she jumped when she felt Will take her hand softly.

"I'm sorry, lovely," he said, and all of his aggression melted away in those three words. He lowered her arm, then put a finger under her chin so she'd look up at him. "I'm sorry."

She took a shaky breath and still stepped back from him, wrapping her arms around her torso. Knowing what was coming next, and knowing it wouldn't get any better, Angelyn steeled herself.

"You go ahead, Miss McKinlee," Irvin said. He'd created enough space between them, standing back by the fire and busying himself with working the wrinkles out of his violet tunic. "Let him hear the rest from you."

Slowly, she met Will's gaze. It was hard to believe that, hours ago, they'd been surrounded by thousands of cheering soldiers. The sharp noises of hundreds bustling around outside the building were still constant, but for some reason while she gathered her courage, it felt like the background sounds amplified, grinding into her ears and setting her more on edge.

"Sarrett said that a spy of his told him about where to ambush your supply line the night of the siege," she said softly. "The spy was sent north, into the area where The Forts are located. Sarrett described the man accurately and knew his name. . .Travok McKinlee."

Will shook his head, then ran a hand along his jaw, not saying a word.

"I tried to send men north, right away, to keep Josh and the rest of the rebel families safe because I know how twisted and violent and heartless Travok is," she insisted. "But Irvin didn't think it was necessary. He made me promise to not tell you about his torture of Sarrett's children, if he sent a man to make sure Josh wasn't in danger. Travok should face *me*, not our son. I have to keep him away from my boy–"

"And you learned all of this three days ago?" Will whispered. His tone was quiet as well, but there was enough strength behind the question to cut her off.

Angelyn just nodded. She knew what he was thinking; when he'd gotten back from Kaladir the first time, he'd unearthed some unsettling information about Cybarys, along with a lot of difficult questions. He knew he couldn't fix this city without putting his daughter at risk.

During those nights before he went into the digsite with Devaki, they had shared deep, personal stories with one another. Her recollection of the night Joshua was conceived, Will's experience losing his mother. All of that sat, unspoken, in his gaze, and she felt tears fill her vision.

"I don't talk much about myself." He told me that in Kaylyn. Telling me a story about his past that he'd written in that journal meant only for Devaki was something he had "to work up to" was what he said weeks ago. It took so much for him to trust me, and I was hiding things from him while he opened his heart.

"I didn't know how you would react if I said something," she began. "I was afraid, Will. It was so much, to learn he's alive, after all these years, and that he still poses a threat to Joshua. . ." She put a hand over her mouth, unable to continue.

"Why did you force her to remain silent about such things?" Will looked at Irvin when he asked the question, his voice starting to rise to a more demanding level.

Irvin scoffed. "Because of this!" He waved his arms, demonstrating the unseen tension in the room. "I told you not to make an enemy of me, Miss McKinlee."

"You cannot and *will not* shame me for trying to take care of my son!" Angelyn snapped back. Every bit of hurt she felt from Will she shifted and countered in Irvin's direction. She would not let herself be beaten down by this man who justified even the worst actions in the name of freedom. "With the snow that's fallen by now up north, there's no way we'll be able to reach or help those people. Just because you lost a child–"

Irvin slammed a fist against the mantle, displacing several books and loose sheets of paper. At that moment, Angelyn knew she'd gone too far. "You realize," Irvin hissed, "that the only reason why you wanted a messenger, no, an entire troop of rebel soldiers sent north is because you were ashamed to learn your husband is alive, working for our slimy Lieutenant. Because your poor son might run into his sorry excuse for a father, your embarrassment of a spouse, you wanted to risk our soldiers.

"You thought, Miss McKinlee," Irvin continued, pointing a finger in her direction, "because of your newfound status, that you could order me to send away vital men without Will knowing, so you could make sure your teenager, who wants nothing to do with you, is safe. Or. . .maybe you're more than embarrassed at your traitorous ties. It's been your plan all along to take our fighters from us in our hour of need. Because you're just like your husband, nothing but another spy. Travok wormed his way into our forces up north while you got in bed with our leader–"

"Irvin, that's a stretch, even for you," Marselle interjected.

"It's more than a stretch," Will growled. "It's enough to get him in serious trouble."

Irvin rolled his neck back, staring at the ceiling for a few seconds as if looking for his patience amongst the cold stones. "I'm sorry if I thought that a family dispute with a single spy wasn't as important as an enormous incoming military threat. I was focusing on what actually mattered: breaking Sarrett."

"We do *not* harm children!" Will cried. Angelyn found that when he shouted, every muscle tensed in her body like she'd been hit. "Regardless of the benefits, no matter the reward you gained, that is a line you will not cross. You will send them home, or at least somewhere safe for them, immediately."

Irvin glanced at Marselle, who gave him a firm nod. "Of course. What I've learned from that man will make a huge difference in the upcoming battle. I guarantee it."

"At what cost?" Angelyn murmured. She imagined her son at risk once more, despite being in a place where the rebel families were supposed to be hidden. She thought of Devaki, nearly bleeding to death under the city. And she thought of the harsh weight of that enchanted piece of rock Will kept close to his chest. They were all payments that the people bearing rebel violet were not aware of, below the surface of it all.

But like the night that Marselle had confessed to her everything she did so Will could shine like a proper leader, the heavy weight pressed down on Angelyn with increasing strength. She caught Irvin's eye, and his next words made her feel like he could somehow read her mind.

"I've done what I've done for the sake of everyone in this damned king-dom. So does Marselle. You want to stand there, Angelyn, high and mighty, next to Will? You want to take my place of authority from me because you sleep next to him at night? Fine. But Will knows full well what I do in dark dungeons to keep this cause alive. Even if he needs to push me around every so often to help his conscience. You better adapt the same mentality and sweet smile in public if you want to live through this."

Angelyn gave Will a worried look. She knew there was a precarious balance here, between what he could do in front of his followers and what others had to do for practicality's sake behind closed doors. When he'd learned the truth of the tangled mess that had enveloped her the last few days, it broke her heart to see that she'd hurt him when it had been so hard for him to be vulnerable with her.

All of this, she thought miserably, *right after I told him that I love him.*

Will put his hands over his face, rubbing his thumbs along his temples. Angelyn watched his right hand slide down to his left forearm where a fresh Strength Rune had been cut. She had wondered why he'd done such a thing when his Touch was gone. *And what,* she wondered, *does he need strength for now?*

He reached into the front of his jerkin and pulled out a black stone. His fingers were barely long enough to wrap around its edges, but instantly, a bright golden light pierced the room. Angelyn flinched as the glow of the ancient magic dominated all else.

Irvin froze and Marselle stepped back till her curls pressed against the wall.

"There are things at play in Rhethos that are far bigger than hurt feelings," Will began. "Believe me, brother," he added in Irvin's direction, "if I had a choice, I wish it was as simple as marching on Kaylyn to get you your revenge and push us closer to The Bradford himself. But the damned Goddess. . ." He grimaced, and Angelyn saw his knuckles go white against the uneven stone in his grip.

"Beyond personal struggles that you've all brought up just now, I still trust each of you greatly. So I'm going to tell you about this Dead Magic because I've kept the full truth from everyone, including Devaki. *That* is what really matters right now. Do you feel that?"

He held the Dead Rune out till his elbow locked, his palm covering the shape carved in its surface. Once again, like the previous evening, Angelyn didn't want to be anywhere near it. From the pale expressions on Irvin's and Marselle's faces, she guessed they felt the same.

"It wants blood. Human sacrifices, for Cybarys," Will said. "There are only singular written copies of them left in the world, which used to be held by Temple Leaders in ancient times. This you know. But what I discovered under this city the first time I made it to the Harvest Room is The First Bradford created a spell using all five of the Dead Runes at once that twisted this magic.

"Back when the Great Sea formed, he broke the Goddess, weakening her into two pieces: the Mother who is worshiped across the sea today, and the Core Aspect who only dwells in places where her Dead Magic can still be found. That's the monster we faced last night in Kaladir.

"The goal of that man's spell long ago was to create and control the ultimate amount of power that could either make or break anything, including the Goddess herself, whom he saw as an oppressive ruler. In fact, back then . . .she was the slave master that many Rhethosians fear today.

"The First Bradford's goal was to either imprison or kill Cybarys. When I almost died down there, she did more than give me a vision; she offered me the same power. If I submit to her, she will make me as strong as she is by eliminating the Mother Aspect."

Silence fell and Angelyn had to take a seat in the chair nearest the fire. The overwhelming entirety of what he'd divulged hit her, including a sharp pang of pain for poor Devaki, whose heart was likely broken when she learned such things about the deity she adored.

Angelyn rubbed a hand against the base of her throat, sudden nausea hitting her while she processed Will's words. "So," she began, "That's why the Rhethosian Captain was digging into Kaladir's remains? So he could find these pieces of Dead Magic for his master, to easily eliminate the rebellion and anything else that could possibly question him?"

"No, no," Irvin said, shaking his head. "Will, you told us this spell she showed you either destroys *or* creates. The person using this magic chooses, yes? So if you submit to the Blood Goddess' chains, she'll have you use that energy to kill her weaker half, I suppose. But if you find them and cast this spell yourself, without becoming her slave, you could channel that energy to create. . .what exactly? My head hurts."

"I really don't know," Will murmured. "I don't know enough. Gardain, if I choose to share all of this with him as well, could likely find more answers in his research. But right now, I'm more concerned about doing what we can to defeat Caldrell swiftly enough that these Dead Runes don't come into the fight. I've told Devaki this already, but my initial goal is to find all of these before The Bradford does."

"I'm sure Devaki wanted you to destroy that rock, right?" Angelyn asked quietly. "And instead you kept it." *And that's why she hates you right now,* she finished in her mind.

A flicker of pain rushed across Will's face. He nodded.

Angelyn sighed, then another question hit her. "Do you think it's fair to say that, if Cybarys spoke to you, Will, that she also spoke to The Bradford?" Angelyn didn't look at him when she spoke, not sure if he'd even want to meet her gaze right now. "Could she have tempted him with the same offer, and that's his goal that we're just getting in the way of with this fight?"

"That is a safe assumption," Will replied somberly while Irvin let out a string of curses. "He already thinks he's a god," Will added. "Why not use this Dead Magic to truly make himself one?"

Angelyn shivered. She couldn't imagine a world like that and truly didn't want to. Since Will had set foot in her old home, she had heard the metaphor of Rhethos' rebirth used many times. Now, however, it seemed as though they were facing the potential breaking of the world itself.

And there's no way Will would seriously consider the Goddess' offer, would he? Angelyn thought, hating it when the realization hit her that she didn't confidently know the answer to that question.

Will exhaled slowly, shifting the Dead Rune in his hand until it rested against his chest. When he took a step forward, eyes on Irvin, the older man shrunk back. "You've been with me since the beginning, brother," Will said. "So I need you to know all these facts, even if you've crossed a line. I have never lied to or hidden anything from you, and to start now would doom us all."

Will held the rock tighter in his hand, and Angelyn almost thought she saw the Dead Rune's light intensify, calling for blood to be given to its master. "My child almost died so that we could find this piece of stone. And she is, no doubt, spiritually broken after discovering its origins and its purpose. She did, indeed, beg me to destroy it the second we found it. But I didn't. Do you know why?"

Will waited for a moment, but, for once, Irvin seemed at a loss for words. "Because I hope there is a way I can use this twisted, old piece of magic for good. Just like how we've done good here in this towne. Though there's a nasty part of me that wants to use it in the destructive way it was intended.

"I am capable of the things you do in dark dungeons, brother. For Rhethos, I'd be capable of even worse. In fact, part of me knows that the Core Aspect of Cybarys would love to see me march to Kaylyn, spill every last drop of Sarrett's blood, carve the shape of this Dead Rune into my chest, and use its power, hoping that it will break Caldrell in two. If I did that, I might win Rhethos, but I would lose everything else. The love of my only child, the respect of my people, the worthiness of this woman. . ."

His attention darted to Angelyn for only two heartbeats. "But we must be united under the same moral banner. And even though I'd like to crack your head open sometimes, Irvin, I'm better than that."

"Thank the Goddess for that!" Irvin breathed, his voice a bit shaky as if he was still trying to take in all that Will had said. "With what Sarrett has confessed about his Captain, I know we have a chance of outmaneuvering Caldrell, especially if we act on our current plans right away, before the entirety of his army can mass in Kaylyn."

Will gave him a curt nod, though Angelyn could tell that he was still struggling inside. She knew that he liked to focus on clear facts he could control and distinctly respond to, not the complicated unknowns that the Goddess forced into his life.

Several sets of footsteps approached, deep shadows running over the windows before a knock came at the door. Two men entered the room, and Angelyn recognized one of Moore's officers, as well as a rebel soldier she didn't know.

"All of your initial messengers have been sent, Master Will," announced the rebel. "And troops are being organized to head to the tree line, as ordered."

"Master Moore has set the command for the banners to be changed on Towne Centre as well," said the officer. "Soon, all of Rhethos will see that we have joined forces."

Angelyn glanced at Will when this detail was shared. She knew that, over the last month, out of respect for Moore's resistance, Will had not replaced the colors flying from the castle turrets. Now, it was the final physical piece of victory in Lorington.

"That's something we should step outside to see, I think," Marselle said. She'd been silent during most of the exchange, but Angelyn knew better than to think that the woman had not been paying attention to every detail: information was a huge part of her trade and she would bet that Marselle would act on what she'd learned within these four walls.

They followed the two soldiers out of the barrack, back into the busy outdoors. Angelyn marveled at how the sun had now descended below the walls, shedding a final orange richness on the frosty western side of the city. *Were we really in there for hours?*

Her gaze shifted up to the castle in the distance, and she put up her hand to shield the left side of her face from the fading sunlight. There, along the soaring gray stone, were flowing shades of strong, rebellious violet.

They were the final banners.

"You now have the entirety of northern Rhethos officially supporting your cause," she said to Will. "There's still a chance we'll come out of this alive."

He stood beside her, his neck craned back as he stared in the same direction. Tentatively, she reached out for his hand. He gripped her fingers, but only for a second before letting go.

"And we'll face the Captain together, with Moore's support and Sarrett's knowledge, and take him down," Irvin added. He wrapped his arms around himself in the cold, though steadfast determination stood strong in his words.

Will gave them a resolute smile. "You're both right. And, even with the Goddess complicating our fight, one piece is clear to me now more than ever: each of us is important. Every drop of blood in our bodies matters and we get to choose when we spill it, or if we spill it at all."

CHAPTER FORTY-SEVEN

VALSARA'S SECRETS

There were ways to escape the desert's heat. One could function only at the coolest times of day, or one could live in the coveted homes that always sat in the merciful shade. But in the spiraled towers of the Silk Palace, raised above the rest of the city, the sun always shone, and so did the oppressive heat.

Beneath Valsara, however, there was cool, clear air and flowing water. As with any thriving arid city, its life lay underground, tapped into the precious natural water sources found far beneath the sand. Hundreds of years ago, Armellans had engineered powerful water distribution systems, sloped down to sea level cities like Valsara.

The man who walked through those waterways now was doing much more than escaping the desert heat.

Back in ancient times, he thought as he went, *these interlocking tunnels were supported with seasonal spells that kept them running . . . but those Dead Runes haven't been used in too long.*

He sighed. Blessing Runes weren't strong enough to create the power of archaic magic. A person's life sacrificed every so often to ensure the survival and blessing of all compared to weaker, modern magic where the caster had to actively, faithfully bleed to achieve a result?

It was a pitiful comparison.

Nowadays, it was a struggle to maintain the water tunnels that flowed underneath the sand's baking surface. Workers bustled by in the poor lighting, and many of them nodded to him with respect as soon as they saw who he was. There was no suspicion in the workers' eyes; whatever he was doing down here was the work of the Goddess, and not the concern of any commoner.

The men moved about the tunnels, putting up supports, testing water levels, and leading Goddess Touched to places where Strength or Protection runes might help, temporarily.

Soon enough, things will be better, he thought. *Stronger.*

He made his way around another bend in the narrow stone walkway and down into a closed-off section of the tunnels. This was a good place to meet individuals who would stick out in the glare of the sun above. After all, he'd spent the last sixteen years building an incredible fear of those across the sea and an incredible love of himself amongst the people.

Armelle's Temple Leader couldn't be seen with Rhethosian military men.

It was unusual to meet in person, and risky to say the least, but after the reports had reached him of what had happened in Lorington, things had escalated in a way he hadn't expected. No thanks, of course, to his Goddess damned cousin who'd thought it her "destiny" to aid the rebel cause in Rhethos.

"Good, you're here," rang out a voice, its foreign accent sounding sharp against the cool sandstone walls.

In the darkness before him, in front of a pile of old, caved-in bricks stood three figures in heavy cloaks. He knew it was winter in Rhethos at this time, but here across the sea, the men wore such coverings to hide their pale skin, not to keep warm.

The man in front continued, "We've been told you have questions, ones you couldn't write down in the usual code?"

"Which of you is from Lorington?" Sehran Tarran posed the question slowly, pronouncing the Rhethosian location with efficiency for one who never said such places aloud.

The figure to the right stepped forward, and Sehran had to strain his brown eyes to see that it was actually a woman. Her light brown hair was almost as light as her skin, accenting dark Rhethosian Blue eyes.

"I'm sure you can imagine that I was not pleased to hear the initial report of what happened in your city several days ago," Sehran began. He adjusted the shoulders of his silk robes as he spoke, not keeping eye contact even though he felt them staring back. "There are a small number of these pieces of magic. For one of them to be held by the rebellion and its master is a severe loss for us."

"Our Captain can take what the rebels found easily," the Rhethosian soldier replied. "We're sure Will and his people have no clue what they dug out."

"That was one of my questions that I did not want answered on paper," Sehran said. Now he caught the eye of the woman from Lorington, who had trouble holding his gaze. "How much do they know? They have been an annoyance up until now, but their success where Caldrell recently failed makes them a real threat. How does your Lord feel about that?"

"Ask him yourself," muttered the Rhethosian man with a shrug. "Caldrell says you and The Bradford have been close for years."

"I'll be sure to," Sehran returned smoothly. "Your name?"

The woman glanced up at him, then pushed a piece of hair out of her eyes. "Tamsyn Norring," she said shortly.

Sehran never understood Rhethosian names and chose not to repeat that one while still remembering it. "My question still stands."

"Since we set sail two days ago, Will and the rebels had not said anything to indicate they understand Kaladir's purpose," she replied. "They only announced that they 'lifted the Goddess' curse' from it. The entire towne loves the rebel leader, just like all of the northern region. By now, they have likely clashed with the Captain's men outside Kaylyn, not far from Lorington."

Sehran sighed. He could never understand why Rhethos' leader chose to put such an unstable man as head of his military; time and again, he'd communicated with The Bradford regarding his recent choices. But what really mattered was that digsite. Kaladir was all but ruins according to Caldrell's men's reports. Maybe Tamsyn's information was right: the rebels were clueless to what they had found.

"Our Lord wanted us to take advantage of this in-person exchange to assure you that there is nothing to worry about," announced the Rhethosian man in the silence. His old, deep voice echoed off the sandstone brick walls of the tunnels, eagerness in his tone.

That did not convey the reassurance Sehran was sure the man was somehow trying to share. The soldier sounded all too used to bootlicking, which never impressed men like Sehran, used to faithful devotion from his followers. He was Cybarys' chosen ruler on this earth, of course.

In his opinion, too much irresponsible use of Sahma in Rhethos led to bad leadership. Yet their Lord's hold was strong, more secure in ways than the one Sehran held over Armelle. The Bradford merely dictated in a more fearful, militaristic way than Sehran did, mainly with the terror of "The Blood Goddess" as his focus.

But people like these military men and this spy of a woman had no real concept of what was at stake. They were insignificant, ignorant pieces in an enormous machine that he'd intricately, secretly built his entire life.

He had broken innumerable laws and blasphemed in ways that would shock his people enough to have them gather and revert to the old ways of bleeding people dry for unthinkable crimes. There were countless hours of digging, through books and legends and actual ruins like those of Kaladir, to find something that resulted in the ultimate magic.

These people before him served a master who had the same goals. They'd spent years surreptitiously scouring both of their kingdoms to find what could give them pure, unchecked power.

It all came down to one question: if the Goddess was completely eliminated, who could hold them back from being the highest beings themselves?

The untimeliness of the rebellion, however, took more effort to deal with than Sehran originally thought. Since the time of The First Bradford, such uprisings always caused a bit of trouble, both in Armelle and Rhethos. This would be no different and would be squashed like all the others, no matter how much of Rhethos now stood behind Master "Will."

"Thank you for your message," Sehran said, adding a tone of finality in his voice. "It was vital to hear such updates in person. Tell your Captain and his Lord that everything still moves forward as planned for us. We wait to see reports on what happens in Kaylyn Towne."

The men and the woman both nodded, seemingly satisfied that they wouldn't be questioned any more in this dank, dark place. Sehran caught the woman's dark blue eyes again, however. "You," he added offhandedly, "Miss Norring. I'd like to speak with you before you return to Lorington. There are several questions Mistress Koresti will have for you. I will have someone summon you when she is ready."

Tamsyn swallowed visibly but nodded. It was good for a spy to be nervous sometimes, and he had a feeling underneath her uncertainty was more knowledge about the latest city the Rhethosian rebels held. She'd likely be more malleable under different circumstances.

Sehran handed off a few coded missives meant for both Caldrell and The Bradford, then made his way back to the surface. There was someone else he'd much rather be speaking with now that these matters were taken care of, and an intelligent man didn't keep his mistress waiting, least of all during a mealtime.

He did not have to brace himself for the heat like most would; in a memorized pattern, Sehran wove through the water tunnels up into one of the storehouses underneath the palace. From there, he could feel the late day's sun before emerging on one of the main floors. Even here, however, there wasn't the level of sweltering heat many were used to.

There were wind systems at the top of this turret, as was the case with most of the spiralizing structures of this ancient building. The specially designed parapets caught the wind and filtered it down into the floors below, bringing a breeze and relief from the sun for those living and serving indoors. He reveled in the soft wind on his face, pressing back the tight bunches of his black curls. There was a long climb ahead of him.

The curved sets of stairs rose higher than the rest to the Temple Leader's private dining quarters. But the decadent meal didn't matter, and the illustrious setting wasn't important. The woman he met there held a light that dimmed all else. Koresti had been the better half of his world for twelve years.

After their meal, they sat together in front of a large open window, overlooking the blue overcast of the desert's night. She'd chosen to wear one of his favorites: a blood-red piece of silk, cinched in just the right places at her neck and waist. It didn't take long for Sehran to share the details of his meeting in the water tunnels with her.

"You're not troubled by the one who calls himself Will now?" Koresti asked. "Truly?" Her dark eyes, almost black in this light, swam with calculative concern.

Sehran shook his head. He knew that she could tell when he was lying, and he admired that about her. Cool, precise observation was a tool he possessed as well, and with her by his side? No one got a single sliver of deception past them.

But that did not mean he told her everything. That would be a poor move, no matter how much he trusted her.

"Will doesn't concern me. In fact, with what I have learned, I'm convinced it is time to reveal the true connection between my friend and the rebel," he answered. He ran his hand down the bare skin of her back, weaving his fingers through the thick ropes of her long braids.

"Tell me why, my love," Koresti prompted gently.

"Because they are getting closer at the digsite in the east desert. And I do not have much need for The Bradford any longer."

She blinked a few times, the sharp line of her jaw falling open slightly. But that was all Sehran was willing to share, no matter how much she leaned into him, trying to pry more details from his eyes, her fingers toying with the edges of his robe. He shrugged her off, then took her hand and kissed her palm.

"I have something more important to share, anyway," Sehran said. He always had at least two pending tasks, each equally important, to send in her direction if she asked too many questions about other subjects he wanted to keep private.

Koresti raised one eyebrow at him, aware of the distraction but eager to hear more nonetheless; he never asked anything meaningless of her or shared anything that wasn't of value.

"It turns out there is a final piece of the puzzle," he said, "one that I did not know of until mere days ago."

"Days?" Koresti repeated skeptically. "But it's taken years, almost two decades to gather what we now know, and all of it is enough to tear apart our very history. There can't be *more*."

"I felt the same. But remember: Cybarys herself still has a hand in all of this. Until we can harm her, we must be cautious. . .especially when she speaks."

Koresti looked stunned, a rare occasion, until the brief moment passed and skepticism showed in discerning lines around her dark eyes. "What have the monks told you this time?"

"You wouldn't believe the amount of Sahma and Goddess Touched it took," Sehran scoffed. "But Cybarys finally shared something new."

Koresti sat closer to him on the cushioned settee, gripping his fingers. Besides the select group of monks present during these "offerings," no one but her knew of what he spoke. Those monks were bound by strict vows of silence invoked by Sehran himself, thanks to his extensive knowledge of Armellan scripture.

Sometimes, when he was desperate, when he needed an edge over the years, Sehran did such things. But it was so rare, because any slip, any whisper of a rumor to the public would destroy him.

Temple Leaders were more often than not Goddess Touched members of the royal family. They usually had direct, flawless connections to Cybarys. But because Sehran's rise in power was so tragic and sudden, he had no such gift and had to work hard to show his "devotion" to their deity.

Which meant getting in touch with the Goddess in different ways. To reach her took gathering many Goddess Touched individuals, from each of the last two or three generations, and giving them copious amounts of Sahma. The locked basement of his city's temple filled with the smoke, not an uncommon situation when supplicating Cybarys, but what they didn't know was how much of the plant's oil was also infused in their drinks.

That put them into such a state that they didn't realize how much they bled. They thought it was a dream when someone, usually a lost soul found on the streets, was cut open for the Goddess' pleasure. Oh, how that poor individual would bleed and bleed till they merely slipped into an unconscious state from which they never woke.

Then, with sickening amounts of blood offered to her, Cybarys could be coerced to speak. And her message would come through Sehran's Goddess Touched subjects who would never remember the words they spoke. Last time, only days ago, Cybarys had told him about something that shifted his many plans.

"What did she say?" Koresti repeated, more insistently this time.

"There is a boy, in Rhethos," Sehran said quietly, "who holds an heirloom as old as the Dead Runes themselves. The family line of the fifth man, the one who broke The First Bradford's spell at the last moment, ended across the sea. They hid that final piece, the fifth rune in addition to the four we have been searching for, that unlocks the spell's true potential to kill Cybarys."

"What?" she breathed, eyes wide. "Does such a thing truly exist? And a *boy* has it?"

"Yes."

"Are . . . are you certain?"

Sehran had to smile, despite the severity of such a weighty piece of information. Koresti never stumbled over words, always confident in the way she spoke and acted. It was a rare moment of triumph he breathed in while toying with the brass prayer bracelets on her wrists.

"This changes everything," she continued in awe. "I had hoped that the four Dead Runes themselves could be enough, as the Goddess herself isn't whole as she was back then. But this . . ."

"It will give us exactly what we need," Sehran confirmed. "I want you to help me find this boy. Use any resources you think necessary." He took hold of her face and brought it close. "I would only trust you with such a task while I handle other matters."

"Of course, my love," Koresti grinned, sincerity behind the words. Already, there were sparks in her eyes, as if she were imagining pulling and guiding countless threads in her webs to make such a thing happen. "I will waste no time."

Sehran nodded, then sighed. "This development has made me think of that day when Cybarys spoke to him and me." He faded off for a moment, knowing that Koresti was aware of who he meant. "We nearly died in those caves that day, long ago," he murmured. "Exploring where we shouldn't have been, but because we nearly died, the Goddess could reach us and give us that vision that's never left my mind for decades."

"Find the Dead Runes," Koresti confirmed with a nod, "submit to the Goddess, and become a god at her side."

Sehran shivered when she said the words that had tempted him since his youth. Everything. . .everything led up to this moment. And now the final piece would let him choose what to do with the power of The First Bradford's spell.

"I know the two of you agreed to share the power back then, as you do now, as Armelle's and Rhethos' respective rulers," Koresti continued. She sat up next to him, and it only took her a moment to catch his eye and slowly form the question he knew she'd ask next. "Sehran, The Bradford," Koresti began. "Does he know of this revelation? About the artifact and the fifth rune?"

He had debated, for days, on what to do in this regard. He hadn't slept, in fact, since his latest "offering" to the Goddess to learn such a secret. This was a crossroads in his Fate's String, one he knew he'd reach one day.

Sehran and The Bradford had been partners, bound by spilled blood the night that Devaki Tarran was born. They were equally ambitious and bloodthirsty, yet Sehran knew, since they were young, that he himself held a higher intelligence than the current Lord of Rhethos.

Cybarys had given *him* this final clue. And Sehran did not see the need to share it.

"No," he answered her. "Nor will he."

Koresti smiled, a bright expression full of lust and pride that made him pull her closer. He kissed her fiercely, then stood with her hands in his. It was only a matter of time now before everything in the world changed.

THE END

ACKNOWLEDGMENTS

Oh, the second book in a series. . .when the stakes have been raised, the complications have begun, and the juicy deepening of a story comes to life. Because of these beautiful yet challenging facts of what happens in *The Strings of Fate*, this is equally the most thrilling and most difficult writing I've done. It wouldn't be here in all its bloody glory without the following patient, talented souls.

Betsy Snider and Cara Shaw, you are top of the list for my "messy middle" of my trilogy. Over the years, life grew beyond small meetings in our homes and weekday hours spent carefree at local libraries (often debating story structure at a too-loud volume.) Despite our families and careers growing, both of you still provided the brutal honesty needed for my artist's soul to take on the depth Rhethos deserved in these pages. I cannot thank you enough.

Now, it may be odd to acknowledge, but my next important mention is Post Partum Depression. This book was crafted mainly in the time periods after both of my daughters were born. After facing uniquely complicated pregnancies, I encountered a lot of judgment, shame, and guilt within myself and from those around me as I started motherhood. Along with PPD, my heart was brought to a dangerous low . . . and yet, now on the other side, I can see these previously crippling challenges as gifts that made the content of this book possible. So, thank you, "fourth trimester," for breaking me down and building me back up into the better storyteller that's always been inside of me.

Lastly, I want to take just one more paragraph to thank "my authors." All of my editing clients over the years have trusted me with the most vulnerable parts of themselves in their rough drafts of their books (both fiction and non-fiction). To walk beside you in your authors' journeys, polishing your writing and honing your voices, has been the biggest honor. Each of you have left little, vital sparks of yourself in me, ultimately inspiring me to continue with my own books. That magic of teamwork, collaboration, and support of one another helps define who I am and (by the end of it), who my characters are, too. Thank you! I love all of you so much.

ABOUT THE AUTHOR

Hannah R. Lyon is an international bestselling author who has worked in the writing industry for eight years. As the mother of Rhethos, she explores deep meanings within her fantasy series that span across the fiction world into the struggles and triumphs of reality.

As the founder of Castle Lyon Editing, Hannah works with authors, helping them find their voices while polishing powerful manuscripts across genres. She lives in the smoky mountains of North Carolina, where her free time consists of indulging in story-driven video games, spinning classic rock and roll vinyl, and raising her two Elven Sprites of daughters.

You can find her on Facebook at www.facebook.com/ladylyon19, on Instagram at @LadyLyon19, and on her websites at www.hannahrlyon.com, www.freedomforrhethos.com, and www.castlelyonediting.com

REVIEWS

"You will be sucked into this remarkable fantasy story with lightning speed! Lyon's characters inspire me to keep going in my own life and bring magic into each day. Go on this journey filled with strong women and see yourself in a different light."

—Janet Cheney, MA English Literature, bestselling author of *So Many Freakin' Secrets*

"Hannah Lyon is a top-notch writer. Her vocabulary and precision of language elevate her writing far above what is found on the shelves these days. Much like Robert Jordan, she started her series in a place that was familiar, but this book really extends on her foundation and shows us that her story *is original* with complex twists. I couldn't put this book down. It's easily my favorite new fantasy novel I've read all year."

—Jared Godfrey

"Lyon's masterful story-building takes you on a journey to unveil the dark secrets of Rhethos. *The Strings of Fate* brings us the gritty wickedness of forbidden magic and makes you question how you might respond in your darkest moments. Readers will discover what they're willing to sacrifice, leaving them eager for the final installment of the series."

—Finn O'Malley, bestselling author of the *Keeper of Elements* series and GLOWup series

"Hannah is a magnificent storyteller who builds an incredibly realistic world and a deep web of intricacies. Her well-developed characters kept me entranced, reading into the wee hours of the night. Everybody can find someone they will relate to in this book. I am eagerly awaiting the outcome of her final book of the trilogy!"

—Jerel McLain, author of *Mixed Tape: The Soundtrack of a Life*

"This book brought me into an amazing space of intriguing fantasy! I was mesmerized by the characters that led me into a world like no other. It made me feel breathless!"

—Deborah Wiener, feng shui consultant, international award-winning speaker

"The palpable feeling of hope and sacrifice on different levels with deep personal dilemmas will tug at your heartstrings. *The Strings of Fate* continues to wage rebellion in Rhethos for change with all its challenges and sacrifices along the way to love, trust, and understanding. There is always a cost to gain freedom and equality, even if you wear rebel violet. In Rhethos, that price is often paid in blood, but even a Goddess might go too far."

—David Walker

"Prepare to be hooked—again! *The Strings of Fate* is a high fantasy adventure with teeth, engaging character development, and plot twists that will make you ponder your own destiny and choices. Hannah Lyon's world-building in book two in the *Freedom for Rhethos* series takes you on another thrilling, epic ride that keeps you spellbound with magical events. I couldn't put it down!"

—Bridget Cook-Burch, *New York Times* bestselling author, founder of Your Inspired Story

"Here is a captivating fantasy novel offering a vivid, thrilling, immersive story. Magic, mystery, and marvel await fans of the *Freedom for Rhethos* series! You'll be on the edge of your seat until the very end."

—Maureen Ryan Blake, TV host, international bestselling author of *Step Into Your Brilliant Purpose*

www.ingramcontent.com/pod-product-compliance
Lightning Source LLC
Chambersburg PA
CBHW051132300726
48978CB00011B/241